Just a M

Just a Matter of Time

BY

La Rhonda Simmons

www.bookstandpublishing.com

Published by
Bookstand Publishing
Morgan Hill, CA 95037
3782_5

ISBN 978-1-61863-403-0
Library of Congress Control Number: 2012920788

Printed in the United States of America

Jade

Eli and I wasted no time getting inside my apartment. We had just come from *PF Chang China Bistro*, one of my favorite restaurants. While we were there, we couldn't keep our eyes or hands off of each other. So Eli paid the check and we made a mad dash for the door.

As soon as we were inside my apartment, he jumped my bones.

"Damn baby, you've had my dick hard all night. I can't wait to fuck you", he whispered in my ear.

"Oooh, I want you too Eli. My pussy is so wet for you", I moaned.

With that said he pulled my dress up and started sucking on my nipples. Considering, I wasn't wearing a bra, it was easy access. He took each nipple in his mouth, making me moan with desire.

After he had my nipples standing at attention, he pulled me into the dining room.

"Sit down", he ordered me, pointing to the dining room table.

I did as I was told and hopped onto the table. He pulled down my panties.

"Now lay back and open your legs", he instructed.

Once again, I obliged. Before I could lay my head on the table, he had his face between my legs, tasting my honey pot.

"Oh shit, that feels soooo good", I yelled out. I could hardly control myself. He used his tongue with such expertise. It was like nothing I had ever felt before.

"Jade baby, you taste so good. I could eat you all night", he whispered between licks.

"Ooooh...eat my pussy baby. Oh...eat that shit!" I screamed.

The more he licked, the harder I grabbed his head. It was feeling so good I wanted to put his whole face in my pussy.

1

And just when I thought I couldn't take anymore, he did something with his tongue that let me know the end was near. He started sucking on my clit and fingering me with his thumb in perfect sync. "Oh yes baby. That's it! Don't stop! Don't stop! Oh fuck...don't stop!"

I tightened my legs around his neck. My back arched. And even though I tried to hold it in, I climaxed. I let out moans that I'm sure my neighbors heard. Afterwards, Eli was standing there with a satisfied grin on his face.

"Damn Eli, whatcha tryin' to do to me? Hell, I'm already hooked", I said after catching my breath.

"Well, you aint seen nothing yet baby". He grabbed my hand and pulled me off the table. "Let's go to your bedroom."

I followed him to my bedroom, where my queen size sleigh bed awaited us. Once we were in there, Eli took off his clothes. I bit my bottom lip as I watched him undress. He had an amazing body to go with his handsome face. Standing at six feet tall, he was built like an athlete. Being a personal trainer had a lot to do with that. His perfectly toned arms and legs accented his rock hard abs. There wasn't an ounce of fat on his body. His skin was like Hershey's chocolate; dark and creamy. He had the prettiest white teeth that I had ever seen on a man. He wore his hair in neat locks, which he kept pulled back. Ellison Turner was the epitome of fine.

As he stood before me in his nakedness, his manhood reached out to me. And I eagerly accepted it.

"Come here you. It's time for my dessert. You know how much I love chocolate." I took him into my mouth. He let out a gasp. I sucked his dick like it was my favorite lollipop. With skills of a porn star, I worked his shaft with my lips and tongue. Of course I couldn't leave out his balls. I gave them the attention they deserved.

"Damn baby, you're sucking the hell outta this dick. You're gonna make a grown man cry", he moaned.

I stopped briefly. "I just want to make you feel good baby." I continued working my magic on Eli, until he pulled my head away.

"Jade, I can't take anymore. I need to get inside of you before my dick explodes!"

Eli pushed me back on the bed and entered me with great force. As he plunged deep inside of me, I was overcome with pleasure. No man had ever pleased me the way Eli had. Our sex was like poetry in motion. I wrapped my legs around his waist, needing to receive every inch of him.

"Oh Eli baby, you feel so good inside of me. This is your pussy baby. It's all yours....oooh, I'm getting ready to come. Keep going baby.... I'm almost there.....That's it!" My body jerked as I cried out in pleasure.

Within seconds, Eli followed, releasing his love juice inside of me. Neither one of us moved at first. I stroked his hair, which had come undone during our lovemaking.

"That was incredible baby. You are one amazing man Ellison Turner", I told him.

He kissed me on the lips. "And you are one amazing woman Jade Peterson. Now, let's go take a shower."

The next morning, I woke up to a muffled voice coming from my bathroom. I turned over and realized Eli wasn't beside me. I didn't want to eavesdrop on him, but from the tone of his voice, he seemed upset. I got out of bed and tiptoed over to the bathroom door. Just as I reached the door, he swung it open. I jumped back, because he startled me. "Good morning baby", I greeted him.

He looked at me with a concerned look on his face. "So are you eavesdropping on my conversations now?"

I acted surprised. "I wasn't eavesdropping. I had just walked to the door when you opened it. I heard you on the phone and I was coming to see if everything was okay."

He gave me a weak smile. "Boo, you know I'm just trippin'. I know you wouldn't eavesdrop on my conversations."

He walked pass me and started putting on his clothes.

"So is everything okay?" I asked him. I didn't want to ignore the subject at hand.

"Huh? Oh yeah...uh everything's fine baby", he answered weakly.

I could tell he was lying, but I wasn't going to force the issue. I would just have to accept his answer.

"I was going to fix us a little breakfast before I got ready for church-"

He cut me off. "Oh no, I can't stay. I really gotta go. There are some things I need to take care of." He pulled back his locks and secured them with a twisty.

I put on my best pout face. "You can't stay for a little while?"

"I'm sorry Jade. I'll make it up to you...I promise." He kissed me on the cheek and rushed out the door.

After I locked the door behind him, I went back to my room to find something to wear to church. My thoughts went back to Eli's weird behavior. Who was he talking to on the phone? Why was he in such a hurry to leave? It was probably nothing. So I put those thoughts out of my mind.

Sierra

I slipped out of my church clothes and put on my favorite pair of jeans and a t-shirt. Jade, Taylor and I had spent the morning at church. Afterwards, we went to Starbucks to chat and catch up on each other's lives. We did that as much as our schedules allowed.

I went downstairs to join my family. My five year old daughter Shelby was watching Dora the Explorer, as usual. "Mommy look, it's Dora!" She excitedly pointed at the television.

I went into the kitchen where my husband Tyler was preparing dinner. "Um, something sure smells good."

My husband was an excellent cook. Don't get me wrong, I could hold my own in the kitchen, but Tyler actually enjoyed cooking. He was always experimenting and trying new recipes. I couldn't wait to see what he had put together.

"I made your favorite, chicken and eggplant lasagna." He gave me a sexy smile.

"Well, what did I do to deserve that? Or shall I say what did you do?" I eyed him suspiciously.

He threw his hands up in the air. "I didn't do nothin' baby. Ya' knows how much I loves cookin' fo' you n' Shelby. I gots to keep my womin' fed." I laughed at his hillbilly talk. "Now you gone an' git tha' youngin' an' I'll fix ya'll up a mess o' somethin'."

I had just tucked Shelby in for the night. When I walked into my bedroom, Tyler was sitting on the bed reading the Herald Sun. I admired him from the doorway. My husband was a very attractive man. He was considered "high yellow" with "good hair". He had the most beautiful green eyes. People always said he looked like Rick Fox or Ginuwine.

5

He looked up from his paper. "Shelby all tucked in?"

"Yeah, she's probably already asleep."

"I hope she doesn't have any bad dreams tonight."

"Yeah, me too. It always freaks me out when she wakes up screaming in the middle of the night."

"I'm sure she'll be alright though. All kids have bad dreams at some point or another."

"I hope you're right."

"I am. Stop worrying."

"Okay...baby, I'm going to go take a shower. You wanna join me?"

I took off my clothes and was standing there naked. Tyler stared at me with lust in his eyes.

"Of course I do. How can I refuse an offer like that?

When we were in the shower, Tyler lathered my body with strawberry scented shower gel. He used his soapy hands to caress my body. First, he started with my breasts. Then he pulled me close to him and rubbed my ass. We took turns caressing and stroking each other until we finally couldn't take it anymore.

As soon as we stepped out of the shower, we were making out like two horny teenagers. It had been two weeks since Tyler and I had been intimate. So I was ready, willing and able. Tonight was going to be a night, he'd never forget.

"Come here, with your sexy ass", he told me. He was now lying on the bed with his arms out.

Instead of getting on the bed with him, I stood in the middle of the floor. The look of confusion on his face turned to pleasure when I started dancing seductively. I rotated my hips like a belly dancer and shook my ass.

"Damn baby, I had no idea you could move like that", he said softly. His manhood was growing larger with each move.

"Well, there's more where that came from." I squeezed my breasts together and stroked each nipple with my tongue.

Tyler let out a groan that let me know I had him

where I wanted him. So I decided to go in for the kill. I took my middle finger, dipped it inside my wet hole and put it in my mouth. "Um, that tastes good."

I walked over to the bed. "Are you ready for the time of your life?" I asked him. Tyler shook his head like a little kid. "I sure am."

We shared a passionate kiss. The chemistry between us was like none I had felt in a while. Since it was so intense, I decided it was time to make my move. Tyler had his eyes closed, enjoying the kissing. He was moaning as if we were already having sex. I grabbed his rock hard shaft. Instead of sitting on it like I usually did, I put it in my mouth. What a bad idea. Tyler pushed me with such force I almost fell off of the bed.

"What in the hell are you doing?" he screamed at me.

"I-I w-was just trying to make you feel good Tyler!" I screamed back at him.

"No, you were acting like a-a slut!"

"A slut?" I couldn't believe he let that come out of his mouth.

"You heard me. You're my wife Sierra...not some dirty little whore. Why would you do something like that?"

"Tyler, I know I'm not a whore. What is wrong with a wife trying to please her husband?"

"I don't like it. It's ...dirty, nasty, filthy and...well...it's just not right", he said crossing his arms.

"We are married for Christ's sake!" He was really irritating me. "There's nothing wrong with a married couple having oral sex, Tyler! Besides, we've never tried it. So how do you know you won't like it?"

"It's not just a matter of not liking it Sierra. It's just something I don't think we should be doing." He was adamant about the subject.

"I think it would spice up our sex life." I looked down at my hands because I didn't want to see the look on his face.

"Oh...so that's what this is about. You think sex with me is boring?" He sounded hurt.

"I never said that Tyler. It's just that-"

7

He cut me off before I could finish my statement. "You think I'm boring Sierra. You didn't have to say it. I can read between the lines."

"Tyler sweetie, listen to me." I cupped his face with my hands. "All I'm saying is that I want to try new things. We've been together for ten years; married six of them. You're the only man I've ever been with. Sometimes things can seem routine. Oral sex is a natural act between couples. I know in the past when I'd bring it up, you'd always change the subject. But I thought if I at least tried it, you would like it. And maybe even do me in return."

He looked me dead in my eyes. "Well, you were wrong. I'm not gonna like it because I'm not gonna try it. And if you want to try new things, maybe you should try them with someone else!" He moved my hands, grabbed his pajamas and stormed out of the room.

I sat there in total shock. What was the big deal? He acted like I wanted to stick something up his ass. As a married couple, we should've been able to experiment with sex. Hell, everybody was having oral sex except me and Tyler. And from the sound of it, he wasn't changing his mind. I climbed into bed, hoping Tyler would come back. He never did.

Taylor

"Taylor Morgan, you are one fine sista." I said out loud while admiring myself in the full length mirror of my spacious walk-in closet. I did that often. Unlike most women my size, I liked my body. I'm what's considered full-figured. I am a size sixteen with curves and an ass that could stop traffic. My perky 38 D's drove my husband insane. I don't like to brag, but my body has always been my asset.

I slipped out of my three piece Escada suit and my Chloe pumps. I didn't have any other plans for the day. So I decided to have a nice long warm bubble bath. I filled the garden tub with warm water and poured in some vanilla scented bubble bath. Then I lit all the candles around the tub. I slid into the tub and let the sudsy water caress my voluptuous body. I laid back and closed my eyes to relax. This is exactly what I needed.

Suddenly, I felt a hand on my right breast. I opened my eyes and saw my husband kneeling down beside the tub with a big smile on his face. "Hey sweetie. When did you get in? I thought you were out golfing with some business prospects."

He was massaging both of my breasts. "Well, I was. But I cut it short. I wanted to come spend some time with my beautiful wife."

I stroked his cheek. "How sweet."

"Taylor, I know I haven't been spending a lot of time with you lately. But as soon as I close this deal, things will be different."

That was the story of our marriage. After this deal, there would be another one. David was a sharp business man. When he went after something, he got it. He didn't become a multi-millionaire by sitting on his ass. I never complained about his work. After all, I benefited a great deal from it. "It's okay David. I know how important your business deals are."

He stood up to dry his hands on a towel. "But nothing's more important than you Taylor. And don't you forget that."

"I know sweetie. I also know you are a workaholic. But I knew that when I married you, so I've learned to deal with it." I stood up in the tub. "Baby, can you hand me that towel?"

His eyes lingered over my entire body before he gave me the towel. "God, you're beautiful. I am one lucky man."

I started drying off when, he took the towel out of my hands and let it fall to the floor. In one swift move, he was sucking on one of my nipples.

"Um baby, that feels good." I closed my eyes as he licked and slurped on each breast. He licked a trail down to my belly button. He wrapped his hands around my waist and pulled me down. So I was now sitting on the edge of the tub. With his hands, he opened my legs. Within seconds, his sandy blonde head was buried between my legs. David always went wild when he went down on me.

"Oh, I love eating this sweet, juicy black pussy", he managed to say between licks.

"Um and I love it when you eat this pussy. Oooh Daddy, lick Mama's pussy. Lick it baby. Oh God, that feels so damn good!" I screamed.

David was an expert pussy eater. Sometimes he would do that all night without even attempting intercourse.

He kept licking and I kept enjoying. The pleasure was getting so intense. I opened my legs even wider, as he feasted on my dessert. "Don't stop Daddy! Mama's gonna come! That's it Daddy!"

My body jerked as David continued eating me. Most of the time, I had to literally push him off of me. "Damn baby, that's enough." I was out of breath.

David stood up and looked down at me. My juices were shining around his mouth. I handed him the towel off the floor. He bent down and kissed me on the lips. Then he wiped his mouth. I loved tasting myself on his lips. For some reason, it turned me on.

"I'm gonna go downstairs and see what Hazel left for us to eat. I think she fixed something before she left yesterday." He handed me the towel and turned to leave.

Before he walked out the door, he said, "I love you Taylor."

"I love you too, baby."

I watched him walk out the door. Do I really love David? No, I love his money. I do care for him a little and wouldn't want anything to happen to him. He's a good man and he treats me like the queen that I am.

Sometimes, I can't believe how I lucked up with David. We had met two years ago at a function at the *Durham Marriott*. I was working for an escort service. This old geezer had hired me to be his date. He had to bail out, when his wife showed up. I was looking too good to leave, so I went to the bar and ordered myself a drink. From behind me, I heard, "What's a beautiful woman like you doing sitting here by yourself?"

I turned around to see one of the most gorgeous white men I had ever seen. I smiled at him. "My date bailed out on me. His wife showed up, so he rushed out before she spotted him. Of course, I had no idea he was married."

"That's too bad." He pulled out a stool and took a seat. "Do you mind if I join you?"

"Sure, why not? But it's no big deal. It wasn't anything serious. Plus, I bounce back pretty quickly." I took a sip of the margarita the bartender had given me.

He looked at me with lust in his eyes. "I'm sure you do bounce back quickly. I'm also sure you can have any man you want."

I laughed at his comment. "Well, I wouldn't say that. But I will say that I don't have any trouble getting a man's attention."

"Well Ms..."

"Johnson, Taylor Johnson"

"Well, Ms. Taylor Johnson, you've sure got my attention. And I would love it if you'd spend the rest of the evening with me." He patted my hand.

"That would be fine with me. But it would be even better if I knew your name."

He looked embarrassed. "Oh, I'm sorry. I'm David Morgan." He handed me a business card he had taken out of his suit pocket.

I held out my hand to shake his and glanced down at the card. "Well, it's nice to meet you David."

I knew I had hit the jackpot when I saw *Morgan Corporation* on his business card. He owned tons of property throughout Durham County. I had once heard he was one of the wealthiest men in the state. I pretended not to be impressed by his money. But I knew it was only a matter of time before I would have him wrapped around my finger.

Sure enough, after having dated for only six months, he asked me to marry him. I happily accepted. I quit my job at the escort service, which David knew nothing about. That would always be my little secret; among other things.

So David and I have been married for a year and a half. I couldn't be happier. I live in a big house, drive the BMW 745 that I've always dreamed of, and designer clothes, shoes and handbags fill my closet, that's the size of my old bedroom. My mother always told me, I'd never have anything. Well, I proved her wrong. And all I have to do is be the best wife I can be. What more could a girl ask for?

Jade

I couldn't believe that Eli had not called me. After he left my apartment yesterday, I made several attempts to contact him. Every time I called his cell phone, I got his voice mail. I was beginning to worry, because he always kept his phone on. I was getting ready to try again when there was a knock on my door. "Come in."

"Hi Jade. Mr. Lawson has asked that everyone meet in the conference room." My co-worker Judy popped her head in my office. She was a petite white woman with freckles, red hair and glasses too big for her face. "He said he had an important announcement to make", she continued.

"Thanks Judy. I'll be right there." I wondered what was so important. There had been talk of a merger or an expansion. As long as my pay wasn't cut and I still had a job, I didn't care one way or the other. *To The Max Ads* was one of the best private advertising agencies in the Triangle. I had been working there for three years. I worked in the accounting department.

When I reached the conference room, everyone was taking their seats. Mr. Lawson walked in behind me. "Good morning everyone! Thanks for joining me. I know you all have a lot of work to do, so I'll get to the point."

Mr. Lawson was always about business. His being the owner had a lot to do with that I'm sure. He was a decent looking man for his age. He still had all of his hair, even though it was graying. Expensive suits and shoes were always a part of his wardrobe.

He continued, "You may or may not know that Robert will be leaving us next month. He has taken a position with a company in Dallas."

Robert acknowledged everyone with a big smile. "His position as operations manager will need to be filled. Any of you may interview for the position. But of course, the most qualified person will get the job."

It could have been my imagination, but I could've sworn that Mr. Lawson looked directly at me. This is the break I have been waiting for. The pay is a big jump from my current salary, which isn't too bad for a single black woman with no kids. But most importantly, I am the most qualified person here.

"Mr. Lawson, when will you start the interviewing process?" Paige, the office slut asked. The rumor was that she had slept with half the men in Durham. That even included some of the company vendors. She was always prancing around in her too short for work skirts and showing way too much cleavage. And she was as fake as that tore up weave in her head. I tried to get along with all of my sisters, but she was one that I couldn't deal with for too long.

"I'm glad you asked Paige. In the next couple of weeks, I'll start holding interviews. I want the position filled before Robert leaves. I'm sure he'll want to give some pointers to the person that's going to fill his shoes." Mr. Lawson directed his attention to Robert.

"My position in Dallas doesn't kick in until June, but I'm actually leaving towards the end of May to get settled in. That will give me about two weeks to help train the new operations manager. I wish all of you the best of luck!" he said as if he was an announcer.

Mr. Lawson stood up and buttoned his jacket. "Unless someone has more questions, that will be it for now. Good luck everyone."

Most of my co-workers hurried back to their offices. I wanted to congratulate Robert on his new job. Before I could reach him, Paige intercepted. "Congratulations Robert! You must be so excited. We're all going to hate to see you leave, but we're also glad to have a chance at your position. So what company-"

I couldn't take another second of her babbling. "Excuse me Robert, I just wanted to say congratulations and good luck."

"Thanks ladies. I really appreciate it. Well, I guess I better get back to work." He walked off, leaving me standing there with Paige.

I was about to walk off until she opened her mouth. "Jade, are you going to apply for the position?" Not giving me a chance to respond, she said, "I am. I know I'm very much qualified for it. It's practically mine already."

I knew she had lost her damn mind. She would get that position over my dead body. Plus, she was nowhere near qualified. "Paige, I don't mean any harm, but I don't think you're qualified for the job."

She looked at me like I was crazy. "What's that supposed to mean?" she asked.

"It's kind of self-explanatory. You have not been here long enough. And the qualifications don't require being in a horizontal position...if you get my drift."

If looks could kill, I would have died on the spot. She tossed her raggedy weave over her shoulder and hurried out the door. That would shut her up for a little while.

When I got back to my office, I dialed Eli's number again. His voice boomed from the other end. "Hey baby what's up?"

I was glad to hear his voice, but I pretended to be mad. "Don't what's-up-baby-me. Where have you been and why haven't you returned my calls?"

"What's this, twenty questions?" He was getting all defensive again.

"Eli, I was really worried about you. I called you several times and left several messages. I was just wondering what was going on okay?"

"I was really tied up boo...had to take care of some things...no need for concern", he said casually.

"Well, you know after yesterday when you left in such a hurry, I just -"

He cut me off. "Can we drop that Jade? It wasn't that serious. Everything is cool. Like I said, I had to take care of some things."

I changed the subject. "So what are you up to?"

"I'm sitting here trying to figure out a way to ask my girl if she wants to have lunch with me today", he said playfully.

"I'd like that Eli. We haven't had lunch together in a while," I said.

"I know baby. Meet me at *Ruby Tuesday's* on 54 at one o'clock. I'll see ya' then...peace." Then he hung up.

When I hung up with Eli, I felt much better. Even though, we had only been dating for six months, it felt like we had been together much longer. He was so caring and charming. I was falling in love with him day by day.

But there were some things that did bother me. I had never met any of his friends or family. He was always talking to people on his phone. But when I asked him about friends, he claimed he didn't have any. He was secretive when it came to discussing his family. He said he just didn't get along with any of them.

Maybe I was being paranoid and making a big deal out of nothing. Besides, Eli treated me so good. Plus he was fine as hell and the sex was banging.

When I walked into *Ruby Tuesday's,* I saw Eli sitting at the bar. Some half-dressed female with bright red hair was smiling in his face. He was staring at her like he wanted her for lunch. He didn't even notice that I had walked up.

"Um-um," I cleared my throat to get his attention.

You would've thought he had seen a ghost. "Oh. Uh Jade. Hey baby...I didn't see you come in."

I looked over at his company. "Yeah, I noticed. You seemed preoccupied." She rolled her eyes at me. "I'm Jade Peterson, Eli's girlfriend. And you are?"

"This is Asia, Jade. She's an old friend of mine," Eli blurted.

She didn't even acknowledge me. "Well Eli, it looks like my time is up. It was nice seeing you again. Look me up sometime. You know where to find me." She looked me up and down before she sashayed away.

"Baby, I'm starving. Let's go eat." He wrapped his arm around my waist, acting as if nothing had happened.

I wasn't letting him off the hook that easy. "Eli, who in the hell was that little hussy?" I asked.

"Aw man, Jade. She's nobody."

"She didn't act like nobody to me. You were practically all over each other when I walked in."

"Look Jade. I'm gonna be honest with you. She once had a thing for me, but I wasn't feeling her like that. I like classy women like you. She was in here with some of her friends and we just happened to run into each other while I was waiting for you. Baby, you're the only woman I want."

He sounded so sincere. And he had never given me any reason to doubt him.

"Well, I didn't like the way she was looking at you...or me for that matter. Next time, I might not be so nice. I may be classy, but I can get street if I need to."

He pulled my chin up and looked me in my eyes. "Baby, there won't be a next time. Then he kissed me on the lips.

I smiled at him. "It better not be."

Eli had a serious expression on his face when he said, "Jade Peterson, I love you with all my heart. I'm not gonna do anything to lose you...okay? Now let's go eat."

I followed Eli to our table. All through lunch, I thought about what he had said. He confessed his love for me. Since we had been dating, he had never said anything like that. He actually said he loved me. Now I knew I had nothing to worry about.

Sierra

Tyler was still angry with me. He was gone when I got up this morning. He had even taken Shelby to daycare. I tried calling him on his cell phone, but it would go straight to voicemail. I really didn't think he was going to get so angry. I really thought I could seduce him. I had been trying for years to get him to engage in oral sex. He always flat out refused.

Tyler and I have been together for ten long years. He had walked into the spa I was working at the time. I was about to close up, which is something the owner allowed me to do from time to time.

"Excuse me sir, we're just closing for the day," I informed him.

"You can't be! I need to be serviced bad," he pleaded.

I shook my head at him. "I'm sorry. You can come back tomorrow and I will be more than happy to help you."

He came closer to me. "Ma'am, I'll pay you double. I am in so much pain right now. I don't think I can wait until tomorrow."

"Well if you're in as much pain as you say, you may need to go see a chiropractor instead of getting a massage," I explained.

"There's nothing wrong with my back. I'm just tense and figured a good massage would ease the tension. And I don't think I can sleep tonight with all this tension in my back and shoulders."

I stood there, not knowing what to say or do. He could've been some psycho or sexual predator. He smiled at me. "Just thirty minutes...PLEASE."

I couldn't resist that smile or his charm. So against my better judgment, I locked the front door and escorted him to the back. Lucky for me, he wasn't some psycho or sexual predator. Before he left, he asked me out.

At first, I hesitated. My relationship with men hadn't been the most exciting up to that point. I never went on dates and I didn't particularly show interest in them. It wasn't because I was gay or anything. I just knew that I wasn't going to be going through one sexual fling after another. I always felt that most men were only after one thing and I wasn't about to be giving it to them. I had decided that the man I gave my virginity up to was going to have to prove that he was worthy.

I went out with Tyler and one date turned into many dates. The next thing I knew, we were a couple. After dating for four years, Tyler asked me to marry him. We got married right away. We didn't see a need to drag out our engagement. We knew we were soul mates.

For our two year anniversary, he surprised me with my very own day spa. He had chosen a vacant spot in the *Kroger Shopping Center* on Martin Luther King Jr. Parkway. My place does pretty good, but I'm always trying to build clientele.

Tyler has always been supportive of me. That's one of the reasons I love him so much. I just wish I could get him to see things my way when it comes to sex. Don't get me wrong, I'm no sex freak or anything like that. I just feel that our sex life lacks a little something. It's just so boring and routine. Something just has to change.

The bell on the entrance door signaled someone had entered the spa. "Welcome to *Sierra's Day Spa*, how may I help you?" Jazmin, my receptionist greeted.

A tall, gorgeous, brown skinned female with long hair walked up to the counter. "Yes, I need a full body massage," she said with confidence.

"Do you have an appointment ma'am?" Jazmin looked down at the appointment list.

"No. Do I need an appointment?" She asked, with a little tone in her voice.

"Actually, you do have to make an appoint-"

I decided to interject before things got out of hand. "Is there a problem Jazmin?"

Before Jazmin could respond, the female

answered. "Yes, I'm trying to get some service and your clerk wants to give me the run around."

I put on my friendliest voice. "I'm sorry for any inconvenience ma'am. What time is your appointment?" I asked, knowing she didn't have one.

"She doesn't have one," Jazmin spoke up.

I saw her roll her eyes at Jazmin. I didn't want to lose a potential client, so I made a decision. "Look, Miss..."

"Montague, Alexis Montague." She smiled sweetly.

"Okay, Ms. Montague, we do require appointments, but I will do my best to get you some service. Now what can I do for you?" I spoke with my most sincere voice.

She glared at Jazmin. "Well, like I was telling her earlier, I would like a full body massage. That wouldn't be a problem...would it?"

"Actually Ms. Montague, you're in luck. I'm the massage therapist and I don't have any appointments scheduled right now."

She had a look of satisfaction on her face. It was a look that said she was used to getting what she wanted.

"Just follow me and I'll get you settled." I turned to Jazmin. "You know to hold all of my calls and take messages."

I showed Ms. Montague to one of the massage rooms. Soothing sounds of the ocean greeted us as we entered the room. I lit the many aromatherapy candles that were scattered throughout the room. I was about to leave so Ms. Montague could get situated. When I turned around, she was getting undressed. She unbuttoned her blouse, revealing naked breasts.

"Um Ms. Montague, you can wait until I leave, so you can have some privacy," I told her.

"What's the point? You're going to be touching and rubbing all over my body in a few minutes. Besides, we're both adults." Then she let her skirt drop to the floor. I gasped. She wasn't wearing any panties either. Now she was standing in front of me completely nude. I couldn't help but stare at her. She had a body to die for. Long, lean legs, rock hard abs, and full perky breasts were all wrapped up in smooth flawless skin. She was drop dead gorgeous and she knew it.

"I guess you can hop up on the table since you're ready now," I instructed.

She got onto the table and slid under the heated blanket. "Umm...this is heavenly," she sighed.

"Yeah, it is nice isn't it?" Do you want me to do your back first or last?" I asked.

"I think I want my back done first. I'm so tense back there."

"Ok... I need you to lie on your stomach."

She did as she was instructed. So I started the massage.

"I need you to do my ass as well", she mumbled.

"Excuse me? Did I hear you correctly?" I asked.

She lifted her head up and said, "I said I want you to do my ass."

"But Ms. Montague, we don't do that-"

"Please call me Alexis dear."

"Okay, Alexis. We don't do that here. That part of the body is off limits. We can be slammed with unwanted physical contact lawsuits and all sorts of things."

She turned around to look at me. "I don't care about all of that. I'm a lawyer and I have no intentions of filing any type of complaint. I'm asking you to do it, so it shouldn't be a problem. I'm paying you for a service and if I have to pay extra, I will. If I'm satisfied with the service, I'll be your number one client. And let's not forget all the other clients I will send your way."

She had me there. I needed all the clients I could get. I had my fair share, but I needed more. My goal was to have the top day spa in Durham. Even though, I felt uncomfortable with her request, I had to do it.

Throughout the massage, she kept moaning. If you hadn't known any better, you'd swear she was getting sexed. A one hour massage seemed like a two hour massage. But I was getting paid, so what the hell?

"Alexis, you're all done. I'm going to leave so you can get dressed. There's no rush. So take your time." I left her and returned to the front.

A few minutes later, she was back up front. "You know, I never did get your name," she said as she stopped at the counter.

I felt embarrassed. "Oh, I'm sorry. My name is Sierra." I handed her one of my business cards.

"So, you're the owner as well?"

I smiled proudly. "Yes, I am."

"Like, I was saying earlier, I may be able to send a lot of clients your way."

"That would be great. I'm always looking for new clients."

She looked down at her watch. "Well, if you have time, maybe we can go to the coffee shop next door and talk."

I didn't know anything about this Alexis person, but something about her was intriguing. She was arrogant and confident and I envied her. "Sure...why not. Just let me get my purse."

She grabbed my arm. "Don't bother. It's on me." She walked out the door and I followed her.

Taylor

"Damn Exodus! Are you trying to turn a bitch out or what?" I was nearly out of breath.

My plaything Exodus had just fucked me like my loving husband couldn't. David could eat the hell out of some pussy, but a sista like me needed some black dick in her life. To make matters worse, Exodus is one of David's employees. I know I'm wrong, but Exodus is fine as hell. And let's not talk about his skills in the bedroom. There's no way I'm letting that Mandingo go.

He was stroking my arm lightly. "I told you Taylor, you need to leave that white boy and get with a real man."

I looked at him like he was stupid. "Don't start that shit again, Exodus. I've done told you that I'm not leaving David."

He sat up to look at me. "Why not? You don't love him. He can't fuck you the way I can."

I laughed at his silliness. "Who said I don't love David?"

"Taylor, you know you don't love that man," he said with conviction.

"Whether I love him or not is beside the point. The fact is I'd be a damn fool to leave David over some dick! Do you not realize that he is a multi-millionaire? And unless you can keep up the lifestyle I'm used to living, stop talking stupid!"

He got up in my face. "Oh, so now I'm just some dick to you?"

This conversation was plucking my nerves. "Exodus, you knew from day one what this relationship was about. You came into this knowing it was all about sex. Don't act like you aint getting nothing out of this little arrangement. That Movado watch sure as hell didn't come from the tooth fairy. And I don't hear you complaining about those designer clothes and shoes that pop up into your closet. Now, if you're developing some feelings you don't need to be developing, I advise you to get them in check."

He sat there like a child on punishment. "I'm sorry baby. I don't know what came over me. I guess I'm just jealous because that white man got a fine sista like you. But you do take care of a brotha. So I really can't complain."

I got up and started putting on my clothes. "Well, your apology is accepted. Now you better get back to work before David starts looking for you."

"Aw, I aint worried about that. David ain't that type of boss. As long as you're making paper, he's cool." He started putting on his clothes. "So when can I see you again?"

"I'm not sure. I'll call you. I gotta go." I kissed him on the lips and was out the door.

It had been a while since I had done some serious shopping. A shopping trip to New York was what I wanted, but I'd have to settle for the mall. Even though, I lived closer to *Northgate Mall,* I didn't really like going there. So I headed for the *Streets of Southpoint* mall. As soon as I walked into the designer section in *Nordstrom's, some* pieces caught my eye. I started browsing and selecting things I wanted to try on. I noticed two ritzy looking white ladies watching me. I kept choosing merchandise, not really looking at the prices. It didn't matter what it cost. If I wanted it, I was going to get it.

Before I could get the salesperson's attention, the two ladies went up to her and started talking to her. I sat back and waited for them to finish. Then I noticed they were all staring at me. The salesperson walked over to me. "Excuse me ma'am. Can I help you with something?"

"As a matter of fact, you can. I would like to try these things on. So can you please get me a dressing room ready?"

She looked at me like she didn't understand what I was saying. "You want to try all of those on?"

"Yes, I do. Is that a problem?" I didn't like the way the conversation was going.

The two ladies were standing behind her like they

were her bodyguards or something. "Uh. No it's not a problem. It's just that it would be easier if you took in a few pieces at a time. You can leave the rest out here and I'll get them for you when you're ready." She sounded nervous.

I wasn't going to trip and let the hood come out of me. So I calmly took the items I wanted to try on first and left the rest. While I was in there, I could hear the two women talking to the salesperson.

The first lady said, "I think she's up to something. You might want to call your security officer. I don't trust her."

The second lady chimed in. "Did you see that fake designer bag she's carrying? I know the real from the fake. I'm sure she has no intention of buying any of that stuff. She probably can't afford a thing out of this department. She wasn't even looking at the prices. She definitely looks like a thief to me."

The salesperson spoke up. "Well, she hasn't really done anything wrong yet. I'm pretty sure she won't buy all of those things, but I can't say anything to her. I may get in trouble."

"Why wait for her to rip you off? I guarantee you she doesn't buy one piece of merchandise. I know her type. They come in and try on stuff they know they can't afford. They're either going to steal it, or they're just window shopping."

I barged out of the dressing room, surprising the hell out of all three women. "Let me tell you bitches something. First of all, the only things fake I see are your tits." I looked at the one with her boobs busting out of her top. Second, I can afford to buy anything in this damn mall. You don't know who the hell I am. If I was a white woman, not a damn thing would be said. But because I'm black, you assume I don't have any business being here."

They were looking at me like they were afraid I was going to hurt them. But I wasn't going to stoop to that level. Then one of them said, "Look honey, you don't have to pretend with us. It's okay. Everybody can't wear expensive clothes." She looked at the other one with a smirk on her face.

The average person would have cursed them out and left the clothes there, but not me. I had to prove a point. Before I met David, I had to sell my ass and do what I had to do to get nice things. Those same type of women use to look at me like I was out of place. They didn't know that I was spending my rent money to buy clothes that I really couldn't afford. But things are different now. I had money, and lots of it.

I handed the young clerk the clothes I had in my hands. I walked over to a rack and picked up five more items. I put them on the counter along with the other items I had previously left. "Can you ring these up for me? Or if you don't want the commission, I can give it to someone else."

She stumbled behind the counter with a look of shock on her face. She started ringing up the merchandise, while the two snooty women stood there and watched. By the time she finished ringing up my items, my total had come to over fifteen hundred dollars. When I pulled the cash out of my wallet and counted it out to the clerk, I thought the two women's jaws were going to drop to the floor. I used cash because I didn't want David being nosey by trying to track my credit card spending. He was always lecturing me about all the clothes I buy.

I rolled my eyes at the women and grabbed my bags. "Next time, don't be so quick to assume that you know what a person's financial status is. And you might want to close your mouths before something flies in them." I walked out of the department, leaving them standing there with the shock still on their faces.

On my ride back home, I thought about the experience I just had. It felt good to be able to go in any store and pick out anything I wanted, without worrying about the cost. I was so poor growing up. It was always just me and my mother. I never knew my father. Hell, I don't think my mother even knew who my father was. But anyway, I never had the latest fashions. I would end up with clothes from the thrift store or some yard sale. My mother always bought stuff for herself first. She always said that she needed work clothes, but I never seen her go to work.

My mother was a beautiful woman in her day. She was curvy and voluptuous, like me. Men were always swooning around her and she enjoyed every minute of it. There was a different man at our house almost every night. I gave up trying to remember names and faces. They would always go straight to her room. She would tell me turn the television up loud in the living room. I was told to stay in there until she came out of the bedroom. As I got older, I realized what kind of work my mother did. She was a prostitute. Those men coming to our house every night were paying her for her services. Apparently she was cheap, because the place we lived in was a dump. Everything was either old or broken.

Everyone in town seemed to know what my mother did for a living. When we would be out in the town, I use to hear them talking about us behind our backs. My mother always held her head up high, like nothing bothered her. She always tried to portray this certain image. She was always dressed nice, with her high heel pumps and short dresses. She never left the house without her makeup or her hair done. She always said a lady had to look her best at all times, because no man wanted a lady who didn't look worth nothing. She looked fabulous and I looked homeless.

The girls in school always teased me. They would talk about my clothes and my mother. I got into so many fights defending her. I didn't care that they teased me, but I couldn't take them talking about my mother. She was all I had. My mother wasn't as loyal to me as I was to her. She would constantly tell me that I wasn't going to amount to anything when I grew up. She'd say 'You aint gonna be shit, 'cause yo' momma aint shit.' I'd always come back with, 'You're wrong Mama. I'm gonna be a doctor or a lawyer. You'll see. I'm gonna make you proud.' She'd shake her head and say 'Taylor the only thang you got going for you is yo' body. You just like me. You gonna have a big ass and some big titties. And as long as you got those, men will always fall at yo' feet.

Don't go getting yo' hopes up 'bout bein' no lawyer or no doctor, 'cause that shit is for white folks.'

So I stopped talking about being a doctor or a lawyer or anything else respectable. My mother was right about my body. I blossomed when I was about twelve. One of my mother's friends took notice. He had come by one night while my mother was gone out on a date. When I told him my mother wasn't home, he forced his way into the house. He got real close to me. I could smell the alcohol on his breath.

"Taylor, you sure have grown up girl. My, my, my...just look at ya'. You got a body just like Gwen's", he said rubbing his hands together.

I didn't feel comfortable with him being there, so I asked him to leave. "Mama's not gone be back for a while, so you might as well go now."

"I'll just wait for Gwen to come back. I aint in no hurry." He kept coming closer and closer to me, until he had me pinned against the wall. His breath stunk so bad, I felt as though I would throw up. "Please get away from me or I swear I will scream", I threatened him.

He just laughed. "Scream if you want. No one's gonna hear ya'. Even if they did, do you really think anyone is gonna help ya'?"

He was right. No one would come, even if I screamed to the top of my lungs. So I did the only thing I could think of. I kneed him between his legs so hard, he stumbled to the floor. He looked up at me with fire in his eyes. I became really scared, because I didn't know what he was going to do.

"You little bitch! You gonna get it now. I wuttin' gonna do nuttin' to ya' at first, but now you done fucked up. Ima put dis here dick up in dat young pussy."

I started to run, but he tripped me with his foot and I went tumbling to the floor. He grabbed my ankle and pulled me to him.

I started screaming, "Get off of me you ole pervert!"

He ignored me and started pulling down his pants. I sat there, not knowing what to do. I was too scared to try to run again. Before I knew it, he was naked from the waist down.

"Ya' know it's been a long time since I had me some young pussy. I'm really gone enjoy dis", he said rubbing his chin.

He pulled up my nightgown and yanked off my panties. He had the evilest look in his eyes. It was as if I was staring the devil in the face. I tried one more time to stop him from hurting me. "Please Mr. Bobby, don't hurt me. I promise if you stop, I won't say anything to Mama about this."

He looked at me and started laughing. "You aint telling Gwen shit no way. And even if you do, she won't believe ya. I'll tell her dat you jus' makin' up stuff like young gals do." He then forced me to open my legs. He took his middle finger and inserted it into my vagina. I had never felt anything inside my vagina, so it was very uncomfortable.

He started laughing. "Oh, I think I got me a virgin here. Dis is gone be betta than I thought...ooowee!"

"Of course I'm a virgin. I'm only twelve." I started trying to get up when I saw him stroking his penis. He slapped my face and told me not to move again. I did as I was told.

He took my virginity right there on the living room floor. It felt like my insides were going to burst. I cried and screamed when he first forced himself in me. Then when I realized it wasn't going to do any good, I stopped. I just laid there and let Mr. Bobby have his way with me. I prayed that Mama would come home and save me, but she never did. When Mr. Bobby was finished with me, he put his clothes back on and the only thing he said was, "If you tell anybody 'bout dis, you will be sorry. Dis is our little secret."

He walked out of the house like nothing had happened, with me still lying on the floor. I was there for a minute, still in shock. The pain between my legs was so bad, I couldn't move at first. Then I realized something was trickling down my butt cheek. I put my hand there to see what it was. It was blood. I started crying again. I knew what sex was, but I never imagined my first

LaRhonda Simmons

experience would be like that. I was no longer a virgin, and I knew my life would never be the same. I got up off the floor and headed to the bath room. I cleaned myself up before my mother got home. Just as Mr. Bobby had instructed me, I never said a word to Mama or anyone else.

Every time I thought about Mr. Bobby, I got mad. I let him do those things to me. It didn't stop at that one incident. Since I didn't tell Mama about the first time, he did it again and again. It went on for about six months. Every time he knew Mama was going to be gone, he would come over and have his way with me. Each time he would say the same thing, "You know what da deal is. You bed not ever tell Gwen 'bout us." It finally stopped when he just disappeared. There were rumors that someone had stabbed him to death. The other rumor was that he got killed in an automobile accident. Either way, I was happy, because I knew he would never hurt me again.

Even though, he wasn't around to hurt me, the others were. Many of my mother's men friends started showing interest in me. I started thinking that my mother was in on it. She always wanted me to be extra nice to them. And sometimes she would tell me to change into something else when one of her new friends was coming over. It always seemed like the next time they came over, she would just happen to be gone. And that's when they would force themselves on me. Then she would always bring me a gift from them afterwards. I hated thinking that my mother would do something like that, but all the evidence pointed in that direction. I guess she was getting too tired and too old to keep selling herself, so she resorted to selling her daughter.

A tear ran down my cheek as I thought about the things my mother put me through. A part of me hates her, which is why David or none of my friends know about her. I told them she died when I was younger. To me, she is dead.

30

Jade

A week had passed since Mr. Lawson had announced the opening of the operations manager position. Mr. Lawson had interviewed everyone that was interested in the position. I think my interview went pretty well. I was feeling very confident. Those Mr. Lawson were interested in would have a second interview with him and Robert. Everyone was walking around brown nosing and kissing Robert's ass, because they knew he had some input on who would get the job. I wasn't into ass kissing. It just wasn't my thing. If I couldn't get the position based on my skills, then I didn't want it.

Paige, on the other hand was around here grinning like her life depended on it. Her skirts got shorter and her tops got lower. I believe she even started stuffing her bra, because her cleavage looked fuller than usual. Earlier today, she had the nerve to come into my office asking about my interview.

"So Jade, how did your interview go?" she asked.

"It went fine Paige. Why do you ask?" I rolled my eyes at her.

"Oh, I was just wondering. Mine went very well. Mr. Lawson was impressed with how much I've taken in since starting with the company. He said I was a quick learner and very aggressive."

I sat there watching her, wanting to slap that smirk off of her face. Instead, I spoke. "That's all fine and dandy Paige. Why you felt the need to come in here and share that is beyond me. Frankly I couldn't care less about your interview."

She smacked her lips. "Jade, you're just intimidated by my presence-"

I cut her off before she could finish her sentence. "Bitch, let me tell you something. Jade Peterson isn't intimidated by anyone! I never have and I never will be. I have way too much self-confidence and self-esteem for that. And even in my weakest moment, I couldn't be intimidated by the likes of you. Go get that tore up weave done, wipe off some of that clown makeup, and invest in a pumice stone for them crusty ass heels before you come up in my face talking about some intimidation."

She got closer to my desk and looked me dead in my eyes. "We'll see if you talk all that shit when I get that position. I just came by to give you a heads up. I didn't want you getting your hopes up, because that position is going to be mine...whether you like it or not. So you better get used to it." Then she strolled out the door.

That was really bugging me, because she was talking a little too confident for me. I don't care how much she has taken in. There is no way she is qualified to do that job. There are only two other people that I could see getting that position over me. Nancy is one of them. She has been here as long as I have. Her department deals with the actual clients, figuring out what they want *To The Max Ads* to do for them. Carlos is the other person that has a chance. He works in marketing. He's in charge of getting all the details together and setting up the ads. So if anybody else gets that position, it better be one of them.

Hell, why am I tripping off that shit Paige said? I know she isn't qualified. So I'm not going to let that bitch scare me. Besides, it's way past time for me to be going home. I had stayed a little late to finish some things I didn't want to deal with in the morning. I grabbed my purse and a file that I needed to drop off at Mr. Lawson's office.

Everyone was usually gone by now. So I was a little surprised when I got closer to Robert's office. I heard muffled voices, followed by moaning. The closer I got, the louder the moaning got. The door was cracked open. I got the shock of my life when I peeked in his office. Paige was riding Robert like she was on a mechanical bull. He was sitting in his chair and her back was to the door. She still had on her clothes, but her skirt was pulled up around her waist. He had his underwear and pants dropped to the floor around his ankles. I didn't even move. I just stood there watching and listening like a voyeur.

"Paige, you're a big slut just like they say you are. But you got some good damn pussy! I don't know why you waited so long to give me a sample", he said almost out of breath.

"Sometimes, you have to wait until the time is right", she said in between moans.

"Are you sure this has nothing to do with my position Paige?"

"Of course I am. I've always been attracted to you. Like I said, you have to wait for the right time."

I hope Robert wasn't falling for that. Paige didn't give a damn about his ass. That bitch would stop at nothing to get that job. She was in there fucking Robert's brains out so he would consider her for his position. How was I supposed to compete with that? I was tempted to bust in there and let them know what I had seen. But I decided against it. I would have to handle the situation differently. I just wished I had a clue how. Then it hit me. I reached into my purse and pulled out my cell phone. Thank heaven for camera phones. I got close enough to take a few shots without them seeing me. I was able to get a few shots where you could see their faces enough to tell who they were. They were so into what they were doing, they didn't even notice me. When I had enough shots, I left them to continue their little activity. I walked off feeling very pleased with myself.

When I got home, Eli was outside my door waiting for me. I was surprised to see him, because he didn't tell he was coming over. "Hey, what are you doing here?" I asked him.

"Well, how the hell are you too?" he asked with his sarcastic voice.

"I'm sorry baby. I'm just surprised to see you, that's all. You didn't say you were coming by." I unlocked the door and entered my apartment.

"Are you expecting someone else? You don't seem too happy to see me." He followed me into my apartment.

I reached out to hug him. "Of course I'm not expecting someone else. You know you are the only man in my life. Like I said, I'm just surprised...pleasantly surprised to see you."

I started taking off my shoes and my jacket to get comfortable. He was just standing there watching me with this funny look on his face. "So what's up baby? What do you have planned for the evening?" I hung my jacket on the coat rack next to the door.

"Nothing, really. I just wanted to come spend some quality time with my baby. I thought maybe we could just cuddle up on the sofa and watch a movie or something. Is that cool with you?" He flashed that killer smile.

I had plans of coming home, taking a bubble bath, ordering a pizza and curling up with a good book. But there was no way I could resist him. "Sure babe. That's cool with me. You don't mind if I take a shower first, do you?"

"Yeah, that'll work. While you're doing that, I'll go grab us some grub. Is Chinese food okay?"

"Anything you choose is fine with me Eli. You can take my key in case I'm still in the bathroom when you get back."

He left to go get the food and I jumped in the shower to wash away the day's stress. I was still thinking about what I had witnessed in Robert's office. I knew Paige played dirty. I just had no idea she would stoop so low. Now I just had to figure out what I was going to do with those photos. All I know is that by the end of the week, everyone at *To The Max Ads* is going to know what a slut Paige Smith really is. Jade Peterson, you are one smart bitch.

Eli came back with Chinese food and an armful of DVDs. He had all the old movies I like. He had *Purple Rain, The Color Purple, and Boomerang.* "So you trying to get some tonight or what Eli?" I asked him.

"What makes you say that Jade?"

"I guess you got these movies for yourself huh?"

"Hey, I like old movies too. You're not the only one that watches old black movies."

"Yeah, but if memory serves me, someone told me they didn't see the point of watching all those old movies over again, because times today were nothing like that."

He started laughing at my comment. "Damn Jade, you got me there. I do remember saying that, but I didn't expect you to remember that shit. In all seriousness, I figured you would get a kick out of these movies. I know how you like this stuff. So I decided to make tonight about you. Is that okay? Can't a man think about someone other than himself sometime?"

"Yes, I guess he can. You know I was just teasing you. You should know you don't have to do anything nice for me to get some of this." I pointed between my legs. "This is always yours to do as you please with it...within reason."

He leaned close to me. "I'm glad you feel that way, Jade. 'Cause I plan to do a lot of things with it." Then he started kissing me.

"Wait, Eli. Our food is going to get cold. We got all night to do any and every thing you want to do." I pushed him away and started opening the food he had brought in.

We ate our food and watched two of the movies. It felt good to be cuddled up on the sofa spending quality time with Eli. We were always going out. I figured I could get to know the real Ellison Turner this way.

"Eli, you never want to talk about your family. Why is that?" I know I had asked him the same question before, but that was a while ago.

"Jade, you just don't believe in letting up do you? I could swear you've asked me that question before. And I could swear I've already given you an answer." I could hear a little agitation in his voice.

"Yes, Eli...I have asked that question before. But that was a while ago. I figured now that we've been together a little longer you wouldn't mind divulging that information. I've told you everything about me and my family. Yet, I don't know a damn thing about you. It's like you're living some secret life or something. Is it so wrong for me to want to know about the man I'm involved with?"

He took a deep breath. "No Jade. It's not wrong for you to want to know something about the man you're involved with. But what is wrong is for you to keep asking me about shit that obviously makes me uncomfortable. I'll tell you about my family when the time is right. And right now, I don't feel the time is right. I'm begging you not to bring this shit up again, because no matter how many times you ask me, I aint saying shit 'til I feel like it."

I could tell I had struck a nerve. He sounded like he was angry with me. I just didn't understand what the big deal was. What could be so bad that he didn't want to tell his girlfriend? But no matter how bad I wanted to know, I wouldn't bring it up again. So I decided to let it go. "I'm sorry Eli. I promise I won't bring it up again. You can tell me when you're ready for me to know."

With that behind us, Eli and I made our way to my bedroom. I climaxed so many times, I lost count. No man had ever sexed me the way Eli did. There was no way I was going to mess things up with him. Whatever he didn't want me to know, I'd just have to live with it. As fine as he was and the way he pleased me in bed, I'd be a fool to let him get away. With that in mind, I laid back and let him rock my world for the rest of the night.

Sierra

Things with me and Tyler had gotten a little better.
And by that, I mean we were at least speaking again.
Things in the bedroom were still the same. I didn't try to
persuade him to have oral sex anymore. When we had
sex, I just laid there and let him do his thing. Sometimes,
it felt like he was doing a chore. There was no passion at
all. It was like he was just going through the motions. He
didn't care if I enjoyed it or not. I was unhappy and there
was no hiding it. I had started spending more time at the
spa.   Then I realized I was neglecting Shelby in the
process. I couldn't let my baby be a part of me and Tyler's
problems.   So I started spending extra quality time with
her. I would take off work early and we'd catch a movie or
go to the park.

Alexis was starting to come around a lot. She
would come into the spa almost every other day. One day
she would get her nails done. Then the next day, she
would get her hair done. Then another day, she would get
a pedicure or a massage. But I wasn't complaining. She
had plenty of money to spend and I was eager to accept it.

One day she came in to get a massage. After I
finished servicing her, she asked me a question that kind
of surprised me.   "How would you like to go out or
something...kinda like a girls' night out?"   She had a
desperate look on her face.   It was almost like she was
begging.

"Uh, sure. Why not? I just have to check with my
husband to make sure he doesn't have anything planned
for us." Hell, I knew he didn't have anything planned. He
never had anything planned.

She sounded excited.   "Great!   Here's my home
number. Just call me when you find out for sure. Maybe
we can catch a movie or go out to eat. Is that okay?" She
wrote her home number on the back of a business card.

"Sure...that would be fine." I took the card from

37

her. I was really looking forward to hanging out with someone new. I mean, I loved getting together with Jade and Taylor, but it was always nice to make new friends. I called Tyler and told him about my plans. He said he would pick Shelby up from daycare.

I drove up to Alexis' house in *Garrett Farms* after she gave me directions over the phone. She had a really nice place. When she opened the door, she looked as if she had just stepped off a runway in Paris. "Wow...you look great", I told her. I felt underdressed in my black slacks and chiffon gold blouse. She was wearing a red dress with spaghetti straps, with a plunging neckline that showed plenty of cleavage.

"So do you. Please come in." She escorted me inside. Her home was beautiful. It was decorated with expensive looking African art and sculptures. As we walked, our heels clicked on the shiny hardwood floor. I felt like I was in an art museum.

"You have a lovely home, Alexis. This art is magnificent. I don't think I've ever seen such a beautiful collection in one home."

"Why thank you. I've collected it over the years. Some of it, I've bought from different galleries or stores. And I've actually gotten some of it from my trips to Africa." She was glowing as she talked about her art.

"You've been to Africa? That must have been exciting. I've always wanted to visit, but it's much too expensive for me and Tyler. It would take us a long time to save for a trip like that."

"Well dear, you never know what may happen. Business seems to be going well for you. I'm sure one day you will be able to squeeze a trip in somewhere. It's all a matter of planning."

"That would be a dream come true."

"Well, sometimes dreams do come true. I just need to finish my makeup and I'll be ready. You just wait here and make yourself comfortable." She pointed to what looked like her den, while she went upstairs.

As I waited, I studied some more of her beautiful art. She had great taste. There was an oil painting of her over the fireplace. It was a very good likeness. Even though, she was smiling, her eyes looked sad. Then I noticed a photo of her and a very handsome man. They looked like they were on a beach somewhere. Once again, she was smiling, but her eyes appeared sad. I was always told that a person's eyes told their true feelings. I wondered if that was her husband. She had never mentioned a husband...but then she didn't really discuss her personal life. Actually, she was quite mysterious.

"So, are you ready to go?" she asked from behind me. I turned to acknowledge her. She had an evening bag in her hand and a shawl wrapped around her shoulders.

I looked down at myself. "I feel so underdressed Alexis. You're all dolled up and here I am in some pants and a blouse." I felt like canceling the whole evening. I couldn't go out with her looking like that.

"I told you, you look fine. I always get carried away when I go out. I've always been that way. Anytime I get a chance to wear a sexy dress, I take advantage."

I took her word for it and we were on our way. We hopped into her silver Mercedes and headed to *Angus Barn*. Tyler had taken me there once. I thought it was overrated. I could go to *Outback Steakhouse* and be just as content. But since I wasn't paying, I had no complaints.

When we first got there, we were both kind of quiet. I felt a little uncomfortable at first. I didn't know what to talk about with her. All the other times, we discussed business. So I didn't know how to strike up a conversation that wasn't business-related.

"So...how long have you and Tyler been married?" she asked after taking a sip of her wine.

"Well, we've been together for ten years and married for six of them."

She took another sip of her wine. "That's a long time."

"You seem surprised."

"Well, you know these days it's not often you find

39

that kind of longevity in young couples." She said that like it was from experience.

"I never heard you mention a husband. Are you married?" I figured I could find out who that handsome man was in the photo.

She hesitated before she answered. "No. Um...well, not anymore. My husband and I split up last year."

"Oh, I'm sorry to hear that." I didn't know what else to say.

"It's okay. I've learned to deal with it. We were married for five years and I caught him with someone else in our home. I was devastated at first. I couldn't believe he would do something like that to me. But you know what's funny? All the signs were there. Sometimes we as women ignore things that are right up under our noses. We see what we want to see."

"That's tough. Do you guys still keep in touch with each other? I mean do you at least still speak to each other?"

"He calls me every now and then just to see how I'm doing. He says he never meant to hurt me. He couldn't control his self is what he told me. Some things are just meant to be was his reasoning...But anyway, enough about me and my pitiful life."

After we finished dinner and drove back to her house, she invited me back inside. I was about to tell her it was too late and I would take a rain check. But then I realized I had no reason to go running home. Tyler wasn't going to notice if I was home or not. Once inside, Alexis made a pot of coffee. We sat in her den and struck up another conversation.

"So what do you and Tyler do for fun?" she asked like she was conducting an interview.

"Well, it depends on what you consider fun." I took a sip of my coffee.

"You know...like going to the movies or concerts...or things like that. I know you have a little one. Does that stop you from going out like you want to?"

"Shelby has no bearing on our not going out. Tyler has really gotten kinda boring lately." As soon as the statement left my mouth, I wished I could take it back. I didn't feel I should be discussing my marital problems with a stranger. So I tried to clean it up. "What I mean is that Tyler has been throwing himself into his work. So we haven't been doing too much of anything lately."

She gave me a look that said she knew I was lying. "It's okay Sierra. When you've been together as long as you have been with Tyler, it's bound to happen if you don't spice things up a little."

"Do you have any suggestions or ideas?" I needed all the pointers I could get.

"Well, you could do things like role playing or bringing toys into the bedroom. Anything like that may help."

I was clueless about it all. "What exactly is role playing?" I knew I sounded like a naïve teenager.

"You pretend to be someone other than yourselves while you're in the act." She had a devilish grin on her face.

"Okay...so who are you pretending to be...celebrities, people you know...who?" I just didn't see the point.

She laughed at my ignorance. "You can pretend to be anybody you want to be. For example, Tyler can pretend he's your doctor and you're his patient coming in for a check-up. Once he examines you, one thing can lead to another. Or you can pretend you're a teacher and Tyler is your student. You make him stay after class because he was being a bad boy. Then you show him what happens to bad boys...if you know what I mean."

That role playing stuff really had my attention. It was starting to sound interesting. But I knew Tyler wasn't going to be down for any of that stuff. He liked to keep things simple. And that was part of the problem.

She interrupted my thoughts. "Does that sound like something you think you can handle?" I paused before I answered her. "Yes, it's something I'd be interested in trying. Now Tyler, that's another story."

"You don't think he would be willing to spice up your relationship?"

I felt like a patient talking to her shrink. "I know he wouldn't be willing to try it. You see...Tyler and I..." I stopped for fear I had said too much.

She reached out and touched my knee. "Sierra, you can tell me. I promise you, I won't judge you or think any less of you."

I had never even discussed me and Tyler's sex life with Jade and Taylor. So how could I open up to Alexis? There was just something about her that made me feel like I could tell her anything. She acted as though she was really interested and wanted to help me. I took a deep breath. "Tyler and I have never had oral sex."

She gasped. "Are you serious?"

"I'm sorry to say that I'm very serious." I was looking down at the floor. I felt so embarrassed.

"I didn't mean to sound so shocked, but I am really surprised. I thought everyone was doing that."

"Yeah. Everyone but me and Tyler."

"Do you mind my asking why?" She had a confused look on her face.

I took a deep breath before answering. "Because Tyler thinks it's disgusting and degrading."

"Oh really?" she said in a sarcastic tone.

"Why did you say it like that?" I asked, curious as to why she had sounded that way.

"It's just that these days men don't find too much of anything disgusting or degrading. Like I said before, I'm just a little shocked."

"Well, I guess Tyler isn't like most men. He refuses to budge on that subject."

"Have you tried being aggressive with him? Maybe just doing it?"

I went on to tell her about my attempt to seduce him and how it backfired in my face. She really couldn't believe he was so upset with me. "Honey, it aint too many men out there that don't want their dick sucked. Your husband must be really old-fashioned."

"I don't know what you want to call it, but I call it BORING!" I threw in a fake yawn.

"You know Sierra, that's terrible. A young woman

who is vibrant and sexy like you shouldn't have to go through stuff like this...especially when you're married."

She called me sexy. I didn't consider myself sexy. I knew I wasn't an ugly duckling or nothing. I just always felt I lacked the self-confidence to be sexy.

"Sex is very important in a marriage", she continued. "It's more important than most people are willing to admit. That's a big factor in a lot of failed relationships...other than money."

"Is that why you think your husband cheated...because of lack of sex?" I asked that question without thinking. So I tried to take it back. "I'm sorry Alexis. That was an inappropriate question. You don't have to answer that."

She put her hand up. "It's okay. I'll just say this and leave it at that. Our sex life wasn't the problem. My husband just wanted someone else."

That was my cue that it was time to go. It was getting late and I really needed to get home. Alexis and I wrapped up our conversation and called it a night. On my drive home, I thought about Alexis and how I felt we were going to have a great friendship. I could tell that we were going to be spending a lot more time together.

Taylor

Here I was getting ready for another one of David's dinner parties. Every time he closed on a major business deal, he threw an extravagant party. I had to grin and smile in those snooty ass people's faces. Most of those fake bitches wanted to be in my shoes, married to one of the wealthiest men in Durham. That little secretary of his really struck a nerve in me. I know she has a thing for David. And I've had to put her in her place on several occasions. She wouldn't miss one of David's parties for nothing in the world. I wasn't threatened by her or anything. Her little skinny white ass couldn't hold a candle to me. But sometimes, I felt like she was reading me or something. It was as if she could see through my act. She was always asking me questions that I had already answered. She kept asking me where I was from and asking me about my family. One day I just flat out told her to mind her own damn business. She just looked at me with a smirk on her face.

David walked in interrupting my thoughts. "Baby, you look incredible." I was wearing a red evening gown that accented my full figure. I picked it up just for the party. I had chosen gold shoes and accessories to tone down the red. "Thank you sweetie. I was hoping you'd like it. I wanted to look my best for your dinner party. I know how important these dinner parties are to you."

"You know you always look great to me. I always feel so lucky to have you on my arm." He kissed me on my cheek.

I finished touching up my makeup and dabbed some *Bulgari* perfume on my pulse points. I noticed my husband was still standing behind me watching me. "Is something wrong David?" I asked.

"I just wanted you to know how much I appreciate you, Taylor. I know when I'm trying to seal a deal, I'm not around as much as I should be. You're always so understanding and you never complain. A lot of women would be bitching and moaning, yet still enjoying the luxuries that come along with it. You're always so supportive and I love you for that. And not just for that, but for being you." He reached in his jacket pocket and pulled out a long rectangular velvet box. "This is a token of my love for you Taylor Morgan."

I took the box and opened it. Inside was the most beautiful gold and diamond necklace I had ever seen. David had bought me a lot of nice jewelry. Next to my wedding ring, the necklace was the nicest piece he had ever given me. "Oh David, this is beautiful!" He took it out of my hand to put it on my neck. "But it's not as beautiful as you."

I took off the gold necklace I was wearing. It didn't have nothing on the one David had just given me. I turned around so he could put it on my neck. Once it was around my neck, we both stood there admiring it. It was just what my dress needed. "It looks perfect on you, Taylor. I'm glad you like it."

I turned around and gave him a long passionate kiss. He seemed surprised. "Is that what I have to do to get kisses like that? If it is, then I'll be bringing home expensive jewelry more often."

"You know you can get those anytime you want", I teased. He kissed me on the forehead. "Well, that's good to know. But you know I was only teasing you. If I thought you were only after my money, I would've never married you." Then he walked out.

I stood there a minute, thinking about what he had just said. He was so sure of my love and loyalty to him. Sometimes, I actually feel bad for cheating on him and being with him for his money. Then I had to remind myself that as long as he never found out, things would be okay. I'm not a stupid girl. I just had to keep playing my cards right.

The party was going as well as planned. As usual, the turnout was incredible. No one important would miss a David Morgan affair. The food was exquisite and the music was mellow. The guests were really enjoying themselves. Of course Exodus was there looking sexy as hell. He kept giving me the eye from across the room. I didn't have on any underwear, so I could feel myself getting moist each time he looked my way. When I got the chance, I grabbed him and pushed him into one of the many vacant rooms downstairs. David was so wrapped up into his guests; he would never notice I was gone.

"Damn Taylor, you looking so fucking good in that red dress!" Exodus was all over me once we were alone. "Shit, you're not looking so bad your damn self. You look so sexy in that tux." I started massaging his crotch area.

Exodus grabbed my hand. "Stop that! My dick is already hard as a brick and it aint shit I can do about it right now."

I was now sitting on a chair that was nearby. I started feeling my breasts and moaning out loud. He walked toward me. "Taylor, cut that shit out. Someone might come in here."

I pulled up my dress and opened my legs to show him that I wasn't wearing any panties. "Damn girl, you sure are bold. And you're dripping wet...but all jokes aside, you need to get your ass up and let's get outta here."

I grabbed his arm. "Wait...don't you want to taste a little bit? I know you do. You've been watching me and teasing me all night. Now is your chance to get some of what you've been craving for."

He rubbed his chin. "You know I want you bad as hell, but I just don't think this is a good idea. You got a house full of guests, not to mention that your husband, my boss is out there."

"I thought you liked to live dangerously. Besides, no one is going to come in here. I did have enough sense to lock the door. David is out there entertaining his guests. He probably hasn't given me a second thought." I was determined to convince him to play a little.

With a bit of hesitation, he got down on his knees. Within seconds, his face was buried between my legs. I wanted to scream out as he used his tongue and mouth to pleasure me. It wasn't long before I was jerking and shaking from an earth shattering orgasm. "Whoa, I really needed that", I said before pushing Exodus' head from between my legs. "I haven't come like that in days."

"That's because you aint had your pussy ate like that in days. You know nobody can get down like me", he boasted and then flicked his tongue out at me.

I sat up on the chair. "I hate to burst your bubble, but David is an excellent pussy eater. He's proven that the myth about white men is true. You might have the biggest dick, but David is the champion when it comes to the oral skills."

He looked at me with anger in his eyes. "So what was all that shit about not coming hard in days?" I laughed at his jealousy. "Exodus, don't get so defensive. I haven't come like that because I haven't had sex in days. David's been really busy, as you know and we just haven't had the time."

He got up in my face. "It doesn't matter any way, 'cause he still aint got shit on me. He may be able to eat the pussy better, but he'll never be able to get up in them guts like I do."

I pushed him out of my face. "You know what Exodus, you're being really petty right now. I don't know why you think you have to keep comparing yourself to David. You and I both know that our sex is off the hook."

He pulled me up off the chair. "I told you, I just hate to see that white man with such a fine sista like you. I don't care how much money he got. That shit just gets to me."

"Well, you already know why I'm with him. So chill out with that shit. Plus, you know you can get this anytime you want it." I pointed between my legs. "Anyway, we better get out of here before David notices I'm gone." I fixed my dress and made sure my hair was in place. I gave Exodus a long kiss before we walked out. When I pulled away from him, he grabbed my face. "Taylor, I love you girl."

And before I knew it, I said, "I love you too Exodus." Then he walked out the door. I stood there for a few minutes thinking about what I had just confessed. I think I had just opened a can of worms.

I was on my way back to join the others, when I was intercepted by Autumn, David's secretary. "Hi Taylor, have you seen Exodus around anywhere? I noticed you both got missing, so I thought maybe you two were together."

I put my hand on my hip. "No Autumn. I haven't seen Exodus around. Maybe you should spend less time thinking and more time minding your own damn business. I thought we've had this conversation before."

She flung her hair over her shoulder. "I don't know why you're getting so upset. I just asked a simple question."

"Autumn, there was nothing simple about your question. There is no reason for Exodus and me to be together. Just like, there is no reason for you and me to be having this conversation. Both of you work for my husband. So I suggest you stick to your job, before you lose it." I pointed my finger in her face.

"Now Taylor, I know you're not threatening me. David wouldn't dream of getting rid of me. I am the best thing he's got. I was with him before you came along and I have no plans of going anywhere." She rolled her eyes at me and crossed her arms over her chest.

I got closer to her so no one would hear us. "Let's get one thing straight. You are his secretary. I am his wife. Secretaries come a dime a dozen, but a woman like me is one in a million. I know you got a little thing for David. You keep fucking with me, your ass will be out of a job so quick, you won't know what hit you."

She backed away from me. "I'm not going to stand here and listen to your empty threats. Besides, you may want to watch who you make threats to. I know a lot more than you think I know."

"What in the hell is that supposed to mean?" I questioned her. "Don't you worry about that", she snapped.

"Hell, I'm not worried. But I do have a little bit of advice." I looked down at her chest. "You might want to consider a bigger bra, because those fake titties look like they're about to escape." I left her standing there with her mouth open.

"Darling, where have you been? I've been looking all over for you", David asked me as I rejoined him. "Oh, I had to freshen up", I lied.

I started mingling with the guests, pretending to enjoy all of the small talk. The whole time, I kept thinking about Autumn's comments. What did she mean she knew more than I thought? That bitch didn't know shit about me. Then she had the nerve to try to accuse me of being with Exodus. Maybe she had seen us together or something...or maybe Exodus was running his mouth. I needed to talk to him and find out what was up.

Just as I was about to go find him, he walked up. "Hello, Mrs. Morgan", he said loud enough for everyone to hear. I whispered, "You don't have to be so obvious. It looks like you're trying too hard. Just act natural." I glanced around to make sure no one was listening. "Have you said anything to Autumn about us?"

He made a face at me. "Hell naw. I aint said shit about me and you to no one. Why you ask me that?"

"She asked me had I seen you and she thought maybe you and I were together since we both disappeared." I kept looking around to make sure the coast was clear.

"Fuck that bitch. She's just trying to figure shit out. She probably mad 'cause I won't give her ass no play."

I was surprised by his comment. "So, she got a thing for you or something?"

He looked at me and laughed. "That trick throws herself at me...and David too. She be wearing them short ass skirts to work and them low cut tops...titties be all over the place. None of the other women at the office like her.

"What about the men in the office?" I meanly wanted to know about him and David.

He smacked his lips. "Man, nobody don't want that flat ass Autumn. I mean, there are a couple of guys

49

that will probably get with her. David aint got but one thing on his mind at the office and that's m-o-n-e-y. And I damn sure don't want her. You may like white meat, but I like my meat dark."

"Well, she better watch herself. She fucking with the wrong bitch", I said through clenched teeth.

"I turn my back for one minute and you try to steal my wife away from me", David's voice came out of nowhere.

I looped my arm around his. "Honey, you know there's no way any man could steal me away from you."

Exodus rolled his eyes at me before saying, "David, I don't have enough money or class to compete with you. You're the man."

David playfully punched Exodus on his arm. Aw come on Exodus. You're the one that's got it going on." He then turned to me and said, "Almost every woman at the office got a thing for ole' Ex here."

Exodus gave me an innocent look. "David's exaggerating a bit."

"Don't be modest Exodus. You're not married. It's okay to have women vying for your attention." He nudged me in the arm. "I think he has a different lunch date every day." If I didn't know any better, I'd swear my husband was trying to piss me off.

I gave Exodus a look that let him know I wasn't too happy. Who in the hell was he going to lunch with every day? We only got together for lunch maybe once or twice a week. He had a lot of explaining to do. I know I didn't have a right to be mad at Exodus. But I was very jealous when it came to him...more so than with my own husband.

"Most of the time, I go and hang out with some of my buddies or I go to the gym", Exodus explained, as if reading my mind. I just rolled my eyes at him.

David took my hand. "The reason I came looking for you is because I want to make a toast." And as if on cue, the waiters came around with trays of champagne.

David cleared his throat and yelled out, "Attention everyone! I'd like to make a toast." He turned to me. "To my beautiful wife Taylor, who has been so supportive of me and my business ventures. I know I don't spend as much time with her as she would like, but I want her to know that I love her very much and I wouldn't trade her for anything in this world." He then lifted his flute in the air. "To Taylor Morgan."

Everyone took a sip of their champagne after oohing and aahing over David's heartwarming toast. His words almost put a tear in my eye. He was always so emotional when it came to his feelings for me. I just could never bring myself to get on that level. I kept it simple and basic.

Exodus was watching me with a look of disgust. I scanned the room and noticed Autumn was looking at me as well, with a look I couldn't quite figure out. Then she looked at Exodus, then back at me and then at David. What was all of that about?

Jade

My plan had been a success. I got the photos downloaded from my phone to the computer. Sierra and I made a slide show with them. I sent emails to every employee in our company, with the slide show attached. I was careful to send it from an email address that couldn't be linked to me. I even sent Paige one, so she could see her photo shoot. That was the hot topic of the day. It had gotten so bad, that Mr. Lawson called an emergency meeting in the conference room. Paige had the nerve to show up.

Mr. Lawson stood up at the head of the table. "As you're all aware, we've had quite an interesting morning. I'm sure everyone has received or viewed the very explicit photos of Paige and Robert. I'm not really sure why they were sent or who sent them. Right now, that's not really the issue." He rubbed his head, as if he was thinking really hard. "This is a very serious matter."

Everyone was glancing at Paige. She sat there as if nothing had happened. She looked at me and had the audacity to smile.

Mr. Lawson continued. "I've never had to deal with anything of this nature. So I'm not quite sure how to handle it. Do I go as far as to terminate employment? Or do I do some form of corrective action?" He looked at Paige. "Paige, what do you have to say about the matter?"

She twirled her hair with her fingers. "Quite frankly Mr. Lawson, I don't see the point of this meeting. To me, you're making the situation out to be bigger than what it really is. If I was a shy or timid person, I'd be feeling embarrassed right now, but I'm not. Plus, what I do in my personal life is my business." The girl had lost her damn mind.

Mr. Lawson cleared his throat. "Young lady, you can't be serious! First of all, you were still in my place of business. Second, you were being intimate with a man who just happens to have some input on who gets the position you just interviewed for. And last, but certainly not least, this filth has been circulating throughout the office all morning."

Paige looked at me before saying, "I think the person responsible for this should be reprimanded. I just think it is plain rude to spy on someone while they're having a personal moment." If I didn't know Paige was crazy before, I definitely knew it now. Everyone was looking at her like she had lost her damn mind. Mr. Lawson looked like he was going to blow his top.

I knew he had lost it, when he slammed his fist down on the table. "Paige, I think you should leave the room. I can't believe how nonchalant you're acting. I'll deal with you later. You're excused."

She got up from the table, rolled her eyes at me and did her little prance out of the room. Mr. Lawson sat quietly for a few seconds before he spoke again. "What Robert and Paige have done is very serious…but what puzzles me is who took those photos. Why would anyone want to do something like that?"

My heart started beating faster. I didn't think he would dwell on who took the photos. All I was thinking about was getting even with Paige. Now, my job was on the line also. But I made sure there was no way the emails could be traced back to me. Hopefully, he wouldn't get too wrapped up into finding out who sent them.

As if reading my mind, he said, "But I'm not going to get too involved in trying to figure out who sent the photos. The truth is, whoever took them uncovered something that shouldn't be happening. I'm going to handle the situation the way I see fit. But I'm telling you all now, I want all of those emails deleted and I don't want to hear any more about those photos. Do I make myself clear?" Everyone said, "Yes sir" in unison. Then Mr. Lawson excused us.

About two hours after we left the conference room, Paige came storming in my office. "You conniving bitch! I know you had something to do with those photos!"

I looked up at her with the most innocent look on

my face. "Paige dear, I don't know what you're talking about. I had nothing to do with those photos."

"You're lying and you know it. You knew that I was going to get that job, so you figured out a way to get me out of the picture." She put her finger in my face.

"You better get that deformed finger out of my face before I break it. The only way you were going to get that job is by doing what you got caught doing...screwing your way to the top."

"Well, I hope you're satisfied. Mr. Lawson fired me!"

It was hard for me not to smile. "Paige, you brought this on yourself. You were the one in there screwing Robert's brains out. Whoever took those pictures just confirmed what a slut you really are. Maybe now, you will think about the decisions you make before you act on them."

She got closer to my desk. "You may think that you've won, but you are not going to get away with this. You chose to screw with the wrong bitch. I promise you, you haven't seen the last of me...remember that!"

Before I could respond to her little threat, she stormed back out the door. The expression on her face was so serious. As deranged as she sounded, I should've been scared. But I wasn't going to let an emotional wreck like Paige put fear in me. She was just blowing smoke because she had lost her job. To hell with Paige.

Sierra

It had been a couple of days since I had opened up to Alexis about my sex life. Once I got home that night, I felt like I had betrayed our marriage by discussing it with someone else. She had called me several times, but I kept avoiding her calls. One day, she had even come by the spa, but I was with a client. So I didn't get to talk to her. I was going to try to avoid her as much as possible, until last night happened.

I had already tucked Shelby into bed. Tyler was in his office on the computer, as usual. I took a nice warm bubble bath. Afterwards, I covered my body with scented body oil. I put on the sexy piece I had picked up from *Victoria's Secret*. With my black stilettos on, I walked downstairs to my husband's office. He had his back turned to me, so I called his name. When he turned around, his eyes almost popped out of his head. His manhood bulged in his pants. "Wow...Sierra, you look good!" he said, not taking his eyes off of me.

I put my hands on my hips. "Oh, do I now?"

"Y-yes y-you d-do", he stuttered.

"Well, why don't you show me how good I look? Come here." I motioned him to me with my finger.

He quickly turned off the computer and came to me. As soon as he came close to me, I stopped him by putting my hand up to his chest. "Before we go any further, I need to know if you've been a good little boy today."

My husband looked at me like I had lost my mind. "Excuse me?"

I repeated, "I said have you been a good little boy today?"

"Is this some kind of joke, Sierra?" He sounded irritated.

"No sweetie, it's no joke. Once again, have you been a good little boy today?" I knew I was pushing it.

He came closer to me. "I don't know what kind of games you're playing, but I'm not interested."

I dropped my hands to my sides. "Tyler, I was just trying to do some role playing. That's all. Why do you always have to spoil everything?"

"Role playing? Why in the hell do you want to role play? You have been watching too much damn TV or something."

I grabbed his arms. "What's wrong with a little role playing Tyler?"

He pushed my hands away. "I don't want to do any damn role playing Sierra!"

"Why do you have to be so close-minded about everything Tyler?" I sat down on the futon against the wall.

"I'm not being close-minded. I'm being realistic. What normal couples do role playing?"

I couldn't believe him. "Tyler, role playing isn't so unusual. Lots of couples do it to spice things up in the bedroom." I sounded like I really knew what I was talking about.

Tyler threw his hands up in the air. "There you go with that again. Why are you so obsessed with our sex life here lately?"

"Tyler, I'm not obsessed. I just want to try new things. I feel like I'm missing out on something. You know you're the only person I've ever been with. And I'm not saying that I'm tired of you. I'm just tired of the same ole routine." I stood up to go to his side.

He walked away from me and sat back at his desk. "You satisfy me plenty...but apparently, I don't satisfy you."

I walked over to him and touched him on his shoulder. "Tyler, don't try to turn this into something that it's not. All I'm saying is that I feel like we could use a boost in our sex life. I enjoy making love to you. You are my husband and I love you very much."

"You love me, but you don't find me sexually attractive anymore...right?" He asked that question with the most sincere look on his face. I had to step back to look at him. "Are you crazy? Tyler, you are the sexiest man I know. Look at you. You are drop dead gorgeous. Any woman in her right mind would be attracted to you. I notice how they're always staring at you whenever we go out."

He smiled a little and then said, "You're exaggerating, but it did make me feel good."

"No, I'm not exaggerating. It's the truth. But I'm the one that should be concerned. Sometimes, I wonder if you still find me sexually attractive. Really I don't know what to think anymore. Our sex life went from frequent to almost nonexistent. What's going on Tyler?" I looked at him and waited for a response.

He rubbed his face with his hands. "Sierra, there's nothing going on. Hell, I think you're the most beautiful woman in the world. I guess we just see sex in a different way. I'm fine with our sex life and you're not. Maybe you're at your sexual peak or something. I just know I'm not down for all that crazy sex stuff you're trying to throw on me. I just want to keep it simple." And without even giving me a chance to respond, he walked out and went to bed. I was left standing there in my sexy lingerie and stilettos looking stupid.

Now, I really needed someone to talk to. Alexis was my only option. I didn't have any appointments scheduled until later in the evening, so I decided to give her a call. When I got in touch with her, she said she didn't feel like coming out, but I could come by her house for a while.

When I arrived at her house, she was wearing a very sheer dress. It was one of those fancy gowns that you see women in old movies wear. In her hand was some type of drink. "Why haven't you returned my calls Sierra? I was worried about you", she said after inviting me in.

"Honestly, Alexis, I was kind of embarrassed about the stuff I had told you. I didn't know if I could face you again."

She gave me a funny look. "That's silly. You have no reason to be embarrassed. As I told you then, I'm not here to judge you. Besides, you felt comfortable enough with me to confide in me. And that says a lot." She took a sip of her drink.

"Thanks for not judging me. I really appreciate it. I've never even told my two best friends about me and Tyler's sex life. As far as they know, everything is good." I glanced down at her drink. She must've noticed. "Oh dear, where are my manners? Would you like something to drink?" she asked.

I threw my hand up. "Oh. No thank you. I have to drive back to the spa. Plus, it's too early for me to be drinking."

She walked over to the mini bar. "Don't be ridiculous. Honey, in my world it's never too early to drink. One drink won't hurt you."

"I guess one drink won't hurt me. I'm not much of a drinker. So give me something that's not too strong." I watched her pour something in a glass. Without asking her what it was, I took a sip. It burned my throat at first.

She laughed at my reaction. "Just take your time and savor the flavor. After a couple more sips, it won't be so bad." And she was right. Before I knew it, I had drunk two glasses of that stuff and was working on my third. I was starting to feel really good and I kept laughing for no reason at all.

I started telling Alexis about my episode with Tyler the night before. She sat there and listened as I went over every detail. After I finished my story, she came and sat directly beside me on the sofa. "You know it's a shame that a woman as sexy as yourself should have to put up with a man that doesn't appreciate you or your body."

She took the glass out of my hand. I reached for it. "Hey, I wasn't finished with that. Why did you take my drink?"

"I think you've had enough. Just sit back and relax", she ordered and started taking off my shoes. I tried to get up. "Alexis, what are you doing? I need to get back to the spa soon."

She pushed me back on the sofa. "You're in no condition to drive. I'm going to take care of you." She then proceeded to remove my pants. I knew I had gotten a little tipsy, but I wasn't to the point where I couldn't have stopped her. For some reason, I didn't want to stop her. I sat there and let her undress me.

After she got me completely nude, she whispered in my ear, "That husband of yours doesn't know how to please you. I can please you the way you want to be pleased."

For a split second, I wanted to protest to what she was trying to do. I wanted to tell her that I wasn't into women and that I loved my husband. The words wouldn't come out. My mouth wouldn't open.

Before I could muster up the courage to say something, her mouth met mine. Her lips were so soft and sweet. She used her tongue to force my mouth open. Within seconds, our tongues were entwined. She kissed me like I had never been kissed before. I could feel my body heating up and my nipples getting rock hard.

She then started kissing me on my neck. That sent chills through my body. I couldn't believe what was happening. I had to stop her. "No Alexis...this isn't right. You're a very attractive woman, but I'm not gay."

She ignored me and kept kissing me on my neck. Then I felt her fingers on my thigh. She slowly made her way between my legs and I felt her fingers caress my private parts. "Stop it! Get away from me Alexis!" I yelled and pushed her away from me.

She looked at me with surprise. "Why are you tripping Sierra? I'm only trying to make you feel good. You know you want this to happen. Just give me a chance to show you how a woman is supposed to feel. If you don't like it, then you can ask me to stop."

"I'm asking you to stop now." I covered myself up with my shirt. She pulled the shirt away. "Be honest with me and with yourself. Didn't you like the way I was making you feel?"

I didn't answer her. I just looked down at the floor. "Why won't you answer the question?" Before I could respond, she said, "I'll tell you why you won't answer. It was feeling good to you. You hate to admit that, because you think that might mean that you're a lesbo. I know you're not gay. Neither am I. But you are a very sexy and attractive woman who doesn't know what it feels like to have her pussy licked. I feel that it is my duty as your new friend to help you out. I promise you, you will enjoy it."

She then forced my legs open and spit a wad of saliva on my pussy. Then she placed her head between my legs and started doing her thing. When her tongue first made contact with me, I felt as though I would pass out. I had no idea that it could feel so good. I started moaning and groaning like I never had before. "Oh my God Alexis. That feels soooo good. Please...don't stop...don't ever stop!" I opened my legs even wider for her. The sound of her slurping on me echoed through the room and turned me on even more.

"You like the way that feels don't you? I told you I could make you feel good", she said between licks.

I was breathing hard and panting. "Yes, I love the way it feels. I think I'm gonna cry!" I yelled.

Then she inserted two fingers inside of me, while still feasting on me. That was it for me. "Oh Alexis, you're gonna make me come. Oh God...don't stop...don't stop!"

She was moving her fingers in and out of me real fast and sucking on my clit. I had never in my life felt anything so intense. "Tyler could never make you feel like this. I know what you want and need." Alexis stopped for a few seconds to express herself. Then she put my legs over her shoulders. "My goal is to make you come harder than you ever have in your life." Then she started eating my pussy and fingering me again.

Within minutes, my body was shaking and shivering. "Oh God! I'm coming...I'm coming...oh yes, Alexis...that's it...that's it!" I grabbed her head and held it between my legs until my orgasm subsided.

Alexis sat up and wiped her mouth with her gown. "So, how was it Sierra?" She had a big grin on her face.

I had to catch my breath before speaking. "Hell, it was fantastic! Didn't my screams give it away? I have never come so hard in my entire life. I'd say you definitely reached your goal."

She rubbed my leg. "I'm just glad to see that you

enjoyed it."

I looked at her and realized what I had just done. I let another woman have her way with me. What in the hell was I thinking? It had to be the drinks, because I would've never done anything like that sober. Alexis must have noticed the concern on my face. "What's wrong Sierra? You don't look so well." She still had her hand on my leg.

I pushed her hand away. "I can't believe I let you talk me into doing that. What did you put in those drinks?"

She laughed before saying, "Sierra, I didn't put anything in your drink. I can understand how you feel. That's sometimes the first reaction for a woman who has her first encounter with another woman. I had the same reaction my first time."

"I thought you said you weren't gay. You lied to me!" I started trying to put my clothes back on.

She grabbed me. "I'm not gay Sierra. But you are not the first woman I've ever been with. It was a long time ago. You are the first woman I've been with since her. Don't be upset with me."

"Why me? Why did you decide to be with me?" I wanted to know.

She took my hands in hers. "I'll be honest with you. When you opened up to me that night, I kind of felt sorry for you. I just couldn't believe that as sexy as you are, you had never experienced oral sex. I wondered what I could do to help you. When you told me about your ordeal last night with your husband, I decided right then what I had to do."

"So, you really think I'm sexy? I've never considered myself as sexy."

She put her hand on her hip. "Are you kidding me? Sierra, you are a very sexy woman. Don't tell me that your husband doesn't tell you that either?"

"Yeah, he tells me sometimes. But it's usually before we have sex. And I always wonder if he's being sincere or if he just feels obligated to say it."

She pulled me up off the sofa. "Well, I'm being

sincere. You are very sexy." She guided me into the foyer, where a full length mirror was hanging. "Look at yourself. How can you not think you're sexy?"

I looked at myself. I mean really looked at myself. Alexis stood behind me and cupped my breasts. "Look at those full perky breasts." Then she rubbed my stomach. "And that flat stomach." She turned me around. "And check out that round tight ass. Girl, you got it going on."

I gave her a warm embrace. "Thanks Alexis. I really needed that. You know exactly what to say to make a person feel good."

"Honey, I'm just telling the truth. Every woman is sexy in her own way. And don't you forget that." She grabbed both of my hands. "And with your permission, I'd like to show you just how sexy you are again.

I followed her back into the den. She licked my body from head to toe for the next hour. I had one orgasm after another. Things would've gone on longer if my cell phone hadn't started ringing. It was Jazmin calling to tell me that my appointment was waiting for me. I jumped up and threw my clothes on.

"I'll call you later Alexis. I want you to know that I really appreciate everything you've done for me", I told her while putting on my shoes.

She licked her lips and said, "No problem. It was my pleasure. Just don't get missing on me okay?"

As I rushed back to the spa, thoughts of what happened weighed on my mind. I was still in shock that I had been with a woman. But did that really count? I mean, it wasn't like I did anything to her. All I did was kiss her. She did all the work, while I enjoyed it. It didn't matter anyway. No one was ever going to know about my little incident. That was something I would be keeping to myself. Besides, it wasn't like it was going to happen again. It was just a onetime thing.

Taylor

"Taylor, I'm still mad at you for not inviting us to your husband's little dinner party. You think we're too ghetto or something?" Jade whined.

"Jade, I don't know why you keep bringing that up. That was two weeks ago. You don't see Sierra tripping about it. So why are you?" I said before taking a sip of my lemonade.

"Sierra and I are two different people. Plus, I like to mingle with the rich and famous", she replied, dabbing her mouth with a napkin.

I waved my hand at her. "Girl, you know you need to quit. Them folks aint famous. Most of them do have more money than they can spend though. Honestly, those dinner parties are boring. Plus, you wouldn't fit in."

She put her hand on her hip. "And what in the hell is that supposed to mean? If your ghetto ass can fit in, I know I can too."

I laughed at her response. "Jade, you know I'm just messing with you. And why I gotta be ghetto?"

"I don't know. I guess you were born that way." She laughed at her own joke.

"Enough talk about that. Why did Sierra say she couldn't make it tonight?"

Sierra never missed our monthly chic fest. That was our time to catch up on each other's lives and just hang out. If you missed it, it better be for a good reason. Tonight, we had decided on *Firebirds*.

"She said something about having to do some things at the spa."

"At this time of night? That seems so odd don't you think?" I asked, resting my chin on my hand.

She answered nonchalantly, "I guess...I don't know."

I snapped my fingers at her. "Jade, you don't think Sierra's been acting strange lately?"

She shrugged her shoulders. "No. Not really. I haven't noticed anything different about her. I mean, she does seem a little more upbeat to me. That's all."

I chewed the salad in my mouth before replying, "Well, I say something's up. She hardly ever calls me anymore. And when I call her, she's always too busy to talk to me."

Jade rolled her neck at me. "She does have her own business, you know. Not everybody has a filthy rich husband taking care of them Taylor Morgan."

I rolled my eyes at her. "I'm aware of that Jade Peterson. That never stopped her before."

"Maybe business has picked up for her and she doesn't have the time she use to have Taylor."

"You could be right. Maybe I'm just making a big deal out of nothing. I can't expect things to always be the same."

We continued to chat for a while. Then I noticed Sierra enter the restaurant with a very attractive woman. They were laughing and chatting like old buddies. "Hey Jade, check it out. Look who just walked in." I pointed in the direction they had gone.

Jade turned around to look. "Isn't that Sierra? What is she doing here and who is that woman she's with?"

I put my napkin down on the table and scooted to the end of the booth. "I don't know, but I'm about to find out."

Jade grabbed my hand. "You just can't go barging in on her and her guest."

I snatched my hand away. "The hell I can't. We have a right to know why she stood us up, don't we?"

"Damn Taylor, you act like she's married to us or something", she whispered.

I sat back in the booth. "It's not like that Jade. I just want to know why she lied to us. That's all."

"As far as you know, that could be a client she's with and they're here to discuss business."

I looked at her like she was crazy. "She owns a spa for Christ's sake. What kind of business would they be discussing?"

Jade popped her lips at me. "You are hopeless, you know that?"

I guess Sierra spotted us, because she was headed our way, with her guest close behind. "Hi, you guys."

Jade smiled and said, "Hello Sierra." I mumbled a weak, "Hi."

She stood there for a moment, not saying anything. Then Jade cleared her throat.

"Oh, where are my manners? You guys, this is my friend Alexis Montague." She grabbed her friend's arm. "Alexis, this is Jade Peterson." She pointed to Jade. "And this is Taylor Morgan."

Alexis held out her hand to shake Jade's hand and then she shook mine. "It's nice to finally meet the both of you."

Jade responded by saying, "We're pleased to meet you too." I threw in a fake smile, not to be rude.

They were about to walk away, when Jade opened her big mouth and said, "Why don't you guys join us?" I stomped her foot under the table.

Sierra glanced at Alexis. "Well, we have a lot of business to discuss."

Alexis waved her hand at Sierra. "Oh, that's no problem. We can discuss business anytime."

Sierra gave her a look, I couldn't quite comprehend. It could have been my imagination, but it seemed like she didn't want them to join us. "Well, if you think it's okay, then I guess we'll join them", Sierra weakly replied.

Jade summoned the waitress over to inform her of our new guests. We were eating appetizers and salad, so our main dishes hadn't arrived yet. Sierra and Alexis placed their orders and requested that their food arrived with ours.

After the waitress left, Jade spoke up. "So...where do you two know each other from?" She directed the question to Alexis.

She flipped her hair over her shoulder. "One day, I walked into her spa. She serviced me and we've been friends ever since."

"Why haven't you ever mentioned her to us Sierra?" I glared at Sierra.

It took her a moment to answer. She looked at Alexis before replying. "Uh...I-I guess I just never got around to it. You guys are always so busy and I've been very busy myself, with business and all."

"It's okay if you haven't told them about me Sierra. I'm not upset, so I don't know why anyone else should be." She threw me a look and continued, "Besides, she's mentioned you all to me."

Jade gave me a look before replying, "It's okay Sierra. We understand how it could have slipped your mind." She then turned to Alexis. "What kind of business are you in Alexis...if you don't mind me asking?"

"Of course I don't mind. I'm a lawyer. Right now, I'm in the process of opening my own law firm. I'm trying to close a deal on this office space downtown." She laced her fingers together and placed her hands on top of the table.

Jade leaned in closer to the table, like she was really interested. "I know you're excited. So, what's the hold up?"

Alexis cleared her throat. "I'm waiting on David Morgan to come down on the price of the space. We've been going back and forth on the price. David Morgan is a big-"

"We know who David Morgan is!" I snapped.

She glared at me. "Well, I didn't know. Most people who aren't in the business have the slightest idea who David Morgan is."

"Well, I know David very well." I looked her dead in her eyes.

"So, you know him in a business sense?"

I held up my ring finger. "Actually, I know him in a personal sense. He's my husband."

She tilted her head to the side. "Excuse me?"

"You heard me. David is my husband." I kept waving that big rock in her face.

She gave me a skeptical look. "That's funny. I've

never seen you at any of his functions."

I sat up in the seat. "Are you calling me a liar?" I turned to Sierra. "Girl, you better talk to your friend. She got a lot of nerve."

Sierra rolled her eyes at me. "Calm down Taylor. She didn't mean anything by it." She then touched Alexis on the arm. "David is her husband."

Alexis looked at me and asked, "So, how long have you two been married?"

"That's irrelevant. The point is he is my husband. And I don't think I should have to sit here and be questioned by you." I sat back in the seat and crossed my arms.

Jade questioned me, "Taylor why are you making such a big fuss over nothing?"

I glared at her. "I'm making a big fuss because this woman here is calling me a liar in so many words. I have no reason to lie. Her friend here..." I pointed to Sierra. "...should have told her already."

Sierra stood up. "Taylor, I never told her, because it never came up. I can't believe you're acting this way. I will not sit here and let you disrespect Alexis any longer!"

Alexis grabbed her arm. "It's okay Sierra. I can understand how it may have sounded like I was questioning her. Let's just sit here and enjoy our meal." She then turned to me. "I'm sorry if I offended you Taylor. It won't happen again."

Everyone was looking at me. I guess they were waiting for me to accept her weak apology. I wasn't about to say everything was okay, because it wasn't. That bitch had insulted me and I wasn't about to just let it go.

Jade spoke up. "Taylor, didn't you hear Alexis apologize to you?"

I looked at Jade. "Yeah, I heard her."

"Well, aren't you going to say anything?"

I rolled my eyes. "What's there to say?"

Sierra spoke up. "You could at least say-"

Alexis cut her off. "Let's just drop it okay? It's no big deal."

Once our food arrived, I sat in silence. The others

were chatting like longtime friends. I wasn't about to sit there and pretend to enjoy the company. Jade was laughing and smiling at everything Alexis had to say. There was just something about her that I didn't trust. I just couldn't put my finger on it.

"You know what Taylor; you were being a real bitch back there at the restaurant. What was all that about?" Jade was grilling me on the ride back home.

"Listen Jade, I don't have to explain my behavior to anyone. I'm a grown ass woman", I snapped at her.

"Yeah, you're a grown ass woman who was acting like a child. It's a good thing Alexis is so down to earth. Anyone else would've left after cursing your ass out."

She was the one who needed a good cursing out. That hussy was acting like it was humanly impossible for David to be my husband. She acted like I was making it up or something. Gonna tell me she aint never seen me at any of his functions. Hell, I haven't ever seen her ass at any." I was getting mad all over again.

"Taylor, that didn't mean she was calling you a liar. It just meant that she had never seen you before. Only you could take something like that out of context." Jade was trying to defend her again.

"It's not always what you say. It's how you say it. And like I said earlier, Sierra should've already told her that he was my husband if they're such good friends." I turned my BMW into Jades' apartment complex.

"Believe it or not Taylor; everything isn't always centered around your life." She opened the door and got out.

"What is that supposed to mean Jade?" I asked.

"You figure it out Taylor", she answered and closed the door. Then she walked off.

David was in his office when I got home. He was looking over some papers when I came in and hadn't noticed my presence. I walked up to him and he almost jumped out of his chair. He quickly put his papers away. "Taylor, what are you trying to do...give me a heart attack? You scared the hell out of me."

It was always funny to hear my husband curse, because he rarely did. "I'm sorry sweetie. I thought you heard me come in. What are you looking at?"

He took off his reading glasses. "Nothing important really. I was just looking back over some stuff to make final decisions on, that's all. Where have you been?"

I went over and sat on his knee. "I just had dinner with Jade and Sierra...and Alexis." I put emphasis on Alexis' name.

He gave me a puzzled look. "Who's Alexis?"

"She's a friend of Sierra's. Apparently, she knows you too. She's waiting for you to give her a final price on an office downtown so she can open her law firm." I waved my hand in the air in a mocking manner.

David laughed at me. "Oh. That Alexis. Alexis Montague. What a character. She wants me to come down on the price. I've already cut the price twice. I can't go down any further. I hear she's quite the lawyer."

I smacked my lips. "Yeah, she's quite something. She had the nerve to question me when I told her you were my husband."

He wrapped his arms around my waist. "What do you mean question you?"

"She acted like she didn't believe me David. It was as if she was saying that it was impossible for that to be true. Of course, Sierra defended her...Jade too. I was making a big deal out of nothing is what they told me." I pointed to myself.

David started rubbing my back. "You didn't make a scene did you Taylor?"

I gave him a surprised look. "No, I didn't cause a scene. Yes, I let that little hussy know how I felt. Then she had the nerve to give me a little weak apology. All I know is she's got Sierra acting all different."

"Sounds like someone may be a little jealous", he teased.

I laughed at his remark. "Me, jealous? David, don't be ridiculous. I have no reason to be jealous of anyone." I stood up to leave.

"Don't get all bent out of shape. I was just joking."
He stood up and stretched.

I gave him a quick kiss on the lips. "Well, I'm
going to bed sweetie. Don't stay up too late. Momma
might want some loving later."

"Since you put it that way, I won't be far behind
you." He started straightening up his desk.

I walked towards the door. When I got in the hall, I
peeked back in to see David stuffing the papers he was
looking at in a drawer and locking it with a key. He then
put the key in his pocket. What were those papers and
why was he hiding them? I needed to know.

Jade

I was getting settled into my new office. That's right. I am now the operations manager. Everyone in the office had congratulated me and told me how much I deserved the position. Mr. Lawson had to train me though. After all the stuff that went down with Robert and Paige, Robert decided to just go ahead and leave for Texas. That was probably the best decision.

Even though Mr. Lawson seemed uptight and serious, he had quite a sense of humor. Working so close to him for the past week had been an eye-opener. He was a sharp business man and was very passionate about his work.

I had started getting very strange phone calls for the last couple of days. They would call every hour and either breathe heavily into the phone or hang up. It was really starting to irritate me. I started thinking that maybe Paige was involved, but then I thought better of it. I'm sure she has forgotten all about me and has moved on with her life. My thoughts were interrupted by the telephone ringing. "Hello, this is Jade speaking. How may I help you?"

Silence

"Hello! Can I help you?"

Silence

"Who is this and what do you want?"

A man's voice boomed through the telephone. "Bitch, don't raise your voice at me!"

I was flabbergasted. "What did you say?"

He responded. "You heard me! Just watch your back!" Then there was a dial tone.

I sat there in shock for a few minutes. What was all that about? My mind was spinning out of control. I didn't recognize the voice and I had no idea who it could've been. As far as I know, I hadn't pissed anyone off; other than Paige. Someone was obviously trying to scare me.

I'll give them credit. They had done a good job. Now, I would be looking over my shoulder every second.

Eli and I were having dinner at *Chili's*. I had just decided to tell him about my mystery phone call.

"So who do you think it could be Jade?" he asked me after drinking some of his tea.

"Eli, I told you I have no earthly idea who it could've been. That's why it's such a shock to me. I've been receiving calls for the last couple of days."

"Why are you just now telling me this?" He seemed upset.

"Today was the first time they said anything. All the other times, they would just breathe heavy into the telephone or just hang up when I answered." I rubbed my temples to try to ease the headache that I felt coming on.

"So how many times in all have they called you?"

I shook my head in frustration. "I don't know. Maybe four or five times a day. Look, can we just drop this? I don't want to spoil our night talking about that jerk."

He looked at me and hesitated before answering. "Sure babe. If that's what you want. Just promise me that you won't keep nothing like this from me again...and I'll drop the subject."

"I promise." I placed my hand on top of his. Then our waitress came to take our order. She looked directly at Eli when she requested our order. That was the second time she had done that. When she took our drink orders, she did the same thing. I didn't say anything then, but it had become clear that she was ignoring me. The ladies were always checking Eli out when we were out together, but this chic was really pushing it.

Eli must have noticed my displeasure. "Hey babe, what are you getting?"

I glanced at the menu one more time before responding. "I think I'll have the salmon."

She didn't take her eyes off of Eli. "I just love your hair", she said to him.

"Uh...thank you", he responded without looking at her.

She twirled a lock of her hair with her fingers. "I just think dread locks are so sexy."

I cleared my throat, hoping to get her attention. She still ignored me and kept talking to Eli. "So how long did it take them to get that long?"

Eli refused to look in my direction. "Um, about eight years, I guess."

I had had enough. I was ready to go off on her. Then I decided I would wait for our food. I had heard too many stories of servers doing stuff to your food when you pissed them off. I cleared my throat again. This time, Eli looked in my direction. I gave him a dirty look.

"Uh, I don't mean to be rude, but we'd like to go ahead and place our order now", he finally spoke up.

She playfully hit him on the arm. "Oh, I'm so sorry. I'm just going on and on about your hair, and you're ready to get your food. Let me get this order in and I'll be right back." She looked at Eli before walking away.

As soon as she was out of earshot, I started going off. "What in the hell was all of that about?"

He gave me an innocent look. "Babe, what are you talking about?"

"Don't play dumb with me Eli. That little heffa was practically all over you." I was fuming inside.

"Aw, come on Jade. You are really bugging. She just said she liked my locks. It's no big deal. Women are always complimenting me on my locks and you know that shit."

I put my hand up to my chest. "I'm not bugging. How can you be so nonchalant about this? Yeah, I know women are always sweating you about your hair, but this bitch was being very disrespectful to me. She wouldn't even acknowledge my presence. And if she keeps it up, I'm going to have to put her in her place."

When our food was brought to our table, Miss Thing wasn't far behind. "Is there anything else I can do for you?" She looked directly at Eli. And the way she asked him that, had nothing to do with the service.

I had taken all I was going to take from her. There was no way I was going to keep letting her push up on my man right in front of my face. I just wasn't going out like that. Before I knew it, I was going off on her ass. "What you can do is get your trifling ass out of my man's face."

She looked at me like I had astounded her. "Excuse me?"

I came back at her. "You heard what the fuck I said. Ever since we sat down, you have been all up in his face."

"Ma'am, I'm just doing my job."

"Don't give me that bullshit. He is not the only person at this table. You haven't acknowledged me once."

"You know, you black women are all alike. As soon as there's a pretty white woman around your man, you feel threatened. It's not our fault if y'all are insecure and can't keep your men from looking at us. The truth is you know deep down inside they all want a white woman anyway."

I couldn't believe she went there. I knew we were causing a scene, but I didn't care. That bitch had crossed the line and I was about to let her know a thing or two. "Let's get one thing straight. I am by no means threatened by you or any other white bitch. I wasn't going to turn this into a black and white thing, but you took it there. I am very secure with myself and know that I'm a beautiful black woman and proud of it. If anything, it's the white women like yourself, who want black men so bad, you'll do anything to get one to pay attention to you. This one is mine. So I suggest you go sniffing around another one."

She rolled her eyes at me and before she could say anything else, I threw my glass of water in her face. She was quite surprised and didn't know how to react. I guess someone had gone to get the manager, because she was on her way to our table.

"Is there a problem here Cindy? She asked the waitress. Then she looked at us, after she noticed the water on Cindy's face.

Cindy pointed at me. "She threw water in my face. And I was just doing my job."

I spoke up before she could finish her lie. "She was not doing her job. She was ignoring me, but giving my boyfriend here complete and excellent service...and I didn't appreciate it. Now, I know I may have gotten a little carried away with the water and everything. But she turned it into a black and white issue. So, I lost my cool. That, I apologize for."

The manager looked at Cindy, who was looking down at the floor. "Cindy, you have been warned about this before...several times. I cannot keep having this conversation with you. I have given you more than enough chances to get your act together. This is it. You are finished here."

Cindy tried to protest. "But Deb, I need this job. I promise it won't happen again."

"I'm sorry Cindy. You've struck out. I told you before to get your hormones in check, but apparently you have not."

Eli spoke up. "Listen, I'm sure my girl wasn't trying to get her fired. This has gotten out of hand."

"I understand your concern sir, but this isn't the first time this has happened. She knew that she was on thin ice here. So she brought it on herself. I do apologize for your inconvenience. Your meal is on the house tonight. Enjoy the rest of your evening. Then she went back into the kitchen. Cindy stormed off behind her.

I was kind of pissed with Eli for sticking up for Cindy like he did, but I didn't say anything. He had a certain look on his face. I couldn't tell if he was angry or embarrassed. He just sat there in silence for a minute or two. I had to break the silence. "So are you supposed to be upset with me Eli?"

He tilted his head to the side before answering. "Naw, Jade. I'm not upset with you. I just can't believe things went down like that. Did you have to throw the water in her face?"

"It was either that or my fist." I laughed.

He laughed too. "I guess the water was the better choice."

We finished our meal making small talk. We both were still kind of in shock over the night's events. Eli had seen a side of me that he had never seen before. I didn't want him to think that I was some psycho that would go off at the drop of a hat.

"Listen, Eli. I'm not some crazy bitch or anything like that. That chic just really pissed me off. It was bad enough that she was being disrespectful towards me. But when she said all of that about us black women, I lost it. Even though a lot of brothas have went astray, I have never felt threatened by white women. When it comes down to it, black women represent beauty in all ways."

Eli placed his hand on mine. "You don't have to explain yourself Jade. I can understand why you were upset. I know that black is beautiful. There's nothing in this world sexier than a black woman. From the different shades of your skin, to the many hairstyles you wear, to the variety of shapes and sizes of your beautiful bodies, nothing can compare."

I laughed at his statement. "For a minute there, I thought you were going to break out into a poetry reading."

"So now, you're making fun of me?" He poked out his lip like a little kid.

"No, I'm not making fun of you Eli. I just never heard you say anything like that before. Do you write poetry?"

He laughed at my question. "Me, write poetry? Nah, it's nothing like that. That's just something that came to me."

"Well, if I didn't know any better, I'd say that was something pre-written." I looked at him skeptically.

Before he could respond, his cell phone started ringing. At first, he acted like he wasn't going to answer it. I spoke up. "Aren't you going to answer that?"

He stood up. "I need to take this outside. It's a very important call. I'll be right back." Then he walked outside.

I sat there trying not to get upset. I just didn't understand why he had to take that call outside. I was feeling that he was hiding something from me again.

He came back in smiling like everything was cool. "Now where were we?" he asked after sitting down.

"Who was that on the phone Eli?" I asked him.

"Nobody important Jade."

"But you said it was an important call before you went outside to answer it." I was starting to raise my voice a little.

He leaned closer to me over the table. "Yeah, it was an important call to me. It had nothing to do with you, Jade."

"But why did you have to take it outside? Were you trying to hide something from me?"

He took a deep breath and ran his fingers through his locks. "Damn Jade, you just don't let up do you? Can't a man have a little privacy without all the questions? Maybe I took the call outside so I could hear better. Did you think about that? I mean after all, we are in a noisy restaurant."

He laughed, mainly to himself. There is one negative thing about black women."

"What's that?' I asked

"Y'all are nosey as hell." He got up from his seat and placed a tip on the table. "Let's ride", he said and then walked out of the restaurant.

I sat there for a few seconds, feeling like a fool. When I got outside, he was standing by the car. I knew I had messed up with all the questions, so I had to make things better.

"Look Eli, I'm sorry." I placed my hand on his back. He didn't respond. We both stood in silence for a few minutes.

I tried again. "Eli, I really am sorry. Sometimes, I don't know what comes over me. I don't want to push you away. Please accept my apology."

He turned around to look at me. "Jade, you are one of the most fascinating women I've ever dated. But you seem obsessed with asking too many questions. I don't have to hide anything from anyone. If I feel you should know something, I will tell you."

I wrapped my arms around his waist. "I guess I keep thinking about some of my past relationships. I was always being lied to or cheated on. Sometimes it's hard not to think about that Eli. Don't you understand where I'm coming from?"

"Yes, I understand where you're coming from Jade. Hell, we've all had bad relationships. But you can't let that shit control your life. Just trust me baby. You're my boo. I promise you, I won't hurt you." He kissed me on my forehead. I felt so much better.

Our ride back to my apartment was a silent one. I don't know what was on Eli's mind. But I was thinking about what he had said. I had to let go of the past. Why did I keep comparing Eli to old boyfriends? No one had ever treated me like Eli did. I knew that I needed to back off. I didn't want to blow it with Eli. Any woman would be tickled pink to have Eli in their life. I had him in mine and I was going to mess it up if I didn't get it together.

When we got to my apartment, we sat in the car for a few minutes. "Are you coming in tonight, Eli?" I asked hopefully. I didn't want to be alone.

"Not tonight. I got something I really need to do. Maybe another night."

I tried not to sound upset. "Okay. Will you at least walk me to my door?" I thought maybe I could change his mind once I gave him that goodnight kiss.

When I got ready to open my apartment door, it just swung open. Eli entered first. I cut the light switch on and almost passed out. Someone had broken into my apartment. Stuff was strewn all over the place. My leather couch was cut up. All of my art had been knocked off the walls and broken. My television screen had been smashed, along with my DVD player. I ran into my bedroom. It was a disaster area also. Most of my belongings in there had been torn and smashed. I just broke down and started crying. Eli tried comforting me. "Everything's gonna be okay baby. Calm down."

I snatched away from him. "How in the hell can I calm down Eli? Someone has come into my apartment and destroyed almost everything I own. Look at this place. How could anyone be so cruel?"

He grabbed me more forcefully. "Jade, I know you're upset, but you have got to pull yourself together.

What we need to do is call the police. You have insurance on your stuff don't you?"

"Um, yeah I do. I have renter's insurance. I never thought I'd have to use it. I just can't believe this shit." I started pacing back and forth. Eli went to the phone and called the police.

"Let's go outside and wait for them to get here. This place is depressing." He grabbed my hand and we headed outside.

Once we were outside, Eli asked, "Do you think this had anything to do with those phone calls you've been getting?"

I shook my head. "No. Not really. I think this was just a random act of vandalism."

He gave me a skeptical look. "Have there been other cases of break-ins or vandalism around here lately?"

I pondered his question before answering. "None that I know of."

"So how can you be so sure that this had nothing to do with those phone calls?"

I took a deep breath. "I just don't think they're connected. Besides, how would that person know where I lived? People at work don't even know where I live. I mean, my address is on file like everybody else's, but it's my old address. I never had the chance to update my records."

Eli pulled me close to him. "I hope you're right. But I just don't want you to dismiss the fact that the two could be related."

I was about to respond, when a police car pulled into the parking lot. "Good, they're here. Now, I can get this over with."

The female officer inspected every inch of my apartment, taking notes in the process. When she had inspected all she could, she started questioning me.

"So, who discovered the break-in?"

I raised my hand in the air. "I did. Well, when I went to unlock the door, I noticed it was already open. He was with me." I pointed to Eli. "He pushed me to the side and entered first."

Eli continued. "We turned on the light and discovered the mess."

The officer jotted something on her pad. "Does anyone have a key to your apartment...other than yourself Ms. Peterson?"

I thought for a moment. "Um...my best friends Taylor and Sierra do. But I know they didn't have anything to do with this. It's not like they use them. They just have them for emergency purposes."

The officer looked at Eli. "Is he your boyfriend?"

Eli spoke up. "As a matter of fact I am."

"Do you have a key to her apartment?"

"No, I don't."

I jumped in. "I just never got around to giving him one. Why do you ask?"

She jotted something else on her pad before answering. "I just have to weigh all options. There doesn't seem to be any forced entry. So either you didn't lock the door or someone used a key to get in. That's why I asked you who had keys to your apartment."

"Well, I didn't do it if that's what you're getting at officer", Eli snapped.

I tugged him on his arm. "Eli, baby, I don't think that's what she was trying to say. She's just trying to gather all of information she can."

She closed her notepad. "Well, I think my work here is done. Ms. Peterson, please feel free to contact us if you think of anything else." She reached in her pocket and handed me a card.

"There is one more thing officer", Eli said. I gave him a warning look. He ignored me and continued. "She has been receiving some threatening calls at work."

The officer took out her pad again. "Why didn't you mention this before Ms. Peterson?"

I rolled my eyes at Eli. "Because, I didn't think it was relevant."

She wrote in her pad again. "Why don't you let me be the judge of that? What exactly is being said on those calls?"

"They pretty much started out breathing on the

phone or not saying anything at all. Then today, they told her to watch her back or something like that", Eli jumped in before I could answer her.

She looked at him. "So, you were there?"

"No, I wasn't. She told me about it tonight at dinner."

She turned her attention back to me. "You don't think too much of these phone calls do you?"

Eli jumped in. "No, she doesn't She doesn't think they're a big deal and is not taking them seriously."

She asked, "Do you have any idea who it could be?" She put her hand up to Eli before he could respond for me.

I answered reluctantly, "No, I don't."

She closed her pad again. "They may or may not be connected. Once again, if you think of anything else, give me a call. Y'all have a good night...what's left of it. Then she was out the door.

"I'll stay and help you clean up so you can get some rest, if you want me to", Eli said as he started picking up stuff.

"What happened to your thing you had to do? Did you change your mind?" I questioned him.

"Forget that Jade. Your place was broken into. How could I leave you in your time of need? What I had to do can wait." He sounded so sincere.

"It doesn't matter anyway, because I'm not staying here tonight. I feel so violated. I don't know when I'll feel comfortable staying here again." That was my chance to see where he lived. He just had to volunteer his place. It was the obvious thing to do.

Instead, he said, "Where are you going to stay then Jade?"

I was almost too upset to speak. "I guess I'll call Taylor and ask her can I stay with her and David for a few days."

He rubbed my back. "Yeah, I think that's a good idea. Why don't you go ahead and call her. I'll wait for you outside."

Once he was outside, I went to my bedroom to

pack. I threw a few things that weren't destroyed in a duffel bag. I went into my bathroom and discovered that my bathroom mirror had been broken. I grabbed a few toiletries and hurried out. When I was done packing, I called Taylor.

"Hey ho, what's up?" she said as soon as she answered.

My voice cracked. "T-Taylor, c-can I stay with you f-for a f-few days?"

She realized I was crying. "Sweetie what's wrong?"

I tried to stop crying so I could tell her what happened. "S-someone broke into my apartment t-tonight."

"Oh my God. Are you okay?"

"Yeah, I'm okay."

"Did they take all of your stuff?"

"Believe it or not, they didn't. They just damaged everything. It wasn't your typical break-in."

"That's odd. But of course, you can stay with me...as long as you need to. You shouldn't be by yourself. I'll even come pick you up."

"No, that's okay. I'll drive myself. I'll be there shortly. Thanks Taylor. You're the best, you know that?"

"You're my girl. That's what friends are for. I'll see you when you get here." Then she hung up.

When I got outside, Eli was waiting by his car. "Come on, I'll drive you to Taylor's."

"I'm driving myself Eli. Besides, I'll need my car for work tomorrow." I started towards my car. He tried to block me. "You can't be serious. You're going to work tomorrow?"

I pushed him out of the way. "Of course I'm going to work tomorrow. I still have a job to do."

He grabbed my arm. "Your apartment was just broken into. How can you think of going to work?"

"Yes, my apartment was broken into, but I'm okay. So, there's no reason for me to stay out of work. Now if you will excuse me, I'll be leaving now." I pulled my arm out of his grasp.

"You are one stubborn woman Jade. But I guess

that's one of the reasons I love you. Give me a call tomorrow to let me know how you're doing okay?" He held out his arms for a hug.

I gave him a long hug. "I'll talk to you tomorrow. And thanks for staying with me until the police came. I really appreciate it."

"It's no big deal. What kind of boyfriend would I be if I just left you here?"

The same kind that wouldn't ask his girlfriend to come stay with him in her time of need, I thought to myself.

I watched him drive off. I hopped into my car and made my way over to Taylor's. I thought about my apartment and the events of the night. Whoever broke into my apartment really did a number on me. It would take a while to get my place back in order. But at this point, I didn't know if I could spend another night in there.

Sierra

I had started spending a lot of time with Alexis. Even though I had no intentions of ever being with her again, it kept happening. It was if she had some special powers over me. Every chance I got, I was letting her feast on my goodies. It had gotten so bad I didn't even want to be with Tyler anymore. I still didn't consider myself gay though. It wasn't that I preferred a woman over a man. It was just the way Alexis took her time pleasing me. At times, I had to literally push her off of me when she'd get started. The time that I knew would come, crept up on me while we were lounging in her den.

"So Sierra, when and if ever do you plan to return the favor?" she asked me after popping some popcorn in her mouth.

I tried to play innocent. "What are you talking about Alexis?"

"Don't play dumb with me. You know what I'm talking about", she replied and hit me with a toss pillow.

I was still playing the innocent role. "No really, what are you talking about?"

She grabbed my arm that time. "Sierra, I've been eating you out for quite some time now. I was just wondering if you ever intend on doing me."

"Do you have to be so graphic? There is a better way of saying that, I'm sure." I rolled my eyes at her playfully.

She laughed. "You don't have a problem with the way I say it when I got your legs spread open and my face is buried between them. It's not a problem when this hot wet tongue is lapping on that pussy like a kitten on some milk. So don't give me that bullshit now. The question again...when are you going to eat my pussy?"

I took a deep breath before responding. "You know this is new to me. I've never done anything like that before. Hell, I wouldn't even know what to do."

"I have no problem showing you. All you have to do is think about licking an ice cream cone or a lollipop. And make sure your tongue is really wet." She stood up to remove her pants.

I sat there for a few seconds staring at the floor. I was kind of nervous and a little unsure if I wanted to take it to that level. The thought of putting my mouth on another woman's private parts made me feel queasy.

She must have sensed my uncertainty. "Look Sierra, if you don't want to do it, don't. Why shouldn't I want the same thing you want? I'll just go on eating your pussy forever, not knowing what it would feel like to have you do the same thing to me. If you want to be selfish, I guess you have that right." She was really putting a guilt trip on me.

I ran my fingers through my hair. "Please don't say that. I'm not trying to be selfish. If I'm a little hesitant, it's because I'm nervous. Like I said before, I've never done anything like this. But if that's what you want, then that's what I'll do."

She immediately dropped her pants to the floor. She stepped out of them and took off her panties. She then lay down in the floor and opened her legs in front of me. "Just take your time and remember what I told you. Think of it as an ice cream cone or a lollipop."

I took a deep breath before taking the plunge. I parted her lips with my fingers and got close to her. I could smell her sweetness. She had a scent of her own, which kind of made my mouth water. I stuck my tongue out to meet her moistness. I heard her sigh when my tongue made contact with her private parts. And before I knew it, I was eating her like a pro."

She was like a wild animal from my tongue action. It was kind of hard to go on because she was moving around so much. "Oh God, Sierra. Eat my pussy, you bitch! Eat my pussy!" She was squeezing my head with her thighs. "Don't stop you little slut! Don't fucking stop...yeah that's it! Oh God, that feels so fucking good!!" The more she screamed and begged, the harder I licked her pussy.

I never knew I would enjoy giving another woman oral pleasure. Tasting her juices in my mouth, made me want to go on forever. "You like me eating your pussy Alexis? Is this what you wanted?" I stopped long enough to ask her.

She answered back. "Yeah baby. This shit feels so good. I'm gonna come! I'm gonna come! Don't stop! Don't stop! That's it! That's it! I'm coming! I'm coming!" Within seconds, she was bucking like a wild horse.

After I stopped munching on her, I asked, "Are you satisfied? Did I do okay?"

After she caught her breath, she replied. "Shit, you did better than okay. Girl, you ate this pussy like you've been doing it for years. Not bad for a first time. Not bad at all."

"Thanks, I guess." I didn't really know what to say. I used a spare napkin to wipe my mouth.

She put her panties and pants back on. "Are you going to be okay with what happened? I mean, are you going to have a problem if I want you to do it again?" she asked.

"Honestly Alexis, I can really say that I enjoyed that. Of course, I was kind of hesitant in the beginning. But once I got a whiff of that pussy, it was on. Something happened to me and I'm not quite sure what it was." I looked her in the eyes to let her know I was serious.

She smiled at me. "Girl, that's what killer pussy will do to you. But all jokes aside, deep down inside every woman has lesbian tendencies."

I gave her a funny look. "Seriously, they do. By nature, we're supposed to crave and want a man. But no matter how sexy or how fine a man is or no matter how much he has rocked your world, nothing beats a woman's touch. I was once told that a woman can eat pussy better than any man. At the time, I didn't believe it. Later, I found out for myself. A woman can eat pussy better because she knows what it's supposed to feel like. She knows how much to suck on the clit or how much pressure to apply. While she's eating that pussy, she's imagining that it's her pussy being eaten."

I took everything in that she had said. "I never looked at it that way. Even though you're the first person I've experienced that with, I can't say I agree with you."

"You may not agree with me, but there's some truth in what I say. Believe me. Almost every woman imagines what it would be like to have another woman eat her pussy. No matter how straight they claim to be or how much they say they love dick, that's always a secret fantasy. Between your girlfriends Taylor and Jade, one, if not both of them have that secret desire. Of course, they would never own up to it." She looked at me as if she was waiting for me to dispute what she said. I sat there for a few seconds, digesting it all in. Maybe she had a point. Otherwise, how could I have let all the stuff that happened happen?

We talked for a little bit longer. She told me more about her encounter with the other woman she had been with. I told her more about Tyler and how we had met. It was getting late and I knew Tyler would be wondering where I was. I helped her straighten up the den before cutting out.

Alexis and I never kissed, held hands or anything like that. That would be too much like a relationship. And what we had wasn't a relationship. I mean, we were friends. But the sex thing was just for fun and convenience. She liked pleasing me because my husband wouldn't and I liked accepting. I guess now we'd be pleasing each other. I didn't consider what we were doing as cheating. We were simply two friends having fun with each other from time to time.

Of course by the time I got home, Shelby was fast asleep. I hated that I didn't get to tuck her in. I could see one of her Dr. Seuss books on the floor beside her bed. I was pretty sure she had asked Tyler to read it to her before she went to sleep. I was standing in the doorway admiring her, when Tyler walked up behind me. "I see you finally made it in." I couldn't tell if there was sarcasm in his voice or not.

"Yeah, I was over at Alexis'. We were discussing business and just chatting." I had never mentioned her name to him before. I had been referring to her as my new friend.

"So is this Alexis person the new friend you've been spending so much time with lately?" he asked with annoyance in his voice.

"Tyler, I don't want to argue tonight, okay?" I threw my hands up in surrender.

He started walking towards our bedroom. "Who said anything about arguing?"

I followed him. "It's just that you have that tone. Baby, what is going on with us? Why can't we sit and have a decent conversation like we use to?"

"Things started going wrong when you kept badgering me about doing things I didn't feel comfortable doing. I would say no and you'd get all upset and call me boring", he said while taking off his shirt.

I walked up to him and put my arms around his waist. "Tyler, I know I've been hounding you about our sex life lately. I promise you, I won't ask you to do anything else that you don't want to do."

He eyed me suspiciously. "So, you don't want to experiment with oral sex anymore?"

I smiled at him. "I do, but it was unfair of me to keep asking you to do something that you didn't feel comfortable doing. I've accepted the fact that it's not going to happen. Like you said, it's not the most important thing. What's important is how much we love each other."

He kissed me on the forehead and then said, "I'm glad you came to your senses. I hated not being close to you."

"Me too", I mumbled into his chest. "Now why don't you go jump in the shower and I'll give you one of my special back rubs. You know it's been a long time since I've given you one of those."

"Yeah, I could sure use one of those. My neck and shoulders are very tense from sitting at the computer all day and night." He removed the rest of his clothing and headed for the shower.

As he was walking into the bathroom, I yelled, "Tyler, you know I love you, don't you?"

He turned around to look at me. "Yes Sierra, I know you love me. And I hope you know that I love you too."

While he was in the shower, I set up the massage table that I kept at home. I pulled out my oils and got everything ready. It was so nice to be talking to him again. We had been walking on eggshells for too long and I was glad to put an end to it. My family was back in order. I had the best of both worlds now. I had a caring husband who loved me deeply. And I had a woman that was working me over like a giant lollipop. What more could a girl ask for?

Taylor

It had been a week since Jade started staying with us. She was my girl, but I wasn't use to having another woman in my living quarters other than Hazel the housekeeper, but she didn't count. Whoever broke into her apartment really had her ass paranoid. She had been back over there only once. And that was to get more clothes. She hadn't really said much about the break-in since that night. I tried not to bring it up because I didn't want to upset her. I decided that I would try to cheer her up by taking her shopping.

"Jade, have you heard anything from the police about the person or persons who broke into your apartment?" We were on our way to *Streets of Southpoint*.

"Girl, please. You know I'm not gonna hear shit from them folks. I'm just another young black girl whose apartment got broken into. Now on the other hand, if that was somebody like you and David, that shit would be on the damn news", she said and rolled her eyes upward.

"Jade, don't say stuff like that", I replied.

"Hell, its true and you know it."

"I'm pretty sure they treat all cases the same. That's their job."

"And I'm pretty sure you're full of shit right now."

I stuck my tongue out at her. "Kiss my voluptuous ass. Anyway when do you plan on moving back into your apartment?"

"Who told you your ass was voluptuous? And why are you asking me about when I'm moving back into my apartment? You trying to tell me something?" she asked.

"David, among others thinks that my ass is voluptuous. And no, I'm not trying to tell you anything. I just simply want to know how long you're going to let this jerk run your life."

"I'm not letting him run my life. I just need more time."

"How much time?"

"I don't know."

"You can't live with me and David forever."

"A week is not forever."

"You've got to face the music sooner or later, preferably sooner."

"I'm aware of that Taylor. Like I said, I just need a little more time."

"Just remember, time waits for no one."

"Neither does a foot in the ass."

"Fuck you, Jade."

"No, fuck with me." She balled her fists up and shook them at me.

I slapped at her fists. "Seriously Jade, I'm not trying to tell you what to do, but you need to get your life back. You won't even go in there to get everything back in order. What are you afraid of?"

She blew air out of her mouth. "I wouldn't say I'm afraid. It's just that I feel funny being in there. Some stranger invaded my personal space and it just freaks me out. I just keep imagining them rambling through my things, touching them and it gives me chills. I guess it's hard for you to understand."

Oh, I understood what it was like to have someone invade your personal space. I knew what it was like to have someone invade your body. My thoughts went back to my childhood and how all those men had violated my body. I went through things that no child should have to go through. One night in particular stood out in my mind. I was sitting on the couch watching television. My stomach started cramping like crazy. I looked down at the mound in front of me. The time had come. My baby was ready to enter the world. I stumbled off the couch and went to my mother's bedroom door. "Mama, I think it's time!" I yelled.

I didn't get a response. Another cramp hit me again. I knocked on the door with my fist. "I think it's time Mama!" I yelled even louder.

The door swung open real fast. My mother's friend Earl was standing there half naked. "Girl, what you yellin' 'bout? Can't you see grown folks is handling they bizness?"

I was holding my pregnant belly. "I think it's time. I think my baby is 'bout to come out." I was fourteen and scared to death.

"Well, what you want us to do. We aint no damn doctors." He stood there glaring at me with a smirk on his face.

I tried to peek over his shoulder. "Mama! Please help me! I'm in pain out here!" I yelled. Then all of a sudden, I felt a trickle of liquid run down my leg. "Oh my God! Something's happening to me!"

My mother appeared from behind Earl. "What is it Taylor? You out here carrying on like the world is coming to an end."

The liquid was coming down my leg faster. "Mama, it's time! The baby is coming. We need to get to the hospital." I didn't know much about giving birth, but I knew enough to know that we needed to get to a hospital.

My mother barged out of the room. "Chile, we aint going to no damn hospital. Who you think gonna pay for this shit? We gonna deliver that baby right here. If yo' fast ass wasn't messing 'round with them no good boys, you wouldn't have gotten yo'self knocked up. Plus, I'm too young and too fine to be a grandma."

Earl chimed in. "I know that's right."

I rolled my eyes at them. It hurt me to hear my mother say things like that, especially when the truth was that one of her friends got me pregnant. I had never been with anybody but them. Deep down inside, I wanted to believe that she didn't know. I wanted to tell her the truth and defend myself. Instead I said, "Mama, you don't know nothing 'bout delivering no baby."

"Taylor, you don't know what I know." She turned her attention to Earl. "We gonna need some hot water, some towels, and some old sheets." Earl scurried off to get the items she requested.

I grabbed her hand. "Mama, I'm scared."

She shooed my hand away. "Oh, hush chile. Too late to be scared now. Everything is gonna be alright. I got this under control. Just do what I tell you to do."

Once Earl got the sheets, she fixed a pallet on the floor and made my lay down. The cramps started coming faster and harder. The pain was almost unbearable. I had never in my life felt anything so painful. Even when Mama's friend Mr. Bobby raped me, it didn't compare to that pain.

"Oh Mama, it hurts so bad. Make it stop!" I reached for her hand. She let me squeeze it for a few seconds until the pain stopped. Then she went into the kitchen. When she came out, she had a glass of water in her hand. She shoved some pills in my face. "Here, take these. They'll help with the pain."

"What is it Mama?" I asked her.

"Don't ask so many questions. Just take the damn pills!" I could hear the irritation in her voice.

I pushed them away. "I don't want to take something if I don't know what it is. I heard that certain drugs can hurt your unborn baby. I don't want to hurt my baby."

"I don't give a damn what you heard. I guess you can let them labor pains keep whupping yo' ass. Don't matter to me. I'm not the one in pain. But if you want to feel better, I suggest you do what I tell you to."

Being a fourteen year old that trusted her mother, I took the pills. The pain in my belly increased and I could feel hands and movement between my legs. After a while, I was in and out of consciousness. Later when I finally woke up, my mother and Earl was standing over me. My mother had this look on her face that I'll never forget.

I touched my stomach. The mound was gone. It hurt between my legs a little. "Where is my baby?" I asked my mother.

She ignored my question. "How are you feeling Taylor?"

"Where is my baby Mama?" I asked her again, with a little more force.

She looked at Earl. Earl looked at her. She looked back at me.

"Answer me Mama! Where's my baby? Is

something wrong? Is it a boy or a girl? I hope it's a girl. I'm gonna name her Destiny if it is."

"Taylor, you've just been through a lot. You need some rest. Take a nap."

I tried to get up unsuccessfully. "I don't want to rest. I want my baby. Why won't you let me see my baby?"

Earl blurted, "Yo' baby is dead."

I couldn't believe my ears. I lay there for a few seconds, before saying anything. "Did you say my baby is dead?"

My mother spoke up. "I'm sorry Taylor. She was dead when we pulled her out of you."

Tears started running down my cheeks. "She can't be dead Mama. How can she be dead?"

My mother started stroking my hair. "I wish there was something I could've done Taylor. But there was nothing I could do."

I pushed her hand away. "I told you we needed to go to the hospital, but you wouldn't listen. Now, my baby is dead!" I started crying uncontrollably.

"Taylor sweetie, nothing could be done. Even if we took you to the hospital, the outcome would have been the same."

"She can't be dead Mama. I heard her cry."

She glanced over at Earl before saying, "When did you hear her cry?"

I wiped my eyes with one of the sheets. "I was blacked out, but I could still hear certain things. And I heard my baby cry after she was born."

"You were just 'magining things. There was no cry, 'cause your baby was dead. I know it hurts right now, but you'll get over it. You were too young to have a baby anyway. Now, get yourself some rest, so yo' stuff can heal. Just cause you just gave birth don't mean I'm gonna let you slack up on yo' chores."

My baby was never mentioned again after that night. For the first few months, I kept having dreams of a baby crying. I knew I would never know what really happened to my baby. Then just like Mama said, things went back to normal. Her male friends kept violating me and I kept letting them. So, I wouldn't pop up pregnant again, Mama took me to the clinic to put me on birth control pills.

On the way to the clinic she told me, "We can't afford to let you slip up pregnant again. Aint too much I can do to stop you from being fast. You gone be just like yo mama...always got to be in the company of a man."

I tried to protest. "But Mama, I aint did nothing."

She laughed at me. "So, you like the virgin Mary? How you get pregnant if you aint did nothing?"

I took a deep breath. "Mama, I have something to tell you. It's about your-"

She cut me off. "Taylor, don't start telling a bunch of lies. I don't like it when you lie. I don't want to hear a bunch of nonsense about what you think is going on. We got to eat. So, don't start saying stuff that you don't mean."

That had confirmed what I had been thinking all along. She knew what was going on. And from the sound of it, she had allowed it to happen. I was her meal ticket. And as long as I stayed with her, it would continue to happen.

"So are you going to help me or what Taylor?" Jades voice snapped me out of my thoughts.

"Uh...I'm sorry Jade. What did you say?"

"Are you daydreaming or what? I said are you going to help me get my apartment back in order? I just can't do it by myself. Girl, they did a number on my place. It will take at least a day and a half to get things back in order."

"Sure, I'll help you. Anything to get you out of my place."

"So, it's like that? I thought we were cool."

"We are cool. I just want my space back."

"Bitch, please. That house is so big; you can't even tell I'm there. You got more bedrooms than you'll ever use."

"It's just the fact of knowing you are there."

"Damn. Does the fact that I'm there really bother

you that much Taylor?"

"No, it's not like that. It's just that I don't feel comfortable with another woman being in my house around my husband."

"Hell, it's not like he's there that much. Besides, I would never do you like that. You're my girl."

"I believe you. But I was always told that you should never dangle a bone in front of a dog and not expect him to try to take it."

"What in the hell is that supposed to mean Taylor?"

"It means having you in my house around my husband may be a temptation that he may not be able to overcome. It's not that I don't trust you or my husband. But shit does happen, even when we don't intend for them to happen. After all, he is a man and you are attractive. He may see you one night in your sexy lingerie and the next thing you know, y'all are fucking each other's brains out."

"I guess I see where you're coming from. But trust and believe me, I wouldn't do anything like that. Besides, I don't do white men. Girlfriend, I love the brothas 'cause they got the biggest-"

"Bitch, don't even go there. That is such a myth. Not all brothas are hanging and not all white men have little dicks. I've had some brothas that needed a magnifying glass to see theirs. And I've been with some white men who had dicks that would put some brothas to shame." Unfortunately, that didn't apply to David, but she didn't have to know that.

She let out a sneaky laugh. "Does David fit into that category?"

"Why are you all up on my husband's dick? You don't hear me asking about the size of Eli's dick do ya?"

"I've already told you, I don't do the white thing. And I don't care if you ask about Eli. I will proudly tell you that homeboy is packing."

"Oh really?"

"Yes. Really. And he can work it like nobody's business." She glanced over at me. "But let me hush,

96

'cause you may want to find out for yourself."

I rolled my eyes at her. "I got enough on my plate already. And like you said, I wouldn't do anything like that."

When we pulled into the mall parking lot, I decided that I wanted to go back to *Nordstrom's*. I wanted to see if my little friend was working. She was the first person, I seen when we walked into the designer section.

I startled her when I walked up behind her. "I see we meet again..." She had turned around and I glanced at her name tag. "...Sara. I hope we won't have any problems today. I brought my friend along and we plan to spend a lot of money. It would be wise of you to make this a pleasurable shopping experience."

Jade stood beside me. "We? We don't plan to spend anything." She pointed at me. "She's the one with the money. No offense Sara, but I'm a TJ Maxx slash Marshalls slash Ross shopper. I can't afford this stuff in here."

Jade and I spent the next three hours shopping. Sara was at our beck and call. But it was well worth it, on her part. I tried on so many outfits, I lost count after fifteen. I had to convince Jade to let me treat her to an outfit or two. She was being all proud and didn't want to let me do my duty as a friend. By the time we were finished, I spent well over twenty-five hundred dollars. That surely put a smile on Sara's pale face.

Afterwards, we went to the food court and grabbed something to eat. After we had been sitting for a while eating and people watching Jade spoke. "Taylor, can I ask you a question?"

"Sure, what's up?"

"Do you think it's normal to be involved with someone and not know anything about them?"

I wasn't the right person to be answering that question. "Uh... I guess it depends on what you mean. Can you elaborate on that?"

"Well, let's just say that you are involved with someone exclusively, yet you haven't met any of their family or friends. You don't even know where this person lives. And every time you ask them personal questions, they get all upset or defensive. Their reason for you not meeting their family is because they're waiting for the right time. When you ask about their friends, they say they don't really have any, but they're always having private conversations with people on their cell phone."

"Let's cut to the chase Jade. Are you referring to Eli?"

She looked down at her food, like she was embarrassed. "Yes, I am."

Now, I knew I hid some things from David, but what she was talking was some serious stuff. "You're kidding, right?"

She shook her head. "I wish I was. We've been dating for six months now, yet I feel like I don't know anything about him."

"Six months isn't really that long. But there are certain things you should know by now. Like, where he lives, if he has any kids, and where he works, if he works. Now, the meeting the family thing may be a little touchy. Men tend to drag that process out as long as they can. They only do that if they're really serious about a female; not saying that he isn't serious about you. Then you know as far as mothers are concerned, no woman's ever good enough for their sons." David's mother came to mind when I said that last statement. "Jade there is such a thing as privacy. But there's also such a thing as sharing information with your mate. You better start asking some questions, and fast."

She put her hands on her hips under the table. "Don't you think I have? I told you, he gets all defensive and starts saying that I'm invading his privacy. Then he tells me that he'll tell me about his personal life when he's ready. Sometimes, I feel like I'm making a big deal out of nothing. I remind myself of how he treats me when we're together and how awesome the sex is. Then other times, it bothers me that I don't really know that much about him. I feel like he could be hiding something major from me or he doesn't feel close enough to me to share his private world with me. What should I do Taylor?"

"Now, you know I'm not the one to be giving advice to nobody. If the shit backfires, you're the one to get blamed for it. Only you know what is best for Jade. All I can say is follow your heart. If that doesn't work, then follow your gut. But I will say this...if it was me, I would want to know more about him than what you know. And if he didn't want to tell me, I would find out on my damn own."

She put some thought into what I said. "You're right Taylor. I got to do what's best for me. I'll find out on my own."

I started gathering my trash together. "Enough about Eli. When do you want me to help you with your apartment, so I can get you the hell out of my house?"

Jade

After a week and a half, I was able to move back home. It felt weird being back into my apartment. Taylor had kept her word and helped me get it back in order. Actually, she was going to pay her housekeeper Hazel to do it, but I told her I didn't feel comfortable with a stranger going through my things. So she threw on a pair of sweatpants, something I didn't think she owned, and helped me clean up.

They destroyed all of my things. The main things that were destroyed were my living room and bedroom furniture. Some of my clothes were destroyed, along with some art and other miscellaneous things. I was able to order new furniture and have it delivered to my apartment. Once I received the check from my renter's insurance, I could replenish my savings account.

Eli had come by one of the days we were cleaning up. Taylor started grilling him. "So Eli, where are you originally from?"

He glanced in my direction before answering. "I'm from Durham. Where you from?"

"Oh, uh...I'm from a small town near the coast", she replied.

"And what small town would that be?"

"I'm sure you've never heard of it. Most people haven't."

"Try me. I know of a lot of small towns in North Carolina", he said without missing a beat.

Taylor had an uncomfortable look on her face. "It's called Shallotte."

"Yeah, I've heard of that place. It's not too far from Myrtle Beach, right?"

"Yeah, it's thirty minutes from Myrtle Beach, as well as Wilmington."

"I told you I know a lot about North Carolina."

"Do you have any brothers or sisters", she asked

him.

"Yes."

"Any kids we should know about?"

He gave me another glance. "Are you always this nosey...or did Jade put you up to this?" he asked her.

"Jade didn't put me up to anything. I was just making conversation, trying to get to know the man my best friend's spending all of her time with. Is that a problem?" she asked, rolling her eyes.

Eli answered back. "I wouldn't say it's a problem. But I will say that I'm a very private person So, I won't be answering too many more of your questions."

"If that's how you want to be about it my brotha, that's fine with me. No hard feelings on my part." She reached out to shake his hand.

He took her hand in his. "It's okay...and I'm sorry I snapped at you. You didn't deserve that. Like I said, I'm just a very private person."

"I guess I can be woman enough to accept your apology. Besides, maybe I did get a little nosey. But we're cool, right?"

"Yeah, we're cool."

Then his cell phone rang. Once, he finished his hushed conversation, he kissed me and rushed off. Taylor and I just looked at each other. Once he was gone, Taylor asked, "Does he do that a lot?"

"I have to say yes. He does it more than should be allowed."

"Girl, something is definitely up with him. Jade you are slipping or you're just in denial. Now, I can see why you would be 'cause homeboy is fine as hell. I'll give him that. They broke the mold when they made his ass." She started licking her lips seductively.

"Hey ho! Keep your eyes off my man. Do I need to watch you when he's around? You were talking all that shit about me being in the house with your husband. Hell, I guess I need to keep you away from Eli", I said playfully.

She started laughing. Girl, you know I'm just tripping with you. But on a serious note, something just aint right with your boy. And considering that I know you like I do, you're not going to be satisfied until you find out what it is."

And she was right. I was determined to find out what the real deal was with Ellison Turner. The question was ...how?

Sierra

Things were still going well with me and Tyler. We had even taken Shelby to the park and the movies one day. He spent all day with us. And he kept telling me how much he loved me and appreciated me. Things were finally back to normal. Of course, there was still no exciting sex, but that was okay. I still had Alexis for that.

Now, I was at the spa. I didn't have any clients for the next couple of hours. So I sent Jazmin to lunch while I watched the front and kept up with the appointments. I was just tidying up a bit. I walked over to the manicure/pedicure section. Three women were getting pedicures and chatting with each other. I caught the middle of their conversation.

"Are you talking about that fine ass brotha with the locks?" the female with the short blonde hair asked.

"Yeah, that's the one", the female with the weave down her back replied.

The female with the natural asked, "The fitness trainer?"

"Yes, we're all talking about the same Eli. Eli Turner is his name", Ms. Weave answered back.

"So, he's still up to his old tricks", the one with the natural said.

Ms. Weave replied, "Girl, please. That fool aint ever gonna change."

I realized they were talking about Jade's Eli. What was he up to? I had missed some of the conversation, but I needed to know what they were talking about. So I listened in some more.

The blonde chimed in, "One of my friends had a session with him. She said he hit on her as soon as he walked in the door. She gave him some though. She said he had the biggest thing she had ever seen in her life." They all started laughing.

"Yeah, I heard homeboy was hung like a horse. I

wouldn't give him any though. He is such a dog." That was Ms. Weave.

The female with the natural rolled her eyes. "Can you imagine how his wife must feel? She knows that her husband aint no damn good, yet she stays with him and puts up with it."

"Girl, that's how that black dick do them white women. 'Cause I don't know too many sistas that would put up with that shit."

"Oh yeah. I did hear he was married to a white woman. They're taking over."

"Don't get me started on that. That's a whole other story. But anyway, I even heard that he had seduced her best friend. They said before she knew it, he had her on all fours, rocking her world. The sad thing is their kids were in the next room. The wife walked in on them. They said she beat the shit out of her friend. It was a big mess." The blonde shook her head in disgust.

I couldn't believe what I was hearing. Not only was Eli married, he had kids. I knew Jade had no idea. She would never date a married man. That wasn't her style. And I heard her say that he didn't have any kids. He was lying to her all the way around.

"So, how many kids do they have anyway?" the female with the natural asked.

Ms. Weave answered. "Well, he has a son from a previous relationship. But they have three kids together. His son is like twelve or thirteen. And their kids range from six months to six."

The female with the natural laughed. "Damn, who are you Barbara Walters? You got all the juice don't you?"

"I just know a lot of nosey ass people. Plus, I love to gossip about other folks' lives. It makes me feel better about my pitiful little life." They all laughed again.

"I wonder who his latest victim is. Cause you know there's always one", the female with the natural stated.

"My cousin Asia said she saw him in *Ruby Tuesday's* not too long ago with this brown-skinned chic with short hair. She introduced herself as his girlfriend.

She said Eli was just standing there, being his usual
arrogant self", Ms. Weave said.

"I'm sure she's some female that has no idea who
he really is. He's done filled her head with a bunch of lies.
Now I know, some men can be dogs, but he just takes the
cake. I think he's like a sex addict or something."

"Ms. Weave asked, "What in the hell is a sex
addict? Aint no such thing."

The female with the natural chimed in. "Actually,
it does exist. A sex addict is someone who is actually
addicted to sex. It's a real sickness, just like alcoholism or
drug addiction. They can't control their urges. Sex is
their answer to everything. They can be happily married,
but still go out and cheat. Some even stoop to the level of
paying for sex. Sometimes porn plays a big part in some
of their lives. There are just so many levels of it."

Ms. Weave looked like she was amazed. "I never
knew it existed. I just thought the world was full of dogs
and perverts. Now I know that some of them may be sick
dogs and perverts."

"I'm not saying that all people who cheat are sex
addicts. I'm just saying that it does exist. I don't know if
Eli is a legitimate case for sexual addiction. I just hope
that any female that comes into contact with him uses
protection. Cause there's no telling what that fool got.
AIDS is out there and it don't care who you are."

I couldn't listen to any more of their conversation.
I needed to tell Jade everything I had just heard. She
would be crushed, but it was something that I needed to
do. From what I could tell, she was really falling for Eli.
He had her nose wide open.

I was sitting there trying to figure out a way to tell
her, when I heard the bell on the door ring. Alexis walked
in. "Hi Sierra. What's up? I just thought I'd drop in to
say hello." She smiled at me, and then frowned when she
realized that I wasn't smiling.

"Why the long face? Is everything okay with
Tyler?" she asked.

"It's not that." I guided her back to the reception
area, so we could have some privacy. "I just heard

something and I don't know how to handle it."

"Well, tell me what it is and maybe I can help you", she said with a worried look on her face.

"Jade has been seeing this guy for the past six months or so. Those three women in there were talking about him. Come to find out, he has a wife and kids at home."

"How do you know it was him they were talking about Sierra?" she asked.

"Because they have the same first and last name, the same career, and the description is the same. It's got to be the same person. There can't be that many coincidences."

"Let's say it is the same person. How do you know that Jade doesn't already know his situation?"

"Alexis, I know Jade. She would never date a married man."

"Maybe she's embarrassed and doesn't want you to judge her", she replied.

"Trust me. She doesn't know. And she even once said that he didn't have any kids. The sad thing is that she's really into Eli."

Alexis looked like she had seen a ghost. "Did you say Eli?"

"Yes, I did. Do you know him?"

"Eli Turner?"

"Yes."

"The fitness trainer?"

"Yes."

"You could say that I know him. He gave me a few sessions a while back." She shook her head from side to side.

I thought about what one of the females had said about him jumping her friend's bones as soon as he came into her place. "Did he hit on you?"

She paused a second before she answered. "Yes, he did."

"And?" I motioned with my hand for her to continue.

She took a deep breath. "And...we ended up

having sex right on the floor of my den. It was some of the best sex I ever had."

"I take it you weren't still with your husband?" I asked.

"No. It was right after we had split up. So I was kind of vulnerable. Eli made me feel desirable. Of course, I knew nothing was going to become of it. It just felt good to have a man look at me the way he did, again. After the first session, I was having him over every week. I didn't even pretend to be interested in the workout session anymore. He knew that it had become all about sex." She was staring off into space as she talked.

"So basically, you were prostituting him?" I asked in a tone that I knew sounded judgmental.

She rolled her eyes. "Yes, I guess you could say that Sierra. I was paying him for sex that was better than any workout I've ever had. It's not something that I'm proud of, but at the time, I was satisfied."

"So what happened? Why did you stop?" I asked.

"One day, I just decided that I didn't need him anymore. I had gotten my self-esteem back. So, I called him and told him that I didn't need his services any longer. Of course, he tried to talk me out of it. I told him my mind was made up. He told me if I changed my mind, I knew how to find him. That was the last time I talked to him."

I was still in shock. This city was too damn small. I decided not to say anything else about her situation. I didn't want to sound like I was lecturing her. Who was I to lecture the woman that I was having an affair with? I decided to get back to the original subject.

"So what am I going to do about Jade?" I asked her.

She looked me dead in my eyes and said, "Nothing."

"What do you mean nothing?" I asked

"Sierra, the worst thing you can do is tell a woman that her man is cheating. No woman wants to hear that...especially from another woman."

"But it's more than him cheating Alexis. He's

married!"

"It doesn't matter."

"So what am I supposed to do...just sit here and say nothing?"

"Yes, that's exactly what you're supposed to do."

"She's my best friend. How can I stand by and let this go on without telling her? It's just not right."

"I understand how you feel Sierra. But I promise you, it's the right thing to do. If you say something, you're putting your friendship in jeopardy."

"I don't understand."

"Let me explain. First, she won't believe you. She'll say you have the wrong man or you misunderstood. You didn't actually see him with his wife. You just overheard a group of women talking. So you don't have any evidence. She'll ask him if it's true. He'll say no and then you become the bad guy. The only way she'll believe it is if she sees it with her own eyes. So that's what needs to happen."

I didn't feel good about what she was telling me. But she was probably right. I just felt bad for Jade, because I knew how she felt about Eli.

"So if she does find out and tells me, am I supposed to tell her that I knew all along?" I asked her.

"No, you can't say anything. She'll be upset with you for not telling her."

"Okay, now you're contradicting yourself."

"Sierra, I know it doesn't make sense. The thing is she'll think she's upset with you for not telling her and she'll feel like a fool. But the truth is she really didn't want to hear it from you. Just act surprised and be supportive. It's all a part of being a woman. We are some weird individuals."

She really had me confused, but I decided to just take her word for it. "Okay Alexis. I'll do what you said. I just hope you're right."

"Of course, I'm right. I almost forgot the reason I came by. I want to invite you to dinner tonight at my place. I hope you can come. It's really important that you're there." She leaned closer to me.

"I'll have to see if Tyler has any plans. I'm quite sure he doesn't. What's the occasion?" I asked, while straightening papers on the counter.

"There's no occasion. I just thought I'd prepare a special dinner for us tonight", she replied and then winked at me.

When Alexis opened the door, a lump caught in my throat. She looked breath taking. She was wearing a gold dress that hugged her curves in just the right places. As always, there was a plunging neckline that revealed much cleavage. The sides were made of a chiffon material that went down the length of the dress. So it was obvious that she wasn't wearing any underwear. Her hair was done up in a bun, with a few curls dangling down the sides and front. And as usual, her make-up was perfect. The perfume she was wearing seemed to be made for her. When I finally found my voice, I said, "Alexis, you look absolutely gorgeous."

She smiled and said, "Thank you. So do you. Please come in." She stepped back so I could enter the house.

As soon as I walked in, I could smell a nice aroma coming from the kitchen. I walked into the living room and was surprised to see a very handsome gentleman sitting on the sofa. Alexis came in behind me. "Sierra, this is Boris. He's a very dear friend of mine." He stood up and extended his hand. "Boris, this is my good friend Sierra." I shook his hand.

"Why don't you two sit down and get acquainted with each other? I'm going to run and check on dinner." Alexis then hurried off into the kitchen.

I smiled at Boris, wondering why he was there. Alexis never told me there would be another guest. I decided to be nice and try to strike up a conversation. "So, Boris what do you do for a living?"

He smiled at me with pretty white teeth. "I'm a dancer."

"A dancer?"

"Yeah, you know a stripper." He stood up and did a quick move for me, gyrating his body in a very sexy way.

"Oh...I see. Will you excuse me for a minute?" I stood up before he could see the embarrassing look on my face. I headed to the kitchen to talk to Alexis.

As soon as I entered the kitchen, she asked, "How's it going with Boris? Isn't he fine?"

I ignored her questions. "Alexis, what in the hell is going on here? Why is that man here? You never mentioned him before."

"Nothing's going on. He's here because I want him here", she replied before adding a vinaigrette dressing to a mixed salad.

I took a seat on one of the stools at the island in front of her. "He said he's a stripper."

She looked up at me. "And...what's your point?"

"There is no point. He just caught me off guard. He even gave me a little sample of his work", I replied shaking my head in disgust.

Alexis started laughing. "Oh did he? Lucky you."

"Alexis, this shit is not funny. I'm leaving." I stood up to leave.

"Come on Sierra. Don't be a party pooper. Please stay. I want you here." She pushed me back down on the stool and kissed me on the lips.

"Is everything okay in here?" Boris' voice came out of nowhere.

Alexis answered. "Sure Boris. Everything is fine." She then turned her attention back to me. "Are you guys ready to eat?"

I didn't answer her. Instead Boris spoke up. "I know I am. Everything smells so good. What are we having?"

Alexis went to the oven and pulled out a dish. "We're having baked salmon with rice pilaf and a tossed salad with a homemade vinaigrette dressing. And for dessert, I made a strawberry cheesecake."

"Um, that sounds good", Boris said rubbing his stomach and licking his lips.

The dinner was quiet for a few minutes. Everyone was enjoying the meal. I didn't really know what to say, considering I felt very uncomfortable in Boris' presence. I noticed he kept stealing glances at me when he thought I wasn't looking. Alexis, who was sitting directly across from me, kept giving me seductive looks.

I took another sip of my wine before I decided to break the silence. "So Boris...how long have you known Alexis?"

He looked over at Alexis before answering my question. "I'm not really sure-"

Alexis interrupted him, "We've known each other for about eight months, Sierra."

I gave her a dirty look. "How did you meet?"

"We met on the job."

"Exactly who's job? Yours or his?"

She gave me a steely look. "Does it matter?"

"I was just trying to make conversation, Alexis." I spoke through clenched teeth.

Boris clinked his fork on his wine glass. "Ladies, ladies...there's no need for all the tension."

Alexis looked at him and smiled. "You're right Boris. I do apologize for my behavior." She then looked at me, waiting for me to apologize as well. I just rolled my eyes and took another sip of my wine.

We finished our meal with them chatting with each other. I ate in silence, trying not to spoil the night. I was still trying to figure out the purpose of Boris being there. I had to admit that he was very attractive. But something about him didn't set too well with me. I think it was the fact that he seemed as dumb as a rock. When God was handing out traits, he took good looks, a killer body and skipped on the brains. What he and Alexis had in common, I had yet to find out. Even through Alexis' delicious dessert, I was quiet.

Alexis made the mistake of asking him how business was going. He started talking about how the women are all over him at the club when he's dancing. He explained how their husbands and boyfriends couldn't keep them excited like he does. He went on and on about how hard it is to be so sexy and good looking, because the women see him as this perfect man, and he's not. Hell, I could tell them that. He'd have to have a brain for that.

"Are you okay Sierra?" Alexis finally asked after my long period of silence.

"Yes, I'm fine Alexis", I responded after finishing up my last bite of cheesecake.

"Well, you've been very quiet tonight. That's really unusual."

"That's because I really don't have much to say tonight." I then glanced over at Boris, who was busy stuffing his face with his second piece of cheesecake.

Alexis gave me a scolding look. "If you don't say anything, Boris is going to take it personally."

"I really don't care-"

She cut me off before I could finish my sentence. "Why don't we go into the den to get more comfortable? Sierra, you and Boris can get to know each other better."

Why did she keep saying that? I had no desire to get to know Boris any better. I had seen all I needed to see and I knew all I needed to know. Boris was the first to get up. When he walked out of the dining room, I said, "What are you up to Alexis?"

She looked at me and smiled. "I'm not up to anything. Why must you be so suspicious of everything? I'm just trying to get you out of that circle you're in...that's all."

"What circle?" I had no idea what she meant.

"You know that little circle called your life. You need to get out and meet new people...other than Tyler, Jade and Taylor. And the people at your spa don't count because they work for you. Broaden your horizons." She then walked out to join Boris in the den. I followed.

Boris had taken off his shoes and gotten very comfortable. I sat down in the other seat, while Alexis went over to the mini bar. "Would you guys like something else to drink? I have another type of white wine I picked up the other day."

We both said we wanted to try it. After serving us, Alexis went over to the entertainment center and put in a CD. Within seconds, jazz music filled the room. Alexis then came and sat down on the couch beside me. Boris had his legs wide open and I could see the bulge under his pants. Alexis saw me looking and smiled.

"So, Sierra, you have your own beauty shop huh?" he asked before adjusting his manhood.

"Actually, it's a day spa", I corrected him.

"What's the difference?" he asked.

"The difference is that at my place you can get your hair done, get your nails and feet done, and get body massages of all types, facials and so much more. A beauty shop is usually just centered around hair."

He threw his hands up in the air. "Well, I'm sorry for the mix up. No hard feelings."

"It's okay. It's a common mistake people make."

"So, what a brotha gotta do to get serviced?" He flashed that perfect smile.

"Just call the spa and make an appointment", I said nonchalantly.

"What if I want you in particular?" he asked.

"Just let the receptionist know who you want to service you and she'll let you know what times they have available."

"I'll have to remember that", he said and put his index finger up to his head.

I forced a smile. "Great!"

He drank the last of his wine in one gulp. He then reached into his pocket and pulled out what appeared to be a cigar. After lighting it up, he took a puff of it and passed it to Alexis.

"I didn't know you smoked cigars Alexis", I said.

"It's not a cigar Sierra. Well, technically it is a cigar, just not the kind you think it is. It's a blunt." She took a long puff and smoke came out of her nose.

I looked at her confused. "What exactly is a blunt?"

She looked at Boris and they both started laughing. "You can't be that naïve Sierra. A blunt is a cigar filled with weed."

I let out a gasp. "You don't mean marijuana do you?"

"Of course I mean marijuana", she said rolling her eyes at me.

I tried to take it out of her hand. "You can't smoke that stuff Alexis. You're a lawyer for Christ's sake!"

"I can do whatever I damn well please. Besides, it's harmless Sierra. They've made it legal in some states for medicinal purposes."

"It is harmless Sierra. Maybe you should try some. It will help you relax", Boris said.

I rolled my eyes at him. "I don't want to try any. I heard what that stuff can do to you. I don't want any part of this." For the second time, I attempted to leave.

Alexis grabbed my hand. "Sierra, please don't leave. I want you to stay." She then passed the blunt back to Boris.

"Look Alexis, I just don't feel comfortable being here. First, you spring him on me." I pointed to Boris. "And now, you got drugs in the house. This is just too much for me to handle."

She put her arms around my neck and said, "Sierra, my intentions were not to make you feel uncomfortable. And I wouldn't do anything to harm you. All I'm asking is for you to relax a little." Then she gave me a full kiss on the lips.

For some reason, Alexis could get me to do almost anything she wanted me to do. I begin to realize that it was hard for me to say no to her, especially when she kissed me. I would probably sell my soul to the devil for her.

"Try it. You'll like it", Boris said, as he held the blunt out to me. I hesitated before taking it out of his hand. They both sat watching me as I looked at it for a few seconds.

"Just take a puff and don't swallow the smoke", Alexis coached me.

I put the blunt to my lips, took a puff and started choking on it. I coughed for a few seconds, with tears coming out of my eyes. "This stuff is awful", I stated when I finally stopped coughing.

"You didn't take your time", Boris said. "Try it again. It takes practice to get it right."

So once again, I put the blunt to my lips. I took a

long slow puff. I didn't really like the taste it left in my mouth, but at least I wasn't choking on it again. I passed it back to Boris. He took another puff and passed it to Sierra. She convinced me to take another puff. Before I knew it, we had passed that blunt around and were working on another one. Between the wine and the marijuana, I had started to feel really good. I had never been so relaxed in my entire life.

"Boris, why don't you give Sierra and I a private show?" Alexis said before putting her hand on my thigh.

He stood up. "Sure...why not?" He started taking off his clothes, with the exception of his underwear. His body was perfect. I always thought my husband had the best body on any man, but Boris' body took the cake. There wasn't an ounce of fat on him. It looked as if his body had been chiseled by a sculptor. And from the looks of things, he wasn't lacking in the penis department. He walked over to the entertainment center, showing off a tight ass, and placed another CD in the CD player. A more upbeat song came on, and he started moving his body to the beat. He came over and stood directly in front of us and continued his routine.

I looked over at Alexis. She had one hand between her legs, while the other was still on my thigh. I don't know if it was the marijuana, the wine, Boris' show, or seeing Alexis touch herself, but I was getting hotter by the minute. I don't know what came over me, but I leaned over and started kissing Alexis. She eagerly accepted my kiss, by moving her hand between my legs. I opened my legs further to allow her easy access. It wasn't long before we were kissing and touching each other as if Boris wasn't in the room. And when she started taking off my dress, I didn't object. As soon as she had me completely naked, she removed her clothing. Boris was still shaking his ass as if he was oblivious to what was going on in front of him.

Alexis whispered in my ear. "Sierra, I want you bad. I can't wait to taste you. But I need you to do something for me."

"What is it?" I asked.

She kissed me on the lips before replying. "You

were right. Boris is here for a reason. I want you to fuck him."

I pulled away from her. "You want me to fuck him? May I ask why?"

"Because it will turn me on", she cooed.

I shook my head. "I don't know if I can. I mean, you know I'm inexperienced. Tyler's the only man I've ever been with."

"He knows that Sierra. I told him you were bored with your husband and how you've never sucked a dick, but wanted to. I told him everything", she said.

I was feeling embarrassed because Alexis had discussed my personal sex life with a total stranger. "Why did you do that? I feel so stupid."

She put her arms around me. "Don't Sierra. He's not like that. That's why he wants to help you. If it will make you feel better, I'll be with him first. You can watch us. And when you feel comfortable, you can join us."

Once again, I agreed to do something for Alexis. To get me more excited about the idea, she started performing oral sex on me. Shortly after that Boris joined in. I watched him have his way with Alexis. She seemed to be enjoying what he was doing to her. The looks and expressions on her face were things I couldn't relate to when it came to sex with Tyler. She was on her hands and knees, taking every inch of his big penis. The harder he thrust in her, the more she screamed for more. As I sat there watching them, I became envious. I wanted to know that pleasure.

Surprising myself, I jumped up and said, "It's my turn Alexis."

Next, I was the one being pounded. That was a position Tyler refused to engage in. He always said that we were not dogs, so we shouldn't act like dogs. While in that position, I realized how much easier it was to have an orgasm, because Boris was hitting my spot. After a few more strokes, I was coming all over the place. I collapsed on the floor.

"We're not finished yet Sierra", Alexis said as she crawled over to Boris, who was now sitting on the couch.

I was out of breath. "What do you mean? I don't think I could go another round."

"It's not that. Like I said before, I told Boris how you've never sucked a dick. He said you can practice on him." She looked up at him. "Right baby?"

He pointed to his penis, which was still hard as a rock. "He's ready, willing and able."

"Um...that's okay. I'm good." There was no way I was putting another man's penis in my mouth. It was bad enough I had did all of those other things. But I had to draw the line somewhere.

Alexis tried to convince me. "Come on Sierra. You've gotten this far. Don't be like that. You'll hurt Boris' feelings."

The marijuana was wearing off, so I was coming to my senses. "I'm not doing it, okay? There's nothing you can say that's gonna change my mind." I looked up at Boris. "Boris, it's nothing personal. You've done me a great deed already and that was enough for me, but I'm gonna have to pass on the oral sex."

"That's cool with me sis. I'm just glad I could help you out." He stood up and started putting on his clothes. "It's getting late anyway. I need to get outta here. My girl's probably wondering where I'm at. Call me sometime Alexis."

"Sure thing Boris. Thanks for coming over and hanging out with us", Alexis said hugging his neck.

"No problem." He reached out to shake my hand. "It was really nice meeting you Sierra."

I shook his hand, suddenly feeling awkward. "Yeah...it was nice meeting you too."

Alexis grabbed her dress, threw it over her head and walked Boris to the door. When she came back, we sat in silence for a few seconds. Alexis was the first to speak. "How do you feel about what happened tonight Sierra?"

I picked up my abandoned wine glass, took a sip and said, "I feel like you've created a monster."

Taylor

It had been a while since I had been with Exodus.
I didn't want David to get suspicious, so I told Exodus that
we needed to chill out. But a sista was feening for her
Mandingo. So I called him up and told him to meet me.
He had just finished rocking my world and I was lying on
the bed still trying to catch my breath. I could hear him
singing in the shower in the suite we had rented for the
day.

Sometimes, I felt bad for cheating on David,
because he was so good to me. But he just didn't satisfy
me in the bedroom. Sure, he could eat the hell out of my
pussy, but I needed more than that. Of course, he
thought he was a good lover; mainly because I led him to
believe that. One thing I've learned over the years is how
to stroke a man's ego. I would never let my husband
know that he didn't satisfy me. In the beginning of our
marriage, I would masturbate almost every day. I had
every sex toy imaginable and knew how to use them well.
I would moan and scream while David and I were having
sex. Afterwards, when he would fall asleep, I would sneak
into one of the guest rooms and fuck myself until I
climaxed. I did that for a while, until I met Exodus.

I had just stepped outside David's office building,
when he appeared out of nowhere. "Hello beautiful", he
said with a big smile on his face.

I looked around. "Are you talking to me?" I asked
him.

"You're the only beautiful woman I see right now.
And though I may be a looker, I don't consider myself
beautiful. So I guess I'm talking to you", he said flashing
those pretty white teeth again.

I stepped closer to him. "I see you're full of
yourself." He looked like your typical pretty boy.

"There's nothing wrong with having self-confidence
is there? From the way you walked out that door, I can

tell you sure don't lack any", he said matter-of-factly.

I had to admit, he was one of the finest brothas I had seen in a while. He was tall with a chestnut complexion. He had the most beautiful dark eyes and the prettiest lips a man could own. And from the look of his body, I could tell he worked out on a regular basis. I wasn't trying to be taken in by his good looks, so I decided to wrap up the conversation. "Well, I'll just let you be on your way. Have a good day." I was about to walk off, when he grabbed my arm.

"Can't I get your name or something?" he asked. "Maybe we can go out for drinks later tonight." He stood there still smiling.

I laughed at his aggressiveness. "I'm married."

He looked me in the eyes. "And?"

"And that's it. I'm married. That's all you need to know."

"So because you're married, I can't get your name?"

"If you must know, my name is Taylor."

"Hello Taylor, I'm Exodus. It's nice to meet you." He held his hand out for me to shake it.

"It's nice to meet you too, Exodus", I said while shaking his massive hand.

"So, what's up with those drinks? Is tonight not a good night?" he asked with the most serious look on his face.

"Do you not understand English? I just told you that I'm a married woman."

"Happily?"

"That's irrelevant. The point is I'm married."

"That answers my question. You're obviously not happily married", he said folding his arms across his chest.

I got up in his face. "You have no idea what you're talking about. I am a very happy woman. I'm married to one of the wealthiest men in Durham. I don't have to want for nothing. So there's nothing you can do for me, but keep it moving Mr. Exodus."

He looked at me with a smirk on his face. "Well, if

being wealthy is what makes you happy, then I guess you are happy...if what you say is true."

I rolled my eyes at him. "Oh sweetheart, it's true." I looked down at myself. "I mean, look at me. Anyone can see that I'm the epitome of expensive taste, from my hair to my shoes."

"That don't mean shit. I know a lot of people that live ghetto fabulous. They're living paycheck to paycheck, can barely pay their rent sometimes, but they're out here buying designer bags and shoes. And their bank account is in the negative."

"That doesn't apply to me. There is nothing ghetto about me and my account is nowhere near being empty. Honestly, I don't even know why I'm still standing here explaining myself to you anyway." I pointed to him like he was beneath me, just to irritate him.

He licked his lips before responding. "Because you really want to jump my bones right now. I know you claim you're happily married, but I can tell by the way you're looking at me, you want me bad."

"You must be out of your damn mind. That stuff may work for the other women you're accustomed to dealing with, but it doesn't fly with Mrs. Taylor Morgan." I tried to keep a straight face, because he was right about me wanting to jump his bones.

He looked at the building. Then he looked back at me. Then he mumbled to himself, "Naw...couldn't be."

I knew what he was thinking. "Yeah, that's right. David Morgan is my husband."

He started smiling. "So, your husband is my boss. Aint that something?"

"When did you start working for David?" I asked him. I knew I would have noticed him before.

"A few days ago."

We both just stood there staring at each other for a few seconds, until he broke the silence. "So are we going to meet for drinks later or what?"

I met him for drinks that night. Drinks turned into us getting a suite and fucking like rabbits. After that, I knew I could put my toys to rest, because I had found somebody that could keep me satisfied. And he was doing a great job.

Exodus' entrance into the room interrupted my thoughts. He was standing in front of me with his body dripping wet.

"You couldn't dry off in the bathroom?" I asked him.

"Yes, I could have, but I wanted you to get one last look at me before I left. Give you something to think about tonight when you got that white man with the little dick lying next to you."

I rolled my eyes at him. "You have no idea how big my husband's dick is."

"Taylor, don't play."

"David's dick is not little!"

"I know for a fact, it aint got nothing on this", he said and grabbed his manhood.

I was starting to get irritated. "Can we just get off of my husband's dick please?"

"Whatever you want babe."

I don't know why I got so defensive when it came to our sex life and his manhood. Even though he didn't satisfy me, I hated when others said anything about him or questioned his performance. I guess it was loyalty. After all, he is my husband.

On my way from the hotel, I decided to pay Sierra a visit at the spa. I hadn't seen or talked to her since that night at *Firebirds*. She was probably spending all of her free time with that Alexis chic. If she was available, maybe we could grab some lunch.

When I walked into the spa, Sierra was the first person I saw. She and Alexis were talking and giggling like two school girls. Alexis was the first one to greet me. "Hi Taylor. It's so nice to see you again", she said.

I gave a dry, "Hello Alexis."

"Hello Taylor. I'm so glad you dropped by." Sierra walked over and gave me a warm embrace.

Alexis grabbed her purse from the counter. "Well, I better get going, so you two can catch up. Have a good time tonight Sierra." Then she looked at me. "Once again, it was nice seeing you again Taylor."

I gave her my fakest smile. "Same here. Goodbye."
When she got outside, I asked Sierra, "What's happening
tonight?"

"Oh. Nothing really. Tyler and I are just going out
for dinner. We decided it was time for us to spend some
quality time together." She had a sad look in her eyes.

"Is everything okay Sierra? I asked her.

She hesitated before answering. "Everything's fine.
Why do you ask?"

"It's just the look in your eyes. You don't sound
too excited about your dinner date with Tyler. You know if
anything is bothering you, you can talk to me." I squeezed
her hand.

"I'll be honest with you. We were having some
issues for a minute, but everything is okay now. We've
settled our differences. It was just a matter of us sitting
down and communicating with each other. To show me
how much he appreciates me, he's taking me out to dinner
tonight."

"Oh, that's so sweet. Girl, why didn't you tell me
you were having problems? I thought we were friends.
Jade didn't say anything about it either."

"That's because I didn't tell her either."

I put my arms around her shoulders. "You mean
you kept all of that to yourself? It's not good to keep
things bottled up Sierra. You should always talk to
somebody."

"I just didn't want you guys to worry, but enough
of that. Have you seen or talked to Jade in the last couple
of days?" she asked after taking a seat behind the counter.

I followed her and sat in the seat next to her. I
haven't seen her this week, but I did talk to her. She's
probably somewhere trying to figure out what's going on
with Eli."

"What do you mean?" Sierra asked.

I leaned closer to her, so no one could be all up in
our conversation. "Well, she was saying how she doesn't
really know much about him and he's very secretive.
She's never been to his house or met any of his family or

friends and they've been dating for a while.

"What did you tell her?"

"Hell, I told her something was up with him. But you know when you're in love or think you're in love, you don't want to hear anything bad someone else has to say about that person."

She gave me a funny look. "I'm sure there's a reasonable explanation for his actions."

I laughed at her comment. "Yeah, that explanation is that he's married or has a live-in girlfriend."

"Taylor, you can't make those kinds of assumptions without proof", she replied harshly.

"Sierra, what's up with you? Is there something that you're not telling me?" I looked her in the eyes.

"N-no, it's not. All I'm saying is that you can't accuse a man of something without proof."

I could tell she was lying, but I wasn't going to force the issue. "If you say so Sierra. Just remember what I said, you can talk to me if you need to."

She stood up. "I'll keep that in mind. I really need to get back to work."

"Oh, I was coming to see if you wanted to grab a bite to eat."

"I'm sorry. I can't. I have a client coming in a few minutes. Plus, Alexis and I ate earlier." She started scanning the appointment book in front of her.

I stood up. "Oh, I see. Well, I guess I'll just have to catch you another time. Have a good time tonight."

She looked up from the book. "Thanks for coming by Taylor. It was good to see you. Tell David I said hello", she said in tone that was a little too formal for me.

I said my goodbye and was out the door. I didn't know if it was the mention of Eli or whatever was going on with her and Tyler, but I knew that Sierra was acting really weird. Whatever her reason was, I wanted to find out.

Jade

Just like Taylor said, I tried to find out what was up with Eli. Either he was too quick, or I was a terrible detective. I think it was more of the latter. The other night when he was at my apartment, I tried going through his wallet while he was in the bathroom. As soon as I took it from his pocket, I heard him get out of the shower. I didn't want to risk getting caught, so I put it back in his pocket. And it was a good thing that I did, because he came out of the bathroom as soon as I dropped his pants back on the bed. He started eyeing me suspiciously, like he knew I was up to something. I just played it cool like I was watching television.

Then the next night, we both fell asleep on the couch watching a movie. I woke up to the sound of his ringing cell phone. I noticed he had not heard it, so I reached over to grab it so I could answer it. I knew I could have woken him up, but that was my chance to find something out. As soon as I took the phone off of his belt, he woke up. He wrapped his hand around my wrist so tight, I thought he was going to break it.

"Ouch Eli. You're hurting me!" I screamed.

Still holding my wrist, he spoke through clenched teeth. "Bitch, don't you ever get the balls to answer my damn phone! Don't no fucking body answer my damn phone, but me. You dig?"

I couldn't believe he called me a bitch. I had never seen him look so evil. I sat there, not knowing what to say or do.

He spoke again. "I said do you dig?"

"Y-yes...I dig Eli", I finally spoke, trying to wrestle my wrist from his grasp.

He let go of my wrist and started talking. "You bitches think y'all can just answer a man's phone 'cause you give him a little pussy. It's all about respect. That's the problem with women. You're too damn nosey. Think a man got to tell you every damn thing that goes on. Some things aint meant for you to know. You don't see us asking y'all a bunch of damn questions. Why? 'Cause we don't give a fuck. As long as you aint giving up our pussy, we don't give a fuck what y'all do."

I sat there with my mouth open, listening to him talk shit about women. I had no idea what had brought that on, other than me trying to answer his phone, but I didn't think it was that serious. "Eli, why are you saying all of these things? I've never heard you talk this way. Have you been drinking?"

He laughed at me. "Naw, I aint been drinking. I just figured it was time to give you a dose of reality."

"What do you mean?" I asked.

"All I'm saying Jade is that no relationship is all good all the time. For the past few months, you've been asking me a lot of personal questions. I've been telling you the same thing every time. I'll tell you when I'm ready. But you crossed the line when you tried to answer my phone. To me, you were being disrespectful and I don't play that shit."

I grabbed his hand. "Okay, for the sake of argument, let's say I was disrespectful. But did you have to call me a bitch? To me, that was disrespectful."

He stopped putting on his shoes and leaned back on the couch. He took a deep breath. "You're right, Jade. It was disrespectful. I should have never called you out your name. I guess I was just pissed off. I'm sorry baby."

I stroked his cheek. "I'm sorry too Eli. I should have never invaded your privacy by trying to answer your phone. Let's just forget about everything that just happened and enjoy the rest of the night."

He sat up quickly. "I wish we could, but I got to bounce." He then proceeded to finish putting on his other shoe.

"Just like that? You're going to leave just like that? I thought you were going to spend the night."

He stood up. "Naw, I gotta go Jade. I got to take care of some business."

"This time of night? What's so important that it

can't wait until tomorrow Eli?" I pulled on his arm to try to keep him from going to the door.

"That phone call was a call that I've been waiting on all night. Now, I really need to go. And I don't have time to sit here and argue with you woman." he said.

"But you didn't even answer the phone, so how do you know who it was?" I asked.

"It don't matter how I know. I just know. Now stop it with all the damn questions. I'll call you tomorrow sometime...alright?" He kissed me on the lips and walked out the door.

I had to admit that Eli's behavior was stressing me out. I don't know why I just couldn't say fuck him and move on. Well, I knew the reasons. He was fine as hell. Our sex was off the chain. When we were together, I felt like I was in heaven. All relationships can't be perfect.

Work was getting stressful also. The position of operations manager wasn't a joke. It was very demanding and required a lot of work. Plus, I was still getting those crazy phone calls. Only now, there was a female's voice on the other end. My gut told me it was definitely Paige. I got my confirmation today.

I had stopped to the *Food Lion* on highway 55 on my way home from work. I was in the produce section when I heard, "Well well, look who's here."

I turned around to see Paige staring at me. As usual, she had on a pound of makeup, and that tore up weave. The skirt she had on was so short, you could see her butt cheeks if she leaned over the slightest bit.

"I see nothing has changed with you, Paige", I said while looking her up and down.

She rolled her eyes at me. "So, how is the new position going? How does it feel to have that position, knowing you stole it from me?"

"How did you know I got the position?" I asked her.

"I have my resources", she said slyly.

"Well to answer your first question, the job is going great. And to answer your second question, I didn't steal shit from you. You're the one that screwed up. It's not like you were going to get the position anyway. As I said

many times before, you were not qualified!" I shook my
index finger at her.

"Oh, I was just as qualified as you, Jade and you
know it", she replied, while putting her hands on her hips.

I got closer to her face, so other customers couldn't
hear our conversation. "The only thing that I know is that
you're a crazy slut who thought you could sleep your way
to the top and it backfired. Just admit to yourself that
you fucked up and get on with your life. And by the way,
you can stop calling my office."

She gave me a puzzled look. "What are you talking
about? I haven't been calling your office."

"Cut the bullshit Paige. I know it's you, no matter
how hard you try to disguise your voice. At first, you had
some man calling. Now, you're calling yourself. I didn't
want to believe it was you, but now I know it's you. You're
still blaming me for your screw up. All I have to say is let
it go Paige." I turned my back to her and continued
browsing the fruit.

She grabbed my arm and turned me around to face
her. "Like I said Jade, I have not been calling you. Nor
have I had anyone else calling you. You must have pissed
someone else off. I have better things to do with my time."

I gave her a look that let her know I didn't
appreciate her putting her hands on me. "No, you're the
only person that I've pissed off. And I'm here to tell you,
you can call me every day. It's not going to change the
fact that I have the position you wanted and you lost your
job."

She threw her hand up in the air. "If you want to
believe it's me, go ahead. I know it's not me. I'm actually
kind of flattered that you think it is me. It means you're
still intimidated by me. Or maybe, it's your guilty
conscious eating away at you."

"Like I told you previously, I am not intimidated by
you or anyone else. Besides, I'm really tired of this
conversation. I've wasted enough of my valuable time.
Why don't you and your little handkerchief run along?" I
pointed to her skirt.

She threw her head back and laughed. "You're

just jealous 'cause you don't have the body or the self-confidence to wear a skirt like this."

I looked down at myself. "Oh, I have the body. I just got enough sense to know that any skirt so short it will show off a girdle like yours is not one I want to put on."

She looked down and saw the girdle peeking from under her skirt, pulled on it, and walked quickly towards the bathroom.

I spent a few more minutes shopping for the things that I needed. I was thankful when I didn't run into Paige anymore. I paid for my items and went out to my car. I always parked far away in the day time, to avoid my car getting dinged or scratched by other cars. When I got closer to my car, I noticed both tires on that side were flat. I walked around my car and realized that all four of my tires were flat. The word BITCH was engraved on my driver's side door. I dropped all of my groceries to the ground. I don't know why, but I started screaming like a lunatic. No one was paying any attention to me. They probably thought I was some crazy woman since no one was attacking me. I was getting ready to search for my phone, when I saw Paige prancing across the parking lot.

I don't know what came over me, but I walked over to her, looked her dead in the eyes and slapped her with all the power I had. She was caught off guard and dropped the bag she had in her hand as she fell to the ground. As soon as she hit the ground, I was on top of her, hitting and punching her in the face.

"Get off of me, you crazy bitch!" she yelled between punches.

"I'm not c-crazy. You're the one that m-messed with my c-car", I said, almost out of breath.

She was able to get from under me, after she scratched me in the face with one of those fake claws she always wore. Now, she was on top of me, pounding my head against the pavement. I then took my free hand and pushed her to the ground. We were rolling around on the pavement just like two kids.

I heard someone in the distance yell, "Fight!

They're fighting over there!"

She continued to scream. "What is wrong with you, you crazy bitch!"

"Why did you have to go and fuck with my car?" I yelled between hits and slaps.

She was back on top of me. "I have not touched your car!"

I palmed her face. "You've gone too far Paige."

The next thing I knew, we were being pulled apart. We were both panting like dogs. I was kind of glad of the interception, because I didn't know how much longer I could've went on.

By then, we had drawn a little crowd. One female spoke up. "You two should be ashamed of yourselves, fighting out here like this. Y'all grown women, not children."

I found the face to match the voice. "You're right ma'am, but look at what she did to my car."

Everyone looked over at my car. It was ruined. I could hear the gasps and the groans coming from the audience we had attracted.

"I didn't touch her car!" Paige yelled.

"Here we go again with the lies", I replied.

"How could I have done that? You got out here before I did."

"I don't know how you did it, but I know it was you. And you are going to pay for this", I pointed to my car.

"You can't make me do shit. You have no proof that I touched your car Jade. And you have no proof, because I didn't do go anywhere near your car", she said while adjusting her skirt.

I smacked my lips. "Hell, you even sound guilty. You are not going to get away with this."

She bent down and scooped her bag and purse off the ground. "Once again, you're wrong Jade Peterson. All I can say is that whoever you pissed off; they've really got it out for you. So you better be careful."

"Is that a threat Paige?" I asked her with a serious look on my face.

"No. It's not a threat. It's just a little friendly advice. But you don't have to listen to me. Do what you want to. It's your life." She looked at the few people that were still standing around. "It's been real folks, but I think I've had enough excitement for the evening."

"I'm going to get a restraining order against you. And if you so much as come within one foot near me, I'm going to have your ass thrown in jail", I said to her.

Before opening her car door, she yelled, "If that's what you want to do, that's cool with me. Just remember...I have not called you and I did not touch your car!"

I looked over at the small audience. "What in the hell y'all still looking at? The show's over. Go get your thrills somewhere else."

I located my purse on the ground, picked it up and pulled out my cell phone. I just wanted to get home. I would worry about the car later. I dialed Eli's phone and got his voice mail. I tried Taylor's next and got her voice mail. My next try was Sierra. I called her at the spa. Lucky for me, she wasn't with a client. I told her to pick me up and that I would explain everything later. She would never believe it.

Sierra

When Jade called me and said she needed me to pick her up from *Food Lion*, I didn't know what to expect. I do know that I wasn't expecting what she told me had happened. From what she told me, that Paige chic didn't seem too stable. I had a serious talk with her.

"Jade, aren't you a little worried about this Paige person?" I asked her.

She waved her hand at me. "Girl, please. That bitch don't scare me".

"You shouldn't take her too lightly. She sounds like she may have some mental problems."

"Yeah, she got some mental problems alright. She screwed Robert for his position, got caught and got fired. Now, she's taking her anger out on me, because she thinks I'm the cause of it."

I glanced at her out the corner of my eye. "Well...aren't you?"

She smacked her lips at me. "No! I mean...I did take the pictures and distribute them...But I wouldn't have had any pictures to take if she didn't open her legs. I say she got what she deserved."

"I understand what you're saying Jade. All I'm saying is just be careful. As far as you know, she may be the one that broke into your apartment", I warned her.

She sat there for a few seconds, without responding. She looked like she was in deep thought.

"Did you hear what I said Jade?" I asked her.

She snapped at me. "Yes, I heard you Sierra! Can we just drop the subject please? I'm tired of talking about that crazy bitch."

"If that's what you want Jade, darling", I responded.

As if realizing she had snapped at me, she asked in a softer tone, "How's the family?"

I smiled, thinking about mine and Tyler's plans for

the evening. "They're great. Shelby's being as hyper as a five year old can be. I got a babysitter, so Tyler and I can go out tonight. It was actually his idea. We haven't been out in so long. I'm really kind of excited about it, as silly as that may seem."

"It's not silly to still get excited about going out with your husband after being together for so long. I hope I still feel that way about Eli after we've been together that long."

Hearing his name made my stomach drop. "You really like him, don't you, Jade?"

She smiled when she said, "Yes I do. I'm actually in love with him. I've never met anyone like him before. I know he has this thing with his privacy, but the way he treats me outweighs all of that. When we're together, I feel so special and privileged."

Listening to her say those things, made me want to tell her everything I had heard at the spa. "Jade, can I say something?"

She looked over at me, still smiling. "Sure Sierra."

Alexis' voice boomed in my head. 'Don't say nothing. She won't believe you. You'll put your friendship in jeopardy.' Then I realized I couldn't say anything about what I had heard. But she had just confessed her love for him to me. I just decided the best thing for me to do was to keep my mouth closed, no matter how bad I wanted to tell her. "Uh...I just wanted to say that I wish you and Eli the best of luck with your future endeavors."

"Aw, thanks Sierra. I needed to hear that", she said and then stared out the window.

Tyler and I rode to the *Cheesecake Factory* in silence. Not an awkward silence, just silence. He looked really nice in the black slacks and royal blue pullover that I picked out for him. For me, he chose a black sleeveless knit dress with a matching cardigan that showed off my figure.

After the waiter took our orders and walked away, I said, "Sweetie, I'm so glad you asked me out to dinner tonight. It's been so long since we had some quality time alone."

He put his hand on top of mine. "It was the least I could do. I know I haven't been the best husband lately. And I wanted to show you how much I still love and appreciate you. I know this isn't a five star restaurant, but-"

I cut him off. "Don't be silly Tyler. Just spending some time together is all that matters. For a minute, I thought our marriage was in serious jeopardy. But I later realized that all marriages go through rough times. And things will work out, if both parties are willing to work things out."

"And I definitely want to work things out. You and Shelby mean the world to me. And I do want to keep this family together. Once again, I want to apologize for my behavior. Even though, I didn't want to do the things you wanted me to, I could've went about it a better way. I was really nasty to you and I know I said some pretty mean things. Sierra, I apologize from the bottom of my heart. I just hope you can forgive me and we can move on", he said, as he stroked my cheek with his finger.

I grabbed his hand from my cheek and kissed his palm. "Of course I forgive you Tyler. I just hope you can forgive me for being so selfish, by wanting you to do things that you were uncomfortable with. But let's not talk about that anymore. Let's just enjoy our dinner."

"Aw, isn't that sweet?" A familiar voice interrupted our conversation. I looked up to see Alexis standing there, looking stunning as usual.

"What are you doing here?" I asked her.

"This is a free country", she teased. She stood there staring at me with a look of lust in her eyes.

"Where are my manners? Tyler, this is my friend Alexis." I looked over at Tyler, who looked like he had seen a ghost.

Alexis held her hand out. "Hi Tyler. It is really nice to finally meet you."

Tyler didn't respond. I waved my hand in his face. "Tyler, are you okay?"

He cleared his throat. "Uh...y-yeah, I'm okay. It just got hot in here all of a sudden." He then shook Alexis' hand. "It's n-nice to meet you too."

I looked from one to the other. "Do you two know each other or something?"

"No!" Tyler said loudly.

Alexis chimed in. "No, we've never met before, that I'm aware of."

Tyler pulled his chair from the table and stood up. "If you ladies will excuse me, I need to use the restroom."

As soon as he was out of sight, I said, "What in the hell is going on Alexis?"

She sat down in Tyler's seat. "What do you mean Sierra?" she asked in her most innocent voice.

"I've never seen my husband react that way to meeting another woman. Are you sure you two don't know each other?"

"I don't know why your husband reacted that way. You heard him say he got hot. All I know is that we've never met. I guess I just have that effect on men." she laughed.

I rolled my eyes at her. "That shit is not funny, Alexis. That's my husband we're talking about. Maybe I'm just overreacting. Anyway, why did you come here when you knew that we were going to be here?"

She leaned closer to me. "I was jealous. The thought of you being out with him made me upset. So, I just had to come and make an appearance."

"You are being ridiculous Alexis. Tyler is my husband. All we're doing is having dinner", I said.

She rubbed my knee under the table. "But I'm sure you're gonna go fuck each other's brains out later tonight."

I laughed at her choice of words. "I don't know about the fucking each other's brains out part, but there is a chance that we're going to have sex tonight."

She looked around and then said, "Wouldn't you love it if I put you up on this table, spread your legs open and ate your pussy like it was one of these delicious cheesecakes?"

134

"Alexis, please don't start. I want to enjoy my evening with Tyler", I pleaded.

She continued stroking my knee. "What's the matter Sierra? You afraid your pussy is gonna get wet? You know you would love to feel this hot wet tongue on that fat juicy pussy right now."

"I want you to leave. Tyler should be back any minute. I don't want him getting any ideas about us", I said.

She let out a fake laugh. "Don't be naïve Sierra. Your husband won't even consider anything's going on between us. Men are so clueless when it comes to stuff like that. The male ego kicks in and they can't see the truth when it's slapping them right in the face."

"That may be true, but I still want this to be a special evening. He went through a lot of trouble to plan this and I don't want to spoil it."

She leaned in closer again. "If you really want to make it special, come over to my place later tonight. I'll eat your pussy so good, you'll be seeing stars."

I crossed my legs under the table, thinking about her proposition. "I don't know Alexis. I won't make any promises."

Tyler came back to the table. Alexis stood up. "Well, I really hope you can make it Sierra", she said, a little too loud.

"Make what?" Tyler asked.

"I'm having a little get together at my place with some of my lady friends. I guess you could say it's a sister social. We just have some drinks, discuss some books, fashion, and all that other stuff we women love", she lied.

Tyler asked, "Will Taylor and Jade be there?"

Alexis looked at me before answering. "Well, they're welcome to come. I've only met them once, so I wouldn't feel comfortable personally asking them. But I don't have a problem with Sierra bringing them as her guests."

"I can't promise that they'll be there, but I'll try to make it", I said.

"It won't be any fun without you. So please do

your best to come", she said in a very seductive voice, only I caught. Then she turned to Tyler. "It was nice to meet you. Hope to see you again."

"It was nice to meet you too", Tyler responded in a very unconvincing tone, not even looking at Alexis.

I watched Alexis sashay across the restaurant. And then she was out the door.

I looked over at Tyler, who was still looking down. "Tyler, is it my imagination or did you get really uncomfortable when I introduced you to Alexis?"

"Yes, it's your imagination. What I mean is that it may have seemed that way, but honestly, I just got hot all of a sudden. It had nothing to do with your friend Alexis."

I looked him in the eyes. "So, you're absolutely positive that you haven't met her before? Or were you just stunned by her beauty?"

He looked at me with a straight face. "To my recollection, we've never met before. And as far as her beauty is concerned, she's no more attractive than you are. I mean, she is a little flashier than you are, with the revealing clothes and the ton of makeup. I'm sure she doesn't have your brains either."

"For your information, she's a lawyer", I snapped.

He held up his hands in a defensive mode. "Excuse me. I didn't mean any harm. Put the claws away."

"I'm sorry. I didn't mean to snap at you, but you are talking about my friend", I said.

"Exactly, how much do you really know about this Alexis person?"

I was surprised at my husband's question. "What is that supposed to mean?"

"It means what it means. How much do you know about her? How did you meet her? How long have you known her?"

She came into the spa one day for a massage. I ended up servicing her. She gave me her business card. And I guess you could say we just hit it off. Plus, she's sent plenty of clients my way", I responded.

Tyler asked, "So she just popped into your spa one

day? Out of all the spas in Durham, she just happened to pick yours?"

I gave him a funny look. "Is that so hard to believe Tyler? You know as well as I do that I get new clients all the time. Either they've heard about the spa or they just happen to see it on an outing at the shopping center. Why are you tripping about Alexis?"

He took a deep breath before responding. "I've just never seen you hang out or talk to any women other than Taylor and Jade. And you've definitely never socialized with any of your clients like that. I just think you need to be careful about who you choose to socialize with."

"You're right. I've never dealt with any women other than Taylor and Jade. But there's nothing wrong with making new friends Tyler", I said.

"Yeah, but she doesn't seem like your type. Like I said earlier, she's a little too flashy."

I laughed at his comment. "She's no flashier than Taylor and you know it. Taylor won't step out the house unless she's in full makeup and dressed to the nine. Besides, you're judging Alexis without even knowing her. You can't really tell what a person's like from one encounter."

He leaned back in his seat and stared at me. "First impressions make lasting impressions. I don't want you to hang out with her anymore."

I rubbed my chin with my hand. "You can't be serious?"

"Oh, I'm definitely serious", he said, without cracking a smile.

"I won't do it. I'm not going to end our friendship", I said, folding my arms across my chest.

He sat up in his chair. "So, you're going to disobey-"

I cut him off before he finished his sentence. "Tyler Jackson, I'm your wife, not your child. I'm a grown ass woman and I can be friends with whomever I choose to be friends with. I don't tell you who you can and cannot hang out with."

He looked around the restaurant before

responding. "All I'm saying is that you should be careful who you choose as your friends."

"Thanks for the advice, but I think I'm a good judge of character. Alexis is fun to be around and I have no intention of cutting off the friendship. So get used to it", I said and then I walked out of the restaurant.

We rode back home in silence, an awkward silence. I sat there thinking about how Tyler had the nerve to forbid me from being friends with Alexis. I had never seen him react that way to a friend of mine. I had all intentions of going home and letting him make love to me. But the fact of him not wanting me to be friends with Alexis made me want to see her even more. I had to see her and be with her.

As soon as we pulled up to our house, I opened the car door. "Tyler, tell Nikki thanks for babysitting Shelby. Give her this." I shoved some money in his hand. "I'm going out for a while. I'll be back."

"Where are you going Sierra?" he questioned me as I pulled the keys to my car out of my purse.

I opened the door to my car. "Don't wait up for me. Those sister socials can drag on forever sometimes."

He walked towards me. "Sierra, you need to come inside the house with me. It's too late to be going anywhere."

I cranked up the car and rolled down the window. "Kiss Shelby goodnight for me."

"Come your ass inside and you can kiss her yourself", he yelled loud enough for the neighbors to hear.

I put the car in reverse and sped off down the street, with Tyler in the driveway cursing me like a sailor.

When I got to Alexis', she was dressed in this very sexy chiffon robe, with stiletto heels. She had her hair pulled up in a tight bun. And of course, her makeup was flawless.

She kissed me lightly on the lips and said, "I knew you would come."

"How did you know?" I asked.

"Because you can't get enough of this." She flicked

out her tongue.

I decided not to respond. Instead, I smiled at her. She took my hands and pulled me into the den. "I have a surprise for you", she smiled slyly.

I looked around the room to see if any surprise guests were going to pop out. I was hoping Boris wouldn't show up again.

She laughed at my reaction. "It's nothing like that." She opened her robe. I looked down and saw this huge fake penis in the place where her vagina was.

"What in the hell is going on Alexis?" I asked her.

She put her hands on her hips. "It's called a strap-on and I'm going to fuck you with it."

I backed away from her. "You're not coming anywhere near me with that thing."

She grabbed my arm. "Don't be silly Sierra. It's just like a real dick, only better."

"How can it be better than a real dick Alexis?"

She used her fingers to count out each reason. "First of all, it can't get you pregnant. Second, it won't give you any diseases. And last, but not least, it will go long enough for you to come as many times as you want." She then pointed to the strap-on. "This aint no two minute brotha here."

Alexis did as she promised back at the restaurant. She ate my pussy so good, I was seeing the moon, the sun, and the stars. I was begging her to stop, but she kept going. After she gave me that killer tongue lashing, she used that strap-on contraption on me. She let me have my way with it. She gave it to me missionary style, sucking on my tit's the whole time she was giving it to me. Then she let me ride it like I was at the rodeo, giving me every single inch. Then she made me get on all fours and she pounded me with that thing like her life depended on it. She was thrusting in me so hard I thought she was going to touch my stomach.

She was screaming at me. "Do you like it baby? Does it feel good to ya?"

I answered back. "Yeah baby. It feels so damn good. Fuck me harder!"

She pounded me harder and harder. "Is this hard enough? Is this what you want, you nasty little bitch?"

"Y-yes, that's it! Don't stop! I'm gonna come. Baby, please don't stop! Yes, that's it! I'm c-coming!" I screamed as another orgasm took over my body.

Alexis and I collapsed on the floor after it was over. We were both sweating and breathing hard.

"Wow, I never realized what hard work it is to be a man. No wonder they always go to sleep afterwards", Alexis said, while stroking the strap-on.

I laughed at her comment. "I guess it's pretty tiresome doing all that thrusting and pumping, trying their hardest to make that lady come before they do."

We spent the rest of the night, lying in each other's arms, talking and caressing each other and feeding each other fruit. I decided to open up to Alexis and let her know how I felt about our friendship. "Alexis, I'm really glad you came into my life. You have introduced me to things I never thought I would ever experience", I said, after popping a grape into her mouth.

She looked down at me. "I'm really glad you feel that way Sierra. I saw you as this beautiful, sexy woman who lacked the self-confidence every woman should have. I felt that I could help you in my own special way. And as time has gone by, I've grown this attachment to you."

I sat up and stroked her cheek. "Sometimes, I feel closer to you than I do my own husband. He pushes me away a lot, but you pull me in closer to you. You let me enjoy myself. There are no limits with you when it comes to sexuality. I look forward to seeing you and being with you. I think I love you."

She smiled at me so hard, I thought her face was going to crack. "That's great Sierra. I'm so happy to hear you say that." She grabbed my face and kissed me harder than she had ever kissed me before.

I appreciated the affection she showed when she kissed me, but I couldn't help but notice that she never told me that she loved me back. Was it because she was caught up in the moment? Or was it because she didn't feel the same way?

Just a Matter of Time

Taylor

"David, you know your mother can't stand the ground I walk on. Why does she have to visit us this month?" I asked my husband while applying my makeup.

"Look Taylor, I know my mother is a bit hard to swallow. But just try to be nice to her. Show her what a lovely human being you are", he replied and then kissed me on the cheek.

I gave him a sarcastic smile. "I could jump through hoops for your mother and she still wouldn't like me. She never thought I was good enough for you and the fact that I'm a black woman doesn't make it any better."

David gave me a funny look. "Are you implying that my mother doesn't like you because you're black Taylor?"

I took a second to think before I responded. "I'm not saying that ...exactly."

"Well, what are you saying?" he asked before I could finish my statement.

"I'm saying that I'm sure I'm not the type of person she pictured her only son with. Let's be realistic here David. If I was some blue-eyed, bleached blonde like Suzanne, I'm pretty sure we'd get along just fine."

He laughed at me. "That's the most ridiculous thing I've ever heard."

"What's so ridiculous about it? Your mother turned her nose up at me from the very first day we met. She brushed me off like I was nothing. She doesn't treat me like your wife."

I think you're exaggerating Taylor. My mother's just a little...."

"A little what David?"

"She's just a little arrogant and aggressive, that's all."

I gave him an evil look. "That's all? Forget aggressive. Your mother is a snob David. She criticizes everything or everyone that doesn't have to do with a lot of money. And that's not right."

He became defensive. "I don't see you turning your nose up at all the riches you have surrounding you. You walk around in the best designer clothes money can buy. And that BMW out there wasn't bought with food stamps."

I wasn't trying to get into an argument with David, but he was testing me. "I never said I didn't like the fact of being wealthy. Of course, I enjoy the benefits of having money. I just don't look down on people that don't have it. I know where I came from."

He walked back over to me and put his arms around me. "Taylor, I don't want to argue with you, especially about my mother. Just try to be nice to her, for me."

I looked into his blue eyes and couldn't help but to give in to him. "I'll do it for you sweetie...only for you. Is your father coming also?"

"No, he's not coming. He said he has some business to take care of and he can't get away."

"They say the apple don't fall too far from the tree."

"We Morgan men believe in hard work. How else are we going to take care of the women in our lives?"

"I wish your father was coming. Now, I can deal with him any day."

David's father was nothing like his mother. Sometimes, I wondered how a man like him put up with a woman like her. He was always making jokes and he would flirt with me. I caught him stealing glances at my ass and chest a couple of times. Lucky for me, his parents lived in Miami and didn't visit too often. I knew it was going to be a long week. But I was going to try my hardest to be nice to that old winch.

A stretch limo pulled up into the driveway like we were expecting a celebrity. I knew who was going to step out once the driver got out and opened the door. Claire Morgan stepped out looking like a million bucks. She was wearing a red pin-striped pantsuit with black open-toed pumps. On her shoulder was a red and black leather purse. The driver retrieved her *Prada* luggage from the car. She had packed like she was going to be staying for a month.

"Mother, you made it." David swept pass me and rushed out to meet her.

"Of course, I made it. I told you I was coming didn't I?" she replied after pushing a lock of hair out of his face. "You need a haircut dear."

David stood back and admired his mother. "I still wish you would have let us pick you up from the airport instead of having a limo bring you here."

She slapped him on the arm. "Don't be silly. That's what the limo is for. Besides, I love the attention I get when I'm riding in one. And I didn't want to put you through any trouble."

I took a deep breath before stepping up to greet Mrs. Morgan. "Hello Mrs. Morgan. How are you doing?"

She looked me up and down before responding. "Hello Taylor."

"It's good to see you again. We're so glad that you could come", I lied.

She grabbed David's arm. "Well, I figured it was time for me to come and check on my son and see how he's been doing."

David grabbed my hand and said, "Oh, I'm doing just fine mother. Taylor takes very good care of me."

She gave me a nasty look and said, "I'm sure she does, but we all know that there's nothing like a mother's love."

I smiled at her before saying, "That's all fine and dandy when you're dealing with a child, but David's a grown man Mrs. Morgan. He really doesn't need his mother's care when he has a wife who sees to his every want and need."

I watched her face turn beet red, but I didn't care. I wasn't about to let that old goat come in my home and make me feel like I didn't belong there. I like showing respect for my elders, but she was an exception. From day one, she treated me like crap. For starters, she purposely showed up late for our wedding. Then she had the gall to bring David's ex-girlfriend Suzanne with her.

During the reception, she kept telling stories about their relationship to anybody that would listen. I was furious. David didn't have the balls to say anything to her, even though she was being very disrespectful towards me. Thankfully, Mr. Morgan finally spoke up and told her to stop being rude. She just rolled her eyes at him and continued gabbing with Suzanne. She never did say anything else disrespectful that night. She just kept giving me dirty looks throughout the night. And the few times she has visited, she's made it very obvious that she doesn't like me.

"So is that okay with you Taylor?" David jarred me out of my thoughts.

"Um...I'm sorry sweetie. I didn't hear you. What did you say?"

"I said I have some things to take care of at the office. I thought you could take mother out to the mall or something, so you two can spend some time together."

I looked at David like he had lost his mind. "Honey, your mother just got off an airplane. I'm sure she just wants to go inside and get some rest. Flying always makes me tired."

"Actually, I am a little tired. I just need to lie down for a while." She glanced at me and said, "But don't think you're off the hook. I will want to go out when I get up."

After we got Mrs. Morgan settled into her room and David went to the office, I went in my bedroom and locked the door. I needed somebody to talk to. So I called Exodus.

"Hey sexy chocolate", I said to him as soon as he answered the phone.

"Baby girl, what do I owe for this special phone call?" he asked in his sexy voice.

I smacked my lips over the phone. "Now you know I don't have to have a special reason to call you."

"I know. I'm just messing with you. Sometimes it turns me on to see you all riled up", he said.

I laughed at his comment. "Well, you might come all over yourself with the state I'm in right now."

"What's wrong? You sound upset."

"Irritated is more like it. David's mother is in town. She just got here and she's going to be here for a week. She hasn't been here an hour yet and she's already working my nerves."

"That's too bad. And to think you still got another week to go. How are you going to keep your composure?"

I rubbed my pulsing temple before responding. "I don't know Exodus. That woman is such a bitch."

"That's a little harsh isn't it Taylor?" he asked.

I laughed. "You don't know her like I do. She doesn't think I belong with David."

"I have to agree with her on that." he replied.

"Don't start Exodus. I'm serious. She's a racist and David can't see that. She can't accept the fact that David chose me as his wife. She doesn't show me any kind of respect, even when I'm trying my hardest to be nice to her. And if you're not rich, you're nothing in her eyes."

Exodus lowered his voice and said, "Well why don't you let me take your mind off of that ole' bat. I got something here that will make you forget all about your mother-in-law."

"Stop it Exodus. You're making me horny", I said.

"That's the whole idea."

"I can't. She wants to go shopping when she wakes up. So I have to be here."

He started pleading with me. "Come on baby. I really need to see you. My dick is over here hard as a rock waiting to get inside you. I promise I won't keep you too long. Your mother-in-law won't even know you're gone."

I rubbed my pussy through my pants. "You always know what to say to get me excited. I'll meet you at our usual spot in twenty minutes. Don't be late."

I hung up the phone and went to Claire's room to see if she was sleep. I knocked on the door. When I didn't get an answer, I opened the door to see her sprawled out on the bed sound asleep. I left a note for her telling her that I had to run a quick errand, in case she woke up before I got back. Then I was out the door.

When I got to the room, Exodus was laid out on the bed butt ass naked. Neither one of said anything. I just went over to the bed and started working magic on his huge shaft, which was standing at attention. As I worked him over, he was moaning and groaning like it was the best pleasure he had ever experienced.

"Damn Taylor, that shit feels so good. Suck this dick baby. Suck it like you mean it", he cried out in pleasure.

When he felt himself about come, he made me stop. He threw me on the bed and opened my legs. He dove in between my legs and feasted on my pussy like it was his favorite dessert. I grabbed his head as he continued to pleasure me.

"Oh God! Exodus, you're gonna make me come baby! Oh yeah! That's it baby!"

He looked up at me. "You like that shit don't ya? I told you baby, I can get down too. A brotha aint scared to eat no pussy."

I pushed his head back down. "Keep going. Don't stop. Make me come baby."

Exodus continued to devour me until I screamed out in ecstasy. My body was shaking and convulsing from the powerful orgasm I was having. As soon as it subsided, Exodus entered me with his huge manhood and started pounding me with all the power he had. I thought my insides were going to burst. Even though he was rough with me, I found it enjoyable. The pain he was causing me was a big turn on and I had yet another orgasm.

After it was over, I went to the bathroom to clean myself up and freshen up my makeup. No words were exchanged between us. I left out as quickly as I had come in. When I left, Exodus was still lying on the bed, stroking himself.

"Where have you been Taylor?" Claire asked me as soon as I entered the kitchen.

I glared at her. "Didn't you get my note?"

"Yes, I did. But that still doesn't answer my question." She came and stood closer to me.

I rolled my eyes. "No, it doesn't answer your

question, which I feel is none of your business."

She gave me a look of shock before replying. "There's no need for the hostility, Taylor. I just asked you a simple question."

"I'm not hostile Claire. I just don't feel that I need to give you a rundown of what I do with my time", I replied while pouring myself a glass of juice.

She sat down on one of the bar stools. "I thought we were going to the mall today. David did ask you to take me."

I gulped down the glass of juice, wiped my mouth with a napkin and said, "We're still going. The day is not over yet. I took care of a few things early, just so I could take you to the mall."

"How nice of you", she said in a very sarcastic tone.

I responded with, "Yeah, I thought so too. Are you ready to go so we can get this over with?"

"You make it sound as if you don't want to take me", she replied.

I smiled at her and said, "Of course that's not how I intended to sound. I'm looking forward to our little encounter."

She knew I was lying when the words came out of my mouth. Instead of responding, she went back to her room and got her purse.

On our way to the mall, I decided not to try to pretend like I was interested in starting a conversation with her. I glanced over at her one time and she was staring out the window. Claire was very attractive for her age of sixty. Of course, a lot of it had to do with the numerous surgeries she went through. Plastic surgery was her best friend. She had had face lifts, lip injections, brow lifts, several nose jobs and so many more. She could easily pass for a forty-five to fifty year old. Her hair was kept in a short style, which added to her youthful appearance. At first glance, she appeared to be this sweet lovable lady. But I knew the real Claire. She was a snobby racist woman, who thought the world revolved around her. The men in her life were too afraid to let her know what type of person she really was. Someone needed to put that witch in her place.

"Claire, you don't really like me too much, do you?" I asked her breaking the silence.

"What would make you ask such a question dear?" she asked in the most innocent voice.

I glanced at her and shook my head. "Oh, there are plenty of things that make me ask that question. You were late to our wedding. Then you show up with David's ex, who you flat out said should have been his wife. You embarrass me by talking about their relationship throughout the reception. And let's not forget all the times you belittle me and talk down to me."

She turned to me, laced her hands together and said, "Taylor dear, I have no idea what you're referring to."

"Claire, I'm not the dumb bitch you may think I am. You and I both know that you don't want me with your son. So you can stop the innocent act." I was getting more irritated by the minute.

She let out a throaty laugh. "You're right Taylor. I don't want you with David. You're not the right woman for him. He deserves better."

"And how in the hell do you know what's right for him? David's a grown man. He can choose who he wants to be with. And he chose me."

She looked back out if the window. "I had the perfect woman for him. I had handpicked Suzanne myself. She came from a wealthy family, just like David. They were a match made in heaven. Him, the tall good looking man with the deep blue eyes. Her, the blond haired, blue eyed beauty with the perfect body. You couldn't have found a more attractive couple. Then David had to throw it all away over a few minor issues. He discovered that Suzanne liked to snort a little coke every now and then. And she liked sleeping with women from time to time. I begged him not to break up with her. I told him he could adjust to her lifestyle. All he had to do was monitor her cocaine use. And as far as the sleeping with women went, all he had to do was join in from time to time."

I was amazed at what she had said. "Are you

149

kidding me? You were willing to force your son to go through with that relationship, just because she came from a wealthy family? What kind of mother are you?"

She raised her voice. "Don't you dare question my ability to be a good mother. I am a good mother! I'm a mother who would do whatever it takes to protect her son's assets. I'm a mother who would do whatever it takes to make sure her son is with someone who loves him for who he is and not what he has in his bank account."

"Claire, you have no idea who I am or what I'm about. You've never given me a chance. When you look at me, all you see is some poor black girl trying to live off of your son's money. And that's not who I am", I lied.

"Listen Taylor, I may not know who you are, but I know what you're about. You see the difference between David and me is that he trusts everyone. I, on the other hand, trust no one. To me, everyone has an ulterior motive. When you have money, you have to watch everyone around you. You can never tell who your true friends are. You have people pretending to be your friends when really all they want is to be in your shoes. As soon as your back is turned, they're trying to turn your husband against you, by telling lies and things you told them in confidence. Then you catch them in your bed, screwing each other's brains out."

I didn't know what to say. It was obvious she was referring to her own personal experience. I was sorry that she had to deal with her husband cheating on her with her friend, but I wasn't about to let her put me in some category without knowing anything about me.

"I'm really sorry you had to go through that Claire, but-"

"Go through what?" she blurted."

"That little story you were telling…I assumed you were talking about yourself."

She snapped at me. "Well, don't assume anything! You know what they say about assuming don't you?"

"Yeah, I know the saying. You don't have to admit that it was about you. That's your decision. All I know is that you don't like me and you don't have a valid reason as to why", I replied.

She gave me an evil laugh. "Taylor dear, I know more about you than you think. I'm sure I know more about you than David does. This old lady is smarter than you think. I know who you are and what you're about."

It felt as if my heart dropped to my stomach. "W-what do you mean by that?"

She continued laughing. "Let's just say that with all the resources I have, I can find out anything I want to know. It's amazing what you can find out when you have money. I guess it's true when they say money talks."

I tried to remain calm, like I wasn't concerned about what she had said. "I have nothing to hide. So your little remarks don't affect me the least bit."

"Oh, I beg to differ, darling. Some of the things I found out about you, I know David don't know." She looked over at me to see my reactions to her statement. I knew she was calling my bluff.

"If what you say is true, why haven't you said anything to David about it?" I asked her.

"I want to give David a chance to see for himself who you really are. If I just go to him and tell him everything, he won't believe me", she said, rubbing her hands together.

I glared at her. "You are one evil woman Claire Morgan. I don't know what kind of game you're trying to play, but I don't want any part of it.

She laughed her evil laugh again. "I'm not playing any game. This is all real. But I do have a proposition for you."

She had peaked my curiosity. "What kind of proposition do you have for me?"

"How about I don't go to David with all the information I have on you, if you just walk away from him and the marriage?"

"Are you crazy woman? Do you actually think I'm going to leave my husband simply because you asked me to?"

"You didn't let me get to the good part. I will give you one million dollars if you just simply disappear and never come back."

"Witch, you have lost your damn mind. Do you really hate me that much?"

"Okay...make it two point five million, but that's my final offer. I'm talking cold hard cash here...tax free."

"You don't have enough money to pay me off!"

"Bullshit!"

"You are the lowest of the low. It's hard to believe that you are the mother of such a wonderful person like David. I guess he gets all of his good qualities from his father."

She ran her fingers through her short hair. "Stop being so naïve Taylor. You and I both know that everything has a price. You can call me anything you want. But the truth is you would have never married David if he didn't have money. You may have him fooled, but I can see right through you."

"I guess Mr. Morgan's personality is what stole your heart. His money had nothing to do with you tying the knot."

She took a deep breath and said, "John had nothing when I met him. We were both in college in our sophomore year. We started dating and soon fell in love. I later found out that I was pregnant. John said we had to get married, because that was the right thing to do. So we got married and rented a small one bedroom apartment. We decided that it would be more affordable for me to put college on hold and stay home to take care of the baby. John worked part-time and finished college. He landed himself a good job. And before we knew it, we had money coming in faster than we could've ever imagined. John later started his own business. We bought our first house. And the rest, as they say is history. But the point is I was there when John had nothing. I supported him and his decisions. I put my education on hold, so he could see his dreams through. I made sacrifices so we could live a better life."

"I had no idea Claire. So what were you going to school for?" I asked her.

She looked out the window. "Believe it or not, I

was studying law. I was going to be the best lawyer Durham had ever seen."

"So what happened? I mean, why didn't you go back to school after things got better with you and John?"

"John always had a reason for why I shouldn't go back. He kept saying that I didn't need to go back to school because he made enough money to support us. Then it was because David needed a full-time mom at home and I would be neglecting him if I went back to school. So I let him talk me out of following through with my goals." I could tell that she was getting a little emotional.

"How did you guys end up in Miami?"

She looked over at me, surprised that I was even showing interest. "After David graduated from high school, I started talking about college again. I figured John would be all for me going back to school. I was wrong. He said he was against it and gave me no reason as to why. One day, he just decided that we were going to sell our house and move to Florida. He didn't ask me if I wanted to or not. He made it clear that he was the man of the house and what he said went. So we packed up and moved to Miami. David wanted to stay in Durham and go to college here, but John was against it. So he moved to Florida with us and enrolled in school down there. After he graduated from college, he asked John for a loan. He moved back here to Durham and started his own business."

I was truly surprised by everything she had revealed. The whole time, I had thought she was just a little bitch, who had everything handed to her. But she had made sacrifices to get where she was. "Do you resent John for not letting you go back to school?"

"No, I don't resent him. Sometimes I wonder what it would have been like if I did become the lawyer I wanted to be. But then I think about how much John and I do have. I have everything I ever wanted, and more. I raised an intelligent young man, who is just as successful as his father. Things may not have turned out that way if I would have continued to pursue my career."

I reached over and touched her hand. "I'm glad that we got a chance to talk Claire. I feel closer to you now that I know what types of things you had to go through. You and I are alike in some ways."

She pulled her hand from under mine. "We are nothing alike. Don't think that just because I opened up to you a little, my thoughts of you have changed. I still say you are only after one thing. And it's up to me to make sure David sees you for what you really are. It's just a matter of time."

I sat there, not knowing what to say to her. My mind was in a whirl. I knew she was serious about telling David whatever it was she thought she knew about me. I shouldn't have been worried, considering I knew she had nothing on me. But she struck me as the type of person that would do anything to get what she wanted. I guess I would just have to wait and see.

Jade

Eli was taking me to pick up my car from the body shop. They had worked on my car after I had it towed there. That set me back a bit, but I had to do it. I still couldn't believe Paige went that far. I had no idea that position meant that much to her. The position wasn't even all it was cracked up to be. But I did do what I said I was going to do. I went downtown and took out a restraining order against Paige. I told them about the phone calls and what happened with my car. They asked me if I knew for a fact that it was her. I told them no, but I was sure it was her. At first, they were giving me a hard time about the restraining order. I practically begged them to let me file one. I explained that I was fearful of her and what she may do next. I even told them about our little scuffle in the parking lot. So they granted me my restraining order.

"I hope you got that crazy bitch in check", Eli said interrupting my thoughts.

"If you mean she won't be causing me anymore trouble, I hope so too. A restraining order doesn't guarantee nothing will happen to you. It just allows you to call the police if that person comes near you." I pulled the order out of my purse.

Eli gave me a funny look. "You're carrying that thing around in your purse like its money."

"You have to keep it on you so you can show it if you need to. There's no telling when or where that crazy girl may come at me again. So I have to be prepared. Plus, I was told to keep it in my purse."

"I'm still tripping off the fact that you two were out there in the parking lot fighting. Boy, I would have paid to see that one. I aint seen a cat fight in a long time", he laughed.

"Believe me, it wasn't a cat fight. The more I think about it, the more embarrassed I get. I can't believe I was in the parking lot of *Food Lion* fighting like some teenage school girl." I shook my head in disgust.

"I told you, you got a mean streak in you girl", he teased.

I hit him on the arm. "No, I don't Eli. That's way out of character for me. When I came outside and saw my car, something inside me just snapped."

"If it's not true, how do explain the episode at *Chili's* with the waitress?" he asked.

"That bitch had it coming...talking 'bout black women. Plus, I did apologize for throwing the water in her face." I smiled to myself thinking about the situation.

"I'm watching my back, 'cause one day you might just flip on my black ass."

"Just don't fuck me over and you won't have nothing to worry about", I told him.

He took on a serious tone. "As long as you do right, I'm gonna do right."

"Do you have any appointments today? I was hoping we could do lunch or something."

"Actually, I don't have any until later this evening. We can do lunch on one condition."

I took a deep breath, not knowing what he was going to say. "What's the condition Eli?"

He gave me a seductive look. "I'll do lunch, if you are lunch."

"Ummm...that sounds good. I'm definitely down with that."

We picked up my car from the body shop. Eli drove his car and I drove my car back to my apartment. As soon as we were inside, Eli started kissing me on my neck. I could feel the moisture forming between my legs. "Eli, you sure know how to get a girl in the mood", I mumbled between kisses.

"It's easy when the girl is as fine and sexy as you are", he replied, while unbuttoning my shirt.

"Eli baby, I want you so bad", I whispered in his ear

"I want you too baby, but I want to take my time. I don't have anywhere to go, so I'm gonna love you nice and slow." He unzipped my pants and dropped them to the floor.

I wrapped my arms around his neck. "You know what I like don't you?"

"I'd like to think I know", he replied, licking his lips.

"Oh, you know what I like. And you give it to me every time", I said, holding my head back so he could kiss me on my neck.

"I wanna take your mind off that Paige chic. The only thing I want you to be thinking about is how many times you want to come on this dick", he whispered in my ear.

"I'm definitely down with that idea."

"Well, let's go." He picked me up and carried me to my bedroom. As soon as we entered, he threw me on the bed.

"I thought you were gonna give it to me nice and slow", I teased.

"Oh, I am. But I'm gonna give it to you hard at first, get you worked up. And just when you're about to reach your peak, I'm gonna slow it down...make you beg for it", he said while rubbing his manhood.

I squeezed my breasts. "You like for me to beg for it, don't you?"

"Yes, I do", he replied.

For the next hour, Eli and I made love like it was our last time. When he was finished with me, I felt like a new person. I went back to work with a pep in my step. Paige was no longer on my mind.

Sierra

Tyler, Shelby and I were sitting down having dinner together for the first time in about a week. After I ran off to go see Alexis, he didn't speak to me for a few days. I was beginning to wonder if our marriage was about to expire. Every time I left Alexis, I felt guilty when I came back home to Tyler. I knew what I was doing was wrong, but it was like I couldn't help myself. If I could just get Tyler to make me feel the way Alexis did, everything would be fine.

"Shelby, stop playing with your food...if you're finished eating, leave the table", Tyler said with irritation in his voice.

"Okay Daddy", Shelby answered back. "I'm going to play with my toys."

I spoke up. "You better make it quick, because it's almost time for bed." She was halfway upstairs before I could finish my sentence.

I looked over at my husband, who was now leaning back in his chair, rubbing his flat stomach. "That was good, if I must say so myself", he said mainly to himself.

He had made meatloaf with gravy, homemade mashed potatoes and corn on the cob. I had to agree with him. It was delicious. "You do know your way around the kitchen babe. That's the only reason I married you. That and the fact that you were fine as hell", I said.

"So now the truth comes out. All this time, I thought it was because you loved me. You mean you've used me all these years?" He put his hand over his heart pretending he was hurt.

I laughed at him. "You're so silly."

"Yeah, but you like it when I'm silly."

"I do. It makes me think of the old Tyler; the one I fell in love with."

He gave me a puzzled look. "What do you mean the *old* Tyler?"

I took a deep breath. I didn't want to start an argument, but if I didn't answer him, that would be an even bigger argument. "Well Tyler, you've changed a lot."

"I've matured Sierra. There's a difference."

"I don't mean in that way. You use to have a great sense of humor, always making me laugh. Now you act like laughing is the last thing you want to do. We use to talk. Now, you're always on the computer." I looked away, so he wouldn't see the tears forming in my eyes. "I just don't feel like we're close anymore. It's like we're just going through the motions."

He moved his chair next to mine. "Sierra, I had no idea you felt this way. It's just that I've been under a lot of stress at work lately."

"Your job has always been stressful, but you never let it bother you or our relationship before." I looked him in his eyes. "Tell me the truth Tyler. Do you want a divorce?"

He put his hand on my shoulder. "Hell no, I don't want a divorce! Who said anything about a divorce? That's the last thing on my mind. I love you baby. I know we have our problems, but I could never part with you and Shelby. You guys mean the world to me."

"Then, what's wrong with us?" I asked him.

"I didn't know there was anything wrong with us, Sierra. I know we've argued a lot more lately than we use to. But I didn't consider it anything major."

"Tyler, let's not lie to each other. We have been very distant towards each other lately. And every time we talk, it turns into an argument. And if you don't think there's a problem, then we really have a problem."

"Well, if we have problems, they didn't start until you started hanging around that Alexis character," he responded.

"Oh no! I'm not going to let you blame someone else for our marital problems. This has nothing to do with Alexis." Even as the words came out of my mouth, I didn't believe them. On the other hand, Tyler and I were having problems way before Alexis came into the picture. Of course my being involved with her, didn't make them any better. But that was none of Tyler's business. "This is about you and me Tyler. It's about us not spending any quality time together. It's about us not communicating with each other. It's about you spending every chance you get on that damn computer. It's about me feeling that you're not attracted to me anymore. It's about so much more." I was almost in tears by the time I said what I had to say.

He grabbed my hand and kissed it. Then he said, "Sierra, I took my marriage vows seriously. I meant every word of them. There is no way I'm giving up on us. Having a family is the most important thing in the world to me. A man aint nothing without a family. So I'm willing to work this out...if you are. I just can't lose my family."

I was surprised by his reaction. He was really putting a lot of emphasis on family. But I knew it was important to him, considering he grew up without a real one. I wasn't going to disappoint him. If he was willing to put in an effort, so would I. I was going to have to figure out a way to break it off with Alexis. I knew it wouldn't be easy, but I had to do what I had to do to save my marriage.

I stood up from the table. "Hey babe, why don't you clear the table? I'll get Shelby all tucked in and you can meet me upstairs in our bedroom for a little night cap."

He gave me a naughty smile. "Yeah, I'd like that very much. Why don't you slip into one of those little sexy gowns you have and I'll be right up."

I went upstairs to Shelby's room, helped her into her pajamas, and read her a bedtime story. As soon as she was asleep, I went to my bedroom. I could hear Tyler downstairs in the kitchen. He was such a neat freak. He refused to leave one thing out of place in the kitchen overnight. Everything had to be put up in its proper place. Not even a spoon could be left in the sink.

While he busied himself in the kitchen, I slipped into a little sexy number Alexis had given me. It was very revealing. I'm pretty sure she would be furious if she knew I was wearing it for Tyler, considering I had already worn it for her. She said I looked hot in it. So I was hoping to get the same reaction from Tyler. I posed in the sexiest pose I could think of and waited for him on the bed.

When he walked into our bedroom, his eyes lit up. "Damn baby, you look so good. I've never seen that one before. Is it new?"

"Yes, it is. I picked it out just for you", I lied. "Do you like it?"

He laughed. "Hell yeah! Didn't you just hear me say how good you look?"

"Yes, but I wanted to hear it again. A girl can never get too many compliments from her sexy husband."

He walked over to the bed, pushed me back and started kissing me, long and hard. I could feel my body weakening to his kisses. His kisses were full of passion like they use to be. His hand roamed my body as his kisses went from my lips to my neck on down to my breasts.

Then he whispered to me, "Sierra, you're so beautiful. I'm sorry if I made you feel unattractive. You're the sexiest woman in the world to me."

He was making me as horny as hell and I didn't know how much more I could take. "I want you Tyler, baby. I need you now." I was ready for a night full of passionate lovemaking with my husband.

He stood up and I watched him undress down to his sexy body. He then grabbed my ankles and pulled me down to the edge of the bed. He pushed my legs open and entered me with a force I never knew he could. It scared and excited me at the same time. As he thrust in and out of me, I screamed out his name.

Then he started biting and nibbling on my neck. And when he whispered, "Whose pussy is this baby?" I thought I was going to lose it for sure. I wasn't accustomed to him talking to me that way.

But I didn't let him down. I screamed back, "It's your pussy baby. It's all yours!"

After a few more powerful thrusts, Tyler was

jerking and shaking like a mad man. I knew he had reached his peak. And even though I didn't climax, I was satisfied. The passion that Tyler had shown me was enough to satisfy me for the time being.

After it was over, we just lay in the bed and cuddled. And for the first time in months, Tyler didn't go get on the computer. We fell asleep in each other's arms. That's the way things are supposed to be.

Taylor

David's mother had been gone for a few days and I couldn't have been happier. That woman was a piece of work. I was still shocked about her opening up to me the way she did. I had no idea she was interested in anything else other than money. Even though she wasn't my favorite person, I envied the relationship she had with David. You could tell that she really loved him and wanted only the best for him. She would give her right arm to see him happy. The whole time she was here, she was constantly telling him how proud she was of him. And of course, he treated her like a queen. One could say I was actually jealous. I don't ever remember my mother telling me she was proud of me for anything. All she ever told me was how I wasn't going to be anything, because I didn't come from anything. Instead of giving to me like a mother should, she took from me.

I got my first real boyfriend when I was sixteen. I still remember Devin Stanley. He was only one grade ahead of me, and one of the cutest boys in school. He could've had any girl he wanted, but he chose me. I never had any problems getting boys' attention, but I was still surprised when he showed interest in me. The word around school was that he was kind of experienced in the sex department. Thanks to my mother's friends, I was no longer a virgin, but I didn't want anyone to know that. So I portrayed myself as one.

He started asking me about meeting my mother and I kept brushing him off. I was going to put it off as long as I could. Then one day after school, he said "Instead of you riding the bus today, I'm going to take you home."

"I don't think that's a good idea", I replied.

"Why not? I am your boyfriend aren't I? What's the big deal if I give you a ride home? Plus, I can meet your mom", he smiled and put his arm around me.

"That's what I'm afraid of", I mumbled under my breath.

"What was that?" he asked.

"Nothing."

When we got to my house, my mother was in the kitchen cooking. She was singing a ZZ Hill blues song. "Down home blues....down home blues...all she wanted to hear was these down home blues all night long-"

I interrupted her performance. "Hey Momma, I'm home."

She came out of the kitchen. "Whatcha doing home so..."

She stopped mid-sentence when she saw Devin. Her eyes roamed his body from head to toe. She wiped her hands on her apron. "Well, who do we have here Taylor?"

Devin held out his hand. "Hello Ms. Johnson. My name is Devin Stanley. I'm Taylor's ...I'm a friend of Taylor's. I hope you don't mind me giving her a ride home."

My mother shook his hand, holding it a little too long for a handshake. "Please call me Gwen, Devin. It was nice of you to give Taylor a ride home. And to show you how thankful we are we'd like it if you stayed for dinner."

I tried to nudge Devin's foot to discourage him from saying yes, but it didn't work. "I would love to, but I'll have to call home and let my parents know where I'm at", he said.

"Who yo' people?" she asked him before showing him the telephone.

"My parents are Charles and Ruby Stanley. Do you know them?" he asked.

"I know Charles. I went to school with your daddy. He was fine as wine and had the women to prove it. Every girl at *Union High School* wanted a piece of yo' daddy. Red is what we use to call him, 'cause of his complexion. So... where yo' momma from?"

"She's from Charlotte", he answered.

"So Red went and got him a Charlotte woman. I

guess none of the women 'round here was good enough for him." She put her hand on her hip and stared at Devin like he was responsible for who his father chose.

He looked at me and cleared his throat before responding. "Well...uh...I don't know anything 'bout that Ms. Gwen. That was way before I was born."

She waved her hand at him. "Boy, don't pay me no mind. I was just messing with you. I know you aint got nothing to do with who yo' daddy chose as his wife. I'm sure she's a nice lady."

Devin gave an uncomfortable laugh and excused himself to use the telephone. My mother pulled me into the kitchen as soon as he picked up the receiver. "That's a mighty nice little man you got there Taylor. Why you aint never mention him before?"

I blew air out of my mouth. "I don't know Momma. It's no big deal. You don't know all of my friends."

"Don't get sassy with me gal. If you 'round here being fast with some boy, I need to know 'bout it. I done told you, I aint looking for no more surprises." She glared at me.

I smacked my lips. "Momma, don't start that again. You know I did not do"-

She cut me off before I could tell the truth. "What I tell you 'bout telling lies, Taylor?"

"But Momma, you know I'm not"-

I was cut off again, but this time with a slap across the face. "Don't talk back Taylor. I said stop it with the lies. Don't make me repeat myself...okay?"

I was holding my cheek. "Yeah...anything you say Momma."

Devin walked into the kitchen. He saw me holding my cheek. Then he looked at my mother. "Is everything okay?"

My mother spoke first. "Everything is fine. Taylor just gets worked up sometimes and I have to help her get herself together. Nothin' you need to worry your cute little self about."

Devin looked at me like he didn't believe my mother. But I smiled at him to let him know that everything was alright, even though it wasn't. I was used to living a lie.

He looked back at my mother. "My dad said it was cool if I stayed for dinner. I asked him if he knew you and he said yes and to tell you hello."

"Well, that was mighty nice of him. The food is ready if you guys want to eat. I know it's a little early in the evening, but we may as well eat it while it's hot." She went over to the old beat up stove and opened the oven.

Devin and I sat down at our small kitchen table with the mismatched chairs. "What are we having for dinner Momma?"

She came to the table with a plate of fried chicken. "I fried this chicken I got on sale today at *Wilson's* and I fried some potatoes and opened a can of corn."

"Everything sure smells good Ms. Gwen. Looking at all this food makes me realize how hungry I am." Devin licked his lips and rubbed his stomach.

"Well, there's plenty. So don't be shy", she said as she got the rest of the food.

She then took three glasses out of the dish drain. "Devin, I hope you like cherry *Kool-Aid*, 'cause that's all I got to drink...other than water and some things you too young to be drinking."

He laughed before saying, "Cherry is fine."

She fixed our drinks and we all started eating in silence at first. Then my mother had to start asking a bunch of questions. "So Devin, what does that fine daddy of yours do to make ends meet?"

"He works as a longshoreman down at Sunny Point", he responded and took a sip of his drink.

My mother's eyes lit up. "Oh really? He got him a good paying job. So yo' family don't have to want for nothing do ya'?"

Devin glanced over at me. I looked down at my plate. "I don't ever hear my dad complaining about money or bills. But then again, I don't really pay attention to that type of stuff. I know that we're not rich or anything like that."

My mother looked around at our small space and

said, "But I bet you doing a lot better than we are aintcha?"

"I guess it depends on what you consider better Ms. Gwen", he answered.

She let out a sarcastic laugh. "You know what better is...not poor like us. You probably live in some big fancy house with a big garage that hold two nice cars."

I rolled my eyes at her. "Momma nobody cares about that stuff, but you. We're trying to have a nice meal. Why you got to spoil it?" I looked over at Devin. "You got to excuse my mother. She thinks having money is the key to happiness."

"No need to apologize Taylor. I'm not ashamed of what I have or don't have. Ms. Gwen to answer your question I live in a three bedroom house with a two-car garage that I share with my parents and three younger brothers. It's not the smallest house, but it's not the biggest either...but I like it." He stole a glance at me and winked.

My mother sucked her teeth. "I don't care what neither one of y'all say, anything beats living like this." She spread her arms out, while looking around.

I cleared my throat. "Can we please change the subject?" I didn't want Devin to think that Momma was some crazy lady, judging him because his family had more than us.

No one said anything for a while. All you could hear was forks hitting plates and the humming of our old refrigerator. I was so embarrassed by my mother's behavior. I was pretty sure Devin would never speak to me again. I was thinking he would probably go back to school and tell everyone how crazy my mother was.

Then she broke the silence again. "What kind of grades you get in school Devin?"

He chewed the food in his mouth before answering. "I do pretty good. I'm not a straight A student. But I'm on the basketball team, so I have to keep my grades up."

She looked over at me. "So Taylor you done went and got yo'self an athlete? That's real nice."

"It's no big deal Momma", I said through clenched

teeth.

"I guess the apple don't fall too far from the tree. Yo' daddy was an athlete. He did 'em all. He played basketball, football and ran track. I guess that's how he kept that body of his looking so good...um...um." She shook her head and looked up to the ceiling.

Devin smiled and said, "Yeah, my pops was a real athlete. He still has all of his pictures and stuff from when he was playing all those sports.

My mother pushed her plate away from her and rested her elbows on the table. "But you know what comes with being a high school athlete? Fast ass girls. They start sniffing 'round ya like hound dogs."

Devin blushed. "Well, I don't have that problem Ms. Gwen." Then he looked at me and smiled.

Momma interlocked her fingers, sat up in her chair and looked Devin straight in the face. "Boy, you aint talkin' to no fool. I use to be one of them fast ass girls. I know how they are. Plus you a little cutie on top of that."

I was so embarrassed. "Momma-"

"Don't interrupt me Taylor." She looked over at me and then turned her attention back to Devin. "Now back to what I was 'bout to say. You might fool 'round them other fast girls, but my baby is off limits. 'Cause you know everything has a price."

Devin looked over at me. I'm sure he saw the anger and embarrassment in my eyes. "Don't worry Ms. Gwen. I know Taylor's a virgin and I have no intentions of trying to change that."

My mother threw her head back and laughed. "A virgin...a virgin? Taylor aint no-"

I jumped up from my chair. "Momma please don't! You're embarrassing me!" I looked over at Devin, who had a puzzled look on his face.

My mother glanced at me, then back at Devin. "I don't know what lies Taylor been filling yo' head with, but she fast as pump water."

I had heard enough. I couldn't keep letting my mother embarrass me. So I stormed out of the kitchen and ran outside. Within seconds, Devin was behind me.

"What was all that about Taylor?" he asked me after grabbing my arm.

"Look Devin, you're a really nice guy. I know we've been kicking it for the past couple of weeks, but I think we just need to stop seeing each other."

"Come on. Don't be like that. I thought you said you liked me", he replied and playfully punched me on my shoulder.

"I do like you. That's why I got to stop seeing you. You have no idea what you're getting yourself into. What you just witnessed in there is only half of it." I pointed to my house. "It gets much worse."

"Taylor, everybody thinks their parents are embarrassing." He looked towards the house before asking, "Is what she saying true? You aren't a virgin?"

I turned away so I wasn't facing him any longer. "What does it matter?"

"It doesn't matter, but you did tell me you were a virgin", he replied.

I took a deep breath. "It's something I'd rather not talk about. It's a very touchy subject for me and as far as I'm concerned, I'm a virgin."

Devin never brought the subject up again. And of course my mother never apologized for her behavior. But then again, my mother never apologized for anything she did wrong. She always felt she had a legitimate reason for all of her actions. She even had a reason for doing something that would bring an end to me and Devin's relationship.

After the entertaining dinner at my house, Devin and I started spending even more time together. He would always walk me to class. Then he would give me rides home after school when he didn't have anything else to do. This one particular day after the final bell rang, I went looking for him. I looked all over the school trying to find him. I had even asked his friends if they had seen him. No one had, so I gave up my search. Plus, the buses were about to leave and I didn't want to be stranded. When the bus dropped me off at my house, I noticed Devin's car was in my driveway. He never came to my house without dropping me off, so I was surprised to see his car.

When I entered the house, I heard noises coming from the bedroom. It sounded like someone was crying or moaning from pain. I tiptoed across the creaky floor. I looked through the crack in the door. My eyes almost popped out of my head. Devin was sitting on the bed with his pants and underwear down around his ankles. My mother was on her knees in front of him, with his manhood in her mouth. I stood there in shock watching my mother pleasure him. She was moaning and groaning as her mouth went up and down on his penis. He had his eyes closed, telling her how good it felt. She did it like she enjoyed it more than anything in the world. In between sucks, she mumbled, "I bet Taylor can't suck yo' dick like this. It takes a real woman to give a blowjob like this."

He whispered, "Ms. Gwen, I'm about to come. Please whatever you do, don't stop." He opened his eyes and looked directly into mine. "Oh shit!" he yelled, while pushing my mother off of him.

I pushed the door all the way open. My mother looked up at me and smiled. "Hey, what are you doing home so early?" were the first words out of her mouth to me.

Devin had stood up and was trying to pull up his pants. "Taylor, I can explain. It's not what you think."

I looked at my mother and then back at him. "Well, I know what it looked like. It looked like my mother was sucking your dick and you were enjoying it. Let me guess...she forced your dick in her mouth. Or did you trip, fall and your dick just happened to land in her mouth?"

He fixed his belt and walked over to me. "Taylor, please don't be mad at me. Your mother started hitting on me and the next thing I knew she was...well... you know the rest."

By then, my mother had got up off the floor and was sitting on the bed. "Boy, don't try to put all the blame on me." She looked at me. "Taylor, like I told you before, all men are dogs...young and old. I was just testing him. I did it for you."

170

I could feel the tears running down my face. "How can you say that Momma? Everything you do, you do it for yourself!"

She stood up and walked over to me. "Now you know the truth about him. If he did that with me, think about what he doing with all the other girls at school. It's best you found out before it was too late."

My head was spinning and I felt like I was going to throw up. I had so many emotions going through me. I hated my mother for being so beautiful. I hated Devin for letting my mother seduce him. I hated myself for feeling sorry for both of them. I felt sorry for my mother because she didn't know what real love was and didn't want to experience it. The only thing she knew was pleasing men to get what she wanted. I felt sorry for Devin because he wouldn't have been able to say no to my mother, even if he wanted to.

Devin grabbed my hand. "Don't listen to her. I care about you Taylor. Let's go somewhere so we can talk...alone."

I pulled my hand from his grasp. "I have nothing to say to you Devin. I want you to leave. When you see me at school, just keep walking."

"But Tay-"

I cut him off before he could finish saying my name. "Just go Devin!"

He looked at my mother, who was smiling like nothing happened. Then he looked back at me, before walking out the door. I followed him to make sure he was leaving. Once he was out the door, I leaned against it and let the tears flow. I cried like I had never cried in my short life. All the pain that my mother had inflicted on me came out in those tears. I thought about everything that had been said or done to me that shouldn't have been. I looked up and she was in the doorway of the bedroom staring at me.

"Just one question Momma...why?" I asked her through my tears.

"I told you, I did it for your own good. That boy was a no good dog just like his daddy. All them pretty boys are. All he was after was one thing."

"But did you have to seduce him?"

"I aint seduce nobody. He was the one hitting on me. Why he come over here knowing you aint got home from school yet? He claim he was comin' to surprise you, but I know better. He knew I was gonna be here by myself and he wanted a little taste of this ole' honey. Baby, I can't help it 'cause I'm beautiful."

"What kind of mother sucks her teenage daughter's boyfriend's dick? Momma you should be ashamed of yourself! But the sad thing is you're not. You don't care about anybody but yourself. I will never forgive you for this." I stormed pass her and ran into the bathroom.

I heard her say, "Don't get too grown for yo' britches girl. I still pay the damn bills 'round here. And I don't need yo' damn forgiveness."

I knew at that very moment, that as soon as I got a chance, I was leaving that place for good and never coming back. I would no longer have to put up with my mother's lying and conniving ways. But most of all, I wouldn't have to put up with the type of life I was living. I knew that one day, I wouldn't have to want for nothing or worry about where my next meal was coming from. And no one would violate my body...unless I wanted them to.

I looked around me, taking in all the nice things I was now accustomed to. I had come a long way from that old shack in Shallotte. I had been through a lot of men and had worked very hard to get where I was. And I wasn't about to let Claire or anyone else take that away from me. I didn't know what kind of information she had or thought she had on me. Whatever it was, I wasn't going out without a fight. She had better have a good game plan to turn David against me, because good pussy overruled a mother's love any day.

Sierra

I was at the front desk of the spa covering for Jazmin once again. That husband of hers spent more time beating her than he did working. Of course, she denied that she was being abused, but everyone at the spa knew what was going on. At least once a month she would call in "sick". A lot of days, she came in with black eyes or bruises on her body. She always had some excuse for her injuries. Once she had even went through the trouble of saying that she had gotten into a fight with some girl at the club. Kiki, one of the stylists said, "Well we know who won that fight." Everyone laughed, but me. I didn't think it was funny. There is nothing funny about getting your ass beat every day by a man who's supposed to love, cherish, and protect you. I tried several times to get her to open up to me, but she wouldn't. She told me that Jamal would never lay a finger on her and that I watched too much *Lifetime.* Watching *Lifetime* had nothing to do with it. I knew a battered woman when I saw one.

I guess last night he must've really done a number on her. When she called in, it was because he beat her so bad she couldn't cover up the bruises. I just hope he doesn't kill her one day. I was so deep in thought; I didn't hear the bell on the door ring.

"What are you thinking about so hard?" Alexis asked after popping up to the counter.

"Hey, don't you ever work?" I teased her.

She laughed. "Don't you know I make my own hours?"

"Speaking of work, how's it going with that space you want? Is David cracking at all? I know he's a tough negotiator."

She put her fingers to her temples. "Yeah, he's tough alright. But I can be just as tough. I think he's about to give in. I don't think anyone else wants that space. So he's going to have to give into me or he'll end up with a space that he can't sell."

"If you want me to, I can ask Taylor to talk to him for you", I offered.

"No offense Sierra, but I'll pass on that offer. I don't think I'm one of her favorite people. I doubt she'll be trying to get me special favors from her husband."

I laughed at her statement. "Taylor's a good person. Sometimes she comes off a bit harsh...especially in the presence of a beautiful woman."

She gave me a puzzled look. "I don't understand."

"Taylor likes to be the center of attention, which she is used to being. So when a woman who's as equally beautiful is around, I think she feels a little threatened...maybe even a little jealous. Of course, she would never admit to that."

"Enough about Taylor", she replied, while holding her hands up to my face. "I have a surprise for you my dear."

I removed her hands from my face. "What is it this time Alexis? Your surprises always scare me."

She poked out her bottom lip. "Aw come on Sierra. Don't say that. I thought we always have fun when we're together."

I started straightening up papers lying around on the counter. "We do...but...it's just...sometimes, I just don't know what you're going to have me doing next."

"Boring, I am not", she said with a big grin on her face.

I hesitated before asking, "So what is this surprise you have for me?"

"What kind of surprise would it be if I told you what it is? But I will tell you this. It's tonight and you need to look in your closet and find the sexiest, slinkiest black outfit you own, put on your makeup, do your hair and meet me at my house at 8:00."

"So, you're taking me out tonight. What's so"-

She cut me off. "This is not going to be your average date. Just believe me when I say, it will be like no other."

174

"That's what I'm afraid of", I replied and rolled my eyes at her.

She leaned closer to me. "I can give you a little sample of what can happen if you want me to."

I looked around to make sure no one was listening. "Don't start Alexis."

She licked her lips and whispered, "Come on Sierra. Let me lap on that pussy real quick."

"Alexis, this has got to stop. Plus, I am at work", I told her.

"So you don't like it when I eat your pussy, because your husband won't?" she asked.

"Keep your voice down Alexis! Someone might hear you."

She lowered her voice. "You don't want it to stop Sierra. I've given you more pleasure in the last two months, than Tyler has given you in the last two years. Can you honestly say that you want me to walk out of your life and not come back?"

I took a deep breath. I looked down at the floor and up at the ceiling. I looked everywhere, except at Alexis. I didn't want to stop seeing her. Even though Tyler's attitude had improved, the sex was still the same. No matter how hard I tried, I couldn't get totally into it. I loved Tyler and wanted to be with him, but the woman standing in front of me had me hooked. And even though, I told her that I loved her, I wasn't sure if it was lust or love. I did know that my womanhood was getting moist thinking about what she wanted to do to me.

When I didn't respond to her question, she said, "That's what I thought. Now get one of your girls back there to come up here and watch the desk, while I take you back there and please you."

I did as I was told and asked Michelle to watch the desk. I took Alexis back to my massage room. As soon as I closed and locked the door, she shoved her tongue in my mouth. We kissed like we hadn't seen each other in months. She undressed me and gave my breasts the attention they needed, fondling and sucking on them. Then she moved down to the spot between my legs. She pleasured me until I came multiple times. By the time she was finished with me, there wasn't a spot on my body she didn't touch.

Afterwards, I said, "You sure know how to make a woman feel good."

She gave me a sexy smile and said, "An eye for an eye."

I didn't know what the hell that meant, but I really didn't care. I put my clothes back on and ran my fingers through my hair. I examined Alexis and said, "You might want to reapply your lipstick."

She looked towards my private parts. "Yeah, I did leave all of it in your pussy didn't I?"

"You are so damn nasty."

"Yeah, but you like it...don't ya?"

"Actually, I do."

"You still want to give this up?" she asked.

I leaned over, kissed her on the lips and said, "Does that answer your question?"

She smiled. "Yes, it does."

"You stay in here for a few minutes. Make it look like I was actually giving you a massage."

When I walked back out to the front, Michelle and Kiona were talking and obviously hadn't heard me come out.

"She's in here all of the time lately", Kiona was saying.

"And she'll only let Sierra service her", Michelle responded.

"Well you know she's a lawyer. I'm sure that's a stressful job."

"Aint that much stress in the world."

"What you tryin' to say girl?" Kiona asked.

"I aint tryin' to say nothing. I'm saying that I believe that there's more than-"

I cleared my throat. "You two should worry more about your clients and less about mine."

They both jumped like they had seen a ghost. "Oh Sierra, w-we were j-just discussing-"

I stopped Kiona, before she could try to come up

with a lie. "I know what you were discussing. Don't concern yourselves with what goes on behind that door." I pointed towards my massage room.

They both started apologizing.

"Just don't let it happen again!" I snapped. "You girls know how I feel about gossip in the work place. That's how lies get started. What you do on your own time is your business. But while you are in my establishment, you will respect my clients' privacy and everyone else's." I paused to make sure they had taken in what I said. "Do I make myself clear?"

"Yes Sierra", they said in unison.

Alexis came out straightening her clothes. "Boy, I sure needed that", she said a little too loud. Michelle and Kiona glanced at each other.

"You two may go back to your stations", I said in a stern voice.

They both looked at Alexis and then back at me before walking off. Alexis gave me a curious look. "What was all of that about?" she asked.

"Nothing", I replied, waving my hand at her.

"So, we're still on for tonight...right?"

"Yeah, I guess so."

"Good. Don't be late."

When she was gone, I replayed Michelle and Kiona's conversation in my head. If they had their suspicions, what did the others think? Were Alexis and I that obvious? We were going to have to chill out because I couldn't risk Tyler finding out about us.

Sierra

Even after the conversation I had overheard, I was hyped about the surprise Alexis had for me. When I left the spa, I drove straight home. When I pulled up into the driveway, Tyler's car was already there.

I yelled out, "Hello, I'm home" when I walked in the door. I got no response. I walked towards the den where I heard the television.

Shelby was sitting on her bean bag watching TV, eating her favorite snack, Gold Fish. "Hi sweetie. What are you watching?" I asked her.

"*Spongebob*", she answered without looking up.

"Where's your daddy?"

"He's in his office", she replied, again without looking up.

I left Shelby to her TV show and walked down the hall towards Tyler's home office. As soon as he got home from work, he went straight to his office. I always wondered why he even bothered going to work. He spent more time in that office than he did any room in the house, including the bedroom.

I was about to knock on the door when I heard him say, "I'll think of something...don't worry...yeah...I'll see you then...no I can't tonight...I have plans with Sierra...no I can't break them...we'll talk about it later...okay...goodbye."

As soon as he hung up the phone, I walked into the office. He jumped like I had startled him. "Hey baby, what's going on?" I asked him, walking towards his desk.

He leaped up from his chair before I could get any closer. "Nothing honey. When did you get in?" he asked nervously.

"Not too long ago. I saw Shelby in the den watching TV."

He reached out and gave me a hug. "How was your day?"

"It was good. How was yours?"

He let go of me and walked out of the office. "It was great!" he said with a lot of excitement in his voice.

I followed him to the kitchen. "You're in a good mood."

"Why shouldn't I be? I have a wonderful job and a beautiful family", he said and grabbed a beer out of the refrigerator.

I sat down on one of the stools at the island. "What did you do this time?" I asked.

He took a swig of his beer. "Now why you gotta spoil my good mood? I didn't do anything."

I stood up, walked over to him and put my arms around his waist. "I'm sorry baby. The last thing I want to do is spoil your good mood."

He moved away from me, took one gulp of his beer and tossed the empty can in the recycle bin. "I hope you don't have plans tonight."

I smiled and was about to tell him that I did, but I could break them, but he said, "Because I have something I need to do."

I thought about his conversation I had just eavesdropped on. He told the person on the other end that he had plans with me. Yet he was telling me that he had something to do that didn't seem to involve me.

"What exactly is it that you need to do?" I asked him.

"Things related to work...nothing you'd be interested in", he answered.

"How do you know I wouldn't be interested? You didn't bother asking me", I replied.

"Do I intrude on you when you hang out with your friends?" Before I could answer, he said, "No, I don't. All I want to do is hang out with some of my buddies from work."

"That's fine Tyler. I just thought you-"

He cut me off. "Don't wait up for me. I'll probably be out real late."

I put my hands on my hips. "I hate to burst your bubble, but I have plans too."

"What do you mean you have plans? When did this come about?" he asked.

I threw my hands up in the air. "I kept trying to tell you that I had plans, but you wouldn't let me get a word in."

"What are your plans?" he asked.

"I'm ...I'm going out with Jade and Taylor", I lied.

"Well, it looks like you're going to have to cancel your plans. One of us has to stay here with Shelby", he said without blinking.

I folded my arms across my chest. "I'm not canceling my plans."

"I'm not canceling my plans either."

"I guess we're going to have to call Nikki and see if she can baby sit."

"Sierra, this is ridiculous!" he yelled.

"Mommy, Daddy, please don't fight." Shelby had walked into the kitchen.

I grabbed her hand and pulled her back towards the den. "Sweetie, we're not fighting", I told her.

She looked up at me with the most innocent eyes and said, "Then why are you yelling?"

"Sometimes grown-ups yell when they are upset."

"Why are you upset?" she asked.

"It's nothing for you to worry your pretty little head about.   Your   daddy   and   I   just   had   a   little miscommunication...that's all."

"What does that mean?" she asked.

"It's a grown-up word. You just finish watching TV...okay? Your daddy and I need to finish talking."

"You're not going to yell anymore are you?"

"No, we won't sweetie...I promise." When I got to the doorway of the den, I turned around and asked, "How would you like it if Nikki came to baby sit you tonight?"

"Yay! I like Nikki. She gives me lots of candy!" she screamed, while jumping up and down.

I put my hand on my hip. "Oh really?"

She shook her head.

"I need to have a talk with Nikki."

I went back to the kitchen where Tyler was on the

phone. "I'm sorry for such a short notice...I'll pay you extra...thanks Nikki. You're a life saver. See you at seven...thanks...bye-bye." He hung up the phone, turned to me and said, "Lucky for you, she didn't have any plans."

"What do you mean, lucky for me? You got a lot of..." I stopped speaking, put my palms together and put them up to my lips. I took a deep breath before continuing to speak. "Look Tyler, I'm not going to stand here and argue with you. I promised Shelby. Nikki's coming, so neither one of us has to cancel our plans."

He walked out of the kitchen without saying a word. So much for his good mood. I was still puzzled about the lie he had told the person on the phone. It just didn't make sense. But I couldn't worry about that. I had to get ready for the night Alexis had planned for me.

I arrived at Alexis' house 8:00 sharp. She greeted me, looking gorgeous as always. She was wearing a short, but classy black dress with spaghetti straps. Her hair framed her face and flowed over her shoulders.

"You look incredible", I told her as she locked her door back.

"Thanks...so do you."

I had chosen a short black sheath dress. It wasn't as short as Alexis' dress, but it showed off my best feature, my legs. The back was cut out, which I thought made it a sexy little number. "So, do you think this is sexy enough?" I asked her.

She looked me up and down, winked at me and said, "Oh, you'll fit right in."

I was relieved that she liked what I had chosen. Having her approval meant a lot to me. I don't know why, but it did.

"You can leave your car here and we'll take mine", she said.

So we hopped into her Mercedes and were on our way. On the way to where ever we were going. I asked, "So where are we going?"

She glanced at me and smiled. "You'll see when we get there."

We rode towards downtown. Finally, we pulled up to what appeared to be an empty office building. "Is this the spot you're trying to get for your practice?" I asked her as we exited the car.

She gave me a wicked smile. "Not exactly."

"Well what is this?" I asked, sounding like Shelby.

"You are so impatient. You'll see when we get inside."

"Inside? It looks abandoned."

"That's the whole idea", she replied.

I hesitated a minute before following her up to the door of the building. She pushed the buzzer that was located on the side of the door. A loud voice came through the speaker above the buzzer. "What time is it?" he asked.

Alexis looked around before saying, "Aint no party like a twilight party, 'cause a twilight party don't stop."

Within seconds, the door slid open. Alexis hurried in. I didn't move. She stopped when she noticed I wasn't beside her. "Come on Sierra." She motioned me to come on with her hand. "Don't be afraid."

I grabbed her hand and followed her inside. The door closed behind me. The hall was dark, except for the dimly lit lights along the walls. Another door was in front of us. When Alexis opened the door, we entered into what appeared to be a night club. Men and women, all dressed in black were scattered throughout the room. Some were at the bar socializing. Others were standing or sitting in groups, while half-naked men and women served them drinks on black lacquered trays. Music was playing in the background.

I turned to Alexis and said, "So *this* is the surprise?"

She gave me a sarcastic laugh and replied, "Honey, this is just the beginning."

"Hi baby...long time no see", an attractive woman, wearing a cat suit spoke to Alexis.

Alexis hugged her before saying, "Hello Bunny. It's good to see you." Then they shared a quick kiss. Alexis turned to me and said, "Bunny, this is my friend Sierra. Sierra, this is Bunny, an old friend of mine."

I extended my hand to shake hers, but she kissed me on the lips instead. "Nice to meet you Sierra."

"Um...n-nice to meet you too", I said after finding my voice.

Bunny then turned to Alexis and said, "It was good seeing you Alexis. Maybe we'll get up later."

"Yeah, maybe...see ya' around." Alexis responded. She then looked at me and asked, "Do you want to tour the rest of the club?"

"I guess so", I answered.

She led me down a hall, which had several closed doors. The first door on the right read BONDAGE. Alexis opened the door and I followed her inside. I surveyed the room and was shocked and amazed by what I saw. Every person in the room was naked. Three chairs were lined up side by side in the center of the room. In the first chair, a man was sitting with his hands tied behind his back. His eyes were blindfolded and black clothes pins were hanging from his nipples. A female, with breasts the size of watermelons was down on her knees giving him oral pleasure. The chair next to that one held a slim female who was crying out in pain and pleasure. She also had her hands tied behind her back. Two females were knelt down on each side of her biting her nipples, while another female had her head buried between her legs. In the last chair, another male was tied up, while a curvy female was riding him like she was in a rodeo.

Down on the floor beside them, two females were blindfolded and on their hands and knees. One of the females had a chain around her neck, which was being yanked by a tall handsome man, who was stroking on his manhood. Each time, he pulled the chain, she would cough and gag. The other female was being spanked with a belt by a female, who was wearing nipple rings. As the belt hit her naked bottom, she would scream, "Harder bitch, harder!"

In one corner, two couples were watching the whole scene, while fondling each other. I turned to Alexis and said, "This is too much for me...I need to get out of here."

We left all the moaning, groaning, screaming, and spanking behind us. Once, we were in the hall, Alexis asked, "You didn't like that?"

"It's not that I didn't like it....it's just...it's too...uh...its way above my comfort level. I don't see how any of that could be enjoyable. But to each his own, I guess", I replied.

"Well, let's see if you like the next place." She led me to a door with the word HONEYSUCKLE on it. It sounded innocent enough.

We walked into what looked like a feast fest. There was a big circle formed by about twelve men and women, licking and sucking each other. There were women on women, men on women and women on men. Behind all the slurping, sucking and licking, cries of pleasure echoed throughout the room. I had to admit, it was an amazing sight. I stood there for a few minutes, enjoying the entertainment before me. Just as I could feel the moisture forming between my legs, Alexis said, "You ready to move on?"

I hesitated and said, "Yeah...sure."

We walked towards the door. I looked back at the oral fest one last time before walking out.

The next door she led me to read GANG BANGING. I looked at Alexis and said, "There aren't going to be any guns involved are there? I don't like violence."

She laughed and said, "You are so naïve. No, there aren't going to be any guns...at least not real guns. You'll see when you get inside."

She opened the door and the smell of sex permeated my nostrils. Flesh danced with flesh throughout the room. Portable beds with black satin sheets were scattered about. A female, whose skin was like honey was being penetrated in both holes, while giving oral pleasure to another man. Each time the men thrust themselves into her, I watched in amazement at how she was able to keep up the pace, without missing a beat.

On another bed, a man with the biggest penis I

had ever seen...not that I had seen that many, was being ridden by one female, while another female was sitting on his face.

There was another group with a female on her hands and knees being sexed from behind, sucking on another man's penis, while another female was feasting on her goodies. The rest of the beds were full of people enjoying each other. They all looked as if they were comfortable in their own skin, not caring about their flaws or hang-ups. Nothing seemed to matter, except the pleasure they were giving to each other. I watched the men pound the ladies, trying their best to get them to the point of no return. Tongues and lips probed and worked private parts, determined to pull out that ultimate climax. Orgasmic cries echoed throughout the room, making me envious because I couldn't experience that type of pleasure with Tyler.

Once again, my underwear became saturated, and once again Alexis intervened. "Let's go. We got one more stop", she said.

"You mean there's more? What could possibly be left?" I asked.

She licked her lips and said, "Baby, the possibilities are endless."

The next door we stopped at had TWO IS A COUPLE...MORE IS NOT A CROWD on the front. Once inside, the sight of several couples engaging in sex on a bed almost the size of the room greeted us. Suddenly, the music in the background stopped. That's when I noticed a very handsome gentleman sitting in the corner. When the music stopped, the couples stopped what they were doing. The gentleman in the corner started the music again and the couples switched partners.

"They do this all night?" I asked Alexis.

"Until they get tired...or bored, whichever comes first", she answered.

I shook my head in disbelief. "This is crazy. I've never seen such a thing."

"From what you say, there isn't too much you have seen", she teased.

"I'm sorry if I have a boring sex life." I said, rolling my eyes at her.

"You use to have a boring sex life...until you got with me", she corrected me.

I laughed. "You can say that again."

"Come on, let's get outta here."

Once we were back in the hall, I was about to go back towards the bar area. "We got one more stop", Alexis said and grabbed my hand.

"I thought you said that was the last stop."

"Well, it was...kind of. I do have one more place to show you."

I followed her to the end of the hall. We stopped at a door that had H2O posted on it. We walked into what looked like a huge bathroom. Mirrors lined the walls. Four showers were on one side of the room and two large hot tubs were on the other side.

Alexis said, "This is where everyone comes to wash away their sexual sins."

I observed three women hugging, kissing and touching each other in one of the showers. "I can't tell. Looks like they're still at it", I said, pointing at the women.

"At least, they're getting clean in the process", Alexis replied.

In one of the hot tubs, about ten men and women were relaxing and sipping on wine. I noticed Alexis' friend Bunny was in there. When she noticed us, she said, "Alexis, why don't you and your friend come join us?"

Alexis smiled at her and said, "This is her first time here. So I think we better take things slow." She turned to me and winked. "Maybe another time."

Bunny replied, "Suit yourself." She then took a sip of her wine, lay back against the hot tub, while two men stroked her breasts.

I wanted to say something. I wanted to let them know that I was able to handle it just like them. I wanted to experience wet naked bodies touching mine. My nipples were hard under my dress, but I couldn't say anything. I didn't say anything, even when Alexis dragged me out.

Once we were back in the hall, she said, "Are you okay? For a second there, you looked like you wanted to join in on the fun."

"Who me? No...I'm straight", I lied.

We walked back to the bar area, where there were no sexual acts going on. We found a cozy corner and took a seat. Alexis got one of the sexy half-naked men's attention. He came over smiling, displaying perfect white teeth. "What can I get for you beautiful ladies?" he asked.

Alexis smiled seductively at him. "I think I'll have a Long Island Iced Tea."

He turned to me and said, "What about you miss?"

"I'll just have a glass of white wine."

He jotted down our orders and hurried off to retrieve them. As soon as he was gone Alexis said, "So what do you think of the place?"

I leaned back in my seat, folded my hands across my lap. "Well...it's like nothing I've ever experienced before. I can honestly say I was a little turned on by some of it."

"Oh really?" she asked and then leaned closer and touched my knee.

I leaned back up towards the table and rested my elbows on it. "Yes. I was just so amazed at how they were so relaxed and secure with their bodies. They weren't all perfect and no one seemed to care."

She moved her hand higher up my thigh. She then used her fingers to caress and trace the outline of my pussy. Then she said, "Well Sierra, everyone has their own opinion on what sexy is. What you consider a flaw, someone else may consider it sexy as hell. Some men like skinny women, while some like women with some meat on their bones. Some like big breasts, while others consider more than a mouthful a waste. To me, nothing is sexier than self-confidence." She then leaned over to kiss me on the lips. I was about to kiss her until I saw the waiter coming back with our drinks.

"Here you are ladies. A Long Island Iced Tea for you." He placed Alexis' drink in front of her. "And a white wine for you", he smiled. While placing my drink down, he looked directly at me and said, "Can I get you ladies anything else?"

Alexis answered, "No thank you. That will be all for now."

He winked at me before walking away. "Looks like someone's got an admirer", Alexis teased.

"Don't be silly. He was just flirting...like they all do", I replied after taking a sip of my wine. I started looking around, taking in the scenery and enjoying my wine. I saw something that almost made me choke. There was Tyler, laughing and carrying-on with a female and another gentleman. I was about to get up and confront him. Then I remembered where I was and how I had lied to him. I couldn't confront him without getting cold busted myself. What in the hell was he doing there?

"Are you alright girl? You act like you seen a ghost or something", Alexis said.

"Close enough. We have to get out of here. Tyler is over there." I pointed in his direction.

Alexis looked around. "Where? I don't see him."

I snapped, "Over there with the really pretty female and the guy with the bald head!"

"Did he tell you he was coming here?" she asked calmly.

I rolled my eyes at her before answering. "Of course he didn't and I'm sure he wasn't expecting me to be here either...especially after I lied to him. I told him I was going out with Taylor and Jade."

She eyed me suspiciously. "Why didn't you want him to know you were going out with-?"

I cut her off. "Alexis, we can discuss that another time. Right now, I need to get out of here before he sees me!"

She threw her hands up. "Okay. Okay. But we have to be discreet, if you don't want him to see you."

She placed a twenty dollar bill on the table and led me out of the club before we could be seen by Tyler.

As we rode back to her house, all sorts of things were running through my head. Why was Tyler at that club? Who were those people he was with? How did he know about that club? It looked like I wasn't the only one with secrets.

Jade

My mother and I have always had a weird relationship. I loved her to death, but at the same time, I resented her for always treating me like a child. She always said I didn't make the best decisions, especially when it came to men. A lot of times, I chose to not tell her about the relationships I got involved in, unless I thought they were serious. I had decided to tell her about Eli.

She responded by saying, "I didn't know you were even seeing anyone seriously."

"That's because I didn't tell you. You're always meddling", I replied.

She smacked her lips over the phone. "That's what mothers are supposed to do. We meddle to protect our babies."

I rolled my eyes, only because she couldn't see me. "But I'm not a baby. I'm a grown woman."

"You might be grown, but you have no clue when it comes to men", she said.

"Why do you say that?" I asked, as if she had not told me that a million times before.

"Jade, wake up girl. Your history speaks for itself. Plus from what you just told me, it's obvious that this man is hiding something. Don't let infatuation blind you."

"Mom, I don't need a lecture", I responded.

"I'm not lecturing you Jade. I'm just stating the obvious."

I always showed respect for my mother, but sometimes, she could get under my skin. She was one of those people that spoke her mind no matter what. And she was very controlling, which is why she and my father didn't stay together.

"Mom, I'm not infatuated with Eli-"

Before I could finish my sentence, she said, "Good. At least you have sense-"

It was my turn to interrupt her. "I'm in love with

Eli", I said.

"You can't be serious Jade. You don't know anything about this man."

"I know enough!" I snapped.

"You just told me yourself you don't know much about his personal life", she replied.

She was right, but I hated to admit it. "I know Mom. Eli's just real private...that's all. He'll tell me everything when he's ready", I explained.

"Stop being naïve Jade. I raised you better than that. I see I need to pay you a visit so I can meet this Eli character myself", she said.

"Oh no Mom! You don't have to do that", I almost yelled.

"I know I don't have to do it, but I am. If you don't have sense enough to find out what your so-called man is hiding, then I will", she responded.

"Mom, I'm a grown woman. I can handle my own personal affairs", I pouted.

"I'm coming anyway...I need to get out of Richmond for a few days. Your daddy's bugging me."

"Why would Daddy be bugging you? You guys aren't together."

"That don't mean nothing. Your daddy is always in my face...trying to get-"

I interrupted her. "Mom, that's enough. I don't want to know the details. What you and Daddy do is your business."

"You're right. But anyway, I will be down there this weekend. So don't make any plans", she said.

"It's not like I have a choice", I mumbled

"What did you say?" she asked.

"Nothing Mom. I'll see you this weekend", I said dryly.

After I hung up with my mother, I was mad at myself for opening my mouth. I wanted to call her back and tell her she couldn't come because I had already made plans. But I knew that would be pointless. Once my mother made up her mind about something, there was no changing it. She was coming here in a couple of days and there was nothing I could do about it. Now, I just needed to decide if I should tell him or just let him find out at the last minute. If I gave him a heads up, he may decide not to come. But if I spring it on him, it may backfire in my face.

"So what did Eli say when you told him that he was meeting me?" my mother asked me as we were setting the table.

"He didn't say anything", I answered.

She stopped setting the table and asked, "What do you mean he didn't say anything?"

"Just like I said, he didn't say anything", I answered refusing to look up at her.

She let out an exaggerated laugh. "You didn't tell him I was here did you Jade?"

"No, I didn't Mom."

"Are you for real? You invited him over here without telling him that he's going to meet your mother for the first time?" she asked with her hands on her hips.

"So...what's the big deal?" I said nonchalantly.

"You just don't do that Jade."

"I thought if I told him, he wouldn't show up", I explained.

"Why wouldn't he show up?" she asked.

"Because he may not be ready to meet the parents."

"Well, you didn't give him much of a choice now did you?" she said sarcastically.

"Just don't do or say anything to embarrass me."

Before she could respond, the doorbell rang. My heart started beating faster. I couldn't remember when I had been so nervous. I straightened my top and checked my hair before opening the door. When I swung the door open, I was relieved to see Taylor standing there. "Hey girl! You look fabulous...as always", I told her.

She kissed me on the cheek. "So do you."

"Come on in girl. You're the first one here."

"Hey Ms. Janice!" Taylor yelled to my mother. She

stopped what she was doing and walked over to us.

"Hello Taylor sweetie. It's good to see you", she said reaching out to hug Taylor.

The doorbell rang again. I went to answer the door while my mother and Taylor went into the kitchen. Sierra and Alexis stood smiling when I opened the door.

"Hello", they both spoke as if on cue.

"Hey Sierra. It's nice seeing you again Alexis", I said.

Sierra didn't mention bringing Alexis. It's not that I had a problem with it. I just didn't want any quarreling. I was already nervous as hell. I invited them in and joined the others in the kitchen. Taylor was smiling and laughing until she looked up and saw Alexis. Everyone exchanged greetings and Sierra introduced Alexis to my mother.

"Taylor, I see we meet again. How's David?" Alexis asked as if she was toying with Taylor.

I gave Taylor a warning look, hoping she would be nice and not cause a scene. Once she made up her mind that she didn't like you, she made it very well known.

"Yes we do...and David's fine", Taylor responded.

"Tell him I said hello."

"I'll be sure to do that."

Before the conversation could get any faker, I intervened and guided everyone into the living room.

"Jade, your place is really nice. I like the vintage look you got going on in here." Alexis looked around, enjoying my decorating skills.

"Thank you. I really enjoyed putting it all together. I just love the vintage theme. It's so cool", I beamed.

The doorbell rang interrupting our chat. "Now, that's got to be Eli", I said as I ran to answer the door.

I opened the door and was face to face with a big bouquet of flowers. "Oh how sweet", I blushed before taking them out of Eli's hand and kissing him on the lips.

"Hey to you too", he said.

"I'm sorry. I got excited when I saw the flowers."

"Well, when you said you were cooking dinner for us, I thought these would be a nice touch", he replied and peered into the living room.

"What's wrong baby?" I asked innocently.

"Jade if you knew that you were having company, why did you invite me to dinner?" he asked.

"Actually Eli, I invited you for the company."

"I don't get it."

"Well, my mother wanted to meet you, so I invited you over."

"Are you serious Jade?" he raised his voice a little.

"Yes Eli. Please keep your voice down. I don't want them to think that we're fussing."

"How could you not tell me this before I got here?" he asked.

"I thought if I told you, you wouldn't have come."

"So instead, you tricked me over here."

"I wouldn't say that."

"I would. How do you know I wanted to meet your mother?" he questioned.

"I didn't know. She was just so determined to meet you", I answered.

"I'm really not happy with this situation Jade...just so you know."

"Please just do this for me...okay? I invited some friends over so it wouldn't be so uncomfortable for you", I told him.

"Too late for that", he responded in a harsh tone.

"Just relax", I said and pulled him into the living room with the others. "Mom, this is my boyfriend Ellison Turner."

"Hi Ellison. I'm Janice. It's nice to finally meet you", she said and reached out to shake his hand.

"Hello Eli...long time no see", Alexis said to him.

"What's up Alexis?" Eli responded without looking at her.

"You two know each other?" I asked him.

They glanced at each other before Eli said, "Yeah, I was once her personal trainer...a long time ago."

"How long ago?" I asked. I knew the irritation could be heard in my voice.

"I don't know Jade. Maybe a year. I don't keep

track of that stuff", he replied.

"Hmm, this is taking 'it's a small world' to a new level", Taylor chimed in with a smirk on her face.

I gave her an evil look, because I knew she was enjoying the very awkward moment. I don't know why I was so upset. I knew what Eli did for a living. He was always surrounded by beautiful women.

"What's the big deal Jade? You act as if he said they were former lovers or something", Sierra said.

"Sierra's right Jade. Don't spoil this lovely dinner you've prepared", my mother said.

She was right. I had prepared a lovely dinner. I had made fried chicken, potato salad, macaroni and cheese, string beans, collard greens, and corn bread. For dessert, my mother and I made a peach cobbler. I wasn't about to ruin all of my hard work. I escorted everyone into the dining room, while my mother brought in all of the food.

"Baby, everything looks good", Eli said and winked at me.

I threw him a fake smile and said, "Thanks. I hope you all enjoy it." I had dropped the subject about him knowing Alexis, but that didn't mean he was off the hook.

My mother said the grace. She barely got amen out before everyone was digging in. The table was quiet except for forks hitting the plates. I could tell that everyone was pleased with the food.

My mother decided to break the silence. "So Eli what it is that you do for a living?"

"I'm a personal trainer. That's how I know Alexis", he answered.

"So you deal with plenty of women on a regular basis?" she asked.

"Yes, but I also deal with men too. I deal with people who want to get in shape, but don't know how to go about it. I work with them personally and on a one on one basis. I help people to help themselves", he replied.

"How long you been doing that?" she questioned.

"Um...about five or six years, I guess..."

"What did you do before that?" she asked.

"Mom, enough with the questions", I spoke up.

She turned her lips up at me and said, "This is between Eli and me. You just eat your food. Now back to my question."

Eli shifted in his seat. "Before that I had different jobs. My main thing was bartending."

"You ever been married or got any kids?"

Eli looked around the table, and then glared at me before answering. "No, I've never been married...and I don't have any kids."

All of a sudden, Sierra started coughing uncontrollably. "Are you okay Sierra?" I asked.

"Um-um...I'm okay...um-um...my drink just went down the wrong way...I'm gonna go outside...um-um...for some fresh air."

"I'll go with you", Alexis volunteered. They both got up from the table and headed out the door.

I wondered what the deal was with Sierra's outburst. But that was the least of my concerns. I wasn't too happy with the way Eli had responded to that last question. He hesitated a little too long before answering. Before I could voice my opinion, my mother said something.

"You don't seem too sure about your answer Eli."

He looked over at me before replying. "It's not that. I'm just not use to being put on the spot like that. And as I've told Jade many times before, I'm a very private person."

"You've been seeing my daughter for a while now. Even though Jade is smart, she's also naïve."

"Mother!" I yelled.

She looked at me and said, "Let me finish Jade." Then she looked back at Eli. "For the length of time you have been seeing each other, there shouldn't be *that* much privacy. And the only reason someone would be that private in a relationship is if they have something to hide...so Eli, what are you hiding?"

"You know what Jade. I didn't come over here for this. I'm not gonna sit here and let your mother give me the third degree." He then turned to my mother and said,

"No disrespect Ms. Janice, but I don't answer to no one."
He turned his attention back to me. "Jade, I'm out." He
got up from the table and walked to the door.

I followed him. "Wait, Eli. Please don't leave.
You'll have to excuse my mother. She's just being overprotective."

"Jade, you're a grown ass woman. You don't need
protection...especially not from me."

"Come on Eli. Don't do this. I put a lot into this
dinner", I pleaded.

"Don't tell that to me. Tell it to Barbara Walters in
there." He nodded towards the dining room.

"That's my mother Eli and she's only looking out
for my best interest", I defended my mother.

He opened the door. "Call me when you get some
privacy."

Sierra and Alexis were coming in as he was going
out. "Leaving so soon?" Alexis asked

"Yeah, it's getting a little too personal in there for
me", he responded.

"I'm sure it is", Sierra said in a sarcastic tone.

"What's that supposed to mean?" he asked.

Sierra looked at Alexis and then said,
"Nothing...it's just that I know how you men are...that's
all."

I looked at Alexis and then at Sierra. "Is there
something you want to tell me Sierra?"

She laughed nervously. "No Jade. Girl, you know
how men are. They're so private and don't like us asking
them a bunch of questions."

Alexis grabbed Sierra's arm. "Come on. Let's go
back and join the others."

Once they were gone, I turned back to Eli. "What
was all of that about?"

"She's your friend. How in the hell should I
know?"

"Is there something you want to tell me Eli?"

"I already said what I had to say. Like I said
before, call me when you get a free moment." He kissed
me on the cheek and walked out the door.

I was furious with my mother and I was going to let her know that. I stormed back into the dining room. "Mother, how could you ruin my dinner? You knew how important this was to me."

"Jade, I did that for your own good. That boy is hiding something", she replied.

"Just because he didn't want to answer your questions doesn't mean he's hiding something", I argued back.

"Then why did he get so upset Jade? Why did he leave?" she asked.

"You put him on the spot. You made him feel uncomfortable."

She blew air out of her mouth and hesitated. "Jade honey, you better wake up and smell the coffee. Just as sure as I'm sitting here, that man's got a secret. It's just a matter of time before it comes out."

"You're wrong mother...you're wrong", I said almost in a whisper.

She put her hand on top of mine. "For your sake, I hope I am."

Deep down inside, I felt what my mother said made sense. But on the other hand, I knew how Eli felt about me. And there was no way he could be hiding anything from me. My mother just didn't understand our relationship. Eli would never do anything to hurt me. I just had to keep telling myself that.

Sierra

It had been an interesting and crazy weekend. Friday night after Alexis and I left that sex club, we went back to her place. I called home to check on Nikki and Shelby. Tyler still hadn't gotten home yet. I told Nikki I would be out a couple more hours and I would pay her extra for her time.

Alexis and I got undressed and smoked one of those blunt things. By the time we had smoked it all, I was feeling like I could conquer the world. She had made a pallet and we were sprawled out across her floor in the den. She made me watch one of those pornographic movies.

Afterwards, she said, "Sierra by the time I'm finished with you, you're not going to know what boring is when it comes to sex."

"I believe that", was all I could say.

"Stay here. I'll be right back", she said and rushed upstairs.

I sat there thinking about how much Alexis had changed my life. Since I'd known her, I felt a self-confidence I had never felt before. She made me feel beautiful and sexy. Tyler always told me I was beautiful, but it was just different with Alexis. She was always so spontaneous and I liked it. I liked it a lot.

She came back with a small bag in her hand. "I bet you can't guess what's in here", she said and sat back down beside me.

"No, I can't and I'm not even gonna try", I said.

She dumped the contents of the bag out on the floor in front of us. "These are sex toys", she said with a mischievous grin on her face.

I reached out and ran my hands across them. "Wow, there are so many." I recognized the strap-on she had used on me before.

"Yeah, I do have a nice collection, don't I?" She

smiled while admiring them.

"Why do you need so many?" I asked her.

She laughed and then said, "Variety Sierra. Everything in here has its own little purpose." She started sorting through them. "These are ben wa balls." She held up a clear case with two small gold balls in it.

"This is called a purple seal." She pointed to a contraption that had two tips on it. One tip was bigger than the other.

"What's this?" I asked holding up a string with small balls spaced out on it.

"Those are anal beads."

"You mean you actually put that thing in your ass Alexis?"

"Yes I do Sierra. And instead of me sitting here explaining what every toy does, why don't I just show you? That will be more fun...I promise you."

She leaned over to me and kissed me passionately. My nipples hardened immediately. I could feel the moisture forming between my legs. "You know I can't stay too much longer", I explained as she slid her hand between my legs.

"We have plenty of time Sierra. Just relax and enjoy what I'm about to do to you", she said and probed two fingers inside of me.

"Oh...that feels so good. I wish Tyler was this attentive to my needs", I cooed in her ear.

"Like I said before, a woman knows what a woman wants. Let's not talk about Tyler anymore", she replied.

I didn't speak of or think of Tyler for the next hour or so. Alexis used every toy she had on me and I even returned the favor with a few. I never knew I could climax so many times in one session. She had me in positions that I use to only imagine. I felt like screaming to the top of my lungs. The only thing that mattered to me at that time was the pleasure I was feeling. For so long I had heard people talk about sex as if it was the best thing in the world. I never understood what all the hype was about. To me, sex was just sex. Sometimes it was good. Sometimes it was bad. Sometimes, it was over before it started.

Alexis made me see the light. I knew that at that point, I was definitely hooked, and there was no turning back. I was hers; mind, body and soul.

Saturday evening I ventured to Jade's for a little get together. Jade decided it was time for Eli to meet her mother. Or should I say Jade's mother decided it was time to meet Eli? I felt awkward with the whole thing, but I went anyway. I took Alexis with me for support and to make sure I didn't spill the beans to Jade.

During dinner when Jade's mother asked Eli if he was married and he said no, I got choked up. I had to go outside to compose myself. Alexis accompanied me. As soon as we got outside, she said, "Are you crazy? What is wrong with you?"

"I couldn't help it. My drink really did go down the wrong way", I explained.

"I'm sure it did. But it looked like you were reacting to his answer. Jade's probably suspicious of your reaction. You see how she looked at you?"

I ran my fingers through my hair. "I'm sorry. I know how it must've looked. But he's in there lying to one of my best friends, Alexis. How can I just sit there when I know the truth?"

She put her hand on my shoulder. "Sierra, I understand how you feel, but you just have to let it go. I promise you, you'll regret it if you say anything."

"It just doesn't seem right", I said in frustration.

"Yeah, I know...well, at least the spotlight was taken off of me. You see how she acted when she discovered that Eli and I knew each other?"

"Yeah, I could hear the attitude in her voice", I said.

"That's why I was a little surprised that you wanted me to come with you", she said.

"Well, I knew it might be a problem, but I wanted you here to keep me from doing what I was tempted to do...spill the beans."

"I'm glad I came then." She grabbed my arm and said, "We better get back inside before they get suspicious."

As we were going back in, Eli was coming out. I
wanted to tell him that he couldn't run from the truth, but
I didn't. Alexis' words echoed in my head, once more. I
didn't want to lose my friendship, so I kept my mouth
shut about what I knew.

As I sit here now, I realize that things will surface.
Just as her mother said, it's just a matter of time before
she finds out the truth about Eli. I just hope it won't be
too late.

I looked over at Tyler, who was lightly snoring. He
looked so peaceful lying there. A part of me felt guilty
about my little fling with Alexis, especially after the day we
had. We went to church this morning. Afterwards, we
came home and had a delicious meal. And later, we took
Shelby to the park. It was just like old times, us enjoying
each other as a family.

Then the other part of me didn't feel guilty,
because I knew this wouldn't last long. Tyler had been
like a see saw for the longest. Figuring out his mood had
turned into a guessing game. So he was half to blame for
the situation I was in.

Seeing him at that club was still weighing heavy on
my mind. There was no way I could address the issue
without implicating myself. As uptight as he was when it
came to sex, I found it quite surprising to see him there.
Maybe there was a side to Tyler that I didn't know about.
After ten years together, you'd think there would be no
secrets.

Everything would be alright on my end as long as
he never found out about what was really going on with
Alexis and me. As far as I'm concerned, that would never
happen, because he wasn't smart enough.

Taylor

Being at Jade's watching how her mother was so attentive and protective of her made me feel some kind of way. Once again, I was thinking about the so-called relationship I had with my mother. Jade's mother was trying to protect her from the man she loved. My mother did nothing to protect me from anything or anyone. If anything, I needed protection from her and all the men she brought in and out of our lives. I use to hear other girls talking about doing things with their mothers. My mother and I never did anything together...except argue. I would sit at home while she ran the streets with the man of choice.

I spent a lot of time wishing for a normal life. To my dismay, that never happened. After Devin, I was afraid to bring anymore boys home. So I just distanced myself from all boys, whether I was interested in them or not. My mother would've figured out a way to sabotage any relationship I formed. She was just that type of person.

A tear ran down my cheek as I thought about the baby I carried for nine months...the baby I didn't get to see or hold.

I heard David's voice echoing through the house, calling out for me. I wiped my eyes and checked my makeup. The last thing I needed was for him to see me crying. The questions would start and I wasn't prepared to go down that road with him.

"I'm in here sweetie", I yelled out to him.

"Oh, there you are", he beamed as he entered our bedroom. "What are you up to?" He leaned in and kissed me on the cheek.

"Nothing much. Just going through my clothes to see what I need to part ways with", I lied.

"Uh-oh. That sounds like trouble. Any time you part ways with something, I can expect you to go out and come back with twice that amount."

"I have to replace the things I get rid of."

"Can you hold off on the closet clean out?" he asked.

"Why? What's up?"

"I want to take you to dinner."

"What's the occasion?" I asked.

"There is no occasion. I just want to spend some time with my beautiful wife."

I eyed him suspiciously. "And you're sure this has nothing to do with business?"

"I'm sure Taylor. I really want to just spend some time with you."

There were times when he'd say he wanted to take me to dinner and it would end up being a business dinner. We'd get to the restaurant and there would be clients waiting for us. It always pissed me off when he did that.

"So, where are we going?" I asked.

I thought maybe we could go to *Maggiano's*. Is that fine with you?"

"Yeah, that's great. Let me change."

He looked me up and down. "You look fine Taylor."

"I know, but I'm changing anyway", I replied and headed for the closet.

"This is nice David", I said to him after taking a sip of my wine. "I'm glad we did this."

"I knew you would enjoy it", he replied.

"And I'm pleasantly surprised that it has nothing to do with business."

He took a sip of his wine. "I told you I was going to work on spending more time with you. I don't want some man to come and steal you away."

"I don't think that will happen", I assured him.

"David?" a man's voice came from behind us.

I turned to see a tall, dark and fine specimen with the prettiest smile standing there.

"Charles Williams...hey man, how's it going?" David stood up and they gave each other half hugs. "Long time, no see. I guess the rich do lead normal lives",

Charles joked.

David brushed him off. "Aw, don't you even go there. I hear you're not doing so bad yourself."

"This is my lovely wife, Bonnie", he said. For the first time, I noticed the blond-haired, blue-eyed female standing beside him. "Honey, this is David Morgan."

She shook David's hand. "So *you're* David Morgan? I've heard a lot about you."

David laughed. "All good, I hope." He turned to me and said, "This is my wife Taylor."

Charles reached out to shake my hand. "Hello Taylor, it's nice to meet you."

"It's nice to meet you too", I said and gave him a seductive look that only he saw.

"You look so familiar", Bonnie said.

I stared at her and realized who she was. "Oh yes...I do recall running in to you and your girlfriend at *Nordstrom's* while I was shopping one day."

The look on her face was priceless. At that moment, she looked like she wanted the floor to open up and suck her in.

"So you two have met before?" David asked.

I wasn't going to call her out. I had other things on my mind. "Um...actually, we just happened to be shopping in the same department and realized we had some of the same taste in clothes. It was nothing major", I lied.

"That's nice. Maybe you two can get together some time", David suggested.

"Yeah, sure. That would be lovely", I replied, knowing I had no intentions of doing shit with that bitch. Being the woman that I am, I said, "Why don't you guys join us?" I looked over at David. "Is that okay with you sweetie?"

Like I knew he would, he said, "Of course, it's okay."

Charles and Bonnie looked at each other, shrugged their shoulders and both said, "Sure, why not?"

Bonnie took the seat next to David and Charles sat next to me. The scent of his cologne traveled to my nostrils and I felt moisture form between my thighs. Having him sit so close to me, gave me goose bumps. I was weak when it came to fine black men. And Charles was definitely fine. He had broad shoulders and big hands. Hands, that I imagined grabbing my ass, while I rode him to ecstasy.

I looked over at Bonnie. She was your typical bleached blond bimbo. She had cleavage up to her chin, courtesy of a boob job. And of course, she was the size of a twig. Women like her got off on pissing sisters off. They loved walking around with fine black men like Charles on their arm. Obtaining a black man was a big accomplishment to them and they will rub your nose in it. I know I sounded like a hypocrite, but I was with David for one reason...MONEY. He just happened to be white. Race doesn't matter to me. I only see one color and that's green. Some people would say I'm a gold digger. I would say that I'm a woman who enjoys the finer things in life. And I feel that having a man provide them for me is the icing on the cake. After the way I grew up, I deserved it. I also deserved that fine man sitting next to me, and I was going to have him.

The waiter came and took our orders. David and Charles engaged in small talk, while Bonnie and I stared awkwardly at each other. I sat there pondering over how I could let Charles know that I wanted him, without being too obvious. I could only do so much with our spouses sitting across from us. So I discreetly took the toe of my shoe and ran it up and down his leg. He cleared his throat. I continued doing that, getting pleasure out of watching him squirm in his seat.

"Honey, are you okay?" Bonnie asked him.

"Yeah...I'm fine. I just got a little tickle in my throat. And it's kind of hot in here", he replied.

"Why don't you take your jacket off?" she asked.

"That's a good idea", he said and took his jacket off in a hurry.

All through dinner, I played footsy with Charles. And when he responded to my advances by playing with me, I knew he was down for whatever.

Just a Matter of Time

Jade

Having Eli upset with me was no picnic. For days after the dinner, I called him and he wouldn't answer or return my calls. I started to think that he had called it quits. Then this morning I called him, thinking I was going to get his voice mail again. He answered, "What's up?"

"What's up...Is that all you have to say? I have been calling you nonstop for the last two days, only to have you ignore me."

"I've been busy", he responded.

"Too busy for me Eli?" I asked.

"Look Jade, I didn't answer your call so we could argue."

"I don't want to argue either Eli. It's just that I didn't know what to think. I thought maybe you were breaking up with me", I said, my voice cracking a little.

He sighed before responding. "I'm not gonna lie Jade. For a minute, I thought about it...'cause I told you about my privacy-"

I jumped in, "But Eli, I-"

"Let me finish...as I was saying, I'm funny about my personal stuff. But I realized I couldn't make you suffer for your mom's actions...unless you put her up to that shit."

"I promise you Eli, I had nothing to do with that. And don't be so hard on her...she is my mom", I said.

"Okay...but enough of that. Why don't you let me slide through there so I can slide up in something?"

We hadn't spoken in days and the first thing on his mind was getting some. Even though I wanted to tell him that, I knew I wouldn't. I was wanting some action myself. I knew my rabbit and silver bullet were begging to stay in the night stand for a change. I had worked them overtime for the past few days. And as loyal and handy as they are, they don't get me off like Eli does.

"What time are you coming? I asked, while sliding my hand between my thighs.

"Give me an hour...and put on something sexy", he said.

"Don't I always?"

"Yeah, you do", he replied and hung up.

After I hung up, I stripped all of my clothes off and hopped in the shower. After washing my body with *Oil of Olay* soap, I smoothed on *Oil of Olay* in-shower lotion and rinsed off. Once I got out of the shower, I dried off my feet. While the rest of my body air dried, I applied *Neutrogena Foot Cream* to my feet.

Thoughts of my mother popped into my head, like they had been every day since she left. Before she left, she said, "Jade, I know you're a grown woman who can make your own decisions, but I've been around longer than you have. So I've experienced a lot more than you. Sometimes, we women see what we want to see and believe what we want to believe. I consider myself a good judge of character. And I'm telling you that Eli is not what he seems. He's hiding something from you. I just don't quite know what it is. I would give anything to be wrong Jade. And for your sake, I hope I am."

I knew my mother meant well, but I had to live my own life. Eli was the best thing that happened to me...in a long time. I couldn't let her paranoia spoil a good thing. Eli had been nothing but a gentleman to me. Sometimes, he did let his temper show. But most of the time, he treated me like a queen. He deserved to have his privacy respected and I was going to give him that.

I slipped on the slinkiest, sexiest lingerie I could find. I was about to put on a little makeup, when the door buzzed. Hell, what was the point? It was going to get smeared anyway. I opened the door and Eli was standing there with a bottle of one of my favorites, *Real Sangria*.

"Damn baby, you look good enough to eat", he said as I let him inside.

"So do you", I said, looking him up and down. He was wearing dark jeans and a red polo shirt. His locks were pulled back away from his face, showing off the diamond studs he always wore in his ears.

He walked into the kitchen and sat the drink on the table. Before I could get two glasses, he grabbed me and started prying his tongue between my lips. We kissed like two horny teenagers. He tore my lingerie off of me...literally. He's lucky I was in love with him. That piece cost me fifty bucks at *Victoria's Secret.*

When I say Eli licked me from head to toe, I mean it. To top it off, he fucked me in almost every position imaginable. By the time he was finished with me, all the thoughts my mother put in my head were history. And even when he slipped out of my apartment in the middle of the night, I still felt secure with what we had.

Taylor

I had just finished giving Charles Williams the best fuck he ever had in his life...at least that's what he kept telling me while I was riding his dick.

That night after dinner at *Maggiano's,* I managed to slip him my number. He called me the next day asking when he could see me. I told him I'd get back to him. I couldn't seem too anxious. Now, here we were breaking a commandment and I was enjoying the hell out of it.

"So how long have you been married to Barbie...I mean Bonnie?" I asked him.

He laughed at my slip up. "We've only been married for three years...a long three years."

"There weren't any sistas you could settle down with?"

He smirked and said, "There weren't any brothas you could settle down with?"

I took a sip of my rum and coke. "I asked you first."

He stared off into space, twirling his drink in his glass. "There were plenty of sistas who wanted to give me some play. But I was one of those brothas."

"Meaning?"

"I was one of those black men who thought all black women were gold diggers. I use to think that you all were loud, lazy and didn't know how to treat a good man", he responded.

"And now?"

He laughed and shook his head. "Now I know that's a bunch of bull. Gold diggers come in all colors. And any woman can sit on her ass if she decides to."

"Don't tell me your little Barbie doll is not what you expected", I said in a sarcastic tone.

"You picked the perfect name for her. She is so spoiled, it's ridiculous. As long as I'm dishing out money, everything is fine. She doesn't do anything, but shop.

She couldn't even boil water, if you paid her."

I sat there listening to Charles divulge his wife's shortcomings. I didn't feel bad for him though. I couldn't stand black men who had that white women only mentality. So I say he was getting what he deserved.

"...And she is the biggest bitch there is. She looks down on everyone who doesn't have money. I've been through four house keepers in the last six months. No one can put up with her nasty attitude."

Charles was really messing up my groove. I didn't stop by to listen to him bitch and moan about his wife. I had one thing on my mind and that was freaking him like that skinny bitch couldn't.

"And let's not talk about our sex life. When she does decide to give me some, she just lays there like she's dead. There's no passion at all. I think she'd rather lie in bed naked with a designer handbag than me", he continued.

"Let's not talk about your wife anymore Charles", I said, putting my glass down. I took his glass out of his hand and sat it down also.

"So what do you want to talk about?' he asked me.

"Shut up and fuck me", I said, grabbing his dick.

"I'm down with that", he replied showing all of his teeth.

I rode his dick until I came multiple times. He munched on my pussy a little and then I rode his dick some more. He seemed obsessed with me riding his dick, so I asked him why he liked it so much. He said Bonnie only liked missionary style and he liked watching my tits bounce up and down. So I gave him what he wanted. We fucked until we both couldn't go another minute.

Afterwards, he said, "You keep sexing me like that Taylor, I'll have Bonnie's shit packed and ready to go in no time."

"Let's not get carried away Charles. That's your dick talking. Good pussy will do that to you; have you saying shit you don't really mean." I was flattered by his comment, but I wasn't naïve. This was just a fuck...nothing more, nothing less.

212

"Yeah, I guess you're right. It's been so long since I've came that hard, I'll probably say anything you want me to say."

I started putting on my clothes. While he wasn't looking, I slipped my panties under the bed. I wasn't sure if we were in their bedroom. I guess if he was trifling and fucked me in their bed, she would find my panties in due time.

He said, he had sent her out with his credit card, so there would be no chance of her showing up while we were in the act. He was one brave soul to invite me into his home. But if he wasn't worried, I didn't need to be either. I finished putting on my clothes and shoes, while he tidied up and put the place back in pre-sex mode.

"Give me a call sometime", I said to him as he escorted me out the door.

"Oh, I definitely will", he said flashing his sexy smile.

Honestly, I knew I wouldn't be calling him. What we had was revenge sex. Knowing I had fucked Bonnie's husband gave me much satisfaction, whether she found the panties or not. Don't get me wrong, the sex was good. But Exodus was enough to keep me occupied. But something told me that I would definitely be hearing from Charles again.

Sierra

"Good morning Sierra", Kiki greeted me as she walked into the spa.

"Hey Kiki. How was your trip?"

She flipped her hand at me and said, "Girl, I had a blast. I will definitely be visiting the Big Apple again. All we did was shop."

"You didn't go visit any of the sights?" I asked.

She put her hand on her hip and rolled her eyes. "The only sights I wanted to see were the stores in Downtown Manhattan."

"Kiki, you're crazy", I said as I scanned the appointment book, checking to see how many appointments were scheduled for the day.

Kiki came behind the counter and put her purse down. "Where's Jazmin? She's usually here by now."

"There's no telling with her. She hasn't called or anything", I said without looking up.

"I hope she's okay and that crazy ass husband hasn't beaten her again."

I closed my book and turned to face Kiki. I looked around to make sure no one was listening. "This is serious. We've got to do something."

"Sierra, how can we do anything, when she won't even tell us the truth?"

"I don't know, but if we don't help her soon, Jamal's going to end up hurting her really bad...or worse", I said. I got furious just thinking about it. I could put up with a lot of things. A man putting his hands on me was not one of them. If Tyler ever laid a finger on me, he would regret it.

Kiki gave me a serious look. "Do you really think he'll go that far Sierra?"

My mind shifted to childhood memories. Memories that I had stowed away a long time ago. I had decided that I wouldn't let things from my past control my life.

The only person that knew what I went through was Tyler.

I sat down in one of the empty seats. "Kiki, you can never underestimate what a woman beater can or will do."

"But I think most of 'em just like to scare their women and control 'em."

"That may be true...but tragedy can strike any of those times...whether it be intentional or unintentional."

The bell on the door rang, alerting us that someone was entering the spa. Kiki looked like she had seen a ghost. I looked up to see what she was staring at. I saw a sight that horrified me. It was Jazmin and she almost looked unrecognizable. Kiki and I both jumped up and ran to meet her.

"Oh my God Jazmin. What happened?" Kiki asked.

"Did that bastard Jamal do this to you?" I asked her as if I didn't already know the answer. I grabbed her hand and led her to the waiting area.

She took a seat and stared at the floor. "No...Jamal didn't do this. I was..."

"Stop it Jazmin!" I yelled. "You have got to stop lying to us and to yourself. He can't keep doing this to you. Look at your face!"

She looked like she had been in a boxing match with Mike Tyson. Her right eye was so swollen that it was partially closed. She had a small gash under her left eye. Both of her lips were split down the middle.

"You don't understand. He's under a lot of stress", she defended him.

Kiki put her hands on her hips and rolled her neck. "Honey, it aint that much stress in the world. You need to kick that bastard's ass. Matter of fact, I can get my two big brothers to beat his ass for you. You just say the word!"

I put my hand on Kiki's arm to calm her down. "Kiki, that's not going to solve anything." I then turned to Jazmin. "Jazmin, honey I know he's your husband and the father of your children, but no man has the right to put their hands on a woman."

"He only does it when he's had a bad day at work

or when I make him mad....Anyway, he always tells me he's sorry after it's over", she explained.

I sat down in the seat next to her and turned it so I could be face to face with her. Jazmin, I need to tell you something...and I want you to listen." I put both of her hands in mine and took a deep breath.

I was about to talk about something I hadn't thought about in years. But I was hoping that my confession would save someone else's life.

"Do I need to leave?" Kiki asked. The look on her face told me that she didn't want to. I told her she could stay and she sat down anxiously awaiting my words.

"When I was a little girl, it was just me and my mom for a long time. My dad died when I was a baby. My mom said they were supposed to get married, but he died suddenly from a brain tumor. As expected, my mom was upset and she was depressed for a long time. Her main focus became taking care of me. As time went by friends and family kept telling her that she needed to move on and get a man in her life. She kept saying she didn't want or need a man. When I was about eight or nine, she met this man named Sam. In the beginning, he was a perfect gentleman. He was so good to my mom. He helped her with the bills. He used to buy me gifts and take me places. He was the only man my mom had dated since my dad died. Eventually, he moved in. After he moved in, he changed. He started drinking a lot. He stopped being nice to me and he would talk down to my mom, telling her she was a horrible cook and a lousy housekeeper. One day I asked her why she let him talk to her like that. She told me to stay out of grown folks' business and I was not to be disrespectful to Sam because he was older than me. After a while, the verbal abuse became physical." I could feel my eyes starting to water, but I had to continue.

"I remember the first time he hit my mom. I guess I was about eleven or twelve. We were eating dinner. He told my mom he didn't like the sauce she had bought. She told him it was on sale and that's why she bought it. Before I knew it, he slapped her across her face so hard she fell out of her chair. He started yelling at her, saying that's what he worked every day for, to have the things that he wanted and liked. She scrambled to her feet and ran to their bedroom, closing and locking the door behind her. He looked over at me with remorse in his eyes, before he went after her. He started knocking on the door telling her he was sorry and he would never put his hands on her again. She forgave him and they made up."

By now, tears had escaped my eyes. Kiki grabbed some tissues from the reception desk and handed them to me. "Did he ever hit her again?" she asked before sitting back down.

I dabbed my eyes with one of the tissues. I had already opened the wound, so I had to finish the story. "Yes...he did. Not only did he slap her again, he beat her on a regular basis. At first, it was about once a month. Then it was two or three times a month. After a while he was beating her every week, at least two times."

"Did you witness all of the beatings? I can't imagine having to go through something like that as a child", Kiki said, looking sympathetic.

I wasn't looking for sympathy. I saw a woman in need and I felt my experience could help her, so I continued. "I didn't see *all* of the beatings, but there were plenty of nights when I heard them. Once I even tried to jump in and help my mom. I got pushed down in the process. And he told me if I ever got out of line again, he'd see to it that I was sent away to a girls' home. He also told me not to be running my mouth about what went on in our house...so I did what I was told. I kept my mouth shut and did nothing about the abuse my mom was receiving."

"So what eventually happened?" Jazmin spoke for the first time since I started revisiting my past.

I thought back to the day that changed my life forever. A day that made me realize, that you could never underestimate what a person was capable of doing. Through tears, I finished my story. "My mom had finally gotten fed up with the beatings. So we moved out and went to stay with my grandmother. Every day Sam would come by begging my mom to come back. He promised he would stop drinking and get help for his temper. My grandmother would never let him see or talk to her. But one day he came by and my mom decided to talk to him. We begged her not to talk to him. Something inside me told me he couldn't change. She told us she was just gonna go outside and hear what he had to say. My grandmother asked her once more not to go out, but she did anyway."

The tears were flowing faster and faster. I didn't even bother wiping them away. Kiki and Jazmin were both looking at me, waiting for me to finish.

"After about ten minutes or so, I heard what sounded like fire crackers. I ran to the door to see what was going on." I shook my head from side to side, not sure if I could go on. Then I looked at Jazmin's face and knew that I had to finish. "My mom was lying on the ground with blood pouring from her head. Sam was standing over her with a gun in his hand. I just started screaming to the top of my lungs. My grandmother came running out of the kitchen. I couldn't speak. I just pointed outside. Sam just jumped in his truck and drove off...left my mom there to die. My grandmother called 911 and I ran outside to check on my mom. Sam had shot her three times; once in the head, in the chest and in the stomach. She was dead and there was nothing I could do to help her. I dropped to my knees and cried on my mom's chest. I stayed that way until the ambulance and police came."

Kiki walked over to me and hugged me tight. Then she wiped my tears away with the tissue in my hand. "Oh my God Sierra. I would've never thought that you had gone through something like that. You always seem so strong and put together."

"It was over twenty years ago, so I guess I've healed over time. Of course you never forget something like that, but eventually, you have to move on with your life", I explained.

Jazmin reached out and touched my knee. "What happened to Sam? Did they catch him?"

"The police got him at home. When they got there, he was sitting on the porch with the gun lying beside him. They took him to jail and he was later charged for my mom's murder. After serving only five years in prison, he died from liver problems. I guess all of his drinking had finally caught up with him."

"He deserved to die, after what he did. That was karma." Kiki said. She stood up and walked over to Jazmin. "Sweetie, we need to get you to the hospital."

Jazmin shook her head. "No, I don't want to go to the hospital...I'm okay."

Kiki looked over at me and then back at Jazmin. "Have you seen your face?"

"I'm not going to the hospital", she said, with a little attitude in her voice.

The front door opened. Michelle and Kiona walked in talking and laughing. They stopped when they saw us. "What's going on?" Kiona asked, looking directly at me.

When Michelle noticed Jazmin, she put her hand up to her mouth. "Oh my God Jazmin. What happened to you?"

"That bastard Jamal is what happened to her", Kiki said.

Jazmin put her hand up. "Don't Kiki."

"Don't what Jazmin...tell the truth? It's time to face the facts", Kiki replied pacing back and forth.

Everyone was silent for a few seconds, waiting for Jazmin to say or do something. No matter what we said, she was going to do what she wanted to do.

I stood up and said, "Jazmin, since you won't go to the hospital, at least let Kiki take you to the back to try to clean you up a little."

Kiki went to her and took her hand. I stopped them before they could leave. I turned Jazmin to face me.

"I know you can make your own decisions. But I hope you really listened to what I said. I don't want what happened to my mom to happen to you. Think about your children too." I gave her a long hug before she walked off with Kiki.

An hour later, a tall man who looked like he could

be a professional football player walked in the door. I had seen him before. It was Jamal. He walked up to the counter and yelled out, "Where's Jazmin?"

I stood up and walked around the counter to face him. "Why...you come here to finish her off?"

He looked me up and down and sucked his teeth. "Bitch, you need to mind yo' own damn business!"

"As long as Jazmin is working for me, she is my business!" I replied.

He came closer to me, trying to intimidate me, I assumed. "But she is *my* wife", he said, pointing at his chest.

I didn't back down or let him think I was afraid of him. "So that makes her your property or something? You think that gives you the right to put your hands on her?"

"I wouldn't have to put my hands on her if she didn't disobey me", he responded with rage in his eyes.

"Disobey you? Do you know how ridiculous you sound? She is not your child. She is your wife, who should be treated equally." I couldn't believe he was actually saying that. Men that talked like that were cowards. They beat their women, but would never stand up to a real man.

He walked towards the nail area, stuck his head in there and started yelling, "Where's my wife?"

Michelle and Kiona had customers and I didn't need him causing a scene. "You really need to keep it down. Jazmin's not here", I told him.

He came back towards me. "You're lying. I know she's here. Now get her out here or I'll tear this place apart!" he yelled.

I was about to go call the police when Kiki and Jazmin came out of the back. Jamal, what are you doing here?" Jazmin asked him from behind Kiki.

He walked towards her, but Kiki blocked him. "Bitch, you better get out of my way if you know what's good for you!"

Kiki got all up in his face. "Unlike Jazmin, I aint scared of your punk ass", she said with her hands on her hips.

"I don't have time for this. Look Jazmin...I came to tell you that I'm sorry baby." He tried to reach around Kiki to get to her.

Kiki blocked him again. "Well it's too late for sorry aint it? You weren't sorry when you were using her face as a punching bag."

He looked at me and then back at Kiki. "Y'all need to mind yo' own damn business. This is between me and my wife. Now y'all are starting to piss me off!" he yelled.

Jazmin stepped from behind Kiki. "Jamal please don't make a scene...just go", she said softly.

"I'm not leaving without you. Now, let's go!" he yelled again.

Jazmin said, "No...I'm not going with you."

He gave her a funny look and said, "What did you say?"

She answered, "I s-said...I'm not...going with you."

He started laughing like someone had told a joke. "You need to stop trying to impress your little friends here. Once again, bring yo' ass on."

"I'm serious Jamal. I'm not going with you. I can't do this anymore", she said pointing to her face.

"Now, I'm asking you to leave before I call the police", I told him.

He gave me a dirty look and walked towards the door. He looked back at Jazmin and said "You better be home this evening...or I'm gonna show you what a real ass whipping is." Then he walked out the door.

"You did the right thing Jazmin", Kiki told her. "Now let's get downtown and get you a restraining order. That man has hit you for the last time."

Jade

Being operations manager was starting to take its toll on me. Don't get me wrong, I was honored that Mr. Lawson entrusted me to do the job. It's just a part of me wished I had kept my old position. I was happy with that position and enjoyed it a great deal. I didn't have to deal with the stress that came with this position.

My inside line rang, bringing out of my daydreaming. "Hello, this is Jade", I greeted after answering it.

"Hello Jade. I'm free now if you still want to talk to me", Mr. Lawson's voice echoed through the receiver.

"Ok, I'll be down there in a few minutes."

I had spoken to Mr. Lawson earlier and told him that I needed to talk to him. I wanted to tell him how I was feeling about my new position. But as I looked around my office, I was starting to have second thoughts. Next to Mr. Lawson's office, I had the nicest office in the company. Fine art covered the walls. Italian leather and cherry wood furnished the spacious office. I had a view of the flower garden and fountain Mr. Lawson had installed six months ago. And let's not forget the money I was making. Most would say that I had it made. I guess having it made, sometimes comes with a price.

"Well, it's now or never", I said out loud. I stood up and was about to walk out of my office, when Emily poked her head in the door.

"I'm sorry to bother you Jade. Are you busy?" she asked. Emily was the plainest white girl I had ever seen in my life. Long, thin, scraggly hair framed her narrow pale face. She had a long nose and very thin lips. Her wardrobe consisted of long old-fashioned floral skirts with over-sized cardigans. She always wore those cheap looking black flats that looked like they came from *Family Dollar* or *Dollar General*. She never wore any makeup or jewelry. Needless to say, she was definitely a candidate for a makeover.

"I'm on my way to see Mr. Lawson. What's up?" I asked her.

"Well...I have a small problem", she answered, holding up her thumb and forefinger to imitate small.

Since Emily had gotten my old position in accounting, she had become a thorn in my side. I know everyone needs guidance and training when taking on a new position, but she was quite a handful. Almost every day, she was calling me on the phone or popping her head in my office to ask me some trivial question. I had supplied her with all of the resources she needed to do the job, yet she insisted on annoying me.

"Can't it wait?" I asked her. "I don't want to keep Mr. Lawson waiting", I said, irritated.

"Uh...yeah...I guess it can wait", she said, not sounding so sure.

"If it's that important, I'm pretty sure Carlos or Nancy can help you." Then I held out my arm to signal her to leave. "Now, I really have to go."

When I reached Mr. Lawson's office, he was on the telephone. I stood in the doorway until he motioned for me to come in. I took a seat in one of the leather wing back chairs that were facing his over-sized desk.

"So what can I do for you Jade?" he asked, after ending his call.

I cleared my throat and spoke. "Well Mr. Lawson...I'm just gonna come right out and say that I'm having second thoughts about that position."

He didn't say anything at first. He just sat back in his chair and clasped his hands together. We sat in silence for a few seconds. Then finally, he spoke. "Why are you having second thoughts Jade?"

"I feel I may have bitten off more than I can chew. I never realized how demanding this job was."

He leaned up in his chair and rested his elbows on his desk. "Jade, I would have never given you this job if I didn't think you couldn't handle it. You were my first pick", he said.

"I was?" I asked and put my hand to my chest. I

was surprised.

"Yes, you were", he replied.

"What about Nancy and Carlos?" I asked.

"They were considered. But you have something extra."

"What's that?"

"You have that drive and determination I was looking for...I know right now you feel overwhelmed, but that's normal. You've taken on a huge responsibility and it's going to take some time to get used to it. I'm sure Nancy or Carlos would love to take over the position for you. But I don't think you should throw in the towel just yet. Give it some time. I have faith in you Jade", he said.

"So you don't think I'm doing a lousy job?" I asked him.

"No, I don't think you're doing a lousy job. If I have an issue with your performance, I have no problem letting you know", he answered.

"Thank you. I'm so glad to hear you say that", I said, after letting out a sigh of relief.

"Jade, you are one of the best employees I got. So I know you're going to have that position down pat in no time. Just relax and do what you do...okay?"

I was pleased when I left Mr. Lawson's office. It didn't even bother me when I saw Emily coming towards me with papers in her hand. Usually, I would try to go in the other direction or try to duck into an empty office before she could see me.

"Everything is okay now Jade. Carlos helped me with my issue", she said, holding up the papers.

"That's good Emily. I'm glad he could help you", I said before walking off.

"Jade", she called out.

"Yes Emily."

"Do I bother you...by asking you questions all the time?" she asked.

I turned around to face her. "Why do you ask Emily?"

"Well, I just feel that I may get on your nerves sometimes", she said, with the look of a child that no one liked on her face.

That was my chance to let her know how I felt. I could tell her that she was a nuisance and get her out of my hair...for good. But as I stood there, seeing how fragile and pitiful she looked, I started to feel sorry for her. It was obvious that she had low self-esteem and was accustomed to people running over her or taking advantage of her. I knew deep down inside, I didn't want to hurt her feelings, so I lied and said, "No Emily. You don't get on my nerves."

A smile crept across her thin lips and she said, "I'm glad to hear that, because the last thing I want to do is annoy you. You're one of the nicest people here and I admire you because you're a hard worker."

It was my turn to smile. I felt bad for considering her a nuisance, but I had no idea she looked at me that way. "Thank you. I really appreciate that", I told her.

"No problem."

"Well, I better let you get back to work", I said and walked off.

As soon as I stepped into my office, my outside line rang. *"To The Max Advertising*, Jade Peterson speaking...how can I help you?" I did my usual greeting.

"You better watch your back bitch!" a female screamed into the phone.

"Who is this?" I asked.

"Don't you worry about it!" she yelled.

"I know this is you Paige. Stop calling me. I have a restraining order against you!" I yelled back into the phone.

"Nothing's going to help you when I'm finished with you", she hissed.

"Leave me alone, you psycho bitch!" I screamed before slamming down the receiver.

"Is everything okay in here?" I looked up to see Carlos standing in my doorway. I didn't realize how loud I was. I guess he must've heard me.

"Uh...yeah, everything is fine", I lied.

He didn't look too convinced. "Are you sure?" he asked.

I hesitated for a moment and then said, "Actually...everything isn't fine Carlos."

"You wanna talk about it?"

I didn't usually talk about my personal life when it came to my co-workers. It was always about business. But for some reason, I felt that I could trust Carlos. "Come in and close the door", I told him.

He did as I instructed and took a seat in front of my desk. "What's going on? You sounded upset", he said.

"I've been getting these crazy phone calls", I spoke in a low tone, as if someone could still hear us with the door closed.

"Crazy calls?" he asked, with a confused look on his face.

"Yeah...at first they started out breathing on the phone. Then they started calling me names, saying I needed to watch my back."

"Wow, that is crazy...Do you have any idea who it is?"

I didn't know if I should tell him that I thought it was Paige. He would want to know why Paige would be calling me. But I decided to take my chances. "I think it's Paige."

"Paige that used to work here?" he asked.

"Yes."

"Why would Paige be doing that?"

"Let's just say that we didn't get along...and she was upset because I got the job she wanted."

"That still doesn't make sense." he said.

I went on to tell him about the incident at *Food Lion* in the parking lot and about me taking out the restraining order against her.

He started laughing. "There's nothing like a good cat fight. I would've loved to see that."

"It's not funny Carlos. I was so embarrassed afterwards", I said, crossing my arms against my chest.

"You're right. I'm sorry", he said before laughing again.

"You are so wrong...but Carlos can you please not say anything about this to the others? I don't want my personal business circulating throughout the company."

He threw his hands up in the air and said, "Jade, I wouldn't do that. Besides, I'm not into gossiping. That's not my style. I'll leave that to the ladies", he said.

"Oh, so you're a sexist?" I asked jokingly.

"Naw...I just know how women love to talk. I have three sisters", he replied.

"I'm not even gonna go there, because we could be here all day debating."

"You know I'm telling the truth", he boasted.

"Whatever Carlos."

"Well, I need to get back to work and I'm sure you got work to do as well." He stood up to leave.

"Thanks for listening Carlos."

"No problem, I just hope everything works out for you" he said, before walking out the door.

I felt a headache coming on. I needed to get out of the office for lunch. I dialed Eli's cell number. He answered on the first ring. "Hey baby", I said in my sexiest voice.

"What's up?" he asked.

"You busy?"

"Just finishing up with a client."

"Can you meet me for lunch today?"

"Um...yeah, I guess so...something wrong?"

"Sort of...I just really need my man right now."

"Ok...I'll be right there. Just give me a sec", he said to someone in the background.

"Are you listening to me Eli?" I asked him, with irritation in my voice.

He sighed into the phone. "Yes, I'm listening Jade, and I'm also working. I'll meet you at *Chang's*...okay?"

"Okay Eli. See you later...I love-"

He hung up before I could finish my statement. I was tempted to call him back and give him a piece of my mind. But I knew it would make matters worse. We were on good terms and I was determined to keep it that way.

Taylor

When I told Charles to call me sometimes, I didn't think he would be blowing my phone up. He had called me every day, two to three times a day. I had just stepped out of the shower, when I heard my cell phone ringing. I dashed into the bedroom to answer it. I recognized Charles' number on the display screen.

"Hello", I answered before he could hang up.

"Hey sexy", his deep baritone voice vibrated over the phone.

"Who is this?' I asked, pretending not to know who he was.

"You don't know who this is?" he asked.

"No...I don't."

"It's me, Charles."

"Hey, what's up?"

"You."

"Really?"

"Yeah, I was hoping I could see you today", he said, sounding excited.

I hesitated for a moment. "Uh...I don't-"

"Aw, come on Taylor", he said, interrupting me. "Don't be like that. You've turned down both of my previous invitations."

"That's because I've been busy", I lied.

"I understand that, but ever since we got together, I haven't been able to get you out of my mind", he responded.

My stomach dropped. I wasn't expecting that. I understood the power my loving could have on a man. Back in the day when I worked as an escort, I had men confessing their love for me on a regular basis. Of course, I never took any of them seriously. Good sex will make a man say or do anything, especially when they weren't getting it at home. I had no idea how I was going to handle the situation at hand. "Charles, don't even go there", I told him.

"Why not? It's the truth", he replied.

"We're both married...and it was just sex", I said.

"I know that, but I felt a connection with you...something I never felt with Bonnie", he responded, sounding serious.

Dealing with Exodus was enough. I didn't think I could juggle two affairs. I only fucked Charles out of spite. "Look Charles, you're a really great guy, but I don't think we should start something that may get out of hand", I said, hoping he would back down.

"It's already started. It started when you made love to me", he replied.

I had to nip things in the bud...real quick. That's why you had to be careful about who you fool around with. I would usually lay down the ground rules before I gave up the goods. But with Charles, I figured I didn't have to. Now, he was acting like he was in love after one round. "We didn't make love ...we fucked", I told him bluntly.

"How can you say that Taylor?" he asked.

"I can say that because it's true. I was just looking for a good time Charles, and I assumed you were looking for the same thing....good sex, with no strings attached." I couldn't believe I was even having that conversation.

"Honestly, I was just looking for a good time, but after I got to know you, my feelings changed."

"We spent two hours together Charles. Half of that time we were fucking like rabbits and the other half, you were talking about your snooty wife", I explained.

As if he hadn't heard anything I said, he asked, "So are we gonna get together today or what?"

"I can't today. I have plans", I said.

"So when can I see you?" he asked in a tone I didn't quite care for.

"I don't know. I'll get back to you later."

"Yeah, okay."

I really needed to end the conversation. "Charles, I really need to go", I told him.

"Ok Taylor."

"Goodbye Charles."

"Don't make me wait too long", he said with iciness in his voice. Then he hung up.

He was really tripping, but I wasn't about to let him get to me. I had a lovely day planned. I was going to David's office to meet him for lunch. After I put on my makeup, I scanned my closet for something to wear. I decided on my white *Dana Buchman* linen pantsuit. I slipped on my gold *Stuart Weitzman* sandals and checked myself out in the full length mirror. Pleased with what I saw, I grabbed my purse and headed out the door.

"Good afternoon Ms. Taylor", Pedro, the gardener greeted me as soon as I stepped outside.

"Good morning Pedro", I replied. He had started working for David before we got married. Pedro was a young Puerto Rican and super fine. And he kept our yard immaculate. Every now and then, I would catch him sneaking peeks at my breasts or my ass.

"Hope you enjoy the rest of your day", he said and waved at me.

"Oh, I will...you too." I decided to give him a little show before I left. I jiggled my ass extra hard as I walked to my car. And I knew he was watching.

As I stepped out of my car at David's office, a young woman approached me. "Excuse me ma'am...can I talk to you for a minute?" she said. She looked like she weighed no more than a hundred pounds. Her clothes were dirty and worn. Her hair looked like it hadn't been combed in weeks.

"What can I do for you?" I asked her as I closed my car door and set the alarm.

She came closer to me. "Can you spare a couple of bucks, so I can get me something to eat?" Her teeth were brown and her breath reeked of alcohol and tobacco.

I took a few steps back. I usually didn't give money to beggars on the streets, but I reached into my purse and fished out a twenty dollar bill. "Here, take this...and get a job." I handed her the money and walked away.

"Thank you ma'am", I heard her say as I entered

the building.

Exodus was the first person I saw when I walked in. He was actually sitting on Autumn's desk. She was hanging onto his every word. They were so engrossed in their conversation, they didn't even notice me. I cleared my throat to announce my presence. Exodus almost leaped off of the desk when he realized I was standing there.

"Uh...good afternoon T-Taylor", he stuttered.

"I see you guys are working hard", I said sarcastically.

Autumn looked at Exodus, and then sneered at me. "Can I help you Taylor?" she asked.

I gave her a dirty look and said, "No Autumn, you cannot help me."

"Well, what do you want?" she asked with an attitude.

I got directly in front of her desk and looked her straight in the eyes. "What I want is for you to check yourself. You don't need to concern yourself with why I'm here. I know you take me as a joke, but believe me, I'm not. I do not want to have this discussion with you again."

She just sat there staring at me. I guess she had enough sense not to say anything. I had said all I needed to say, so I waltzed on back to David's office.

When I entered, he was sitting at his desk looking over some papers. "Hey sweetie", I greeted him and tossed my purse on the red leather couch.

His face lit up when he looked up and saw me. "Hey! Aren't you a ray of sunshine?"

I walked around his desk and sat on his lap. "You ready to go?" I asked.

"You're anxious aren't you? What's the rush?" he asked me while rubbing my back.

"There's no rush. I just know how you are."

He tilted his head to the side and asked, "How am I?"

"You'll keep stalling and before you know it, lunch time will be over, and we won't go anywhere."

"You think you know me well don't you?" he asked, planting a kiss on my lips.

"I'd like to think I do", I replied.

"Guess who called me earlier?" he asked jumping to another subject.

I shrugged my shoulders. "I don't know...who?"

"Charles Williams."

My heart started beating faster. I pretended not to know who he was talking about. "Who's that?" I asked.

"You remember the guy and his wife we had dinner with at *Maggiano's.*"

"Oh...him...yeah...so what did he want?"

"He called to say he wants to have dinner with us again sometime...and his wife of course."

"Why?" I asked.

David looked confused. "I don't know Taylor. I guess they had a nice time and want to do it again."

"What did you tell him?"

"I told him I'd get back to him, but I'm sure it wouldn't be a problem...it isn't a problem is it?" he asked.

"No...it's just that I didn't really care for Bonnie that much."

"You didn't even give her a chance, Taylor."

"Believe me. I gave her a chance and she blew it."

He patted me on my thigh, motioning me to stand up. "Any way, we can discuss this another time. You ready to go?"

"Yes, I'm ready", I told him and retrieved my purse.

As David and I headed out to lunch, Charles came back into my mind. I didn't know what kind of game he was playing, but I wasn't going to participate.

Jade

"Boy, these ribs are the bomb!" Eli said, licking sauce off of his fingers. "I wish I could figure out what they put in this sauce."

We were at *PF Chang's* waiting on the food we ordered. Eli was munching on his favorite appetizer.

"I talked to Mr. Lawson about my performance today", I told him.

"And what did he say?"

"He said I was doing a good job and I should give it some time."

"Cool", he said and took a gulp of his tea.

"Eli...I don't want to start an argument...but why did you hang up on me earlier?" I asked him.

He opened the wet nap and wiped his hands. "Like I told you on the phone, I was working. My clients pay me by the hour, so I don't have time to be chatting on the phone. If I hung up on you, it wasn't intentional...okay?"

The waiter came with our food. Eli and I sat in silence for a few minutes. He was shoving his food in his mouth like he was in a hurry.

"Eli?"

"What's up?"

"I was wanting to-" I stopped when I saw him looking behind me.

He pulled his chair out, stood up and put his napkin on the table. "Hold up Jade. I see someone I know. I'll be right back."

I turned around to see him walking over to a table in the corner. A very attractive man was accompanied by a very small and petite woman with her head shaved. He and Eli passed a few words and exchanged business cards. Then Eli made his way back to our table.

"Who was that?" I asked as soon as he sat back down at the table.

"No one in particular...just some guy I know", he

answered and dived back into his food.

I noticed the business card sitting on the table. Before Eli could put it away, I snatched it up. "Boris Manlove...Entertainer Extraordinaire ...what kind of entertainer is he?" I asked Eli, who had an irritated look on his face.

"He's a dancer."

"A dancer?"

"Yes Jade...a dancer."

"You mean a dancer dancer or a dancer as in stripper?" I asked

"What difference does it make?"

"None really. I was just curious."

He grabbed the card out of my hand. "That's your problem, you're too damn curious", he said.

"No need to get all testy. He isn't dancing for you...is he?" I asked in a joking manner.

Eli slammed his fist on the table, getting attention from other diners. "Don't even joke like that Jade", he said through clenched teeth. "You know I don't get down like that."

"Calm down Eli. You're causing a scene", I said, looking around the restaurant.

"I'm sorry. I just don't find humor in gay jokes. I'm all about cat...and don't you forget it."

I placed my hand on top of his. "I know you're not gay. It was a tasteless joke and I apologize...now can we change the subject?"

"Fine with me", he mumbled.

"I got another call today", I told him.

"What they say?" he asked.

"Pretty much the same as usual."

"She threatened you again?"

"Yes."

"So you still think it's that chic that use to work with you?" he asked before taking another bite of his food.

"Who else could it be Eli?" I asked in frustration.

He wiped his mouth with his napkin. "What I don't understand is why she would be doing that over a measly job."

"It's not just some measly job. It's a very good job that pays well, for your information", I said defensively.

"But it still doesn't justify her actions. It just doesn't make sense that she would make those calls and damage your car just because you got the position she wanted."

"Crazy people don't make sense Eli. That's why they're crazy", I replied. I couldn't tell Eli the truth about what I had done to Paige. All I had told him was that she got caught sleeping around and was fired. And she became even more upset when she heard I got the promotion. I didn't want Eli to think I was some cold, calculating person who did whatever she had to do to get what she wanted. He saw me as a sweet and caring person and I intended to keep it that way.

"Yeah, I guess you're right", he said, bringing me out of my thoughts. "Crazy people don't make sense."

"I just wish she would leave me alone...it's not that I'm scared of her or anything. It's just that I don't like all that drama. I'm a grown woman and I don't have time for games", I stated.

"Maybe once she sees that she can't get to you anymore, she'll stop."

"I hope you're right. But the crazy thing is, that night at the grocery store when I first confronted her; she swore that she wasn't the one calling me. I was almost tempted to believe her until I went outside and saw my car. It just has to be her. Who else could it be Eli?"

He smiled and said, "Who else have you pissed off?"

Just as I was about to respond to his question, the handsome gentleman came to our table. "Be cool Eli my man. And hit me up sometime", he said.

"I'll do that Boris...take it easy", Eli said and touched his fist to Boris' before he walked away.

"You could've introduced me to your friend", I said.

"Why, so you could drool all over him? I saw you checking him out", he replied.

"He's nice looking and all but he don't have nothing on you", I said trying to hold in a smile.

"Whatever Jade. You know y'all women love guys with them green eyes", he said.

"That kind of stuff don't interest me", I lied.

"Oh yeah, you're all about the personality", he replied sarcastically.

"I am."

His cell phone went off; alerting him he had a text message. He took his wallet out of his pocket and pulled out two twenty dollar bills. "Hey, I gotta run", he said and placed the money on the table. "This should take care of the bill and the tip."

"Where are you going?" I inquired.

"Like I said, I got to go", he replied and stood up.

"But Eli, can't it-"

"I'll call you later Jade", he said before pecking me on the cheek.

I was left sitting there wondering what was so important that he had to run out on me.

Sierra

Kiki had just come back to the spa and Jazmin wasn't with her.

"Where's Jazmin? Is she okay?" I asked her before she could get in the door.

"To answer your first question, she's with a relative...her and the kids. To answer your second question, she's okay, considering..."

"What happened", I finished her statement.

"We did take out a police report and a restraining order against him", she said plopping down in one of the chairs in the waiting area.

"That's a start", I commented.

Kiki gave me a serious look. "Sierra, that was really noble of you to share that story about your mom. I'm sure it's something you don't like to think of or talk about, but I really believe it opened Jazmin's eyes."

"I felt that it needed to be told. It was worth reliving those memories if it's going to save someone else's life", I replied.

"I just pray that she doesn't let him sweet talk her into coming back to him."

"Yeah, me too."

"Is everything okay with Jazmin?" Michelle asked as she entered the waiting area.

"Yeah, she's okay", Kiki and I said in unison.

"Good because she looked bad this morning. That's the worse I have ever seen her", she said.

"Why don't you get the others and tell them to come out here so I can talk to them", I told her.

"Latoya and Kiona are still with their clients, but everyone else is still available", she said before returning to the beauty area.

Once everyone had gathered in the waiting area, I began to inform them about Jazmin's situation.

Before I could finish, Danny said, "I done heard

how that trifling husband of hers done beat her behind again."

Danny was gay and proud of it. Flamboyant was the one word to describe him. He stood at six feet, with flawless skin the color of caramel. He was a work of art, with brown eyes, full lips, chiseled features, and curly hair. He was a fantastic stylist and maintained a loyal list of clients. Once he styled your hair, you were bound to come back.

"Yes Danny...unfortunately her husband beat her again. He really did a number on her this time", I said.

"But this time, we were able to convince her to admit what was going on and get some help", Kiki added.

"Where is she now?" Destiny asked.

"She's with relatives", Kiki answered.

"And her husband came in here this morning trying to make her leave with him. He left after I threatened to call the police", I informed them.

"Poor Jazmin", Destiny said, with a look of sympathy on her face.

Danny tugged on the scarf around his neck with one hand and put the other hand on his hip. "Honey, aint no man putting his hands on me...and if he do, that will be his first and his last time, 'cause I will take a brick to that skull."

"I know that's right" Michelle said, giving Danny a high five.

"I'm giving her some time off so she can get herself together. In the meantime, if her husband comes in here, call the police", I said.

"And do not tell him where she is, because he doesn't know", Kiki added.

"You all can let Latoya and Kiona know what's going on and I'll fill Angel in when she comes in tomorrow", I said before letting them get back to their stations.

I grabbed Kiki's arm. "Hold up. I need to talk to you", I told her.

"What's up?" she asked.

"I just want to thank you for stepping in and

helping Jazmin like that."

"Don't thank me. I would've done it for any woman going through that", she said and walked away.

"Tyler, do you mind if I hang out with the girls for a little while tonight?" I asked while clearing the dinner table.

"So you're going to see Taylor and Jade?" he asked.

"Yes", I lied. I was really going to see Alexis, but I didn't want Tyler to know because I knew it would cause a problem.

As if reading my mind, he asked, "Do you still see Alexis?"

I didn't want him to know that I saw her on a regular basis. But I didn't want to lie to him because I knew it would come back to bite me in the ass. So I said, "Yeah, I see her every now and then. She still comes to the spa to get serviced."

"So you just see her on a business level?" he asked with a suspicious look on his face.

"Honestly Tyler. What do you have against Alexis?" I asked them.

He walked over to the sink, pretending to be cleaning. His body language told me that he didn't want to be having that conversation. But he initiated it, so I wasn't going to back down.

"Well?" I asked after he didn't answer.

"Well what Sierra?" he replied.

"What do you have against Alexis?" I asked once again. I stood directly in front of him.

"I don't have anything against Alexis", he said, refusing to look at me.

"Yes, you do. You don't want me hanging out with her", I said.

"Like I told you before, you don't really know anything about her. And all of a sudden, you want to be her friend, just because she came to your spa", he replied.

I thought back to the reaction he had the night I introduced him to Alexis. "Tyler, were you telling me the truth when you said you had never met Alexis prior to the night at the *Cheesecake Factory*?"

He dried his hands with a paper towel, threw it in the trash and said, "I'm your husband Sierra. And if you don't believe what I say, then we have a problem." He walked out of the kitchen, leaving me there to ponder what he had said. He was right. I'm supposed to trust him, but I couldn't help but to doubt this trust thing. All sorts of thoughts were running through my mind, thoughts I couldn't dismiss.

"Alexis, do you have any idea why Tyler doesn't want me hanging out with you?" I asked her after taking a sip of my white wine.

She flopped down on the couch beside me and crossed her legs, exposing a lot of skin. She was wearing one of those chiffon house gowns she always wore.

"For the umpteenth time...no Sierra!" she yelled.

I sat my glass down on one of the coasters on top of the glass and marble coffee table. "I'm sorry Alexis. It's just weird that he's acting like that towards you. And from what both of you say he has no reason to."

"So what has he said about me lately to have you asking me that?" she asked, lying her head on her arm, that was resting on the back of the couch.

I took another sip of my wine and placed it back on the coffee table. "Nothing, really. Tonight he just asked me had I seen you lately", I replied, hoping she wouldn't inquire about my response.

"And what did you tell him?" she asked.

I hesitated before saying, "I told him yes."

She gave me a penetrating look.

"Okay...I did make it seem like it was only on a business level", I confessed.

"Sierra, it's perfectly okay for you not to want your husband to know that you're spending time with the person you're having an affair with", she stated.

"First of all, he doesn't know about us. And second, we're not having an affair", I protested.

She started shaking her head and making sucking sounds with her teeth. "You can try to sugar coat it all you want Sierra, but it is what it is. You are a married woman who's cheating on her husband. And where I come from, that's considered having an affair. My being a woman, makes no difference", she explained. As she talked, she ran her hand up and down my arm.

I understood what she was saying, but I still didn't want to agree with her. I knew what I was doing wasn't right, but I didn't consider it a big deal. Yet, I knew I could never tell Tyler. The average man would find it exciting and maybe even ask to join in. But I knew Tyler wouldn't see it that way. His feelings and ego would be hurt. He wouldn't be too understanding. He'd say I turned to her because he didn't satisfy me. I had to take what was going on between Alexis and me to my grave.

"You want some more wine?" Alexis asked, jarring me out of my thoughts. I looked at the empty glass on the coffee table. I didn't even remember emptying it.

"Sure", I said, holding up the empty glass. Since becoming involved with Alexis, drinking wine had become a regular pass time for me. But it did seem to help me relax. Tyler and I only drank wine occasionally.

Alexis returned from her mini bar, holding a glass that contained a darker liquid. "What's that?" I asked her, as she handed the glass to me.

"It's a merlot. Try it, you'll like it", she replied before sitting back on the couch.

I took a sip of the dark wine. Its sweet taste was unexpected, yet pleasing to the palette. Before I knew it, I had emptied the glass once again. And once again, Alexis re-filled it with the sweet tasting wine.

The wine began to affect me and I knew there was no way I could drive home. Even though it was late, I decided to wait for the wine to wear off. In the meantime, Alexis and I talked. I mean really talked. I found out a lot about her.

She told me about her childhood. She was from the small town of Shelby. Her mother was white and her father was black, but her mother raised her alone, because her father's family wasn't too happy that he had conceived a child with a white woman. Growing up, she related more to her white background and didn't consider herself black.

She informed me that all of the black girls in school teased and bullied her, because she hung out with the white girls. "They use to call me a stuck-up bitch", she told me through tears.

I wiped away her tears and continued to listen to her share her memories. She went on to say that even the black boys had a problem with her. They use to say that she thought she was too good to be associated with them, because she was 'high yellow'.

"They all judged me without even knowing me, Sierra. They didn't know that my black relatives didn't even acknowledge my existence. I lived what I knew and what I knew was white. And I wasn't about to change just because some stupid kids couldn't deal with the fact that I chose one race over another." She spoke as if she was talking to those kids that judged her.

I wanted to ease her pain. I wanted her to know that I would never judge her and I understood why she chose to live the way she did. I wanted to let her know that she wasn't the only one that had a rough childhood. Instead, I continued to listen.

She started doing some modeling after finishing high school. Then one day, she decided she wanted to be a lawyer, so she packed her bags, moved to Durham and enlisted at North Carolina Central University. She said she chose the HBCU because she wanted to connect with her black roots. There she met her ex-husband Demond, who was like a modern day Black Panther. His consciousness and charm swept her off of her feet. He made her realize she should be proud to be black no matter how her father and his family acted.

They got married after they both graduated. Their dream was to open a law practice together. Now that they were divorced, she was going at it alone.

"Just when you think you know somebody...they do something that changes everything", she said, almost to herself. She was staring off into space with a blank look on her face.

"Alexis, are you okay?" I asked her.

"Uh...yes...I'm fine Sierra", she replied, snapping out of her trance.

"You looked like you were out of it for a minute there", I told her.

Not responding to my comment, she said, "It's funny how you can love someone with all your heart and soul and then realize they don't feel the same way. It's like your whole relationship was a lie."

"Are you referring to your ex-husband?" I asked.

"I gave that man everything he wanted. When he was hungry, I cooked for him. When he was tired, I rubbed his back. And when he wanted sex, I fucked him all night long. Now what do I have to show for it?" She looked over at me. "Memories", she said, answering her own question.

I reached over and pulled her to me and stroked her hair. I really didn't know what to say to her. I couldn't relate to how she felt. Tyler was the only man I had ever loved. So fortunately for me, I had never experienced a broken heart.

She began to sob uncontrollably. It was as if all the pain and frustration had been built up inside of her. I continued to hold her and stroke her hair. I didn't need to say anything to make her feel better. I think my presence alone was enough. We embraced for the rest of the night, until we both drifted off to sleep.

When I woke up again, it was four o'clock in the morning. I jumped up, "Holy shit!" I yelled, waking Alexis.

I grabbed my phone out of my purse. I had six missed calls from Tyler. I started frantically putting on my clothes. "I can't believe I let this happen. Tyler is going to kill me!" I yelled.

"Calm down Sierra", Alexis said, grabbing my arm.

I snatched my arm out of her grasp. "I can't calm down Alexis. I've never stayed out this late before."

"You're a grown woman", she said.

"I'm also a married woman", I said and slipped on

my shoes. "Any way...I gotta go Alexis!"

"Call me or text me to let me know you got home safe", she demanded.

I didn't even give her a chance to walk me to the door. I told her bye and darted outside to my car.

I sped all the way home, hoping I wouldn't get stopped by a cop and that Tyler would be in the bed asleep.

To my dismay, he wasn't in the bed when I arrived home. He was sitting at the island drinking out of his favorite mug. When he heard me come in, he slammed the mug down on the counter, causing the liquid to splash out. "Where have you been?" he asked without looking up.

"I told you where I was going Tyler", I answered, knowing he wasn't going to accept that answer.

"Sierra...are you seeing another man?" he asked, still looking down.

"No Tyler...of course not. What makes you ask something like that?" I walked over to him, stood behind him and placed my hands on his shoulders. I felt him tense up under my touch.

"I called Taylor and Jade. Both of them said they had not seen you. So if you weren't with them, where were you?" He turned around to face me. The look in his eyes was cold. And for the first time, I noticed he had been crying.

I didn't want to lie to Tyler, but I knew I couldn't tell him that I was with Alexis. Instead of answering his question, I said, "So you're checking up on me now?"

"Don't turn this around on me. I wasn't checking up on you. I was worried about you...like a good husband should be!" he yelled.

"Tyler, it's not what you think...I promise."

"My wife stays out all night and lies about who she's with. Then when I ask her where she was, she avoids the question. But it's not what I think", he said as if he was talking to someone else instead of me.

I tried pleading with him. "Tyler, I know it sounds bad, but-"

244

"I'm going to bed Sierra. I waited up for you because I wanted to make sure you were okay. Until you can tell me the truth, I don't want to hear anything you have to say. Goodnight. Or should I say good morning?" He brushed pass me and left me standing in the kitchen.

I knew it wasn't a good idea to try to reason with him. He was upset and I totally understood why. I didn't know what made me feel worse, him thinking I was with another man or me not coming clean about who I was really with. Either way I knew I had to make things right, but it would have to wait. I was tired, so I made my way upstairs. Instead of going to our room, I retreated to the guest bedroom, where I fell asleep as soon as my head hit the pillow.

Taylor

As soon as I left David after our lunch date, I dialed Charles' number.

"I knew you'd be calling me soon", he said as soon as he answered.

"What kind of games are you playing Charles?" I asked him through clenched teeth.

"Calm down my dear. I'm not playing any games."

"Then why did you invite David and me to dinner?" I asked.

"I told you I wanted to see you again. And if that's how I can see you, then so be it."

"Both of our spouses are going to be there Charles. I don't see how that's going to be a substitute for one on one action", I told him.

"It doesn't matter Taylor. As long as I'm in your presence, I'll be satisfied. The love making will have to wait until we can find time...believe me, I will wait", he said.

Listening to him talk made me think of Anthony Brown. He was one of my clients when I was an escort. He wasn't the most attractive man, but he didn't mind spending his money on me. He had a good job and lived in a nice house all alone, because he had never been married or didn't have any kids. The first time he hired me, I accompanied him to a banquet for the company he worked for. After all the other men were ogling over me, he decided he wanted to see me on a regular basis. I was happy to oblige. But then things started getting weird after a while. He started treating me like I was his girlfriend, by trying to tell me what to do and wanting to know my every move. I had to remind him that I was hired pussy to him, nothing more. But for some reason, he wasn't seeing it that way. He started showing up on my other "jobs" causing scenes. I believe he may have been paying Rico, my agent for information because he seemed to always know where to find me. Of course Rico denied giving him information, claiming he would never jeopardize a job like that. But we all knew Rico was all about making money. And when money talked, he listened. Things with Anthony had gotten really bad. I started turning down dates with him. Once I convinced Candy, one of the other girls to take my place. She said when she showed up, he got really pissed. She said he paid her and sent her on her way. He called Rico and went off about how he wanted what he paid for and he didn't want any substitutes. Rico tried to force me to take him back as a client. I told him I would quit if he tried to make me deal with him again. Rico knew he didn't want to lose me, because I was the best girl he had. So he told Anthony that I no longer worked for him and hooked him up with another girl. I never heard from him after that.

Now, I had a lot more at stake. My marriage was at stake, which only meant that my fortune was at stake. I really didn't know how far Charles would go, but I was determined to do what I had to do to keep him from jeopardizing my current arrangement. "Exactly, what is your goal Charles?" I asked him.

"My goal is to spend as much time with you as I possibly can", he said in a serious tone.

"What if I said that may not be possible?" I asked him.

"It would be in your best interest to make it possible", he answered.

"And if I don't?"

"Well...let's just say that I may have to spend that time with David. And who knows what we'll end up talking about, especially when your name comes up."

"Are you trying to blackmail me?" I asked.

"Call it what you want", he said.

"I'm calling it as I see it. I'm hoping you wouldn't stoop to that level", I replied.

"Sometimes, we have to take extreme measures to get what we want Taylor. You of all people should know that."

"And what's that supposed to mean?" I asked him.

"You are married to a man that you neither desire nor love so you can be taken care of financially", he said, as if I had told him that myself.

"You have no idea what you're talking about. You don't know anything about me", I replied with irritation in my voice. He had no right to try poke his nose into my business.

He started laughing before saying, "Take it easy Taylor. It really doesn't matter to me why you married David. As far as not knowing anything about you, I'm trying to change that. I'll look forward to seeing you and David for dinner...I'll be waiting. Enjoy the rest of your day." And for the second time, he hung up on me.

I stood there for a few seconds, still holding the phone to my ear. I couldn't believe Charles was trying to blackmail me. How could I let myself get into such a mess? I was the one to do the blackmailing. I guess Karma had finally found its way to my door. I had to figure a way out of this. It wasn't that I didn't want to be with Charles. I just didn't like anyone having that type of control over me. I had enough of that when I was living with my mother.

"I'll figure something out", I said out loud to myself. "I need a drink."

I was on my way to our fully stocked bar, when I noticed the door to David's office was open. He never left that door open, unless he was in there. I was about to close it until curiosity got the best of me. My thoughts went to those papers he hid that night. Now was my time to find out what they were.

I walked over to his desk and pulled on the drawer I saw him put the papers in. It was locked. I was determined to find out what was in that drawer. I started looking everywhere for a key. I knocked some papers on the floor. When I reached down to pick them up, I saw a little slot on the underside of the desk. Just as I hoped, there was a key in there. I used the key to unlock the drawer. There were papers and photos in there. I piled them on top of the desk. First I scanned through the photos. I could tell they were old. There was one of

David's parents and a little girl. Even though they were a lot younger, I could tell it was them, but I had no idea who the little girl was. Then I came across another one of the same little girl, only a little older. She was decked out in a pink and white dress, white tights and black patent leather shoes. Her hair was tied up in pink and white ribbons. As cute as she was, she didn't look too happy. There were a few more photos of her and a couple more of her and David's mother. I found it odd that David wasn't in any of the photos. I scanned through the papers and nothing of interest stuck out. Then I came across a birth certificate. It was for a Deana Jo Morgan, born to John and Claire Morgan. David never mentioned he had a sister. He always said he was an only child. But I was looking at proof that he wasn't. Maybe something happened…like she died in a tragic accident or something when she was young. Was that her in the photos? Why were David and his family being so secretive about her? Maybe he was just like me. He had parts of his past he wanted to forget about and pretend they never existed. There were so many unanswered questions. I wanted to know who Deana Jo was, but I had to be discreet. I couldn't risk David finding out I had been snooping. He trusted me and I wanted to keep it that way. I put everything back exactly how I found them. Then I thought of how I was going to get information from David without him getting suspicious.

David and I were in bed together watching TV for the first time in weeks. I took it as an opportunity to get him to discuss his childhood.

"Honey, do you regret us not having a baby?" I asked him.

He gave me a weird look. "I wouldn't say I regret it. I'm sure it would be nice to have some little ones running around. But you know I can't have children due to my low sperm count."

"Yeah, I know. I was just wondering if you felt like you were missing out on something", I said.

"With my job, it's probably for the best. I already feel like I neglect you. I couldn't bear the thought of not being around for my children. It's harder on them than it is on adults. They don't understand that Daddy has to work all the time", he said with his voice cracking a little.

"You sound like you're speaking from experience. Is that how you guys felt about your father?" I asked, hoping he would reveal some information.

"My mother was kind of use to it. But it really used to upset me when my father wasn't around. I felt he was putting his job before me. And being an only child didn't help any. It was always just me and my mother. If I had someone to play with, I don't think it would have been as bad. But I've forgiven my father, because I now know if he hadn't been so career driven, I wouldn't be the success I am today."

He had come right out and said he was an only child. There was no tragic story of how he had lost his sister. There was no mention of a sister being confined to a mental institution. He just confirmed he was hiding something.

Jade

"Sierra, what is going on with you girl?" I had just called her spa.

"Nothing Jade. Why do you ask?" she replied.

"Oh, I don't know...I guess your husband calling me in the middle of the night looking for you kind of alerted me that something's going on", I said sarcastically.

"Oh that...well everything's okay now", she said in a way that didn't sound too convincing.

"Sierra...are you having an affair?" I asked her, not sure of what her response was going to be.

"Of course not, Jade. How could you even think something like that?"

"I'm sorry. It's just that when Tyler called and said you told him you were with me and Taylor, that's the first thing that came to my mind...what would you think?"

"Well, it's not what you think."

"So is everything okay?"

"Everything's fine."

"Are you sure?"

"Yes, I'm sure, so can we change the subject?"

"Uh...yeah, I guess so. But remember, I'm here if you need someone to talk to", I told her.

"Thanks, I'll keep that in mind."

"Have you talked to Taylor lately?" I asked her, picking up on the irritation in her voice.

"Not in a couple of days", she said.

We chatted for a few more minutes. She asked me how things were going at work with my new position. I filled her in about my conversation with Mr. Lawson. She told me how good business was going with her. She also told me about Jazmin, her receptionist. I felt bad for her, but was glad that she was finally doing something about the situation. No woman should have to go through that. If Eli ever hit me, I would stab him in his sleep. My mother always told me if a man hit you, he didn't love you.

"Well Jade, my next appointment is here. I'll get with you later", she said.

"Okay girl...and remember what I told you", I told her.

"Okay, bye."

"Bye."

After I hung up the phone, I started thinking about Sierra's behavior. When Tyler first called, I was caught off guard. When I told him Sierra wasn't with me, he thought I was joking at first. I told him that I wasn't joking and I had not seen Sierra since the gathering at my place. I could tell he wasn't too happy, because he mumbled something under his breath. He apologized for calling me so late and hung up.

Then Sierra just acted like everything was smooth sailing. I wanted to believe her when she said she wasn't having an affair, but things weren't adding up. First she lied to Tyler about who she was with. Then when I asked her about it, she just brushed it off, like it was no big deal. I've known Sierra for a long time and I consider her my best friend. All I can do is hope that everything is okay with her.

My inside line rang. "Jade speaking", I chirped into the receiver.

"Hey, I was just checking to see if you were in your office. You have a package", Charlene, the receptionist said, in her usual hyper tone.

"Well, what is it?" I asked.

"I don't know. It's wrapped in pretty red paper and there's no return address. I'll bring it to you."

"Thanks", I said. I had no idea what it could be. I hadn't ordered anything lately. And even if I did, I wouldn't have it delivered to my job.

Charlene tapped on my door, which was already open. We all did that out of respect for each other's privacy.

"Come on in", I instructed her.

She was carrying a box wrapped in red paper with a big white bow on it. She set it down on my desk. I just looked at it for a few seconds, not sure what to do. Maybe

Eli was making up for running out on me at *PF Chang's*. I hadn't talked to him since, even though I tried calling him several times and left a couple of messages.

The suspense was killing me, so I decided to open the package. Then I realized Charlene was still standing in my office. She had a look of anticipation on her face. "Charlene, thanks for bringing this", I said, pointing to the package and giving her the cue to leave.

She hesitated for a few seconds and said, "No problem Jade." She walked towards the door in what seemed like the slowest pace possible.

I knew she was anxious to see what was in that package, considering she was nosey as hell. Everyone called her the office gossip, because she was always in somebody's business, circulating rumors. Before she left my office, she looked back at me. I gave her my 'you can go' look and said, "Close the door behind you."

As soon as she closed the door, I ripped open the package to reveal a cardboard box. "Eli went through a lot of trouble", I said out loud.

I grabbed the letter opener and used it to puncture the tape on the box. Once I opened the box, I removed the crumpled tissue paper and couldn't believe my eyes. There was a *Bratz* doll with a knife through her head. Her hair had been chopped off, along with her hands and feet. I was almost afraid to pick it up, but I noticed a piece of paper underneath it. I picked up the doll long enough to grab the paper.

It was a handwritten note that read: Bitch, you're next! I balled up the paper and threw it in the trash. At that point, I felt like crying. Feelings of regret seeped through my body. Maybe I had gone too far with the photos of Paige. If I would've known I was dealing with a psycho bitch that would be out for revenge, I would've reconsidered the whole idea. I knew she didn't have a chance at getting that promotion. But that day, when I saw her riding Robert's dick, I knew she'd take drastic measures to get what she wanted and I was not about to sit back and let her fuck her way to the top. But now, I was feeling like it wasn't worth what I was dealing with.

She was like a thorn in my side, that wasn't going away.

There was only one thing left to do. I had to tell Mr. Lawson about my involvement in circulating those photos. Maybe he would consider giving Paige her job back and my life could go back to normal. I'm pretty sure he won't be too happy to learn that I had something to do with it, but I just have to confess.

I picked up the phone and dialed his extension. "Lawson speaking", his voice boomed over the receiver.

"Hey Mr. Lawson. This is Jade. Can I come talk to you? It's really important."

I heard him blow into the receiver. "Uh...Jade can it wait until tomorrow? Today is my anniversary. I was just about to cut out. Got something special planned for the wife."

I hesitated before saying, "Sure Mr. Lawson. I guess it can wait until tomorrow."

"Are you sure?" he asked.

"Yes, I'm sure. I don't want your wife mad at me for screwing up your plans", I answered.

"Well, if you're sure, I guess I'll see you tomorrow", he said.

"Sounds good...Happy anniversary Mr. Lawson", I replied.

"Thanks Jade", he said before hanging up.

I looked down at the crazy looking doll. For the first time, I noticed what I assumed was fake blood dried up on both sides of the doll's head. Yes, that Paige was definitely psychotic.

As I was leaving work later, Charlene was still sitting at her desk. I was hoping she would be gone before I left, because I knew she was going to be asking questions. Unlike everyone else, I didn't have a problem with putting her in her place. But I really wasn't in the mood.

"See you tomorrow Charlene", I said trying to zoom by her desk.

"So...what was in that mystery package you received earlier?" she asked, pointing to the box I was obviously trying to hide from her view.

"Nothing important", I answered.

"Well, if it's nothing important, let me see it", she said, holding her hand out for me to give her the box.

I couldn't believe she was being so out right nosey. I felt that was a bit much, even for her. I could've been a bitch and cursed her out, but I decided to keep it professional. "It's rather personal, so I'd prefer not to disclose it."

She turned her mouth up into a frown and said, "Fine with me. I didn't really want to see it anyway."

"Yeah, I'm sure", I said and walked out the door.

As soon as I stepped into my apartment, I dialed Eli's number. I was no longer upset with him for running out on me. I just needed someone to talk to and confide in.

"Hey baby. What's up?" he said when he finally answered his phone.

"Hey Eli...you busy?"

"No. Not at the moment. What's shaking?"

"Can you come by tonight? I really need to see you", I pleaded.

"Oh, I see. You need some of this thug passion", he said in his sexy voice.

"No, it's nothing like that", I replied, hoping not to disappoint him.

"Then what is it?" he asked.

"I'd rather not discuss it over the phone. Are you coming over or what?" I asked, getting a little irritated.

"Calm down baby. I'll be over. Do you want me to bring anything?"

"Yeah, your ears and shoulders."

"It's like that?" he asked.

"Yes, unfortunately it is", I answered.

"Well, I'll see ya' later."

After I hung up with him, I hopped into the shower. I stayed in the shower longer than usual. The hot water felt good spraying my skin. I washed my body three times before finally ending my shower. And because I knew hot showers can dry out the skin, I rubbed my

Carol's Daughter Jamaican Punch body oil all over my damp skin. I threw on a pair of my comfortable pajamas and headed for the kitchen. I opened the fridge in search of some dinner ideas, realizing there weren't any.

"I need to go grocery shopping", I said to my empty fridge. I looked in my pantry and grabbed the box of *Special K.* "This will have to do." I was about to grab a bowl out of the cabinet, when there was a knock on my door.

I looked out the peephole and saw Eli's face. I opened the door to let him in. To my surprise, he had a pizza and beer in his hands. I grabbed the beer out of his hand and kissed him on the lips. "I knew there was a reason why I love you", I told him as I set the beer down on the counter. He came behind me and put the pizza down.

"Is it because I brought beer?" he asked, kissing me on my neck.

"No, it's because you brought food. I was about to fix a bowl of cereal."

"Well, I'm glad I could be of assistance", he said, showing his pearly whites.

I grabbed two paper plates and we sat down and got to work on the pizza. I wasn't much of a beer drinker, but I figured it would relax me a little. So I popped open a can and took a big gulp.

After finishing his second slice of pizza, Eli said, "So what's on your mind baby girl?"

I took another sip of my beer. "Well...I got something really disturbing today...Why don't I just show it to you?" I got up and grabbed the box off the table by the door. "Check this out", I said and shoved the box in his face.

"What is it?" he asked.

"Just open it. You've got to see it to believe it", I told him.

He opened the box, scrunched up his face and said, "What in the hell is this?"

"It's a doll."

"I can see that", he said frowning at me. "I mean

who did this and why?"

"It was delivered to my job today. There was a note inside saying, you're next. I can only assume it's from Paige", I said.

Eli put the box on the counter. "Well if she did that, she's one psycho bitch."

"My sentiments, exactly...and the truth is, I'm starting to get worried", I said, meaning every word.

He started working on his third slice of pizza and opened another can of beer. I could tell he was thinking about something. He took a swig of his beer and let out a burp. He stared at me for a few seconds before saying anything. "Jade, on a serious tip, what's the real deal with you and this Paige broad?"

"That's part of the reason I wanted to talk to you-"

He interrupted me. Now if y'all are lovers or something, I can deal with that." He had a devious smile on his face.

I rolled my eyes at him. "I hate to burst your little fantasy bubble, but we are not lovers. And FYI, I have never had, or will ever have a female lover. So you can wipe that stupid grin off your face", I told him.

He threw his hands up in the air and said, "You can't blame a brotha for trying."

"Can we get back to the subject at hand?"

"Sure."

I went on to explain to him the situation with Paige. I gave him all of the details on what happened and how everything went down.

"So she knows it was you and that's why she's harassing you?" he asked after I had filled him in.

"No, she doesn't *know* for a fact. After Mr. Lawson fired her, she did confront me saying she knew I had something to do with it. And she said I was jealous because I knew she was going to get the position. But there's no way she could've known I did it, because I made sure I covered my tracks", I explained.

"Damn. And all this time, I thought you were so sweet and innocent. I didn't think you had an evil bone in your body. I'm kind of turned on."

"I'm not evil. I just didn't want to see her get a promotion she didn't deserve, just because she let Robert fuck her."

"I can understand that."

"So you're not mad?" I asked him.

"No...why should I be mad? You didn't get me fired."

"Well. I thought maybe you would look at me in a different way."

He pulled me over to him, so I was standing in front of him, between his legs. "Look Jade. I'm not here to judge you. You did what you had to do...Now we can sit here and talk about this the rest of the night...or you can let me take you into your bedroom and fuck the hell out of you. The choice is yours."

"Um, I like it when you talk like that", I said, rubbing his erection through his pants.

He scooped me up into his muscular arms and carried me into my bedroom. As soon as we were inside, we started removing our clothes until we were both naked. Eli pushed me back on my bed and spread my legs. He kissed my clit and spread my lips apart, while inserting two fingers inside me. I whimpered under his touch, not wanting it to end. He feasted on me and stroked my g-spot until orgasmic waves crept through my body.

Afterwards, he shoved his manhood into my mouth and I sucked him until he was almost at the point of explosion. "Turn over", he ordered me. "I need that pussy now."

I did as I was told and got on all fours. Eli entered me, slowly at first. Then he quickened the pace, making me cry out in pleasure.

"Damn, this is some good pussy", he said while smacking me on the ass.

He withdrew from me and said, "Lay on your back."

Once again, I did as I was told. He put my legs over his shoulders and continued stroking me. He was pounding my pussy as if he wanted to put his whole body inside of me. He was panting and breathing hard.

In between breaths, he said, "Aint no woman ever took this dick like you baby...you da' fucking bomb!"

He slowed down the pace and leaned closer to my face. Then he took his right hand and put it around my neck. He continued to pump my pussy while gripping my neck tighter. I was afraid and turned on at the same time.

"This is my pussy", he whispered in my ear. "And you better not ever give my pussy away!" He went a few more seconds before yelling out, "Awww shit!" And from the look on his face, I knew he was coming. He collapsed on top of me and nestled his head on my breasts.

I was happy at that moment. All thoughts of Paige and her psychotic *Bratz* doll were in the back of my mind. Being with Eli made me feel safe and secure. As long as I had him, I knew everything was going to be okay.

Sierra

Tyler was really pissed off with me. This morning, he didn't say one word to me, even after I tried talking to him. I didn't like it when Tyler and I were on bad terms. In the past when we had disagreements, we talked them over and made things right. We never went to bed angry with each other. Tyler always said, "If I die in my sleep, I wouldn't want my last words to you to be bad ones."

Now things were different. And for the life of me, I couldn't understand why. It's like Tyler changed on me overnight. We were always viewed as the perfect happy couple.

I felt that my relationship with Alexis happened because of Tyler. He pushed me right into her arms. Alexis gave me what he wasn't giving me. And I had no intentions of giving her up anytime soon. But I also knew that I had to make things right with Tyler. There's no way I'm going to be in the same house with him, and have him ignoring me. Something had to be done. The only option was to tell him the truth about where I really was. I couldn't keep letting him think I was out with another man.

When Jade asked me was I cheating on Tyler, my heart dropped. And when I told her I wasn't, I didn't consider it a lie. I knew she was inquiring about another man. I felt bad about keeping secrets from her. But there was no way I would tell her or Taylor about my relationship with Alexis. They wouldn't understand. Besides, I didn't need them judging me. Hell, we all had our issues. Jade was sleeping with a married man and didn't know it, even though the signs were there. We all knew Taylor was only with David because of his money and was cheating on him every chance she got.

A tap came on my door, jarring me out of my thoughts. I looked up and was surprised to see Tyler standing there. "What are you doing here?" I asked him and stood up. Tyler hardly ever came by my spa, so I knew it was serious.

"We need to talk Sierra", he said.

"Yes, we sure do", I said.

"You got time to talk?" he asked.

I had just finished my last morning appointment and didn't have another one until later. "Yeah, sure", I answered.

"You got somewhere we can talk?" he asked.

"We can go to the café next door", I said, holding my hand out to let him go ahead of me.

"Can you hold the fort down? I'll be back", I said to Kiki, who was at the front desk.

"Sure thing boss lady", she smiled, showing all of her teeth.

Tyler and I both ordered regular coffee once we got to the café. We sat in silence for a few seconds, just staring at each other. So I decided to jump start the conversation. "Baby, I'm sorry about last night."

"I want to believe you're sorry Sierra, but I can't help but to think that you're not being completely honest with me", he said.

I took a deep breath. "You're right Tyler. I wasn't completely honest with you."

The look on his face was one of total fear. He looked as if he wanted to cover his ears and run out of the café.

"So tell me the truth", he said.

"Well, as you know, I wasn't with Jade and Taylor. I was with Alexis", I confessed and waited for him to respond.

"You're lying", he said without blinking.

"No...I'm not. I went to her house. We had a few drinks and I fell asleep", I said.

"You gotta do a helluva lot better than that Sierra. If that was the case, you would've said that last night", he said, a little too loud.

I leaned closer to him so no one could hear our conversation. "I didn't say anything because I knew you would be upset."

"Upset? Upset? Hell, I was already upset Sierra", he said, loud enough for other people to hear.

I looked around the café. "Keep your voice down Tyler. People are staring at us. What I meant is that I knew you didn't want me hanging out with Alexis."

"So you let me think you were out with another man instead", he said looking directly into my eyes.

"I wouldn't say that I intentionally let you think that. I just didn't want you to know that I lied to you. And I'm truly sorry for that", I explained.

"Are you really?" he asked.

"Yes I am. But you gotta cut me some slack Tyler. You were so adamant about me not being friends with Alexis, yet you haven't given me one good reason why you feel that way. Both of you keep saying you don't know each other. It just doesn't make sense", I said, while shaking my head from side to side.

He leaned back in his chair and looked down at the table. "I just got a vibe from her."

"A vibe?"

"Yes, Sierra. A vibe. I'm pretty good at picking up negative energy from people. I got that from her when you introduced us."

I laughed at him. "Tyler, you really need to stop. Alexis is good people."

"And you know this how?" he asked.

"I *have* spent a lot of time with her. She's told me a lot about herself. Like I said before, she's divorced. She's a lawyer trying to open her own firm. She is-"

"Why did she get divorced?" he asked.

"Damn Tyler. What's up with the questioning? She got divorced because she caught her husband with another woman, and she couldn't deal with it."

"Oh...that's too bad", he said with a hint of sarcasm.

Tyler had never shown that much interest in any of my friends. I still had a strange feeling about the whole situation, but I wasn't going to dwell on it. At least he was talking to me.

"So are we okay now?" I asked, hoping that we

were.

He blew air through his lips. "I would like to say that we are, Sierra. But I'm still having a hard time about you lying to me."

"I said I was sorry and you know my reason for lying to you. I can't take it back. All I can do is promise you that it won't happen again. And what I need from you is for you to stop trying to dictate who I choose as my friends. I think I'm old enough to handle that task myself."

He stared at me for a few seconds. Then I saw a smile slowly appear on his face. "Maybe I've overreacted. I know you're capable of choosing your friends...although the jury's still out on Taylor." We both laughed. He continued. "But anyway...Sierra, I love you baby. And I will do everything in my power to keep this marriage together. Like I've said a thousand times, my family means everything to me. I don't want to live my life without you and Shelby in it. That's the way it's supposed to be...the American dream, a man, his wife, and their children."

I gave him a skeptical look, wondering what book he saw that in. But I decided not to say anything. I didn't want to spoil the moment. Instead I said, "I love you too Tyler and I want us to be together forever. So from here on out, no more secrets or lies."

"Sounds good to me", he said and leaned over and kissed me on the lips.

I eagerly welcomed his kiss, enjoying the softness of his lips. It felt good to kiss him like that. I was really about to get into it until I remembered we were in a public place. I pulled away and said, "I guess we'll have to continue this later."

He smiled and said, "I guess you're right."

We talked for a few more minutes, expressing our feelings for each other. We both made a pact that we were going to work on our marriage by communicating more and compromising. Then he walked me back over to the spa.

"I need to get back to work", he said as we got to

the door.

"Okay, I'll see ya' later this evening."

He pulled me to him and wrapped his arms around my waist. "Maybe I can cook us a special dinner tonight."

"What about Shelby? You gonna call Nikki?"

"There will be no need for that. I want it to be a family dinner", he said.

"Oh...okay."

"You and I can have our special night later", he said in a seductive voice.

"Um, I like the sound of that."

He kissed me on the forehead. "Bye baby. Love ya'."

"Love you too. Bye." I watched him walk to his car.

As I entered the spa, all sorts of things ran through my mind. I was glad that Tyler and I were back on good terms. He really surprised me by coming by. He had actually left work to come talk to me. I smiled to myself at the thought of it.

"Hey Sierra, Ms. Montague is here. She's in your office", Kiki said to me, just as I walked behind the front desk.

"Oh...I don't have an appointment with her, do I?" I asked her, trying to sound professional in case the busybodies were somewhere listening.

"No. She said she needed to see you about a personal business matter."

"Okay. Thanks." I walked back to my office. Alexis was kicked back in my chair like she owned the place.

"What are you doing here?" I asked her before closing the door behind me.

"I came to see you of course", she replied and then licked her lips seductively.

"I know that, but I thought you'd be in court."

She stood up and walked over to me. "That was this morning. I see you had a visitor. I guess he wasn't mad after all."

"Oh, he was mad alright. He was furious with me.

We didn't speak to each other at all this morning. He just came by to make amends. So now, we're okay", I replied. I didn't really want to talk about it with her, because she always tried to turn things around.

To my surprise, she said, "That's nice." Then she reached behind me and locked the door.

"Why did you do that?" I asked her. I had no idea what she was up to. And to be honest, I really wasn't in the mood to fool around with her...not that she didn't look incredible in her plum colored pantsuit. It looked like it was made for her and showed off her perfect figure. But I was really focusing on Tyler. I was happy that we made up and I didn't want to stray away from that.

"Don't play dumb", she said and kissed me on the lips.

I backed away from her. "Come on Alexis. I don't have time for this. I have things to do."

She pushed me up against the door. "I'm not gonna take up much of your time. I just want what I didn't get last night."

Then she forced her tongue in my mouth. Her lips tasted so sweet and I couldn't help but kiss her back. She traced my lips with her tongue and worked her way to my neck. I threw my head back as she unbuttoned my shirt. She pulled it off and hung it on the coat rack. Next, she removed my bra and released my breasts. My nipples hardened, just from her presence. She bent down and kissed each one. She then squeezed them together and ran her tongue over them. My body became weak and I wanted to push her away, but I continued letting her have her way with me.

Alexis suckled my breasts like a newborn baby. Ripples of pleasure ran through my body and I could feel a tingling sensation between my legs. "Damn, that feels so good", I whispered as she continued to suck on my breasts.

"You haven't seen anything yet", she said and proceeded to take my pants off.

"Let me help you with that", I told her and pulled off my pants and underwear.

She still had on her suit. "Aren't you going to take off your clothes?" I asked her.

"No, it's all about you right now", she replied.

She pulled me over to my desk. In one quick motion, she knocked everything on the floor.

"What is wrong with you? Are you crazy?" I asked her.

"Sit down on the desk", she said, ignoring my questions.

Without a second thought, I sat on the desk as she instructed. She opened my legs and put my feet up on the desk. She grabbed the chair behind her, pulled it closer to the desk and sat in it.

"Ooh, look at that pretty pussy", she said, licking her lips.

I couldn't believe how spontaneous Alexis was. Just thinking about it, made my juices flow.

"Um, looks like someone is just as horny as I am", she said and dipped her finger inside me and popped it in her mouth. "Tastes real good", she said. "Like honey."

My heart was beating so fast, I thought it was going to explode. I was so excited and ready for her.

As if reading my mind, she said, "Are you ready for me to eat that pussy?"

"Yes", I whispered.

"I can't hear you", she replied.

"Yes", I repeated.

"Then say it", she commanded.

"I'm ready for you to eat my pussy", I said loud and clear.

She parted my lips and started sucking on my clit. "Oh God, that feels good", I yelled out.

I leaned back and rested on my elbows so I could enjoy the pleasure I was receiving and watch at the same time. Alexis started licking my clit up and down. Then she inserted her tongue inside of me. "Aw shit Alexis...damn, that feels so damn good", I whispered, trying to keep my composure.

She continued to slurp on my womanhood, making me crazy. The more I moaned, the harder she sucked.

And just when I thought I couldn't take anymore, she inserted two fingers inside me. She looked up at me and said, "I'm gonna make you come like you've never came before."

She went back to feasting on me and fingering me. To top things off, she stuck a finger into my asshole, so I was getting triple pleasure and loving every second of it. As she munched on my pussy, stroked my g-spot, and fingered my asshole, I felt like I was in another world. It felt so incredible that I never wanted it to end. Nothing could've stopped me from enjoying that. Tyler could've walked in right then and there and I wouldn't have cared. The world could've come to an end and I wouldn't have noticed.

"Alexis...baby...I'm gonna...I'm gonna...come", I whispered, barely able to talk.

My body tensed up and a sensation filled me from my head to my toes. But the real explosion was between my legs. "I'm coming...I'm coming Alexis", I screamed, and fluids I didn't know existed shot out of me and saturated Alexis' face.

"Oh my God. What's happening to me?" I asked Alexis as the liquid continued to squirt out of me.

"You're coming baby", she said and licked her lips.

After my orgasm had subsided, and I caught my breath, I said, "Damn, I've never came like that in my entire life."

"I don't make promises I don't keep", she beamed.

I laughed at her because my secretions were glistening on her face.

"What are you laughing at?" she asked.

"You may want to wipe your face", I said

"Yeah, you did get me pretty good", she laughed.

"That really freaked me out. I had no idea women were capable of that."

"A lot of women don't know they can ejaculate just like men. I found out a long time ago, watching a porno. I was so turned on and fascinated by it. And the first time it happened to me, I was blown away."

"Well, you sure as hell just blew me away. That

was the best feeling in the world." I stood up. "Let me get you a towel so you can clean yourself up." I walked to the storage closet in the corner. I opened it and pulled out two fluffy white towels. I gave Alexis one of the towels. "You can use the mirror over there." I pointed to the wall.

She looked at the towel and then at me. "You do this often?" she asked.

"What do you mean?"

"You got towels on standby", she said smiling.

I held my hands up and looked around. "Hello...we are in a spa. Towels are part of my business."

"Don't get so bent out of shape. I'm just joking," she said.

"I know you are", I told her.

I cleaned myself up and put my clothes back on, while Alexis cleaned her face and reapplied her makeup. Then I proceeded to pick up the items Alexis had thrown on the floor in the heat of the moment.

"Let me help you with that", she said, rushing over to help me.

"Thanks for helping me clean up the mess you made", I said sarcastically.

"I guess I did get carried away, didn't I?"

"It's okay because it was well worth it."

We put everything back where it belonged; checking to make sure nothing was damaged. And for the first time, it dawned on me that we were pretty loud earlier.

Alexis noticed the concern on my face. "Are you okay?" she asked.

"I was just thinking..."

"About?"

"Do you think they could hear us?"

"Uh...I haven't thought about it honestly."

"We were pretty loud."

"I doubt they heard us. We're all the way back here and everyone is up front...unless there's someone in the massage room next door", she said.

I thought for a moment. "No...uh...Angel isn't here today...so no one should be in there."

"Girl, you worry too much. You need to relax and go with the flow", she said.

"That's easy for you to say. You have nothing to lose", I replied, irritated by her statement.

"So...it's like that Sierra? Because my husband already left me, I have nothing to lose?" she asked with a smirk on her face.

I reached out to her. "No, I didn't mean it like that Alexis."

"Well how did you mean it Sierra?" she said, backing away from me.

"I'm really sorry. It's just that you're always so spontaneous and nonchalant about things. I'm just not use to that. And I don't know what I'd do if Tyler found out about the things that I've done...for you", I explained.

She laughed. "So everything you've done, you did them for me?" she asked pointing to her chest.

"Yes, pretty much."

"So you let me eat your pussy until you came in my mouth...for me? Let me fuck you with a fake dick...for me? Let Boris fuck the hell out of you...for me? And ate my pussy...for me? Well maybe you did do that for me. You don't have to worry about doing anything else for me. I'm out." She grabbed her purse.

I grabbed her arm. "Wait, Alexis. Please don't leave."

She turned around to face me. She looked into my eyes. "Give me one good reason why I shouldn't leave."

I didn't know what to say. I did know that I didn't want her to leave...not like that. Being with her was the one exciting thing I had in my life. So I did the only thing I could think of. I grabbed her face and kissed her with all the passion I had in me.

She didn't respond at first. But I didn't back down. And within seconds, she was kissing me back. Our lips and tongues did a dance that seemed to last an eternity. We stopped to catch our breath. Then I tilted her head back and placed soft kisses on her neck. A moan escaped her throat, which encouraged me to go further. I started unbuttoning the blouse under her jacket. She grabbed my hand. "Wait, Sierra. We can save this for later", she said.

"But I want to now", I whined.

"I want to as well, but I really gotta go", she said, adjusting her blouse.

"Okay", I replied, sounding defeated.

"How 'bout you swing by tonight...or is Tyler gonna have a problem with that?" she asked rolling her eyes.

"I can't. Tyler has made dinner plans for us. And as far as him having a problem with it, that's over with. We have come to an agreement", I explained.

She gave me a questioning look. "Oh really?"

"Yes, he is to no longer question my friendship with you...at all."

"Then he shouldn't have a problem with you coming by tonight."

"I told you, he's making dinner for us. He'd be furious if I cancelled on him. I just can't do it Alexis...not after we just made up...I'm sorry." I could tell she was upset. It was like choosing Tyler over her, but I had no other choice. Postponing Tyler's dinner was not an option. She stood there for a while, not saying anything. She blew air threw her teeth and ran her fingers through her hair.

"Fine", was all she said when she did finally speak. Then she stormed out the door.

I didn't even bother going after her. I didn't want to draw attention to us up front. And to be honest, I really didn't have the strength to deal with her tantrum. She had no right to be upset with me for spending time with my husband, especially after what I had just shared with her. But I wasn't going to let it bother me. I had other things to be happy about. Tyler and I were back on good terms, and that's all that mattered.

Taylor

I was still suspicious of David and his secrets. Though I had my secrets, I didn't like the idea that he could be keeping some from me. He always had a squeaky clean image...at least since I've known him. But I've known him for only a short period of time. There's no telling what skeletons he may have in his closet. The question is would I care? He could be smuggling drugs in the country and using real estate as a front...or he could even have a love child with Suzanne. The truth is I wouldn't care. As long as it didn't affect my financial status, I was okay. I know that shouldn't be my only concern, but I have to be honest with myself.

Though I was seen as a gold digger or materialistic, I didn't intend to turn out that way. I tried not to be like my mother...I really did. But somehow I ended up going down that road. When I first moved to Durham, I met this guy named Brian. Brian was a student at *North Carolina A&T* in Greensboro, but he was staying with his cousin in Durham, while he was doing an internship. Brian swept me off my feet from the very start. He was sweet, caring, and not to mention sexy as hell. From the get go, I let him know that I wasn't looking for a fuck partner, and I was all about a serious relationship. He said he was cool with that because he wanted the same thing.

I made the mistake of having sex with him too soon. After that, things started to change. Or I could say, things didn't go anywhere from there. Our time together consisted of us sitting on the couch watching TV. Then later, after his cousin Daniel would retire to his bedroom, Brian would pull out the sofa bed. We would cuddle for a little while and then we'd get down to business. Afterwards, we would cuddle a little bit more and then I would go home.

That went on for a while, until I realized I wanted more than that. I started asking him about us going out sometime and spending time together outside of the bed. He always had one excuse after another. I finally told him that I couldn't proceed with the relationship if things didn't change. That's when he decided to tell me that he felt things were getting too serious and he was just looking for a good time. I was furious, as well as heart broken. I wasn't in love with him, but I did care for him. Things died out between us, because I stopped calling him. It was five or six months before I heard from him again. Apparently, he thought we could pick up where we left off. He wanted to see me, and like a fool I said yes.

We talked for a little while and then one thing led to another. Afterwards, I was disgusted with myself. He called me the following weekend. He wanted me to come to Greensboro to see him. I told him no and I never heard from him again.

After Brian, I promised myself that I would never let that happen again. But as we all know, sometimes promises are broken.

Leroy Hawkins eased his way into my heart faster than I could blink. I met him at a club in Raleigh, some of my old friends and I frequented at the time. He was a football player at *North Carolina State University*. I was introduced to him by a fellow teammate, who was also a friend of mine. Leroy was tall and very appealing. His confidence and charm won me over immediately. Before leaving the club, we exchanged numbers.

He called me the next day and we had a very intelligent and interesting conversation. He asked me, "Are you looking for a boyfriend?"

I answered, "As a matter of fact, I am."

"Well, I'm your man then", he replied, sounding sincere.

As time went by, I spent a great amount of time at his apartment that he shared with two other teammates. Eventually, we had sex. And just like with Brian, things changed.

When I started requesting more of his time, he would blow me off. Just like with Brian, our time together was spent in his bed, having sex. At least with Leroy, I did spend the night. But I still felt that something was missing, and I let him know. He gave me a crushing blow, by telling me that I was putting too much pressure on him and he wasn't ready to settle down. I reminded him of what he told me on the phone the day we had the in depth conversation. He had the gall to tell me he told me those things to get me to have sex with him. I couldn't believe my ears. I told him I didn't want to have anything else to do with him.

"I just told you what you wanted to hear", he said.

"But, it was a lie...you used me Leroy. You used me. How could you do this to me?" I fumed.

His nonchalant and uncaring attitude made me so furious, I finally ended our conversation. I was so hurt and felt so betrayed. I cried myself to sleep that night.

Even after our conversation that night, he contacted me, wanting to see me. I knew it was a bad idea, so I told him no. But Leroy was very persistent and determined to get his way. He finally wore me down and I went to see him...to talk. That night, we had some of the best sex we ever had. And from that day on, I found it hard to resist Leroy. The sex we had was always so amazing. It was like he knew my body better than any man ever did.

As time passed, I had to take our relationship for what it was, friends with benefits. Even though I was still sexing Leroy, I got involved with other guys along the way, looking for that special someone. And as always, they were all full of themselves and looking to bust a nut.

Then I was introduced to the escort business. After my first "date", I felt I had found my calling. I would be in the company of men and get paid to do it, with no feelings or attachments. I clung to it and never looked back.

And as for Leroy, our relationship was like a rollercoaster. One week I loved him and was willing to accept our arrangement. The next week, I hated him and was ending our friendship...once again. Eventually, he graduated from college and moved back home. Then is when he decided to tell me that he loved me. "You don't miss your water 'til your well runs dry", he told me. It was too little, too late.

After all of my failed attempts to find true love and getting my feet wet in the escort business, I realized that men weren't shit. As much as I hated to admit it, my mother had been right all along. There wasn't going to be a fairy tale ending. Men would always look at me as a sex object. But I did make a promise to myself...one that I intended to keep. I would never let another man use me again. I never let another man get close to my heart again. I put my heart and soul into the escort business. I obtained as many clients as I could and before long, I was making so much money, I quit my regular job at the clothing store I was working. Having money in my bank account gave me a whole new look on life. If a man didn't have anything to offer me, other than a hard dick, he could keep on moving. It became about what men could do for me and not what I could do for them. If you were going to get some of this pussy, you had to pay up. Being poor and broke again was not an option.

After a while though selling pussy began to wear on me. I started feeling cheap and worthless. Plus, I was getting tired of dealing with some of the psychos I would come across. So when I met David, I knew he was my ticket to a better life. And what a life it has been. David showers me with lots of expensive gifts. And I never have to want for anything. Most of all, he worships me.

So whatever secret he may be hiding wasn't going to come between me and my current lifestyle...unless he ends up being some psychopath. Of course, no amount of money is worth losing my life over. But I guess, all I could do was wait and see.

I reached for my cell phone to call David, just as it started ringing. David's office number flashed across the screen. "Hey babe, I was just about to call you", I said as soon as I answered.

"I guess we have a spiritual connection", he laughed.

"Yeah, I guess we do."

"The reason I called is to tell you that we're having

dinner at Charles and Bonnie's tonight."

I couldn't believe my ears. How could he decide that without checking with me?

"Did you hear me Taylor?" he asked, after I didn't respond.

"Yes, I did David", I snapped. "I thought we were going to discuss this before you decided."

"What's the big deal Taylor? Did you have plans or something?" he asked.

"No, I didn't. But apparently, it wouldn't have mattered if I did", I yelled into the phone. The truth was I really wasn't upset with David. I was pissed with Charles for being so damn persistent. He had control and there was nothing I could do about it.

"Sweetie, I'm sorry. I should've asked you first", David said in his calm voice.

I knew Charles wasn't going to give up his quest. And I also knew that David was going to become suspicious about me continuing to turn down his invitation. So I did what I had to do. "It's okay babe. I'm sorry for snapping and yelling at you. I guess I'm just having a bad day. Dinner with Charles and Bonnie will be just fine."

After I hung up with David, I had to wonder how the night was going to turn out.

Jade

I was really nervous about talking with Mr. Lawson about the situation with Paige. But I had already told him I need to talk to him, so I couldn't back down.

My inside line buzzed. "This is Jade", I said into the receiver.

"Hey Jade. It's Mr. Lawson. Do you still need to speak with me?" he asked.

I hesitated a few seconds, not knowing exactly what to say. When I still hadn't answered, Mr. Lawson said, "Jade, are you still there?"

"Uh...yes, Mr. Lawson I'm still here."

He repeated his question, "Do you still need to talk to me?"

"Um...yes, I do...would it be too much to ask you to come to my office? I have something down here that I need to show you."

I knew it was a bold move asking the president of the company to come to my office. But I had brought that doll back with me and I didn't want to take a chance of running into that nosey ass Charlene with it.

"Sure, that won't be a problem. I'll see you in a few."

A few minutes later, Mr. Lawson was at my door. "Can I come in?" he asked.

"Of course you can", I said.

"So what's on your mind? You still having doubts about your job?" he asked as soon as he sat down.

"Well...not exactly. The thing is ...uh..." I pulled the box from under my desk. "Let me start by showing you this."

He opened the box and did a double take. "What on earth is this?" he asked.

"It's a doll-"

"Well, I can see that", he said, interrupting me before I could finish telling him.

"I think Paige sent it to me."

"Why would she do that?" he asked with a confused look on his face.

"Because she thinks I'm the one that spread those pictures around."

"And why would she think that?" he asked.

I was beginning to have second thoughts about confessing. As Mr. Lawson sat there, waiting for an answer, it really kicked in that I could lose my job. I thought about how I would feel if he decided to give me my walking papers and what explanation he would give to the rest of the crew.

But I had to say something. He was sitting there patiently waiting for an answer. "Uh...she thinks that...uh...because I did", I confessed and then looked down at my hands.

Mr. Lawson stood up and paced the floor for a few seconds. He kept shaking his head from side to side. Then he rubbed his forehead and turned to face me. "Jade...I wanted so very much to believe it wasn't you."

I looked up, surprised. "You mean you knew it was me the whole time?"

"Yes, I had a feeling", he said.

"But...how?" I asked.

"You're the only person, other than myself that's ever here after work hours", he said.

"I don't understand."

"It was obvious that what occurred between Robert and Paige happened after office hours. So the person that took those pictures had to be someone that would be here that time of evening. My first guess was you", he explained.

"Why didn't you say anything?" I asked him.

"Like I said earlier, I didn't want to believe it was you. So I just swept it under the rug. But more importantly, why did you do it Jade? I thought you were bigger than that."

Seeing the disappointed look on Mr. Lawson's face made me want to disappear into thin air. The look on his face resembled the one he had the day those photos surfaced. I had to defend my honor.

"I am bigger than that Mr. Lawson. The thing is, after you made the announcement about the position, Paige was so confident that she was going to get the position."

"But she wasn't qualified Jade", he said calmly.

"Yes, I know that. But she just seemed a little too sure of herself. That day when I discovered them in the act, I knew that she was willing to do anything to get that position. And I didn't think it was fair for her to get that position just because she had sex with Robert", I rambled. I could feel tears forming in my eyes. I had no intention of crying, but just talking about it to Mr. Lawson made me upset.

Mr. Lawson sat back down. "Jade, I can understand how that would make you angry, but there was no way Paige was going to get that position, because she was intimate with Robert. I had the final say on who got that position...not Robert. And if he wouldn't have let his little head do the thinking for his big head, he could've told her that as well. I already had in my mind who I was going to give that position to."

The tears were slowly running down my face, because I felt like a fool. I had embarrassed Robert and Paige. Paige lost her job, and there was a chance that I would lose mine as well. "I am so sorry Mr. Lawson", I said before wiping my face with the back of my hands. "I can understand if you want to fire me."

He took a deep breath. "I think if it was anyone else, I would. But I'm just not ready to let you go Jade. I feel you're an asset to my company. Besides...you did come clean about it."

"I have to be honest Mr. Lawson. I only confessed because of what's been happening. And I want you to give Paige her job back, so she can leave me alone", I told him.

"You can't be serious", he replied.

I told him about all of the things that had happened. The phone calls, the break-in and vandalism of my apartment, and the little scuffle in the parking lot of *Food Lion.* He looked at me in disbelief. "Jade, I'm really sorry that you've had to go through all of that, but there's no way I'm bringing Paige back here."

"But you have to-"

He cut me off. "Paige caused her own dismissal by being intimate in my place of business. If I let her come back, she'll think that what she did was okay. And that's not the image I want to project."

I blew air out of my mouth. "I guess I can understand where you're coming from. I just figured if you gave her, her job back, she would leave me alone."

"Are you absolutely sure she's the one doing all of those things to you?' he asked.

"Well the day you fired her, she stormed into my office saying she knew it was me and she said I'd be sorry. I didn't really think anything of it...even after the phone calls and the break-in. But that night at the grocery store when I went outside and saw the damage to my car, I knew it was her. Besides, as far as I know, I don't have any enemies."

He laughed. "And even after all that, you would still want to work with her again?"

I had to laugh too. "I guess that does sound silly."

"Yes, it does. From what you've told me and from the looks of this butchered doll..." He looked down at the doll, still sitting on my desk. "...she sounds like she may not be too stable. So there's no way I want her back in my place of business."

"You've made your point Mr. Lawson", I told him.

He stood up to leave.

"Mr. Lawson."

He turned around to look at me. "Yes, Jade."

"Are you going to tell the others about this?" I asked him.

He gave me a serious look. "The only way they will know is if you tell them. I don't see a reason to inform people about matters that are none of their business."

I breathed a sigh of relief. "Thanks Mr. Lawson."

"Don't thank me Jade. I'm not doing it for you. This company is my heart and soul. I built it from the ground up...and I will not let it be turned into some low class, gossip filled environment." Then he walked out.

I felt so ashamed. It wasn't that I cared about Paige's feelings. Mr. Lawson was right, she deserved to be fired. But I could've handled things differently. Instead of making a slide show for the whole office to see, I could've gone to Mr. Lawson personally and informed him about the situation. The more I thought about it, the more disgusted I got. What I did was tasteless. And I felt I had lost Mr. Lawson's respect.

Sierra

I was pleasantly surprised when I got home from work. Tyler had cleaned up and had dinner in the oven.

"Um...something smells good", I said as I wrapped my arms around his waist. He was in the kitchen making a salad.

He turned around and kissed me on the forehead. "Hey sweetie! I didn't hear you come in."

"Yeah, you were too busy playing Mr. Good Housekeeping."

He laughed. "So you got jokes? You're quite the comedienne."

I wrapped my arms around his neck. "You know I'm just kidding babe. What's for dinner, besides this beautiful salad?"

He started talking like he was a waiter describing a dish to a customer. "For starters, we have baked stuffed pork chops, made with homemade stuffing. Sides include fresh asparagus, cooked in garlic oil and caramelized apples. For dessert, we have key lime cheesecake."

My mouth was watering by the time he finished. "Oooh, that sounds delicious...when did you have time to bake a cheesecake?"

"I didn't. I picked it up from this bakery near my job." He went to the refrigerator and pulled out a plastic container. "Doesn't it look good?" He took the lid off so I could take a peek.

I licked my lips. "Yes, that does look good."

"And it better be good too...as much as it cost. But my girls are worth it", he said, flashing a big smile.

"Aw, how sweet...where is Shelby anyway?"

"She's upstairs in her room watching a movie."

The timer on the oven beeped. "Good, the rolls are ready", he said. He opened the bottom oven and peeked inside.

A double oven was something Tyler insisted on

when we were building our house. Considering how he loved to cook, I knew the kitchen was going to be a big deal. He always said a man was the king of his castle, and he wanted his castle to have a kitchen fit for a king. And it was. Our kitchen looked like it came straight out of a kitchen and baths magazine.

"You really did it up", I complimented him.

"I told you, I wanted a special dinner. Everything's ready, so I'm gonna go get Shelby." He kissed me on the cheek before walking out.

I was so happy that things were good between us again. But my mind kept going back to Alexis. I still had not talked to her since she stormed out of my office. I kept hoping she would call me, but she never did. I hated knowing she was upset with me, but my marriage came first. And I thought we had that understanding. I was going to let her cool off before I attempted to call her. But just in case she decided to try to spoil my evening, I turned off my cell phone.

"Mommy!" Shelby screamed and ran up to me, wrapping her arms around my legs.

"Hey sweetie", I said, picking her up and placing kisses all over her face.

She squirmed in my arms. "That tickles!" she yelled.

"You silly little girl. You're going to make me drop you."

"Okay girls. Settle down. It's time to eat", Tyler said.

"Everything looks so good", I said, admiring the spread he had set up on the table.

We all sat down and Tyler said the grace. We made small talk, filling each other in on the events of the day. Of course, I left out my visit from Alexis. There was no need to volunteer unnecessary information. He said he got off early to prepare our meal, hoping it would be on the table when I walked in the door. I let him know I appreciated all of his hard work. We spent the rest of the meal listening to Shelby talk about the daily adventures of daycare. When she got started, there was no shutting her up.

Tyler and I kept giving each other seductive looks. I knew what was in store...a night of passionate lovemaking. After dinner and dessert, I helped Tyler clear the table. While Tyler loaded the dishwasher, I ran a bubble bath for Shelby. I washed her and let her have a few minutes to play with her bath toys. She put on her pajamas after I dried her off.

"Mommy, can you read me a story please?" she asked in her sweetest voice.

"Of course I can sweetie."

She picked out one of her *Dr. Seuss* books. I read it to her until she fell asleep. Afterwards, I went downstairs to join Tyler.

"You got perfect timing", he said sarcastically.

I grabbed one of the dish towels and hit him with it. "I was upstairs being mommy while you were down here being domestic."

"Yeah, but your job was more rewarding. Cleaning up a dirty kitchen is no fun", he pouted.

"No one told you to cook all that food", I said, hitting him with the dish towel again.

"You weren't saying that when you were stuffing your face", he replied, snatching the towel out of my hand.

"I sure didn't, because it was delicious."

"Okay, so why are you complaining now?"

"I'm not complaining. Remember, you had a problem with all the dishes."

He smiled at me and said, "Shut up and kiss me."

He wrapped his arms around my waist and pulled me to him. And for the second time that day, we shared a passionate kiss.

"Um...you keep this up, I'm gonna have to take you upstairs and have my way with you", he said in between kisses.

"You promise?"

He then scooped me up and carried me upstairs. As soon as we got upstairs, I went to get my massage table. "Put that way", he instructed. "It's about you tonight."

I did as I was told. When I came back, Tyler had candles lit and was filling the tub with water, rose petals and bath salts. Unscented candles were lit around the tub and soft sounds of jazz music played from the portable CD player. Once the tub was full, Tyler undressed me and helped me get into it.

"Tyler, I can't believe you did all of this. I am really impressed", I told him, as I slid into the warm inviting water.

"I wanted to show you that I was sincere about us making amends. Besides, you deserve it." He leaned down and kissed me on the forehead. "Now, you just sit back and relax. I'll be back in a few minutes to wash your back."

I lay back and rested my head on my lavender scented bath pillow Tyler had given me a couple of months ago. I couldn't remember the last time my husband went through so much trouble for me. He used to do that type of stuff when we first got married. But as the years passed, they became far and few between.

I closed my eyes so I could enjoy the water and the soothing sounds of the jazz music. But as soon as I did, Alexis' face popped into my head. She had been dominating my thoughts since she came into my life. Tyler had gone through so much to make my night special, yet I was thinking about my lesbian lover.

"I've got to stop this", I said out loud.

"Stop what?" Tyler asked as he entered the bathroom, carrying two glasses filled with liquid.

"Uh...nothing...I was just thinking about work...that's all", I lied.

"Forget about work. You're supposed to be relaxing." He sat on the edge of the tub and gave me one of the glasses.

"You're right. What's in the glasses?"

"Champagne."

"Let's make a toast."

"To what?"

"To...us."

We clicked our glasses together. "To us", we said

in unison, and took a sip of our champagne.

"You really thought of everything didn't you Tyler?"

"And just think, there's more to come", he said and downed the rest of his champagne.

"Like what?" I asked, knowing what he was referring to.

He smiled at me and said, "Why don't you get out of that tub and let me show you?"

I drank the rest of my champagne and hopped out of the tub.

"I'll be waiting", he said before walking back into the bedroom.

I rubbed chocolate scented body oil over my damp skin, hoping it would tempt Tyler to nibble on all of my body parts.

When I entered our bedroom, Tyler was lying on the bed naked. His manhood was lying limp against his thigh. But as soon as he saw me, it stood at attention. "Looks like someone's happy to see me", I said in my seductive voice.

"Come on over here and let us show you how happy we are", he said.

I went to my husband and he took me into his arms. He made love to me like he did when we first got married. Even though we didn't indulge in any oral pleasure, I was quite satisfied when it was over. I didn't have explosive orgasms like I did with Alexis. But the way Tyler took his time trying to please me was enough. I fell asleep with a smile on my face.

Taylor

David and I pulled up to Charles and Bonnie's house at 7:00 sharp. "I still don't know why you agreed to have dinner with them", I whined.

"And I still don't understand why you're making a big fuss about it", he replied.

"Well, we're here now. So let's go ahead and get this over with." I opened my door and didn't wait for David to open it, like he always did.

We walked up to the door and David rang the doorbell. He looked over at me and said, "You look amazing tonight Taylor."

I had on a royal blue knee length dress that hugged my curves and showed plenty of cleavage. I was hot and I knew it.

I managed to utter a simple, "Thanks."

An older black woman, who I assumed was their housekeeper, answered the door.

"Hi, we're David and Taylor Morgan", David chirped.

"Yes, Mr. and Mrs. Williams are expecting you", she smiled and escorted us inside. "Please have a seat. I'll let them know you're here. While you're waiting, would you like something to drink?"

"No, thank you", we both replied.

She spent around on her heel and went to fetch our host and hostess. David tried to strike up a conversation. "Nice place, huh?"

"It's okay", I responded without looking at him.

"Are you going to act like this all night Taylor?" he asked.

"What are you talking about?" I asked innocently.

"You obviously have an attitude and I hope it's not going to interfere with dinner." He gave me a stern look.

I usually got my way when it came to David. But I also knew when to quit. When he put his foot down, I didn't cross him. Before I could respond, Charles and Bonnie walked in.

David stood up to shake Charles' hand. "Hey man. It's good to see you again."

I threw in my fake hellos and noticed Charles undressing me with his eyes. I also noticed Bonnie looking at me with a dirty look. She probably noticed her husband checking me out.

As soon as everyone sat down, the housekeeper entered. "Sir, everything is ready", she said looking directly at Charles.

"Thanks Ms. Lorraine. We'll be in shortly."

We passed a few more pleasantries and headed to the dining room. I was pleasantly surprised. The table was beautifully decorated. There were orchids in a crystal vase placed in the center of the table. Four place settings, consisting of fine bone china, crystal goblets, linen napkins and gold cutlery awaited us. She even had place cards, which I felt were unnecessary, considering it was only four of us. But it was a nice touch.

"You have a nice home", David said.

"Thank you", Bonnie replied, like she had something to do with it.

"I'm sure it has nothing on that mansion you're living in", Charles joked.

"Believe me, your place is nothing to scoff at", David responded.

I interjected. "Are you two going to compare houses all night?" I was ready to sit down and eat. The sooner we ate, the sooner we could get the night over with.

They both just looked at me and continued talking. Bonnie just rolled her eyes. We all sat down in our appointed seats. I was seated beside David, across from Charles, which I'm sure was no coincidence.

Ms. Lorraine entered the dining room pushing a fancy dinner cart, made of marble and cherry wood. "I have salad for you", she announced. She took each of our salad plates and piled them with the crisp salad. "No need for dressing. It already has a dressing mixed in...made it myself", she beamed.

We all dove into the salad. "Um, this is delicious", I said, surprised by how good it was.

"Yes, this is some of the best salad I've ever eaten", David said and scooped up another fork full.

"What's in it?" Charles asked.

"No, no, no. I can't tell you that. It's a secret...passed down to me by my mother", she said.

"We don't have secrets in this house", Bonnie quipped.

Charles gave her a nasty look, but it didn't seem to bother her. "So are you going to divulge the recipe?" she asked Ms. Lorraine.

Ms. Lorraine looked around the table apologetically. "I'm sorry...but I can't do that. I promised my mother. I had a chance to make it a national product, but I turned it down. My mother's honor was more important to me than having my own personal dressing on the market."

"Well, that's just plain stupid. Who wouldn't want to make lots of money if they had the chance?" Bonnie responded.

"Money isn't everything", Ms. Lorraine shot back.

"I guess that's why you're still just a maid, cleaning up after people who do have money", Bonnie said, with a wicked grin on her face.

Right then and there, I understood what Charles meant by her being a bitch. She was being downright nasty to her housekeeper, for no reason at all. She was proof of how certain people with money acted. David was one of the wealthiest people in the county, but you would never know it by the way he acted. He didn't talk down to people who were less fortunate than him. He never treated people differently. And even though Jade and Sierra accused me of being spoiled and privileged, I would never talk to Ms. Hazel that way...or anyone else for that matter. I knew what it was like to struggle and I didn't turn my nose up to those who weren't lucky enough to get out of their situation.

"I enjoy what I do. It makes me feel useful", Ms. Lorraine explained.

Bonnie laughed. "Oh please. No one can possibly enjoy that...unless that's the only job they can get."

David and I both looked at Charles, waiting for him to put his wife in check. But he just sat there eating his salad like nothing was going on.

Ms. Lorraine took a deep breath and looked up to the ceiling. "If you're implying that I can't get other employment, you're dead wrong. I'm not some dumb ole' black woman who doesn't know anything. I'll have you know...I have a bachelor's degree in business and an associate's degree in food and nutrition. I owned my own catering business for twenty years. I was ready to retire, but I didn't want to shut down the business, because it was so successful, so I turned it over to my two daughters five years ago. After traveling to all of the many places I wanted to visit, I decided I needed to do something with my time. So I took a job as a housekeeper for a lovely couple with three wonderful children. I worked for that family up until two months ago." She looked at Charles and then back at Bonnie. "If you would've taken the time to get to know me like your husband did, you would've known all of that. Now I know I just started working here, but I'm a nice respectful person, who demands respect in return. And I take my job very seriously."

Ms. Lorraine made me even more proud to be a black woman. She was smart and successful, and didn't need to flaunt it. She didn't have to work, but chose to, to keep herself busy. I looked over at Bonnie. She was embarrassed and it showed. And it served her right for running her mouth, not knowing what she was talking about.

Charles was sitting there trying not to laugh. He knew all along that Ms. Lorraine could handle Bonnie, which is why he didn't say anything.

"Now is everyone ready for the main course?" Ms. Lorraine asked.

Everyone said yes, except Bonnie, who was sitting with her arms crossed and a scowl on her face. Ms. Lorraine took our empty plates, loaded them onto the dinner cart and rolled them into the kitchen.

As soon as she was out of sight, Bonnie turned to Charles and said, "How could you just sit there and let her talk to me like that? I will not be disrespected in my own house...especially by the help."

"Bonnie, you're overreacting. She was nothing but respectful towards to you. Besides, you're the one that took it there."

"Of course, you're going to defend your people", she replied.

As soon as the words left her mouth, I felt my blood boiling. I was about to say something, until David touched my leg. He knew I was going to let her have it.

Charles spoke through clenched teeth. "Don't you ever say anything like that to me again. This has nothing to do with race. It's about treating people the way you want to be treated."

Bonnie tried to speak. "But she-"

Charles cut her off. "Don't say another word, unless it's an apology. You are making a fool out of yourself and embarrassing me. So cut it out." He then turned to me and David and said, "I do apologize for my wife's behavior. I don't know what's come over her tonight."

Nothing had come over her. She was acting the way she always acted. She was a prima donna and thought she was the cat's meow. How Charles put up with her was beyond me. But then again, he got what he deserved with his "white women only" rule.

Ms. Lorraine came back in pushing the dinner cart. "Dinner is served", she announced.

She filled each of our plates with what she said was garlic-rosemary chicken, broccoli cheese casserole and penne pasta cooked in a lemon wine sauce. "Oh my! I almost forgot the rolls", she said and ran back into the kitchen.

She came back with a basket of yeast rolls and honey butter. "Sorry about that", she said.

"It's no big deal Ms. Lorraine", Charles assured her. "Everything looks amazing."

"Thank you. I hope it tastes as good as it looks",

she replied.

"Oh, I'm sure it will", Charles said.

"Well, I'm going to leave you folks to enjoy your meal. I'll be back to check on you. Just let me know if you need anything", she said, before retreating back to the kitchen.

It was dead silence for a few minutes. Everyone was enjoying the meal. Even Bonnie was digging in. I guess just because she was a bitch, didn't mean she didn't know good food when she tasted it.

David was the first to speak. "This is incredible. I never knew I could enjoy broccoli so much."

"Yeah, I sure lucked up with this one. It feels great to come home to a nice home cooked meal", Charles said and then looked over at Bonnie. She gave him a dirty look.

"Eating like this is dangerous to my thighs", I said, thinking about the extra pounds I was probably packing on.

"Hmm, I don't have to worry about that type of thing. I've been a size four for as long as I can remember. I can eat what I want and never gain a pound", Bonnie bragged.

"Well good for you. It must be nice not to have any curves or ass to deal with", I replied. That shut her up for a while.

The rest of the meal, David and Charles did most of the talking. They talked about everything from sports to politics. Charles kept stealing glances at me. I kept looking at my watch, wishing the time would go by faster.

Ms. Lorraine came back in to check on us. "Are you guys ready for dessert?" she asked.

David leaned back in his chair. "I don't know if I can eat another bite."

"But I insist...I have peach cobbler, with vanilla ice cream", she said as she cleared the table.

"Homemade cobbler?" Charles asked.

"I wouldn't have it any other way", she answered.

"Well in that case, I guess I can squeeze in a piece", David said, rubbing his stomach.

"After you clear the table, you can take off", Charles told Ms. Lorraine.

"But I still have to serve you dessert", she protested.

"You've done enough already. Bonnie can handle dessert."

Bonnie threw Charles a nasty look, but she didn't say anything.

"Are you sure?" Ms. Lorraine asked.

"Yes. I insist. We'll see you tomorrow."

She flashed a big smile and said, "Thank you so much." She then turned to me and David. "It was nice meeting you."

I said, "It was really nice meeting you as well."

"It was nice meeting you...and your food too", David said.

"Why thank you. You all enjoy the rest of your evening." She turned to Charles and said, "And I'll see you all tomorrow." She walked out of the dining room and a few minutes later, I heard the front door open and close.

"Bonnie, why don't you and Taylor go to the kitchen and fix us all some of that cobbler?" Charles said to his wife.

I gave him a look that let him know I wasn't too happy with his suggestion.

David chimed in. "Yeah, that's a good idea. Give me and Charles a chance to do some male bonding."

I rolled my eyes at him and reluctantly stood up so I could join Bonnie in the kitchen. As soon as we were in the kitchen, she started complaining about having to fix dessert.

"That's what we pay her for. I shouldn't have to do the help's job. I'm not cut out for this type of work", she whined.

"It doesn't seem like you're cut out for any type of work", I said out loud, before I realized it.

She rolled her eyes at me. "Honey, you don't know a thing about me", she said.

"I know that you're a spoiled bitch who thinks you're better than the average person. You've gotten so used to having what you want and wouldn't know an honest day's work if it slapped you in the face", I told her.

"You have some nerve coming up in my home and insulting me."

"I only call it like I see it. And besides, I didn't want to come here anyway."

She didn't say anything, which surprised me. She took the cobbler out of the oven and the ice cream out of the freezer. For a few seconds, she just stood there staring at the food like she didn't know what to do next.

"You're quite pathetic", I said to her.

She smacked her lips. "Don't you dare-"

I cut her off. "Just get me some plates to put this in."

She hesitated for a second, before she started searching through the cabinets for some dessert plates. I located an ice cream spade. Ms. Lorraine already had the cobbler cut into portions. As I fixed each plate, Bonnie stood there watching me. I started feeling uncomfortable with the way she was looking at me.

"What in the hell are you staring at?" I asked her.

"You have some of the most beautiful breasts. Who did them?"

"Excuse me?"

"I said who did your implants?"

I turned around so I was face to face with her. "Sweetheart, these are natural. Don't you know the real deal when you see it?"

"They look a little too perfect to be natural", she said, eyeing them even harder.

I did something that I couldn't believe I would do. I unzipped the back of my dress and pulled it down enough to expose my bare breasts. "Do they look fake to you now?" I asked her.

She stood there with her mouth open, not knowing what to say. I made sure she got a good look at them. Then I pulled my dress up and zipped it back up. I fixed the last of the desserts and put the ice cream back in the freezer.

When I turned back around, I noticed Bonnie still

staring at me, biting her lip in a seductive manner. "Bitch, don't get any crazy ideas. I am all about dick. So get that look out of your eyes", I told her.

She touched me on my arm. "Aw, come on. You haven't ever sucked a cunt before?" she asked.

"Hell no! And I don't have any desire to. Another bitch can't do shit for me!"

"I beg to differ."

"Whatever!"

"Don't knock it 'til you try it."

I poked my finger in her chest. "Let's get one thing straight. I have no interest what so ever in women...and even if I did, it damn sure wouldn't be your pencil thin, fake titty, spoiled, bleached blonde white ass." I then grabbed two of the plates and shoved them in her hands. Then I grabbed the other two plates and waltzed out of the kitchen.

David and Charles were talking about business when we entered. As soon as we put their plates down in front of then, they went to work on the cobbler.

Throughout dessert, between the small talk, Charles and Bonnie both kept stealing glances at me, while David was oblivious to everything except his peach cobbler. At the end of the night, I was glad it was over with.

On the way home, David said he finally understood why I felt the way I did about Bonnie. So I knew we wouldn't be having dinner with them again...and that was fine by me.

Jade

"I knew you were a good girl", Eli said to me after I told him about confessing to Mr. Lawson. He had come over to hang out with me. We ate Chinese food and watched a movie.

"I just needed to clear my conscious", I explained.

"Yeah, that's what good girls do", he teased.

"And I was hoping he would give Paige her job back", I added.

He turned his mouth up at me and said, "Are you for real?"

"Yes", I answered.

"Why in the hell would you want that psycho bitch working with you again?"

I threw my hands up. "I know. I know. That's the same thing Mr. Lawson said...minus the psycho bitch part. I was just thinking it would get her off my back."

"You're better than me, 'cause there's no way in hell I would've confessed."

"Well, like I said before, I just needed to clear my conscious. Excuse me for being honest", I said.

"Don't get all brand new. You weren't so honest when you put those pics out there for everyone in your office to see them", he replied.

"I was honest...I exposed the truth. The dishonesty came into play when I didn't own up to doing it. Anyway, can we please change the subject?"

He shrugged his shoulders. "Fine by me. You're the one obsessed with this shit."

"I'm not obsessed. I just-" The ringing of his cell phone interrupted my statement.

He looked down at the phone and put it back in its holder.

"Aren't you going to answer that?" I asked him.

"No", he said.

"Why not?"

"Because I don't want to."

"That doesn't make sense."

"Damn Jade. This is like déjà vu. Didn't we have this discussion before?"

His phone continued to ring until he silenced it. Within seconds, it started to ring again.

"Somebody's really trying to get in touch with you", I said and rolled my eyes at him.

He silenced the phone again, by turning it off. "Yeah, some folks just can't take a hint", he said. He had a distant look on his face.

"Something you wanna talk about?" I asked.

"No...not really", he answered.

"Eli...do you know how it makes me feel that I'm your girlfriend and you can't even talk to me?"

I had tried to respect his privacy, but I was starting to get a little irritated. Our relationship had no emotional involvement, except on my behalf. He never talked about his feelings or his thoughts...nothing.

"Maybe I'm just one of those people who doesn't like to talk or share feelings", he said, without even looking at me.

I called his bluff. "Well you know what Eli? I don't know if I can continue a relationship with someone who doesn't have an emotional attachment to me."

"What are you saying?" he asked, finally looking at me.

"I'm saying that I'm starting to think that you're not as into me as I'm into you."

He rolled his eyes towards the ceiling and blew air out of his mouth. I sat there watching him, trying to decipher what was going through his head. His body language told me he was thinking hard, wanting to be careful with his words.

"You're wrong Jade. I'm feeling you...hard, probably more than I have for any other woman", he said, looking into my eyes. He looked sincere, like he meant every word he said.

I reached out and grabbed both of his hands. "Then why won't you open up to me?"

He dropped his head and stared at our hands. He waited a few seconds, and then looked back at me. He took a deep breath, and then spoke. "That was my mom."

"Okay", I said, feeling a little confused.

"She's a crack head...has been for a while now. She only calls when she wants money."

I squeezed his hand. "Eli, I'm sorry. I had no idea."

He held his hand up. "I'm not finished. You want to know about me, so I'm gonna tell you. Like I said, my mom's strung out on crack. I don't want to give her money to support her habit. But if I don't, she'll do whatever it takes to get some."

I felt so bad for him. I could honestly say that I didn't personally know anyone on crack. I had always heard how crack destroyed people...and their families as well. I could never understand why someone would even try it, knowing what it could do to them. I tried marijuana once when I was in high school. I didn't really care for it. The boy that got me to try it told me I wasn't smoking it right. I didn't bother to learn. I didn't want to take a chance on frying my brain cells.

"Have you tried to get her help?" I asked him.

He laughed and shook his head. "That's an understatement. But I've learned that you can't help someone who doesn't want to help themself."

I couldn't imagine what he was going through. My mom and I have always been close. Some would say she was always overprotective. And she babied me because I was an only child.

"So how is the rest of your family coping with it?" I was curious to know if he knew his father or had any siblings.

"Shit, they got problems of their own. My little brother is locked up for armed robbery and attempted murder. My little sister got damn six kids by four different men...and word on the street is, she's pregnant again by this low-life she dealing with now. So...as you can see, my family life is fucked up...which is why you haven't met them."

I had no idea Eli was dealing with all that. I was beginning to understand why he was so secretive about his personal life. He was ashamed of his family. But he still hadn't mentioned a father.

"What about your father?" I asked, hoping I wasn't pushing it with him.

"What about him?" he snapped.

From the way he was looking at me, I was hesitant about even finishing the conversation, but I had gotten him to open up and I wasn't about to be intimidated by his demeanor. "Where is he?" I asked.

"That son of a bitch wasn't nothing but a sperm donor as far as I'm concerned", he said, without blinking.

"You said was...is he dead?"

He looked me straight in my eyes and said, "As far as I'm concerned, he is."

"Wow, that's kind of harsh...isn't it Eli?"

He gave me a serious look. "To you...maybe it is. But you don't know what I went through growing up."

"You're right, but-"

He cut me off. "Was your father in your life?"

"Yes, he was...and still is", I told him.

My father was worse than my mother when it came to me. He showered me with gifts and plenty of love. As far as I was concerned, he was the best father a girl could have.

"Well, mine wasn't. He came around long enough to plant two more seeds inside my mother after she had me. She kept letting him come back into her bed like everything was okay. He never spent any time with us kids. It was like we didn't exist...like we were some other man's offspring."

I touched his knee. "Eli, I'm so sorry."

He didn't acknowledge me. Instead, he kept venting. "There were so many times I wanted him to play catch with me, take me fishing or to a game...anything. But, he never did."

"That must've been hard for you", I told him.

"Yeah, it was for a while. But as I got older, it didn't affect me much. I learned to cope by working out, which is how I got into personal training." He had a sad look on his face. And I had never seen him look so vulnerable. But I was still glad that he was opening up to me.

"So how did your brother and sister handle it?" I asked him.

He looked at me like I was irritating him, but he continued talking. "They both handled it in their own way. My brother became a trouble maker. He was always getting into fights at school. He spent more time out of school than he did in school, because he was always getting suspended. Eventually, he dropped out of school and started running with a rough crowd. I tried my best to steer him on the right path, but I was unsuccessful. Because he didn't finish school and couldn't get a decent job, robbing and stealing became a part of his life."

I could see the guilt in his eyes, like he was blaming himself for his brother's choices. "Eli, you can't take the blame for your brother's actions. He made his own decisions."

He gave me a surprised look. "I don't blame myself...I just wish I could've done more for him."

"I'm sure you did what you could. But in the end, it was up to him. He was gonna do what he wanted to, regardless", I explained.

He laced his fingers together and put his hands behind his head. I guess you're right. I just wanted to save him. My hopes were that he'd come to his senses after one of his boys got shot and killed, during a botched robbery. That didn't slow him down one bit. He continued his crime spree...until his luck ran out. Now, he's doing time for attempted murder. He shot the cashier...even after he gave him the money. Fortunately, the young man didn't die."

I shook my head in disbelief. I remembered that incident. It was all over the news after it happened. The poor guy was now paralyzed from the waist down. He was a track star at *Central*, who was working part-time to make some extra money for school. And all because some thugs decided to shoot him over a little cash, he would never run again. Who would've thought that I'd end up dating the guy whose brother pulled the trigger?

"I remember when that guy was shot. It was so sad. His future was ruined...all over a few bucks", I said.

"And I have to live with that every day", he replied.

"Your brother has to live with that. You didn't pull the trigger", I said, trying to get through to him.

"I failed as a big brother...to him and my sister. They looked up to me, but I wasn't able to help them." He sat up in the chair and rested his elbows on his knees. "My sister gave her virginity to the first boy that showed her some attention. She was only fifteen when she got knocked up by that little punk. He dropped her like a bad habit. She ended up dropping out of school also. After she had her baby, she gave up on any hopes of a successful future. And things just went from bad to worse. She kept falling for sorry ass man after sorry ass man, and the babies kept coming."

I felt bad for her. She was leaning toward men for the love and attention she didn't receive from her father. "Do any of the fathers support their children?" I asked, just out of curiosity. It always irritated me to hear how some men impregnated woman and then left them to fend for themselves, after the child is born.

"Not really. She's living off the government...just like so many others in her situation." He paused for a few seconds and shook his head. "I know everyone makes mistakes, but I could never understand how she kept making the same mistake over and over again."

"I'm sure she feels bad about it and regrets her choices." I tried to give her the benefit of the doubt.

He rolled his eyes. "Hell naw, she doesn't have any regrets or feel bad about it....otherwise she would've used some type of birth control. But she is my sister, and I love her. I just wish I could've saved her too."

"It's still not too late, you know. She can get her G.E.D. Then take some courses and work on getting a degree", I explained.

"You just don't get it ...do you? Don't you think I've tried to tell her that?"

I didn't say anything. I just stared at him. He continued. "I've been on her case for the longest, trying to get her to do something with her life...anything, besides having babies for different men, who don't want nothing from life either. Do you know what she had the nerve to say to me once?"

This time I said, "What?"

"She told me I wasn't shit either, because all I am is someone who helps people workout, something they can do on their own."

"But you're so much more than that Eli", I told him.

"Hell, I know that. I told her I enjoyed my work. I get to help those who want to change for the better. I help people get their self-confidence back. And it aint for chump change either...Besides, I'm one of the most sought after personal trainers in the area, because I get results."

I could see the passion in his eyes as he talked about his job. We both sat there for a few seconds staring at each other. Then he said, "I just wish I could get through to her. I wish she was more like you Jade."

I pointed to my chest. "Me...why me?" I asked.

He held his hand out at me. "I mean look at you. You're beautiful and smart. You have a great job...." He looked around my apartment. "...Obviously making good money. You're independent. You're...you just got it going on girl."

I felt myself blushing. I never looked at myself in that way. I mean, I knew I had a wonderful job and never really had anything to complain about. I at times, wished that I had a baby. But that would always be put to rest when I'd see a baby crying to the top of their lungs out in public, with the poor mom looking like she was going to cry as well. As I sat there listening to Eli, I realized my life was good. And Eli made it even better.

"Aw...that's so sweet Eli. I never knew you felt that way", I told him, still smiling.

"Of course I do. I wouldn't be wasting my time with you, if you weren't about nothing", he said.

"Well with all that you said about me, you know

what completes it all?"

"No. What?"

"You...meeting you was the best thing that's happened to me. These have been the happiest months of my life."

He leaned back on the sofa and said, "You're really feeling me...aren't you?"

"Of course I am. And I hope you feel the same way about me."

"You know I do."

"But I like to hear it."

"I can do better than that. I can show you." He stood up and held his hand out to me. "Just one condition...now that you know my family background, you have to promise not to ask me about meeting them again."

I grabbed his hand and stood up. "I think I can handle that", I said and followed him into my bedroom.

Sierra

"Good morning beautiful", Tyler said and gave me a kiss on the forehead.

I tried to look at my alarm clock. "What time is it?" I asked.

"It's almost seven-thirty", he answered.

"Damn, I need to get up." I could taste the stale morning breath in my mouth.

"What's the hurry? You still got good time before you need to be at the spa", he said, sitting down on my side of the bed.

"Where's Shelby?" I asked him.

"She's downstairs eating some cereal."

I stared at Tyler, looking at how incredibly handsome he was. He was wearing a charcoal grey *Sean John* suit with a powder pink shirt and a hot pink and grey tie. Tyler had his own sense of style. He always went to work looking good and well groomed. "You look nice today", I told him.

"Thanks baby", he said blushing.

He looked towards the doorway and leaned in closer to me. "You were incredible last night", he whispered.

"So were you", I said, thinking back on how he made me feel last night.

He was getting ready to say something, but Shelby came running into the room. "G' morning Mommy!" she yelled and jumped onto the bed.

"Good morning sweetie. Did you eat all of your cereal?"

She shook her head and said, "Um hum. *Cheerios* are my favorite cereal in the whole wide world."

"I'm sure they are", I said and tickled her on her stomach. I tickled her for a few more seconds before Tyler said, "Okay princess, we have to go before Daddy's late for work."

"Okay Daddy", she whined. "Have a good day at work Mommy", she said, before jumping off the bed.

"I will sweetheart. And you have a good day at daycare and listen to your teacher." She came and kissed me on the cheek. "Okay Mommy." Then she ran back downstairs.

"Well...I better get going. Have a good day", Tyler said and stood up. He stared at me for a few seconds. I knew my hair was all over my head and I probably looked a mess.

"What is it?" I finally asked him.

"I love you", he said and walked out the door.

I lay in the bed a few minutes more thinking about Tyler's comment. It made me have mixed feelings about a lot of things. I knew that Tyler loved me and I knew that I loved him. Yet, I allowed myself to be seduced by another woman. On the contrary, it wouldn't have happened if things were okay at home.

The look in his eyes was so sincere when he told me that he loved me. If he loved me so much, then why was he at that sex club? But then he could ask me the same thing.

I didn't want to be negative about Tyler's sudden change in attitude, but history had taught me that it wasn't permanent. I guess I would enjoy it while it lasted. I drug myself out of bed and headed to the shower. As soon as I entered the bathroom, I noticed a black velvet box sitting on the vanity. There was a note beside it that read: *'Sorry I didn't get to give you this last night. This is a token of my love for you. Tyler'*

I opened the box to reveal a white gold necklace. A heart made of diamonds dangled from it. "Wow, this is beautiful", I said out loud. I held the necklace up to my neck and admired it in the mirror. Maybe Tyler really was ready for a change.

I put the necklace down and hopped into the shower. As the shower heads sprayed warm water onto my body, my thoughts went back to the night before. Tyler was so attentive and gentle with our lovemaking. It was as if he had discovered my body for the first time. He made me feel like he enjoyed what he was doing and it wasn't just a husbandly duty, like taking the trash out.

If things were looking up for me and Tyler, where did that leave me and Alexis? Would it be fair to keep seeing her when things are going well with me and Tyler? My mind was in a boggle and I had no idea how I was going to handle it.

I stepped out of the shower, dried off and lathered my body down with *Philosophy body lotion*. The day was going to be a laid back casual day. I threw on my favorite pair of *Calvin Klein* jeans and my Jimi Hendrix t-shirt. I pulled my hair back into a ponytail and applied some moisturizer with sunscreen on my face. I didn't feel like putting on any make up, so I just threw on some lip gloss. I slid into my sandals and headed out the door.

I noticed Kiki's Honda in the parking lot when I got to the spa. She has been doing a great job since Jazmin has been out. I had given her a key to the spa. Most days she would beat me in and have everything ready for the day.

As soon as I stepped into the spa, I heard, "Good morning! Aren't we extra casual today?"

I looked down at myself as if I didn't know what I had on. "Yeah, you could say that. After the night I had, you're lucky I even showed up today."

Kiki looked at me, saw the smile on my face and said, "Girl, I aint mad atcha! I wish I could've got some action last night. All I did was watch TV all night...by myself. Now you see that's why I need me a husband."

I shook my head at her. "Kiki, I hope you want a husband for more than that."

She put her hand on her hip and said, "What else they good for...other than giving you a little change every now and then?"

"You are too much Kiki", I told her and put my purse on the counter.

"I'm just telling it like it is", she replied.

Changing the subject, I asked, "Do we have a lot of appointments lined up today?"

She ran her finger down the list. "Well, it's pretty

much steady. We're not overly booked, but we have a decent amount of clients today."

I looked at the appointment book to see how many clients I had, and then I went to the supply closet to check the inventory. I supplied all of the products for everyone in the spa. Of course, the hairstylists did use some of their own products also.

I scanned the shelves and did a double take when I got to the shelf that housed the relaxers, shampoos and conditioners. The count was lower than it should've been. Business had been good, but it hadn't been that good. I didn't keep a to the tee record of the product usage, but I had an idea of what should be there.

"Kiki!" I yelled. "Can you come here for a sec?"

"What's up?" she asked as she entered the supply closet.

"Do you have any idea what happened to the relaxers, shampoos and conditioners?"

"What do you mean?" she asked, looking dumbfounded.

"There are several missing", I said.

"Missing?"

"Yes, there are supposed to be more than this", I said, pointing to the product that was there.

"It looks like the normal amount to me, but then again, I don't really pay that much attention to that." she said.

"Well, it's not the normal amount. I know for a fact that there was more than that", I replied.

She ran her hand through her hair and said, "Maybe the stylists actually used the product Sierra."

I didn't like the way she responded to me...like she had a little irritation in her voice. And her body language was a little on the defensive side. I wasn't going to make an issue of it, so I simply said, "I don't think so."

She shrugged her shoulders and walked out. I scanned the shelves again and it was then that I noticed some bottles of hair dye were unaccounted for. Dye jobs didn't come that often, so there was no reason for that many bottles to be gone.

Maybe I was losing my mind...or maybe I hadn't ordered as much as I thought I did...or just maybe I had a thief in the building.

I walked back out to the front just as Danny and Destiny were entering.

"Good morning, my beautiful sistas!" Danny greeted in his usual dramatic way.

"Good morning", Kiki and I said in unison.

Danny threw his head back and gave me a quick once over. "Either you got some good loving last night or you need to do laundry", he said.

I laughed at his comment and said, "What are you talking about?" I then looked over at Kiki, who had a smirk on her face.

"And I'm going with the first one, seeing how you're glowing like a *Yankee Candle*", Danny responded.

"What is that supposed to mean?" I asked, still playing dumb.

"Girl, don't even try to play dumb with me", Danny said, waving his hand in the air. "I know the look of someone who just got laid real good...besides, you don't usually look this informal."

I looked down at myself. "Well dang...thanks a lot Danny. Now I feel like I need to go home and change."

"I didn't say you look bad. I'm just saying I'm not used to seeing you look this way." He looked at me and winked. "Actually, you look younger."

"If that's the case, I may need to do this look more often."

We all laughed and joked back and forth. Everyone was about to head to their stations.

"Guys, when the rest of the gang gets here, I need to have a quick meeting", I said to them.

I noticed Kiki had a disgusted look on her face, but she didn't say anything. She just grabbed her purse and headed to her station. I grabbed my purse and went to my office. As soon as I entered, I headed straight for the file cabinet. I searched for the invoice for my last order. I located it and the one before it. I looked them over thoroughly. A lot more product was missing than I first realized. The most recent invoice showed that I over ordered so I wouldn't have to order anything for a while. So between that shipment and the one before, my shelves should've been fully stocked, even with great business. Something wasn't adding up and I was determined to get to the bottom of it.

"Sierra, the rest of the gang is here", Kiki said, after popping her head into my office. She was about to walk away, but I stopped her.

"Kiki, are you okay today?"

"Yeah."

"Are you sure?"

"Yes, why do you ask?"

"You just seem different...like you're in a bad mood or something."

"Well, I'm fine", she said and walked off.

I sat there for a few seconds, trying to understand Kiki's sudden change in attitude. Something was bothering her, but I didn't have time to try to figure it out. Besides, she said she was okay. So I had to accept that answer. I grabbed the two invoices and headed to the front.

When I got up there, everyone was gathered in the salon area, laughing and chatting. The only people missing were Angel and Kiona. I would have to talk to them later. I cleared my throat to get everyone's attention.

"Good morning, to those of you that just got here."

Everyone gave their greetings.

I continued. "We have a small...well actually, it's not small. It's pretty big...but anyway, we have a problem." I held up the invoices. "This morning, I noticed quite a bit of hair product missing from the supply closet." I paused for a few seconds to see everyone's reactions. They all seemed surprised. "Now, I know business has been good, but that doesn't account for the product that's missing."

"How can hair product just come up missing?" Michelle asked.

"That's what I'm trying to figure out", I responded.

"And you're sure it didn't get used on clients?"

Latoya asked.

"That was my question", Kiki blurted. "I mean we do work in a hair salon. Of course the products are going to get used."

I took a deep breath. "I know that the products are going to get used, but not at that rate. I ordered extra product last time, so I wouldn't have to for a while. There are several bottles of hair dye missing and I know that can't be from use on clients. We haven't had that many dye jobs."

"So what do you think is going on Sierra?" Danny asked.

"To be quite honest Danny, I'm not exactly sure what's going on. But I do know that something's not right", I told them.

No one said anything else. I glanced at everyone to see if I could detect guilt in anyone's eyes. Everyone appeared to be innocent, so maybe the thief hadn't gotten there yet. I didn't want to come right out and say what was on my mind. So I just decided to drop it for the time being. I dismissed everyone and retreated back to my office.

As soon as I stepped into my office, I heard my cell phone ringing inside my purse. I grabbed it and answered it, without looking at the caller id. "Hello."

"So did you like the necklace?" Tyler asked from the other end.

"Well, hello to you too. How has your day been?" I asked sarcastically.

"I'm sorry...I just assumed you would've called me by now...that's all."

"I'm sorry too sweetie. I just have a lot going on here. I love the necklace. It's beautiful", I said.

"Not as beautiful as you", he said in the sweetest voice.

"Aw, you're so sweet and I am sorry I hadn't called you to say thank you. I had every intention on calling you. I just got side tracked with a major issue here."

"What's going on?" he asked.

"Well...I think I have a thief."

"Really?"

"Yes. A lot of hair product is unaccounted for."

"Oh...I thought you meant cash or something", he responded.

"As far as I'm concerned, it's cash, because this stuff cost me money", I said, irritated that he was taking it so lightly.

"I'm sorry. I didn't mean to imply that it wasn't a big deal. Theft is theft...so do you know who it is?"

"No. Not really. I just had a quick meeting with most of them. Of course, everyone's claiming ignorance."

"Do you have any suspicions about who did it?"

"Honestly Tyler, I really don't", I replied, after closing my office door. "But I will say that Kiki's been acting funny since I discovered the missing products."

"Funny how?" he asked.

"Like she has an attitude or something", I replied.

"Sounds like guilt to me", he said.

"I don't know. I can't see her doing that to me. I trust her."

"Sierra, you trust everybody. That's why you have a thief in your spa", he responded.

Tyler always told me I was too trustworthy and naïve. I didn't consider myself naïve. And I trusted people until they gave me a reason not to. I didn't see anything wrong with that.

"There's nothing wrong with trusting people Tyler...I trust you", I told him.

"I'm your husband. You're supposed to trust me. I have your best interest at heart. These people work for you. They have their own interest at heart", he said.

"Technically, they work for themselves. I just rent them space", I explained.

"Don't get all technical, Sierra. The point is, they're working in your establishment and one of them is stealing from you."

"I know...I know. I'm just in shock right now. I never thought that any of them would steal from me", I said, honestly.

"So what are you going to do?" he asked.

I thought about his question. I had no idea what I was going to do. I knew I had to talk to the rest of the gang. But after that, I had no plan. "I really don't know", I finally said.

"Well, you better come up with something...or they're going to clean you out", he replied.

"You think they would continue to steal from me, even after I've discovered it?" I asked.

"It's a possibility, considering you don't know who it is."

"Yeah, you're probably right. I'm gonna have to monitor it very closely."

"I can't believe you didn't monitor it before."

"I never really had to. Jazmin always took care of that type of stuff."

Jazmin was always so dependable. She handled all the little things I didn't want to deal with. I missed her terribly.

Tyler's voice interrupted my thoughts. "Well, I hope you find out who the culprit is. I need to get back to work. I just called to see how you liked the necklace."

"It's beautiful and I really appreciate it", I told him.

"You deserve it...you really do."

"Thanks sweetie."

"See ya at home."

"Bye babe", I responded before hanging up.

I looked down at the invoices on my desk. "How could I let this happen?" I asked myself out loud.

I had to come up with a plan to prevent any more theft. The supply closet didn't have a door on it. I could have one with a lock put on it, but I didn't want to go through the trouble of redoing it. The thought of keeping the supplies in my office crossed my mind, but I didn't want to take away my privacy. The only thing I could come up with was to make up a product log and have them sign it each time they took something out.

It's a shame that I had to take such drastic measures. But what else could I do?

I just needed to find out who was stealing from me and why?

Taylor

"Taylor, you looked ravishing last night", Charles complimented me over the phone. He had been calling me all morning and I kept ignoring his calls. Obviously, he wasn't taking the hint. I finally decided to answer so he wouldn't be calling me all day.

"Thank you Charles", I said weakly.

"So you wanna hook up today?" he asked cheerfully.

I hated to burst his bubble, but I had no intentions of hooking up with Charles today or any other day. "I'm sorry, but I have some errands to run", I lied.

"You gonna be busy all day?" he asked.

"Pretty much", I lied again.

"Damn, when are you gonna have time for me?" he whined.

"I'm not your wife Charles. I don't have to make time for you", I snapped.

"So, it's like that now?" he asked.

"It's always been like that. But for some reason, you're having a hard time seeing that", I explained.

"You can't just cut me off like that Taylor."

"Oh my God...Charles, we had sex one time. Didn't we have this discussion already?"

"Yes, and I told you how I felt then, but you brushed me off."

"I brushed you off, because I didn't think you were serious."

"Oh, I'm serious...as serious as cancer."

"Maybe it had been so long since you had some black pussy, you lost it when you finally got some more. Did you think about that?"

"Don't patronize me Taylor. Maybe I should call my buddy David and invite him and his wife to dinner again...or better yet, maybe I should tell him about my little fling with his wife."

I laughed at his statement.

"So you think it's funny?" he asked.

"I think you're funny Charles", I told him.

"My intentions aren't to be funny. My intentions are to be heard and taken seriously", he replied.

"Well...as far as you inviting us back to dinner, you can save your invitation. Thanks to your wife being a snob and an asshole, David's decided that he doesn't want to have dinner with you two anymore. And I really don't think you want to tell David anything about me and you. You couldn't handle Bonnie taking half of what you have, once she found out about us. And believe me, if David finds out, so will Bonnie."

He didn't respond right away. I assumed he was thinking about what I said. He knew I was right. Bonnie would take him for everything he had. We both had a lot to lose.

"You think you're so smart, don't you Taylor?" he asked. "And that little stunt you pulled with the underwear didn't work."

"What are you talking about?" I asked in the most innocent voice.

"You know what I'm referring to...leaving your panties under the bed. Ms. Lorraine found them while cleaning up. It was obvious they didn't belong to Bonnie. But considering how she feels about Bonnie, she didn't say anything to her. She gave them to me, along with a disgusted look and said nothing else about them."

"Lucky you", I said with a smirk.

"You wanted Bonnie to find them, didn't you?" he asked.

"Yes I did, but for reasons of my own. It had nothing to do with me and you", I explained.

"What do you mean?" he asked.

Now was my time to tell Charles the truth. I didn't want to hurt his feelings, but he needed to know. "Charles I fucked you to get back at your wife", I said.

"I don't understand", he replied.

I told him about the incident at the mall with Bonnie and her friend. I explained to him how I put my plan into action the night we ran into them at the restaurant.

"So you weren't even attracted to me?" he asked.

"Oh...don't get it twisted. I think you're fine as hell. It's just that I wasn't planning on getting serious with you", I told him.

He didn't say anything at first. He just kept sighing into the phone.

"Charles, are you okay?" I asked him. "I hope I didn't hurt your feelings."

"You know Taylor, the crazy thing is Bonnie has no reason to treat people that way. She came from a trailer park in Burlington where she lived with her mother and five brothers and sisters. She didn't go to college. And when I met her, she was working as a cashier in a grocery store. I was attracted to her the minute I laid eyes on her. So I asked her out."

"Let me guess. You instantly fell in love with her and asked her to marry you", I joked.

"Not quite", he said. "I'm not sure if I ever loved Bonnie. She was what I considered the ideal woman...thin with blonde hair and blue eyes. So I married her. Everything was okay in the beginning. Then she made new friends and her whole attitude changed. She stopped talking to her family. She started looking down on those who didn't have money. I had to remind her several times of her beginnings, but she would always get upset with me and tell me that part of her life was over. I stopped bringing it up and accepted her behavior...even though I knew it wasn't right. Hell, I wasn't born with a silver spoon in my mouth. I had to work hard to get where I am. And I wasn't going to let no one take what I had...which is why I banned black women. In my mind, they seemed to be after my money. So I went on the hunt for a white woman."

"I'm glad you got what you wanted", I said sarcastically.

"Hun...if I only knew then what I know now, things would be a lot different."

"I'm sure they would be", I replied.

"My mother can't stand Bonnie. And it's not because she's white. She said she is a materialistic snob."

"That's an understatement", I mumbled.

"Taylor, do you really have room to talk?" he asked.

"Let's get one thing straight", I said, holding my finger as if he could see me through the phone. "I do love money and having the finer things in life, but I'm nowhere near being a snob. Hell, I grew up poor also. And when I got a whiff of the nice life, of course I didn't want to look back. But I've never treated people differently or looked down on people because they didn't have money. I know what it feels like to be singled out because of poverty. So don't you dare compare me to your wife."

"You still married David for his money", he quipped.

"And your point is...?"

"My point is you're a materialistic gold-digger", he replied.

"No, I'm a woman who was tired of struggling. I'm a woman who saw an opportunity for the good life and jumped at it. It was a life I felt I deserved. You don't know what I went through in my past life. So don't sit here and judge me and think you know who I am, because you don't. No matter what, at the end of the day, I'll never be like that little witch you're married to", I told him.

"You keep saying I don't know you, but that's what I'm trying to accomplish", he said.

I had had enough and it was time to put an end to it. "Look Charles...I really need to go. Like I said earlier, I have some errands to run."

"So we can get up some other time?" he asked.

"Sure", I lied. And without waiting for his response, I hung up the phone.

I walked over to my full length mirror and admired myself. "Taylor, girl, you're gonna have to stop hooking 'em with this good pussy", I said out loud. "Some men can't handle it."

My mind went to me and David's lovemaking the night before. After we came from Charles and Bonnie's, he insisted we have sex. After he ate my pussy for what seemed like an hour, he finally decided to get down to business...or as close to business as he could get. Sex with David was always weird to me. He's the only man I've ever been with who didn't want blow jobs. In the few years we've been together, David never let me suck his dick. It was as if it was off limits or something. He never let me touch it or play with it. I wasn't complaining. I just found it to be a little odd. Then I came to the conclusion that he was ashamed of his size. I had come across some big ones in my life, but I had also come across some little ones.

And even though David was lacking in size, I don't think that's what caused me to be dissatisfied. The sex itself was missing something. If it wasn't for the way he feasted on my goodies, I would never have an orgasm with him.

As I stood there looking at my sexy body in the mirror, I knew I needed to release. I could go to my toy stash or I could give Exodus a call. I wanted some genuine dick, so I dialed Ex's number.

"I need to see you", I said as soon as he answered.

"Well hello to you too", he replied.

I ignored his sarcasm. "You need to find a way to get away...now."

"That won't be a problem. Boss man is pretty cool when it comes to stuff like that. I'll just tell him I got some errands to run", he said.

"Okay, meet me at our spot in an hour", I told him before hanging up.

I jumped in the shower to freshen up and remove David's residue. An hour later, Exodus was rocking my world in our favorite hotel suite. He was giving me what David couldn't and I was enjoying every minute of it.

After going several rounds, we collapsed on the bed and lay there for a while, trying to catch our breath. "Thank you Ex...I really needed that", I said.

"Anytime", he replied, lying on his back with his eyes closed.

I admired his smooth chestnut body. He was always so confident. He wasn't ashamed or embarrassed of his body. He didn't try to cover up or run into the bathroom after it was over like David did. And he didn't care if the lights were on when we had sex. But then again, Exodus had no reason to hide. His body was a work of art. I sat there for a few minutes more admiring him until he opened his eyes.

"What's up?" he asked, eyeing me suspiciously.

"Nothing...just admiring your body", I said.

He flashed a smile. "Yeah, it is a sight to see isn't it?"

"You are so full of yourself", I replied and smacked him on his thigh.

"But you love it baby. You can't get enough of it."

He was right, but I wasn't going to tell him that. Exodus knew he satisfied me and that's all he needed to know. "For your information, I can quit you anytime I want", I told him.

"That's what all addicts say", he replied.

I decided not to respond and let him think I was addicted. I knew the truth and that's all that mattered.

"I'm going to jump in the shower", he said, after realizing I wasn't going to respond to his statement.

I admired his naked ass as he strolled to the bathroom. Why couldn't David have a body or sex skills like Exodus to go along with his money? Things would be so much easier for me if he did.

As soon as Exodus turned on the shower, his cell phone vibrated on the nightstand. I was about to go get him, but then decided against it. For some reason, I was curious about who it could be calling him. I picked up the phone and saw the initials CM, along with a 786 area code phone number on the display screen. I started to answer, but knew that would be crossing the line, so I put it back down on the nightstand. My gut feeling told me that CM was a female. I knew I didn't have a right to be jealous, but I was. The thought of Exodus fucking another woman drove me crazy. I wanted to think that he was loyal to me...even though I knew he probably wasn't.

And what was even sadder was that the thought of David with another woman didn't even upset me.

Honestly, it hardly ever crossed my mind. I always figured that if he had me as his wife, he wouldn't even think about looking at another woman. David isn't a bad looking man. In fact, he's very attractive. But when we're out together, I notice the brothas doing double takes at us. They always look like they're questioning how a white man like David ended up with a sista like me.

"Boy, I sure needed that", Exodus said as he exited the bathroom wrapped in a towel.

"The sex or the shower?" I asked.

"Both. I needed the sex, but I also needed the shower after the sex. Can't go back to work with the boss' wife's pussy lingering on me."

"You had a call", I said, ignoring his last statement.

He grabbed his phone off the nightstand and checked it. He put it back down and started putting on his clothes.

"Exodus, are you fucking someone else?' I blurted.

He stopped what he was doing and looked at me long and hard. "Do you really think you have a right to ask me that?"

"I just want to know", I replied, refusing to admit to him that I had no right.

"If you want to know if I'm seeing anyone, the answer is no...not exclusively. I do go out sometimes, but I don't have a steady girl."

"That wasn't the question. I don't give a damn about who you're *seeing*", I said, using my fingers to imitate quotation marks. "I want to know if you're screwing someone other than me."

He came over to me and kissed me on the lips. "You more than satisfy me", he said.

"You're so full of shit", I told him. "And by the way, you might want to grab some gum or pop a mint. I can taste my pussy on your breath."

"Thanks for the tip", he said and went back to putting on his clothes.

Even though he didn't completely answer my question, I wasn't going to push the issue. It was obvious he was trying to spare my feelings. Little did he know my feelings couldn't be hurt. The life I had led, taught me to keep my feelings in check. You could hurt my pride or my ego, but you couldn't hurt my feelings.

"Well babe, I gotta get back to work", he said, after adjusting his tie in the mirror.

"So, you're going straight back to work?" I asked him.

"Of course. Where else would I be going", he replied, giving me a funny look.

"I was just wondering...calm down", I said.

"You know Taylor. You are really tripping today, so I'm gonna go ahead and bounce."

He kissed me on the cheek and left. I stood there for a few seconds, wondering why I was so-called tripping.

Jade

I felt so much closer to Eli since he had opened up to me. All the doubts and insecurities I had about our relationship had vanished last night. The way he made love to me, let me know how much he really did care for me.

"Jade, Mr. Lawson wants to have a meeting in the conference room in about ten minutes", Judy said after popping her head into my office.

"Did he say what it was about?" I asked.

"No, he didn't", she replied and walked off.

The last time Mr. Lawson called a meeting, he had big news. I wonder what he had to talk about this time. A part of me was afraid that he might expose me about my confession. I know he assured me that he was going to keep it to himself. But what if that was a lie? What if he wanted to embarrass me in front of the others to teach me a lesson? I knew I should've kept my mouth shut. Now all the others were going to think I was evil.

I had to face the music, so I walked down to the conference room. Everyone else had already gathered around the table. As soon as I took a seat, Mr. Lawson came in.

"I see everyone's here, so I'll get straight to the point." he said before sitting down in his chair.

My heart was beating so fast, I was sure everyone could hear it.

"I just received some very upsetting news", he said, looking around the table.

I braced myself and was about to stand up when I heard him say, "I just found out I have prostate cancer."

A round of gasps and moans echoed throughout the room.

"Oh, I'm so sorry Mr. Lawson", I said, after gaining my composure.

"Well, it's not as bad as it seems. I mean, of course

I'm not happy that I have it, But luckily for me, it hasn't spread", he replied.

"That's good to know", Carlos said.

"The thing is, I have to have surgery...if I want it gone", Mr. Lawson said, looking like he was upset.

"That's great Mr. Lawson", Judy said.

"Yes, it is...but you don't seem too happy Mr. Lawson", I said.

He looked around at everyone and rubbed his handkerchief across his forehead. "The thing is...I'm scared to death", he said.

"Are you afraid the surgery won't get rid of it?" Carlos asked.

"No, the surgery is what I'm afraid of", he said and wiped his forehead again.

"Aw, come on Mr. Lawson. You're not afraid of a little old surgery are you?" Carlos joked.

"Let them nip and snip around your region and then tell me it's a little old surgery", he replied.

"All I'm saying is that the surgery is for your benefit. Don't you want to live longer?"

"Men live long healthy lives with prostate cancer. Not all of them get surgery you know."

"Then why are you getting the surgery?" Carlos asked.

"Because if I don't, my wife is going to nag the hell out of me", he said.

We all laughed

"Mr. Lawson, you're going to be fine", Nancy assured him.

"I hope you're right", he told her.

"As you said earlier, many men live normal lives with prostate cancer. My grandfather was diagnosed with prostate cancer. We begged him to have surgery or get treatment. He was as stubborn as a mule. He said he was an old man and when the good Lord wanted to call him home, he was going without a fight. He lived to be ninety-two years old. And old age is what took him from us, not prostate cancer."

"Wow, what an amazing story", Judy said,

sounding as corny as ever.

"So, when are you getting the surgery?" I asked.

"In two weeks. And I'm going to be out for a while after that, to recuperate."

"Not to sound selfish, but what's going to happen to us?" Carlos asked.

"You guys will be fine." He looked at me and said, "Jade's going to be in charge and I'll be keeping tabs on you from home."

When he said I was in charge, my heart dropped. He caught me off guard with that. He hadn't even discussed it with me. I didn't want to be in charge. Being operations manager was one thing, but being the head honcho was another. I just didn't want that responsibility. But what could I do? Maybe I could talk to him about it later.

"Plus, I'm going to hire a temp to take Paige's place until I can get someone permanently", he added, interrupting my thoughts.

"What about my old position?" Emily asked.

Mr. Lawson hesitated before answering. "Technically, you haven't advanced yet. Emily, don't take this the wrong way, but I'm still trying to decide if you're the right person for the position."

Emily's face turned beet red, showing her embarrassment. She didn't say anything though. She just looked down at her hands, which were clasped together on the table. I felt bad for her, but she brought it on herself. Everyone at the table knew she wasn't cut out for my old position. Apparently, she wasn't aware of her lack of capability. To end the awkwardness, Mr. Lawson finally dismissed us.

"Can I talk to you for a minute?" I asked him.

"Sure Jade. What's up?"

I waited for everyone to exit the room before speaking. "Why did you choose me to be in charge when you go out for your surgery?"

"Because you're the operations manager...and you're capable of handling it. Is there a problem?"

"Uh...you just caught me by surprise."

"I know and I do apologize for that."

"Can't you leave Carlos or Nancy in charge?" I asked him.

He took a deep breath, like he was irritated. "Jade, you are the operations manager." He pointed his index finger at me. "Not Carlos or Nancy."

"Yes, I know that Mr. Lawson, but-"

He interrupted me. "I don't think you understand the power or the importance of your position Jade."

"I do."

"No, I don't think you do...operations manager is more than a title. You're kind of like my vice president. That means you're in charge when I'm not here."

I stood there for a few seconds, taking in everything he had said. I should've been flattered, but the truth is I was scared as hell. I was scared because I knew that if I screwed up, I would have no one else to blame.

As if reading my thoughts, Mr. Lawson said, "Jade, you've got to stop doubting yourself. You're a very smart young lady and I know you will do just fine. Now, if there's nothing else, I really need to get back to work. I got a lot of things to do."

Without waiting for me to respond, he walked out.

"So you're going to be in charge the whole time he's out?" Sierra asked me.

I had invited her and Taylor over for a little get together, since we hadn't hung out in a while. I made hot wings, potato skins and bought some *Heineken.*

"Yes, girl", I answered.

"Well, that's great Jade", Taylor chimed in.

"I'm kind of nervous though", I said.

"Why?" Sierra asked, licking sauce off of her fingers.

"Because I've never had that kind of responsibility before", I told her.

"You'll do just fine", Taylor said, after she took a sip of her beer.

All I could say is "I hope you're right."

"She is right", said Sierra.

"Can we change the subject?" I asked, not wanting to keep talking about my job. I only brought it up to see if they were confident in me. I know that sounded silly, but I really needed to know that someone else believed in me.

"So what y'all want to talk about?" Sierra asked.

"I don't know...how's business with Sierra?" I asked.

She put her wing down on her plate. "Well, I think I have a thief in my establishment", she said nonchalantly.

"Are you for real?" Taylor asked.

"Unfortunately, I am."

"Well, you don't seem too upset", I told her.

"I am upset. I've had all day to ponder it. So I've kind of calmed down a little", she explained.

"Do you know who it is?" Taylor asked her.

"No...not really", she answered.

"Girl, give us some details, what happened...something. You're being so evasive", I told her.

She sat back on the couch and told us how she discovered her products missing and everyone's reactions.

"Sounds like Kiki's your thief to me", Taylor said and took a big bite of a wing.

"How do you figure that?" Sierra asked.

"Cause I got good sense", Taylor responded.

I didn't want to say anything, but I felt Taylor was right. From the way Sierra described her behavior, she sounded like she was hiding something and she seemed pretty defensive.

"Well, I think you're wrong. Kiki would never steal from me", Sierra defended her employee.

I spoke up. "Well who else can it be Sierra? You said she has a key since Jazmin's out for a while."

"So because she has a key, that automatically makes her a thief?"

"Yes", Taylor blurted.

"No...it's just that she has access that she didn't have before", I explained.

Sierra shook her head from side to side. "I still

don't think it's her", she insisted.

Taylor put her hand on Sierra's knee. "Sierra honey, you can't put all your trust in everybody."

"You sound like Tyler", she replied.

"They're right Sierra", I said.

She gave me a cold look, but didn't say anything.

"What was that for?" I asked her.

"What are you talking about?" she asked.

"That look you just gave me."

She picked up her beer and took a drink. Then she looked down at the floor. "I didn't give you any look."

"Yes, you did", I said more forceful.

Taylor clapped her hands. "You guys are getting off the subject at hand. The issue is to figure out why Sierra is being ripped off!"

I looked over at Sierra, but she was looking down at her food. I waited for her to look up at me. She looked everywhere but at me.

I finally spoke. "You're right Taylor. We need to figure out who's stealing from Sierra."

Taylor smacked her lips. "I already know who's stealing from her."

"Don't start that again", Sierra said.

Taylor blew air out of her mouth. "Come on Sierra, use your brain."

Sierra rolled her eyes at Taylor. "I am using my brain. And my brain says you're barking up the wrong tree. So can we just drop it with Kiki please?"

I saw Sierra was getting upset and I didn't want to add fuel to the fire. But I wanted to know what her plan was in finding out who was stealing from her. "In all seriousness Sierra, what are you going to do?" I asked her.

"I decided to come up with a product log. They have to sign out any item they take from the supply closet", she said.

Taylor started laughing hysterically. "A product log... a product log? You can't be serious Sierra", she said after she finally stopped laughing.

"What's wrong with that?" she asked.

"You don't honestly think that a thief is going to

write down what they steal from you, do you? Taylor asked.

"What I think Taylor is trying to say is that even if they do sign out what they use, they can easily take more stuff and not log it", I added.

Sierra looked at me and Taylor and rolled her eyes. "Y'all think I'm stupid don't you?"

"No, we don't", I said. "We're just trying to protect you Sierra."

Taylor didn't say anything. She just sat there with a smirk on her face. I continued. "You're just a very trusting person...that's all."

"Yeah, a little too trusting", Taylor chimed in.

Sierra ran her fingers through her hair. "Why does everyone act like trusting people is such a bad thing? I trust people until they give me a reason not to trust them."

"And I trust no one...until they give me a reason to trust them", Taylor said.

"We all know that Taylor", I replied.

Sierra smacked her lips and sat up on the edge of the couch. "Either way, I'm going to try my product log and see how that works."

"Sierra, I'm telling you, you're not going-", Taylor started speaking, but Sierra cut her off. "It's my business and I'll run it the way I want. So can we please just drop it?"

The room was silent except for the music playing in the background. Taylor didn't seem to be upset by sierra's outburst. Nothing ever seemed to bother her. A part of me envied her for that. She always seemed to be so emotionally put together. I carried my emotions on my sleeves. I hated confrontation and Taylor faced it head on. I liked to mediate and resolve issues where Taylor caused conflict and basked in it. I guess you could say Sierra fit somewhere in the middle. We were all so very different. One might ask how we were best friends. I guess our personalities offset each other.

I broke the silence. "So what's going on in the world of Taylor Morgan?"

"Oh, not too much", she answered.

"Any lavish parties you haven't invited us to?" I said sarcastically.

"No smart ass. But I'll make sure that you're the first person on the guest list should one come up again", she responded.

"I'm holding you to that...just so you know."

"I know you are."

"So what's David up to, besides making money?"

Taylor's expression grew serious and she took a sip of her beer, which was warm by now. "You know David. He's always busy making money. That's his hobby."

"That's right up your alley isn't it?" Sierra asked, rolling her eyes.

Taylor didn't respond, which was unusual. She never gave up a chance to put someone in their place. I looked over at Sierra and even she was surprised.

"So what's going on Taylor?" I asked.

"I think David's keeping a secret about his family from me", she said.

Sierra and I looked at each other, then at Taylor. She had always been secretive about her family and her childhood. Once I asked her about her parents. She told me she didn't have any and for me not to bring it up again. I never did.

"So what makes you think that?" I asked her.

"Well...for starters, he always said he was an only child-"

"And?" Sierra asked, cutting her off.

Taylor rolled her eyes toward the ceiling. "You didn't let me finish. Like I was saying, he always told me he was an only child. But recently, I came across some old photos of his parents and a little girl. There was even a birth certificate with the name Deanna on it. I'm assuming that's the girl in the pictures."

"So what did he say when you asked him about it?" I asked.

"I didn't ask him about it", she said.

"To be honest, I didn't just come across the photos. I kind of went snooping in his office", she answered, looking down at the floor.

"What made you do that? I thought David was perfect", I said.

"That night when I got home from *Firebirds*, he was in his office. And he was acting all suspicious, like he was hiding something. Before I left to go upstairs, I saw him shoving some papers in his desk. So when I got the chance, I searched through his desk and I came across those photos and that birth certificate", she explained.

"Maybe she passed away when she was young", Sierra suggested.

"That's still nothing for him to be so secretive about. I'm his wife. He can tell me that. Plus, his parents have never said anything about her either."

"Maybe it's a touchy subject for them Taylor. The death of a family member, especially a child or a sibling can be very traumatic. Some handle it by never discussing it. It's like they pretend it never happened", Sierra explained.

"She's right Taylor. Some people handle tragedies like that by sweeping them under the rug. The less they talk about it, the less it hurts," I added.

Taylor sat silently for a few minutes. Then she said, "I just hate to think that he's being secretive about his past."

I gave her a look and said, "Aren't you kind of being a hypocrite Taylor?"

She rolled her eyes at me and said, "Call me what you want Jade. But you have no idea about what my childhood was like. You don't know what I went through. Everyone didn't have the perfect childhood you had."

I was surprised when I heard Sierra say, "She's right, Jade."

"Why are you taking her side?" I asked.

"I'm not taking anyone's side. All I'm saying is that there may be situations or times in a person's past that they don't want to discuss", she said.

"Keeping secrets", I said.

"Not necessarily. I wouldn't call it that. Just like we said earlier about David, it could be that it's just too painful to talk about."

Sierra sounded like she was speaking from experience. Were both of my best friends keeping secrets from me? Sierra never talked about her childhood either. I was the only one that discussed my childhood. I talked about how amazing my childhood was, hanging out and playing with my cousins. Maybe they felt their childhoods wouldn't measure up to mine and that's why they were a little hesitant about discussing theirs. Or just maybe they both had events in their childhood that they wanted to forget. I thought about Eli and how he hated his childhood because his father wasn't there for him. I know Taylor claimed to not have any parents, but Sierra never discussed hers. Come to think of it, Sierra never talked about anything. If I didn't know any better, I'd say her life didn't begin until she met Tyler.

I felt like asking Sierra about her past, but I didn't want to put her on the spot. Plus the tension in the room was already thick. So instead, I said, "Taylor, why don't you just come out and ask David about the Deanna girl?"

"I can't do that!" she yelled.

"Why not?" I asked.

"Because he'll know that I've been snooping through his stuff", she replied. "I said that earlier Jade!"

"Damn, Taylor. I forgot...I'm sorry. You don't have to bite my head off", I responded, rolling my eyes at her.

She leaned back in the chair. "No Jade, I'm the one that should be sorry. I didn't mean to yell at you."

"Some girls night this turned out to be", Sierra said with a smirk on her face.

We all started laughing. "Are we PMSing or what", I asked in between laughs.

"You sound like the men. Why we got to be PMSing just because we showing a little aggression?" Sierra asked.

Taylor added, "Cause most of the time, it's true."

"Oh, that is so sexist Taylor", Sierra shot back.

"Call it what you want. It is what it is", Taylor replied.

We all laughed again and enjoyed the rest of the

evening without any more arguing. Even though we were all different and had our little spats, I couldn't have asked for better friends. I couldn't imagine my life without them.

Sierra

I surveyed the supply closet, documenting everything that was in there. Last night after I got home from Jade's I came up with a log to use for signing out products. I was going to show it to the gang when they all came in. I'm pretty sure a lot of them wouldn't be happy with the idea, but I had to protect my inventory.

I don't like having to make everyone suffer because of one person's dishonesty, but that's the way it has to be. And after listening to Taylor tell me how naïve and trusting I was last night, I felt like a fool.

After everyone had staggered in, I called them all to the waiting area. "As I told you all yesterday, I discovered missing products", I said as I looked into each of their eyes.

I held up the product log. "I've composed a product log. Every time you take something out of the supply closet, you will sign it out on this."

A chorus of sighs and groans spread throughout the room. Someone even said, "This is ridiculous!"

"Look, I know this may seem petty to you guys, but this is what I have to do", I explained.

"It's like you don't trust us or something", Kiki said. I shook my head at her statement. I couldn't believe she let that come out of her mouth, considering the situation at hand.

"I think the problem is that I trust you all too much", I said.

"That's cold", Kiona replied.

"I didn't mean that in a bad way. I know all of you aren't thieves. But the truth of the matter is, one of you is a thief", I said.

Kiki spoke again. "So because you think someone is stealing, we're all being penalized." She used her fingers to imitate quotation marks when she said the words think and steal.

"I don't *think*, I *know*. The numbers don't lie and most of all, my eyes don't lie", I said.

Danny had his hands on his hips. "So every time I need to get something out of the supply closet, I gotta sign it out?"

"That's correct", I answered.

He threw his hands in the air and said, "This is just too much for me!"

"That's what I'm saying", Destiny added.

"Well, you have two options. You can continue to use my products and sign them out...or you can supply your own", I told them.

They all looked at me without saying anything. I knew it may have appeared to them that I was being a little harsh, but I had to protect my business.

"Sierra, I don't see a problem with what you're doing. If you ask me, you should've been doing that a long time ago", Angel spoke for the first time since I called the meeting.

I noticed Kiki and Michelle rolling their eyes at her.

"I don't have a problem with it either", Latoya said.

"Honestly, I don't see why anyone would have a problem with it...unless they're hiding something", I said, looking back and forth between Kiki, Danny, and Michelle.

I felt that one of them was guilty. I wasn't sure about Destiny. She would most likely be guilty of knowing something and not speaking up. I know I kept defending Kiki to everyone else, but as time went by, I was beginning to think that she wasn't as innocent as I may have believed.

"You wanna start searching our bags before we leave too? Or better yet, why don't you make us carry those clear bags like they do in the department stores?" Danny said with sarcasm in his voice.

"You can be a smart ass if you want Danny. It doesn't bother me. The bottom line is my name is on that door. And if you don't want to abide by my rules, then maybe you need to find a new place to work." I looked at each of them. "And that goes for everyone." I stood with my arms crossed, daring anyone to say something that would piss me off further. When no one said anything, I ended the meeting. They all went back to their stations.

I went behind the counter to check the appointment book. As I flipped through the book, I realized Latoya was standing at the counter. "You need something Latoya?" I asked her.

She interlocked her fingers in a nervous manner. "Actually, I need to talk to you Sierra", she said.

I motioned for her to continue. "Um...can we talk in private?' she asked.

"Sure", I said and motioned for her to follow me to my office. "Close the door behind you", I told her as she entered the office behind me.

I sat down in my chair behind my desk and invited her to sit in one of the chairs facing my desk. "So, what's on your mind?" I asked her.

She looked down at her hands, like she was unsure of what to say. I knew whatever she had to tell me, had to be important. Latoya was an ideal employee. She came to work, did her job and went home. She and Angel were all about business. They didn't get involved in gossip and drama like the rest. It must be something with the hair stylists and nail techs.

"I don't want to start no trouble or nothing like that Sierra", she finally spoke.

"I can't see you as a trouble starter Latoya", I told her.

She took a deep breath. "Well...it's about the situation with the missing products."

I sat up in my seat. "You know who took them?"

"Not exactly."

"Well, what do you know?" I asked her.

"One day recently, I heard Michelle and Kiona talking. They didn't know I was around."

"What did you hear?" I asked, growing impatient.

She continued. "They were saying something about somebody getting caught if they continued to do what they were doing. Then Michelle said no one would get caught because you didn't notice stuff like that and you were too trusting."

"Who were they referring to?" I asked her.

"They didn't implicate anyone. It's like they were trying to talk in codes or something", she replied.

I shook my head and leaned back in my chair. "I can't believe this shit!" I said.

"Honestly Sierra, I didn't think anything of it until you told us about the theft yesterday. I started putting two and two together. At first, I wasn't going to say anything, because I wasn't sure what they were talking about and I'm still not. But I decided you needed to know what I overheard."

"You're right Latoya. We don't know for sure if that's what they were talking about. But my gut tells me it's all connected."

She sat up in her chair and leaned in closer to me. "Sierra, please promise me you won't tell them that I told you anything, because I don't want any trouble."

"I wouldn't do that to you Latoya. I like you too much. Besides, that's not how I operate", I told her.

"Thanks Sierra. I appreciate that...As you can probably tell, I don't really fit in with the little clique. I don't want to give them even more reason not to like me", she said.

I smiled at her. "It's okay if you don't fit into that clique Latoya. You're a very sweet person and I wish some of the others were more like you."

She smiled at me, showing off perfect white teeth. I never realized how pretty Latoya was. She was one of those people who didn't like to draw attention to herself. She wore her hair in a simple ponytail. Her wardrobe usually consisted of jeans and t-shirts. As far as makeup went, she only wore lip gloss and a little mascara. As I sat there and watched her, I saw the potential in her. With a little confidence booster and a small makeover, she could be a knockout.

She started to get up. "Thanks, Sierra. I better get back to work."

"Wait Latoya", I said, holding my hand out. "I hope this doesn't offend you. But have you ever thought about getting a makeover?"

She rolled her eyes toward the ceiling. "And look like those other girls out there? No thank you."

"You don't have to go to that extreme", I told her.

"What do you have in mind?" she asked with a little hesitation.

"You're a very beautiful girl Latoya and I don't think you realize that."

"I've never considered myself beautiful", she replied.

"That's because you're not giving yourself the attention you deserve."

"What do you mean?" she asked

"I bet if you did something to that hair...other than a ponytail, experiment a little with some makeup and spruce up your wardrobe, you'd stop traffic."

She laughed. "I seriously doubt that", she replied.

"See...that's what I'm talking about right there. You have sooo much potential and you don't even know it. Anybody can be born with a pretty face, but it takes someone special to have sex appeal and self-confidence."

I thought about Alexis and how she had impacted my life. She helped me regain my sex appeal and now I was sharing the wisdom with someone else.

"I don't know Sierra. That's just not my style", she said.

"I tell you what ...let me give you my friend Taylor's number. If anyone can help you, she can. She'll teach you some makeup tricks and help you pick out some fabulous clothes." I wrote Taylor's name and number on the back of one of my business cards.

She took the card out of my hand and stood up. "Thanks", she said dryly.

"Latoya, I don't want you to leave out of here thinking badly of me. I just think you're a beautiful young lady and you need to start showing it. Give those girls a real reason not to like you", I told her.

"I'll think about it", she replied and walked out the door.

I hoped I didn't offend her, but it was something I felt needed to be said. Either way, I had bigger fish to fry.

Who and what were Michelle and Kiona talking about when Latoya walked up on them? I was tempted to just go out there and ask them little hussies if they were stealing from me and if they weren't, who was. But I knew I couldn't do that without implicating Latoya.

They couldn't have been talking about themselves though. So that left Kiki, Destiny, Danny, Angel and Jazmin. I knew they couldn't have been talking about Jazmin. And I couldn't see Angel being the guilty one. So that narrowed it down to Kiki, Danny, and Destiny.

Then I remembered every criminal makes at least one mistake. If they were stupid enough to keep stealing from me, they would eventually get caught. It was just a matter of time.

Taylor

"Did I tell you that Charles invited us to dinner again?" David asked me as he poured himself a cup of coffee.

"No, you didn't. What did you tell him?" I asked.

He took a sip of his coffee. "I told him I'd get back to him."

"I thought we agreed that we weren't going to go back over there again."

"I know that Taylor, but I couldn't just come out and say no", he replied.

"Why not?" I asked.

"Come on Taylor. You know I'm not that type of person."

"So what are you gonna tell him?"

"I'll just keep brushing him off or come up with some excuse", he said.

"Eventually, you're gonna have to tell the truth...His wife is a bitch and you don't want to be in her presence", I told him.

"Now Taylor, that's not nice", he said in a scolding manner.

"So you don't feel that way?" I asked him.

"I never said she was a bitch. I just said she wasn't the most pleasant person to be around and she needed to work on her people skills", he explained.

"Well, I still say she's a bitch."

My cell phone rang, echoing Mary J Blige's *My Life* throughout the kitchen. I picked it up and saw Sierra's number on the screen. "What's up chic?" I asked after answering.

"Hey girl. What you up to?" she asked.

"Nothing, just sitting here chatting with David."

"I need a favor", she said.

"Sure, what is it?" I asked.

"Well, one of the girls here at the spa needs your

expertise."

"What are you talking about?"

"Her name is Latoya. She's a very pretty girl, but she just needs some sprucing up. So I gave her your number", she explained.

"Oh, I can definitely handle that...turning an ugly duckling into a beautiful swan", I said, laughing.

"Taylor, she's not ugly. She just doesn't realize how beautiful she can be. Her self-esteem and self-confidence is a little low," she said.

"How old is she?" I asked her.

"I think she's like twenty-one or twenty-two, something like that."

"So when does she want to meet with me?"

"Actually, she didn't say for sure if she was going to call you. But I just wanted to give you a heads up in case she does."

"Oh, okay. That's cool."

"Well, I have to get back to work. I got a client coming soon", she said.

"Ok. I'll talk to you later then."

"Bye."

"Chow."

I ended my call and walked over to David, who was finishing his coffee. "Babe, I gotta head to work. I have an important meeting today", he said before putting his coffee cup in the sink.

I wrapped my arms around his waist. "David, why don't we take a mini vacation this weekend?"

He turned around to face me. "I wish we could, but I have way too much work to do."

"That's always your answer. What's the purpose of making all of that money if you're not going to enjoy it sometimes?"

"Come on Taylor. Don't start that again", he replied.

I could tell by the tone of his voice that he was getting irritated. "All I'm saying David is that we don't travel as much as we should."

"I didn't realize there was a quota", he said.

I rolled my eyes at him. "David, you have a beach house in Myrtle Beach and a penthouse in New York that are just collecting dust. What's the purpose of having them if you're not going to use them?"

"They're there for when we need them Taylor. You know this is a busy time of year for me. You just can't decide to go somewhere at the last minute."

"David, you are your own boss. You can take time off whenever you want to." I stuck out my bottom lip, hoping to persuade him to change his mind. It was always hard for him to say no to my pouting face.

He grabbed me by my shoulders. "I promise we'll do something soon babe."

"When?" I asked.

"I don't know Taylor. I can't say the exact date."

"That's because you know it's not going to happen", I said.

"That's not fair Taylor. You know I always keep my word to you."

"Yes, I know but-"

"Can we talk about this later? I really gotta get going."

He kissed me on the cheek and headed out the door.

Sometimes David made me so mad. He had more money than he'd spend in his lifetime, yet he didn't like spending it. I had always heard that rich people were tight wads. I didn't believe it until I married David.

When we got married, I had visions of traveling the world, visiting all the places I dreamed of when I was a young girl. The only places, he has taken me out of the country were Mexico, Jamaica and the Bahamas. That may seem like a lot to many people. But when you had money like David, the number should've been higher.

I want to visit Europe and Africa and so many more places. I am married to a man with plenty of money and I want to start living like it. After all, I deserve it.

I remember when one of my mother's boyfriends was supposed to take us to *Disneyworld*. His name was Teddy. I was so looking forward to that trip. But of course my mother had to screw that up. She talked him into giving her the money to handle the arrangements. She ended up blowing all of the money on clothes, shoes, wigs and makeup for herself.

When Teddy found out, he flipped out and jumped on her right in front of me. I had to grab a butcher knife out of the kitchen and threaten him with it to get him off of her. He was sweating and his face was all scrunched up like a mad man's.

"What you gonna do with that knife?" he asked me.

I held it up to him. "I'll stab you with it if you touch my momma again!" I yelled.

He wiped the sweat off of his forehead. "Yo' momma owes me money and I want it", he yelled back.

"I told you I spent the money Teddy", my mother said, with blood dripping from her nose.

"Bitch, you used me!" he yelled.

I tightened my grip on the knife. "Mr. Teddy, I think you need to leave", I told him.

He was still glaring at my mother. "I aint going nowhere 'til I get what's owed to me."

"How you gonna do that Teddy? You can't get blood from a turnip. The money is gone", she said, getting up in his face.

I could tell he wanted to hit her again. But he looked over at me holding the knife. "I'm gonna leave, but this shit aint over Gwen!" he yelled and walked out the door.

As soon as he left, my mother turned to me said, "Can you believe him? He got a lot of nerve coming up in my house tripping over a few dollars."

I shook my head in disbelief. "It wasn't your money to spend Momma."

She went into the kitchen and wet a paper towel to wipe her nose. "He was a fool to give me the money in the first place", she said.

"But you knew he was giving you that money to pay for the trip Momma", I cried.

She put her hand on her hip and said, "Well, he should've known better."

"You knew how bad I wanted to go to *Disneyworld.*"

"It aint always about you Taylor. Fuck Mickey, Minnie, Goofy, and all the others. They aint gonna pay no damn bills", she said and turned her back to me.

"It's never about me Momma. You don't think about anyone but yourself. I just can't believe how selfish you are." I still had the knife in my hand. And at that moment, I wanted to thrust it into my mother's back. I could've ended it all right then and there and blamed it on Teddy. That would've rendered me motherless and a child of the state. I decided against it, but I later realized it couldn't have been worse than what I lived through. I stepped closer to her, just as she turned around. "You walking up on me like you wanna do something with that knife. Girl, don't be getting no ideas in that thick ass head of yours."

I smacked my lips. "I aint getting no ideas!"

"Watch your tone girl. You know I'll still knock yo' teeth down yo' throat", she warned. "Now, put that knife up."

Eventually, Mr. Teddy forgave my mother for stealing his money and she forgave him for beating her up. They went on like nothing ever happened. I was furious with my mother for spending that money on herself. And when Mr. Teddy offered to spring for the trip again, she told him that I didn't need to go to *Disneyworld* and she could use that money for something useful, which we all knew meant herself.

When I realized I wasn't going on that trip, I cried. I had never been outside of Shallotte, other than to Wilmington, Myrtle Beach and other surrounding cities. But those didn't count. I wanted to travel to faraway places and experience different cultures. I was tired of being confined to the hick town of Shallotte. I knew that once I escaped that place, I would never go back.

So now that I've got money, there's no reason why I shouldn't be traveling the globe. My mother held me back, back then. And I'll be damned if I was going to let David hold me back now. He's going to have to get it together or I would resort to traveling alone...at least that's what I'd make him believe.

I had no plans for the day and I didn't know what I was going to do with myself. I could go shopping, but I didn't feel like going by myself. Of course Jade and Sierra were both at work. I need to get some rich friends who don't have jobs.

I thought about going through my closet to see if there was anything I needed to part ways with. But I really didn't feel like going through all of those things. Besides, I probably wouldn't get rid of anything. I usually didn't. I still had plenty of clothes with the tags still on them and boxes of shoes I hadn't put on since I tried them on in the store. David always said I had enough clothes to split between twenty women. I loved clothes and shoes, but I think I really just liked the idea of having all of those things. The more I had, the better I felt. I never had nice things growing up, so I made up for it.

I had almost a full day ahead of me with nothing to do. Then I thought about the photo and the birth certificate in David's office. Hazel had the day off and David wouldn't be home for quite a while. So I had time to go fishing for more information.

I entered David's office, looking over my shoulder as if expecting someone to come up behind me. As I sat at David's desk, I admired his beautiful office. Art by local artists covered the walls. One wall had a bookcase that expanded the length of it. Books of all genres filled the shelves. His desk was an exact replica of the one at his office, with the leather chairs to match. David had great taste. He didn't skimp on spending when it came to furnishing his space.

I opened the drawer I had found the items in previously. They were still there, just as I left them. I rummaged through the drawer looking for more things. There were just a bunch of business cards. I tried the bottom drawer and discovered more miscellaneous papers. I was about to give up my search, but then I noticed the four drawer file cabinet in the corner behind his desk. I went to open the top drawer, but it was locked. Damn it! There had to be a key somewhere. I searched through his desk, hoping to locate it. Just when I was about to give up my search, I realized I had not checked the small pull-out drawer underneath the desk.

I looked through the clutter and found a small silver key on a spiral key ring. I tried it to see if it would work. It did. I opened the top drawer, which seemed to be full of real estate papers. Then I tried the second drawer. It too, was filled with files and files of papers relating to David's business. Next came drawer number three. Again, more business related junk. I didn't understand why he kept so much business stuff at his home office. If he had all that stuff at home, what did he have at the office?

I tried the fourth and final drawer. To my dismay, it too had nothing but real estate paperwork. I sat back in David's chair and blew air out of my mouth. There had to be a reason he kept it locked. He could've been hiding his real estate papers, which would've been pointless. I couldn't tell you what any of that stuff meant if you paid me.

I was about to close the drawer when I noticed a big brown envelope sticking up in the back of it. I pulled it out and saw the word *miscellaneous* written across it with a permanent marker. I opened it and pulled out its contents. The first thing on top was a duplicate of Deanna's birth certificate. I studied the piece of paper, noticing the birth date, January 23rd, 1969. David was born in 69, but his birthday was March 19th. I was more confused than ever. How could she be David's sister if they were born in the same year, only two months apart? And she couldn't be adopted because David's parents' names were on the birth certificate. That only meant that David was adopted.

I continued sorting through the papers. There were numerous awards and certificates made out to Deanna Morgan. From what I could tell, she was very smart. Then I came across a stack of old photos with a rubber band around them. I removed the rubber band and scanned the photos. They were all of Deanna, I had assumed at various events. One photo appeared to be at a prom or formal dance. She looked so uncomfortable, like she really didn't want to be there. I studied the rest of the photos. Deanna was a pretty girl, but she was kind of awkward. Even in the photos of her and her parents, she looked uncomfortable. She just looked unhappy. I kept looking through the photos, hoping to see some of David. There were none.

I put the rubber band back around the photos and put everything back in the order in which I found them. I stuffed everything back into the envelope and put it back into the file cabinet. I locked it back and put the key back into the desk.

Before leaving out of the office, I glanced around to make sure everything was in its place. I didn't want to leave any evidence of my snooping around.

I was thirsty, so I went to the kitchen and grabbed a bottle of water. I took a long gulp of the drink before putting it down on the island.

My thoughts went back to Deanna. Where was she? And why was David being so secretive about her? Maybe she *was* dead and talking about her was too painful. Or maybe she turned out to be a disgrace to his family and they disowned her. But as sweet as David was, I couldn't see him turning his back on his sister, even if she wasn't his blood relative.

This discovery had my mind boggled. My husband was keeping a big secret from me concerning his family and it was freaking me out. I guess if you really thought about it, everyone had skeletons in their closet. But I felt I had good reasons to keep my childhood a secret. I hated everything about it and felt no reason to share details about it with my husband, friends, or anyone else I came into contact with.

There was obviously a good reason David didn't want me to know about Deanna. Regardless what it was, I was determined to find out.

Jade

I had spent most of the morning working closely with Mr. Lawson. He was preparing me for when he went out for his surgery. He made running the company look so easy. But I was still a little nervous about it. It was easy for him because it was his company and he'd been doing it for years.

Mr. Lawson was a remarkable man. I had learned a great deal about him. He told me how he started his company. He had worked at another advertising agency in New York as a sales representative many years ago. He said he wanted to venture out on his own and move down south. He didn't get much support from his boss and fellow co-workers. He said they all told him he was making a big mistake and would fall flat on his face. With his savings and wife's support, he headed to Durham and opened up *To The Max Advertising.*

I asked him if he had any regrets. He said "When I first opened the agency, I was expecting the money to just come rolling in, but it didn't. Business was a little slow at first...probably about the first nine or ten months. I was ready to throw in the towel and go back to New York to beg for my job back."

"What happened?" I asked.

"My wife told me she didn't marry a quitter. She said it was unrealistic of me to expect not to have any obstacles or road blocks in my way. She told me she was proud of me for going out on a limb and she wasn't going to sit by and let me give up on something that meant so much to me."

"So what did you do?"

"I did what any real black man would do. I got on my knees and prayed, busted my ass and got this business up and running. And as they say, the rest is history."

Mr. Lawson's and Sierra's success stories made me

proud to be black. It always felt good to see black people in business for themselves. A lot of us were scared to take a chance...scared of failure...scared of success, always wondering what if? And Mr. Lawson was lucky to have a woman like his wife. A lot of women in my generation would've turned their backs on a man who was struggling to get his business off the ground. They don't want to stick out the tough times, but you can be sure that they're around when the money's rolling in. I took pride in not being that type of woman. My parents didn't raise me to be that way. They taught me to be independent and to never rely on a man financially.

"Make sure you can do it by yourself", my mother always told me.

My thoughts always went to Taylor when it came to women, money and men. Don't get me wrong, I love Taylor like a sister. But I've always been against her policy of dating for money. She always said if a man was broke, he could keep on walking. Of course, most women wanted to be financially secure. But I just couldn't see myself being with a man simply because he had money. He had to have something else going for him, other than a fat bank account. As long as Taylor was surrounded by money, she was happy. I often wondered if she even loved David, but I already knew the answer to that. I also wondered what happened in her childhood to make her act that way.

But it wasn't my place to judge Taylor on her lifestyle. She had her way of living and I had mine. Besides, I still loved her just as she was.

My cell phone vibrated inside my purse, which was in my desk. I usually didn't have it turned on while I was at work, but I decided to grab it anyway. The number was marked unknown, but only my friends and family had my number, so I answered it anyway.

"Hello, this is Jade", I spoke into the phone.

There was dead silence. "Hello", I said into the receiver again.

"I bet you think you're hot stuff, don't you bitch?" a female yelled into the phone.

"Who is this?" I demanded.

"Don't you worry about it. Just know that I'm your worst nightmare!" she responded.

"Paige, I know it's you. You're trying to disguise your voice. How did you get my number?"

"Honey, I have my ways and like I told you before, my name isn't Paige."

"Even if you're not Paige, you're calling for her. Whoever you are, please just leave me alone!" I yelled.

"Bitch, raising your voice doesn't scare me. But I will say this. Your wrong doing is going to catch up with you...sooner than you may think."

"I haven't done anything to you", I replied.

"Whatever. Just consider yourself warned", she said before hanging up the phone.

I locked my phone and threw it back in my purse. How in the hell did Paige get my cell phone number? She was really trying to mess with me by calling me on my cell phone. I wasn't about to let her get to me. She was a coward who got her kicks out of making empty threats to me over the telephone.

I walked down to Mr. Lawson's office. His door was open and he was on the computer. He motioned for me to enter when he noticed me standing there.

"You got some more questions Jade?" he asked.

I hesitated for a moment before answering. "Actually Mr. Lawson...I just wanted to tell you that I just received another phone call from Paige."

He gave me disgusted look. "Look Jade, I can't monitor every phone call that comes to this office."

"She called me on my cell phone this time", I responded.

"How did she get your number?" he asked.

"I have no idea Mr. Lawson."

"So what did she say?" he inquired.

"She just threatened me like always and denied it was her."

Mr. Lawson sat up in his chair. "Jade, are you sure there's not more to the story than what you told me? You sure there's not a man involved?"

"I told you the whole story Mr. Lawson. And there's not a man involved. I've been seeing one man for the past few months."

He cupped his hands together and moved them back and forth. "Jade, I really don't know what you want from me", he said.

"I just wanted to inform you on what's going on", I said, feeling frustrated.

"My suggestion to you is to get the police involved, if you're concerned about her coming after you", he said.

"I've already taken out a restraining order against her. So hopefully, she won't come near me", I told him.

"Well...good luck", he replied.

"Thanks", I said and walked out the door.

As soon as I stepped into the hallway, I walked right into Charlene. "Sounds like you got some drama on your hands", she said, with a sneaky grin on her face.

"What are you talking about?" I asked her.

"What's going on with you and Paige?"

"I have no idea what you're talking about Charlene", I said to her and walked away.

She followed me to my office. "You don't have to lie to me. I overheard your conversation with Mr. Lawson", she said with her hand on her hip.

"You shouldn't eavesdrop on people's private conversations."

"It wasn't private if the door was open", she tried to rationalize.

"You're pathetic", I told her.

As if not hearing what I said, she asked, "So what happened between you and Paige that made you take out a restraining order on her?"

I sat down at my desk. "I have a lot of work to do and I suggest you get back to work as well", I told her, without looking at her.

She stood there for a few seconds just staring at me. At first she had a serious look on her face. Then all of a sudden, she started smiling. "I've figured it out. It all makes sense now", she said.

"What makes sense?"

She pointed at me. "You're the one who sent the emails with the pics of Paige and Robert."

My heart started beating faster. If Charlene knew what happened, it would be all over the office before the end of the day. So I did the only thing I could think of. I lied.

"You have no idea what you're talking about. I did not send those emails."

"Something tells me you're not telling the truth. I know what I just heard", she said.

"First of all, you can't assume anything based on bits of a conversation you overheard. Second, the conversation was none of your business", I told her.

She smacked her lips and said, "You don't have to be so nasty about it Jade."

"Oh, I think I do. You seem to think it's okay to put your nose in other people's business...like you have no class", I said, looking directly into her eyes.

"How you gonna tell me I don't have no class? You're the one that sent those filthy pics all over the office", she said.

"See what I mean? You're still saying things that you don't know are facts. My advice to you is to speak only what you know", I said, with firmness in my voice.

She was about to respond, but I cut her off. "Look Charlene, I'm not about to sit here and go back and forth with you. It's obvious that you don't respect other people's privacy and personal business. I'm sure Mr. Lawson wouldn't be too happy about that."

"Oh, so you gonna go running to Mr. Lawson about this?" she asked.

"I don't know...Do I need to?" I asked, tilting my head to the side.

She took a deep breath and said, "No...I guess not." Then she walked out the door.

I sat there still stunned at her boldness. Some people just had no limits. I would never go at someone the way she came at me. She acted like we were buddies and she could say whatever she wanted to me.

Even though I denied sending those photos, I knew

she was still going to tell everyone in the office that I did. She had to be stopped. Everyone in the office respected me and I didn't want my image scarred, just because some busy body couldn't keep her mouth closed.

But I would have to deal with Charlene later. I had more important things to handle, like what I was going to do for lunch.

Sierra

I had spent the majority of the day with clients. I had one appointment after another. Don't get me wrong. I was happy to be busy. That meant more money coming in. I had a little time before my next client, so I decided to sit at my desk and nibble on the fruit salad I had prepared.

"Hello Sierra", a voice came from my doorway.

I looked up to see Jazmin standing there with a big smile on her face. I jumped up to greet her. "Oh my goodness. Jazmin, it's so good to see you. How are you doing sweetie?"

"I'm doing just fine Sierra...thanks to you," she said, still smiling.

I grabbed her hand and pulled her to me. She gave me a warm hug. We held each other for a few seconds before she let go. I studied her from head to toe. Even though she still had a little scarring from her injuries, she looked great.

"You look good Jazmin", I told her.

"Thank you Sierra. I feel good too." She was still smiling, like she couldn't control it.

"Come sit down and talk to me", I said and walked back around my desk and took a seat in my chair.

She sat down in one of the chairs. "So what do you want to talk about?" she asked.

"Girl, don't play with me. Tell me how life's been treating you? Most of all, when are you coming back to work?" I said.

She sat back in the chair and crossed her legs. "Sierra...you don't know how grateful I am to have you in my life."

"Oh Jazmin, that's so sweet. But trust me. It was nothing", I explained to her.

"It was something to me. Your story saved my life." Her eyes started to water and she looked toward the ceiling. "I had been putting up with Jamal's abuse for most of our marriage. It started out the same way it did with your mother. He was verbally abusive at first. Then it moved up to a slap here and there. Before long, I was getting beat down on a regular basis. It seemed to get worse after each baby was born. It was like he'd get jealous of the attention I was giving to the baby. He'd just go off for the simplest things. There were even times he would hit me when I was holding one of the babies."

Tears were running down her face. I handed her a tissue from my desk.

"He didn't ever hurt your girls, did he?" I asked.

She dabbed her eyes with the tissue. "No, he'd never hurt the girls. They mean the world to him. I use to think that if it wasn't for them, he would've killed me a long time ago."

I felt so bad for her. Jazmin was one of the sweetest people I knew. And the thought of her husband beating on her that way put a pain in my heart. "So why did you stay with him so long?"

She looked down at the floor and closed her eyes. For a minute, I thought she had gone to sleep. Then she opened her eyes and spoke. "I stayed with him because he kept promising me he would change. I stayed with him because I wanted my girls to have both parents in the home. I stayed with him because...I loved him Sierra. But I knew what I was going through wasn't normal. Now I sit here and think about all the times I tried to hide the black eyes, the busted lips and the bruises, and it makes me sick to think I let myself go through that. He had this control over me that made me feel like he owned me."

"The important thing is you finally got the courage to leave. While it's good for kids to have both parents in the home, it's never good for them to be around abuse. It scars them in more ways than one. Take it from me."

She let out a heavy sigh. "And I know that now. I just hope it's not too late for them. They've witnessed so many beatings from Jamal", she said and started crying again.

I tried to comfort her. "They're still pretty young.

So it may not be too late for them. Just give yourself credit for leaving when you did. Besides, they can always go to therapy...just like I did", I told her.

"I guess you're right." She laughed and shook her head. "And the crazy thing is he's been begging me to come back to him."

I sat up in my seat. "I hope you're not thinking about it", I said. The same way she left him is the same way she could go back to him.

She smacked her lips. "Of course not! Did you not just hear everything I said? There's no way I'm going back to Jamal. I feel better than I've felt in years. There's no turning back. But enough about me. How are things around here?"

I stood up and went to close the door. I didn't want anyone trying to eavesdrop on what I had to say. Jazmin gave me a funny look when I went to sit back down.

"What's up Sierra? You're acting strange", she stated.

I told her all of the details of what had been going on since she'd been gone. By the time I finished telling her everything, she had a look of confusion on her face.

"Why are you looking at me like that?" I asked her.

She started shaking her head from side to side. "I don't believe this...I knew something wasn't right."

"What are you talking about Jazmin?"

She looked towards the door as if she was making sure it was closed. Then she leaned in closer to my desk. She took a deep breath. "Okay...right before I left, I started noticing some items coming up short."

When she said that, I was really pissed that she hadn't said anything to me. "So why didn't you tell me?" I questioned her.

"To be honest Sierra, I really didn't think anything of it."

I gave her a dirty look. She must've noticed because she said, "What I mean is I thought maybe it was just me. I figured that I had miscounted or maybe the product had gotten used...or maybe my numbers were just off. I don't know Sierra. I can say for sure that the thought of someone stealing it definitely didn't cross my mind."

"Yeah, I know what you mean. I was shocked too. You put too much trust in people and it comes back and bites you in the ass. I built this business from scratch. And to know that someone thinks they can steal from me and get away with it really pisses me off!" I was starting to get upset all over again. I had told myself that I wasn't going to get worked up again, but every time I thought about it, it made my blood boil.

"So what are you going to do?" Jazmin asked, interrupting my thoughts.

I told her about the sign out log. She let out a hearty laugh, just like everyone else. "Do you really think that's going to work Sierra?"

I became frustrated. "Why does everyone keep saying that?"

She stopped laughing. "No hard feelings Sierra, but there's no way some sign out sheet is going to stop a thief."

I smacked my lips. "I know that. I just figured if I got stern with them and put my foot down, they'd know that I mean business and maybe they would stop."

She studied me a few seconds before she said anything. "You know Sierra...I always thought you were too laid back."

She surprised me with her confession. "I'm just a laid back person Jazmin. Everyone knows that."

"It's okay to have a laid back personality. But you've got a business to run...and sometimes folks mistake kindness for weakness. And that's when they take advantage of you."

I thought about what she said. She was right. They all thought I was weak just because I was nice to them and wasn't all up in their space. Well, they were in for a surprise, because a new Sierra was about to unveil.

Taylor

"You look beautiful Latoya", I told her as she spun around.

"Thanks", she answered shyly.

I had just put the finishing touches on her new look. She had called me just as Sierra said she would. And I eagerly accepted her request to help her. When she arrived, I saw how beautiful she really was. I had seen her in passing at the spa a few times. I knew I had to pull out all the stops.

I took her to the mall to go shopping. She was a little hesitant at first, when it came to picking out clothes. When I told her I was going to foot the bill, she began to cry.

"What's wrong sweetheart?" I asked her.

"No one's ever did anything this nice for me before", she said between sniffles.

"I'm sure that's not true", I told her.

"Oh, but it is", she assured me.

"Well, you pick out anything you like and don't worry about how much it costs", I told her.

She stared at me for a few seconds. The she said, "Why are you doing this?"

I said, "Because I can...Now let's get started. These clothes aren't going to pick out themselves."

We spent hours selecting clothes for her to try on. She ended up with a very modest wardrobe that consisted of casual, business, semi-formal and formal attire. We got shoes and accessories to match. Afterward, we went to the *M.A.C* and *Bobbi Brown* counters to pick out makeup.

I spent so much money on her, but I didn't mind. It felt good to be able to help someone who was as sweet and caring as she was.

After we finished shopping, we headed to the food court to grab something to eat. I learned a lot about Latoya. She was a student at *Central*. She was the oldest of five children. Her job at Sierra's spa was a way for her to earn money while she was in school. She was studying to be a lawyer and her ultimate goal was to be a family court judge.

I was really impressed with her. She had her head on straight and knew what she wanted out of life. I asked her about her parents. She told me her mother was a teacher and her father worked for the division of motor vehicles. She said they were very encouraging to her and her four sisters.

As I sat there and listened to her talk about her family, I had to battle the green-eyed monster inside my head. Her family didn't have a lot of money, but they had what I wanted. They had love and unity; something I never had growing up. Her parents encouraged and supported them in anything they chose to do.

Now as she was standing in front of me, I couldn't help but wonder why her self-esteem seemed so low. She kind of reminded me of myself at that age, minus the curves.

"Latoya, can I ask you a question?"

"Sure."

"You are such a beautiful girl. Why do you have such low self-esteem and self-confidence?"

She looked down at the floor and said, "I don't know."

I put my fingers under her chin and lifted her face up so she was looking at me. "Come on Latoya. There's got to be a reason. Do you think you're not pretty?"

"It's not that. I-I just never really thought about it", she said.

"Aw come on. I know you have boys chasing you all over *Central*", I teased.

"Yeah, right. I've never had any boys chasing me", she said. She walked over to look out the window. "I've always been the plain Jane. When all of my girlfriends had boys drooling over them, I was left out." She pointed to her chest. "As you can see, I'm lacking in the breast department."

"And? There's more to a female's beauty than

356

having big boobs", I told her.

"Well, that's easy for you to say Taylor...I mean look at you. You're not lacking in anything."

"That may be true, but that doesn't make me more beautiful than you...or anyone else for that matter. Besides, sometimes having boobs and curves can be a bad thing", I replied.

"I don't see how that's possible", she said.

I grabbed her hand. "Come sit down and let me talk to you."

We took a seat on the settee at the foot of the bed. I begin to tell her my story. "I developed early when I was growing up and it got me attention that I didn't want." I thought about my mother's friends that took advantage of me. I could still see all of their faces in my head.

"What do you mean", she asked.

"Boys were always making snide remarks and all of the girls hated me because I got all of the attention. I even had older men hitting on me."

She scrunched up her face. "Ooh gross."

I laughed at her reaction even though there was nothing funny about it. But I had no intentions of telling her about how I was constantly molested by my mother's boyfriends.

"I just wanted to be a normal teenager. But because I was blessed or cursed with curves and boobs, I couldn't have one. The boys never looked me in the face. They were always staring at my chest or my ass. And I hated it. The truth is Latoya; you really don't want that kind of attention. Take it from me", I told her.

She let out a deep breath. "I guess you're right."

"I know I'm right. You've always had natural beauty. You just needed someone like me to bring it out."

"Thanks Taylor. I really appreciate all of this." She looked down at the clothes and shoes she was wearing.

"Really, it's no problem Latoya. I was glad to help. Now we just need to work on your confidence and you'll be the total package."

"I don't know if I can be confident", she said with a frown.

"What's your GPA in school?" I asked.

"It's a 4.0...but what does that have to do with anything?"

"Do you ever get worried that you won't obtain your degree?"

She gave me a puzzled look before answering. "No. Of course not."

"And why not?"

"Uh...because I consider myself a smart person and I study hard."

"Which means you're confident when it comes to your academics...correct?" She started smiling. "I guess you can say that."

"So the same confidence you have when it comes to school can be used in all aspects of your life."

She got up and walked over to the antique full length mirror. She admired herself a few minutes. "I never realized how bright my eyes are or how full my lips are", she said.

I walked over to her and stood behind her. "It's amazing what a few makeup tricks can do."

"Yeah, but I won't be able to do my makeup the way you did it", she said.

"Latoya honey, you really don't have that much makeup on. And I promise you will be able to handle those simple steps. It will be like brushing your teeth once you get used to it."

Once again, she began to cry. I went to the bathroom and grabbed some tissues off the vanity. I handed them to her and put my arm around her shoulder. "Why are you crying now?" I asked her.

She dabbed her eyes with the tissue. "I'm sorry Taylor. It's just that I'm so emotional right now. You've been so nice to me. I have pretty new clothes and shoes. I don't even recognize myself in the mirror. I guess it's just a lot for me to take in right now."

"I understand." And I did understand. Maybe if I had someone to mentor me, I might have turned out a lot differently. I'm sure I wouldn't have been a high-priced call girl slinging pussy to men I didn't know for all those years. Hell, I would've gone to law school just like Latoya was doing. Instead, I was living off of my rich husband's money.

Up until now, I never had any regrets about the life I've led as an adult. I always figured that as long as I got what I wanted, nothing else mattered. If I had to use men to get it, then so be it. Going to college crossed my mind from time to time. But then my mother's negative comments would pop into my head and bring me back to reality. So I settled for what I did best...until I met David.

"Taylor, did you hear what I said?" Latoya asked, jarring me out of my thoughts.

"Oh, I'm sorry Latoya. What did you say?"

"I said I need to get going because I have a paper to write."

"Oh, okay. I really enjoyed our time together today", I told her.

"Thanks. I did too. And once again, I want to thank you for all that you've done for me. I don't know how I can ever repay you", she said, getting misty eyed again.

"You can repay me by continuing to do well in school and getting that self-confidence we talked about."

"It's a deal", she replied and shook my hand.

We gathered up all the items we had purchased and I helped her take them to her car. She gave me a long hug before she got in the car.

"If you need anything, whether it be makeup tips, fashion advice, or just someone to talk to, don't hesitate to call me", I told her.

"Thanks. I will", she said before driving off.

I went back inside to the kitchen to grab a bottle of water out of the fridge. Hazel was in there preparing dinner. I had completely forgotten that she was there.

"So, who's the young lady that just left?" she asked.

I took a long gulp of my water. "She works at Sierra's spa."

"She's a very attractive young girl", she said as she cut up vegetables.

I downed the rest of my water. "Yes, she is. But for some reason, she's having a problem seeing that."

She scooped up the vegetables and put them in a pan on the stove. "That's too bad. The expectations set by these famous folks are just so high these days that these young girls have no self-esteem. If you're not pencil thin with big titties and plumped up lips, you don't make the cut. And that's a damn shame."

I had to hold in my laugh. Ms. Hazel was so amusing when she talked. She wasn't one to bite her tongue and she said what came to mind, whether she hurt your feelings or not. I didn't really like her when I first met her, because she was always looking over my shoulder. I came to realize that she had a genuine concern for David and was only trying to figure out my intentions for him. So I pulled out my southern charm and eventually won her over. We haven't had any problems since.

"Well, Latoya doesn't have to worry about not being pencil thin. Lots of girls would love to be her size", I said before tossing the empty water bottle in the recycle bin.

Ms. Hazel rolled her eyes to the ceiling. "I know you're not referring to yourself...are you?"

I smacked my lips and ran my hands down my body. "Of course not! I love my full figure", I boasted.

She put her hands on her hips, shook them seductively and said, "I know what you mean."

We both started laughing at her little dance. Ms. Hazel was more than full figured. She had enough breasts, hips, and thighs for three women. She was always saying that a man wanted a woman with some meat on her bones.

"Is that husband of yours going to be home for dinner tonight?" she asked while opening a bag of brown rice.

"As far as I know, he is. I haven't talked to him since he left home this morning. I know he had meetings all day."

"He usually calls if he's going to be late anyway, doesn't he?" She poured some rice in a pot filled with water and stirred the vegetables in the pan.

"Yes, he does. He's considerate like that."

She smiled and looked off into the distance. "He sure is. He's the sweetest man I've ever met."

Ms. Hazel was very fond of David and protected him like a mother hen. She knew him better than anyone. I decided this would be a good time to ask her some questions about him.

"Ms. Hazel, can I ask you a question?"

"Sure honey. What is it?"

"Does David have a sister?"

She turned her head towards me so fast; it looked like it was going to spin off. "Now Taylor, you know David is any only child."

"Yeah, I know-"

She cut me off. "Why did you ask me such a thing?

I ignored her question. "So you've never heard him mention a sister the whole time you've worked for him?"

She wiped her hands with her apron and sat down at the island next to me. "Now if David had a sister, don't you think we would've met her by now?"

"You would think. But what if she was a secret or something?"

She shook her head and stood up to go check the food. "Taylor, you spend too much time alone. Where is this coming from?"

I wasn't about to tell her that I had been snooping through David's office. She would give me a lecture and I really wasn't in the mood for one. "Let's just say that I have my reasons for asking."

"May I ask what those reasons are?"

"Really, I don't want to get into it. Just forget that I asked."

She took the vegetables off the stove and put them on a pot holder. "So you ask me this off the wall question and I'm supposed to just forget about it?"

"Exactly."

"If you say so."

I stood up to leave. "And can you not mention this

to David?"

She hesitated for a second. "Sure, it'll be just between us."

"Thanks", I said and walked out.

I hope I could trust Ms. Hazel to keep her word...at least until I got to the bottom of this mystery girl.

Jade

The time for Mr. Lawson to go out on leave was winding down. We were both as nervous as hell...for different reasons, of course. I made several attempts at convincing him to leave one of the others in charge. It didn't work. He told me he had made up his mind and there was no changing it. So I had to like it, or leave it. I didn't like it, but I damn sure wasn't leaving. I'll just have to accept it and make the best of it. I'm sure Mr. Lawson won't let me fail.

As far as Charlene goes, I took care of her. I went straight to Mr. Lawson and told him what happened. He wasn't too happy about it and called her to his office.

When she came to his office and saw me sitting in there with him, the expression on her face was priceless. She knew it wasn't going to be pretty.

"Could you close the door behind you please?" Mr. Lawson told her after she entered.

She did as she was instructed and took the seat beside me. "You wanted to see me Mr. Lawson?" she asked in the sweetest voice she could muster up.

Mr. Lawson looked at me before answering her. "Yes Charlene. I did. Jade told me about a conversation you two had."

She looked over at me and rolled her eyes. "What about it?"

Mr. Lawson leaned back in his chair and took a deep breath. The look on his face told me he wasn't too pleased with Charlene's demeanor.

"I'm going to say this. First, I expect all of my employees to respect my privacy as well as their fellow co-workers' privacy. Second, I expect everyone to behave in a professional manner. I don't want my place of business turned into a rumor mill." He looked at me when he made that last remark.

"So you're just gonna make assumptions without

even getting my side of the story Mr. Lawson?" Charlene asked, with an attitude.

I had never heard anyone speak to Mr. Lawson like that. We all respected him so much.

"I'm not making assumptions. I'm just stating my expectations...not that I should have to. But apparently, some of you have forgotten that this isn't high school." His tone was stern.

Charlene folded her arms across her stomach. "So you're doing this all because of something she told you?" she asked, tilting her head towards me.

"Do you have a different version?" he asked.

"I don't know. I haven't heard her version yet", she replied.

He sat up in his seat and rested his elbows on his desk. "Exactly", he said.

Charlene looked confused. She looked back and forth from me to Mr. Lawson. Then she said, "What's that supposed to mean?"

Mr. Lawson didn't answer her. Instead he said, "Why don't you tell me your side of the story."

She looked at me before saying anything. "Well, all I was doing was trying to get to the truth Mr. Lawson."

"All you were doing was trying to stir up trouble", I jumped in.

Mr. Lawson glanced at me and said, "I'll handle this Jade." He then turned to Charlene and said, "And what truth were you trying to get to?"

"I just assumed that Jade was the one who sent those pictures around...and before you ask, I came to that assumption after I overheard you two talking." She rolled her eyes at me like I had done something to her. I knew she was pissed with me because I told Mr. Lawson about our conversation. But she had herself to blame.

"So you overheard me and Jade talking and came to your own little conclusion?" Mr. Lawson asked her.

"Well, am I lying?' she asked with a smirk on her face.

I wanted to slap that smirk off of her face. Mr. Lawson was saving her from getting a beat down.

"Can I ask you something Charlene?" Mr. Lawson asked her.

"I guess", she said.

"Why is this so important to you? What does it matter to you?" he asked her.

I could tell his questions caught her off guard. Once again, she looked over at me. I just threw her a fake smile and waited for her answer.

"Um...it's not important to me....It's just that...uh...I just feel that everyone should know the truth", she stammered.

"Paige is gone and so is Robert. It's over and done with", Mr. Lawson said.

"That may be true, but Paige is gone because of her", she said, pointing her finger at me.

I wanted to grab that finger and break it off. I was about to respond to her statement, but Mr. Lawson gave me a warning look.

"Correction...Paige is gone because she had sexual relations in my establishment. And if Robert hadn't been moving away, he would've been out of a job also", he explained to her.

"But no one would've ever known if Jade had not put it out there like that", she responded.

Mr. Lawson took a deep breath and wiped his forehead with the handkerchief he took out of his jacket pocket. "So you think it's okay to break the rules or do unacceptable things as long as no one finds out?"

"No...uh...that's not what I'm saying. People should just mind their business and not worry about other folks' business", she said.

I couldn't control myself. Mr. Lawson was just going to have to do what he had to do. I ripped into her. "You got a lot of nerve fixing your mouth to say that. The only reason we're sitting here now is because you are in my business and because you are a gossiping busy body. Every time something goes on around here, you're the first one to spread it, like you don't have anything else to do. When you're not sure of all the facts, you make up stuff or twist things around."

"I'm not the one spreading sex pictures around the office. So before you start talking trash, you need to think about your wrongdoing. I guess you think because you're always up Mr. Lawson's butt, you can do what you like."

Mr. Lawson stood up. "Okay, that's enough!" he yelled. "I did not bring you in here so you two can argue and sling mud at each other."

"Well, she started it", Charlene whined.

"It doesn't matter who started it. I'm about to finish it. I'm going to be leaving soon and I can't have all of this nonsense going on around here. Going forward, I don't want to hear another word about those photos. Do I make myself clear?" He looked at both of us.

"You won't hear another peep out of me", I said.

We both looked at Charlene. And Mr. Lawson repeated his question. "Do I make myself clear?"

"Yes Mr. Lawson", she answered dryly.

"I don't want to come back and clean house." He looked at Charlene. "I trust that you all will behave like the adults that you are. Now let's all get back to work."

Charlene stood up and waltzed out the office, slamming the door behind her. I just shook my head and wondered how I was going to deal with her while Mr. Lawson was gone.

He looked at me and said, "I hope that's over with."

"Mr. Lawson, I really want to apologize once again for all the problems my actions have caused", I told him.

He sat back down in his chair. "I said I didn't want to hear any more about that. And I meant it Jade. Let's move on from that. What's done is done."

"Okay Mr. Lawson", I replied.

And that was the end of that.

Since then, every time I've crossed Charlene's path, she's given me dirty looks. But the good thing is I haven't heard anyone talking about those photos. I knew it was eating Charlene up inside, not being able to spread what she considered juicy gossip. But I didn't care, as long as my reputation didn't get tarnished. If she decided not to ever speak to me again, it wouldn't phase me none.

Now, if I could just get Paige off my back,

everything would be okay. I had received a couple more phone calls. And I even found a threatening note on the windshield of my car after work one day.

What bothered me the most was the way Eli was acting about the whole situation. He kept saying that she was just trying to ruffle my feathers and I shouldn't take her too seriously. Like I told him, you can never tell what a person is capable of doing. And you should never underestimate what a person will do when they feel they've been done wrong. I guess I should've thought about all of that before I decided to go against Paige. Well, it was too late to think about that. What's done is done. I just needed to figure out how I was going to get rid of that crazy bitch. She just had to be stopped.

But I would have to worry about that later. I was enjoying the time I was spending with my man.

As if reading my mind, Eli said, "Jade baby, you alright over there? You've been quiet all night. What's up with that?"

"I'm okay Eli. I just got a lot on my mind, that's all."

"Don't tell me you still worrying about that crazy broad Paige?" He was smiling, as if he found it amusing.

"That, among other things", I said.

"Other things like what?" he asked, sounding defensive.

He probably thought I was referring to something pertaining to our relationship. But I was over that. I had no intentions of asking him anymore personal questions. Now that I knew more about his family, I understood why he was so secretive. But I was irritated because he acted like he had no idea what was bothering me.

"Eli, you know I've been worrying about being in charge when Mr. Lawson goes out on medical leave. Do you not listen to me?"

"How can I not listen to you when you're whining about the same shit every day?"

I was hurt by his statement and I felt the urge to go off, but I knew that would only make matters worse. "Oh, so that's how you see me...as someone who whines every day?"

"I didn't mean it like that Jade."

"Well, that's how you said it. Considering you are my man, I thought I could talk to you and express my feelings to you. But apparently, I'm getting on your nerves."

"See, I never said you were getting on my nerves. You're trying to put words in my mouth now."

"So exactly what were you saying?" I asked.

He blew air out of his mouth and stared at me for a few seconds. I could see the frustration in his face. "All I'm saying is that you let stuff bother you too much Jade."

I knew he was right, but I couldn't help it. "I'm sorry if I'm not like you and don't care about anything."

He laughed at my remark. "It's not that I don't care. I just don't let shit get to me, especially shit I can't control. Take this Paige for example. You may be right about her being capable of doing some crazy shit to you. But are you gonna stop living because you're afraid? You got to live for the moment and worry about shit when it actually happens. The best thing you can do is be prepared. And as far as work goes, obviously your boss thinks you can handle it. I don't see him leaving his business in control of someone who don't know what in the hell they're doing. You just need to relax and do the best you can, which I'm sure you will. You're a smart lady and I'm confident you can handle it."

I couldn't help but smile. Times like this made me realize just how much Eli meant to me. He always knew what to say to pep me up. And I could tell he was sincere about it.

"You know for a guy, you're pretty smart", I joked.

"I wouldn't call it being smart. I call it keeping it real", he said.

"Oh, okay. I can deal with that...I think."

"I'm gonna request the check...unless you want some dessert or something", he said and downed the rest of his drink.

I loved cheesecake, but I was too stuffed to eat anything else. "No babe, I think I'm gonna have to pass."

"Well hello there, Eli. Long time no see", a tall light skinned female said as she approached our table. She gave me a look of disgust and I returned the favor. Her hair was cut short like mine. She had on a dress that showed off her toned body and her legs appeared to be a mile long.

I looked over at Eli to see his expression. He looked very uncomfortable. "What's up Tosha?" was all he said.

"Nothing much Mr. Turner, besides waiting on you to call me", she replied and looked over at me and smiled.

"Well...uh...I been kind of busy", he said.

"Too busy for your favorite client?" she asked.

"Someone told me you found another trainer", he replied.

"Well, I did for a short time. But you know no one can work this body like you can", she said and ran her hand down the side of her body.

I could feel my temperature rising. I didn't know how much longer I could sit there and listen to her make sexual innuendos to my man. He had a stupid grin on his face, and it appeared that he had forgotten I was there.

"Um-um", I cleared my throat.

"Oh...uh...Tosha, this is Jade. Jade this is Tosha, one of my former clients", Eli introduced us. I noticed he didn't call me his girlfriend, but I wasn't going to make a big fuss about it.

I held my hand out to shake hers. She looked at it like it had fungus on it before giving me a weak handshake. She then turned back to Eli and said, "So when can we get together?"

He looked at me before answering. "Uh...I'll have to check my calendar." He reached into his back pocket and pulled out his wallet. He gave her one of his business cards. "Take this in case you lost my number. We can come up with a time that's suitable for both of us."

"Okay. I'll definitely be giving you a call", she said, giving him a seductive smile.

He pretended not to notice and said, "My rates are still the same."

"I hope they are", she replied and looked towards the entrance where three other women were standing. "Well, I better get going before my girls leave me. And then you'll have to give me a ride home."

I almost said, "Don't count on it bitch." But I knew better.

Eli just laughed it off and said, "Girl, you're crazy. I'll see you around."

As soon as she was gone, I said, "Who in the hell was that Eli?"

Without looking at me, he said, "I told you her name is Tosha and she's a former client. I don't know what else you want to know."

Maybe I was making a big deal out of nothing. After all, she was the one being rude and flirting with him. He was being his usual charming self. If I was going to try to make it with Eli, I had to learn to deal with his career. He came into contact with women every day. A lot of them were overweight housewives who had low self-esteem. And some of them were attractive, sexy women who were hoping for the opportunity to show Eli what they were working with. I couldn't let jealousy and insecurity get the best of me. And I couldn't hold Eli's looks against him. He was an attractive man and women were going to continue throwing themselves at him as long as he looked the way he looked.

"I'm sorry Eli. I was just being jealous. Plus, I didn't like her little funky attitude", I told him. "It's like she was saying things just to piss me off."

"You know how y'all women are", he replied.

"No, I don't. Why don't you tell me how we are", I said.

He shook his head from side to side. "Oh no. I'm not getting into that. I know better."

"Well, you started it."

"Just forget I said anything."

We both laughed and called a truce. Eli paid the check and we headed back to my place.

Once we were in the car, Eli said he wanted to pick up some beer.

"We can just stop to the *Kroger* on MLK", I told him.

When we pulled into the shopping center, I noticed the lights on in Sierra's spa. I knew she was closed. So there was no reason for lights to be on. I pulled out my phone and dialed her cell phone number.

As soon as she answered, I said, "Where are you?"

"Well, hello to you too. I'm at home, if you must know", she replied.

"Is your spa closed?"

"Of course it's closed. Jade you know I close at six. What's going on with you?"

"I'm here at the shopping center and I noticed there are lights on in your spa."

"Are you sure? I know I cut the lights off before I left."

"Yes, I'm sure. You need to get out here ASAP." I hung up the phone before she could respond.

"Is everything okay?" Eli asked.

I had completely forgotten he was still sitting in the car with me. "I don't know yet. The lights are on in Sierra's spa, and they shouldn't be."

"Okay?"

"Someone's been stealing from her and this may explain how they've been doing it", I told him.

"Oh. I see. Well, I'm going in the store."

"Okay. I'm gonna sit out here and wait for Sierra."

"Do you need anything?"

"No, I'm good."

After Eli got out of the car, I turned my attention back to the spa. I tried to see if I could see any type of movement in there. I didn't see anything. I wanted to go in there and investigate, but it wasn't my place and I didn't know what I'd do if I found someone in there.

I saw Sierra's car approaching the shopping center and I jumped out to go meet her. As soon as I reached her, she started fussing at me. "I don't appreciate you hanging up on me."

"I had to in order for you to take me seriously. Plus, I wanted you to get out here right away", I told her.

She looked around the parking lot and scrunched up her face. "That's Kiki's car", she said and pointed at a black Maxima parked a few spaces down from where she parked.

"What would she be doing here this time of night?" I asked, feeling I already knew the answer.

"I don't know, but I'm about to find out", she replied and walked towards the spa.

I followed behind her to have her back in case she needed it. I also wanted to be nosey. As soon as we entered, we heard noises coming from the area towards Sierra's office. Sierra was about to go back there, when a male and a female came out carrying boxes.

"Kiki...Danny...what in the hell is going on here?" Sierra asked.

They both just stood there, not saying a word. They were just as surprised to see Sierra as she was to see them.

Sierra raised her voice. "Somebody answer me damn it!"

I put my hand on her shoulder. "Calm down Sierra", I said to her.

She whipped her head around to look at me. "How am I supposed to calm down Jade? I got two people standing in front of me with their hands full of my merchandise. Merchandise that's been coming up short lately", she said.

Danny was the first one to speak. "It's not what you think Sierra honey."

"Yeah, it's not as bad as it seems", Kiki added, with a nervous laugh.

"It looks to me like you're ripping Sierra off", I said.

Sierra glanced at me. "Thanks Jade, but I can handle this."

Then she turned her attention back to the perpetrators. "I can't wait to hear how you're going to explain this little scenario."

When neither one of them said anything, Sierra said, "I'm waiting."

Still no one said anything. "Okay...since neither

one of you wants to say anything, I'll start with you Kiki, since you're the one with the keys."

"Okay, but I need to put this stuff down. It's getting heavy", she replied.

She and Danny both put the products down on the receptionist counter.

Kiki hesitated a few seconds before speaking. "W-we were trying to get you a better deal on hair care products."

Sierra clasped her hands together. "Let me get this straight....You were taking my products out so you could get me a better deal on other hair care products? Is that what you want me to believe?" She then looked over at me. "Can you believe this shit Jade?"

I didn't say anything, because I knew she really wasn't expecting an answer. Then she started laughing hysterically. "Are you okay Sierra?" I asked her.

She didn't answer. Instead she said, "You guys must really think I'm stupid. I mean, who would actually believe that bullshit you just told me? Only an idiot...so you must think I'm an idiot."

"She's telling the truth Sierra", Danny said.

"You're a liar...both of you are liars", she replied.

She looked down the hall. "I need to go see what damage you've done." Then she walked down the hall.

When she left, I gave both of them dirty looks, letting them know I didn't appreciate them stealing from my best friend.

Sierra let out a shriek and I was getting ready to go see if she was okay. But she came storming out of the back. "Where's the rest of my shit?" she asked, getting up in Kiki's face.

"It's in the c-car", she stuttered.

"I can't believe this! Half of my stuff is missing from back there. I am so furious right now. I trusted you Kiki. How could you do this to me?"

"I told you it's not what you think Sierra", she explained once more.

"Even when Jade and Taylor said it was probably you, I didn't want to believe it", Sierra said, shaking her head.

Kiki looked at me and rolled her eyes. I returned the favor. She had no right to have an attitude considering she had just got caught doing what we had predicted.

"Are one of you gonna be man or woman enough to tell me the truth?" Sierra asked them.

They looked back and forth at each other. Then Danny said, "Okay Sierra, I'm gonna tell you the truth."

Kiki nudged him with her elbow and said, "Shut up Danny!"

"I'm sorry Kiki. I can't do this no more", he replied.

"You better keep your mouth closed if you know what's best for you", she warned.

Danny put his hand on his hip and said, "Heffa' I know you not threatening me. Danny aint scared of no one honey."

Sierra was growing impatient. "Danny, just tell me what's going on."

He took a dramatic deep breath and looked around at everyone before speaking. "Okay...the truth is Kiki and I are trying to open our own salon."

"Okay, what does that have to do with me?" Sierra asked.

Danny put his hand up. "Sierra please let me finish before I lose my nerve."

Sierra nodded her head for him to continue.

"Well, we came up with the idea of-"

"No, *you* came up with the idea", Kiki said, cutting him off.

He smacked his lips at her. "Like I said, *we* came up with the idea of popping into your inventory to build up our inventory. We were trying to cut corners the best way we could."

I knew Sierra was disappointed in them. She treated her staff like they were family. I could see tears forming in her eyes, and she was trying her best not to let them fall.

Her voice came out in almost a whisper. "So you thought it would be okay to steal from me...like I wasn't gonna be affected?"

"I'm really sorry Sierra", Danny said.

Kiki didn't say anything. She didn't seem to have any remorse for her actions. She had her arms crossed and was staring at Sierra like she was the one that did something wrong.

"Sorry isn't good enough Danny", Sierra replied.

He tried pleading with her. "I know what I did was wrong Sierra. I just hope you can find it in your heart to forgive me."

"I want the rest of my shit. And I want you and Kiki to clean out your stations. I don't want to see your faces in my spa again", she said through clenched teeth.

Kiki stormed out the door, almost bumping into Eli, who was just walking in. "Is everything okay in here?" he asked.

Before I could answer, Sierra said, "Hell no, everything's not okay. I just discovered who was stealing from me and I'm very disappointed."

Danny was still standing there looking as if he wanted to break down and cry. I almost felt sorry for him. But then I had to remind myself of what he did. He walked over to Sierra and tried to grab her hand. She stepped back away from him.

"Please don't Danny. Maybe you should go help Kiki bring in the rest of my stuff. And don't try anything slick, like trying to leave, because I will call the cops."

He did as he was instructed and walked out the door.

"Don't even say it Jade. I do not want to hear 'I told you so' right now", she said and walked around the counter.

"Sierra, you know I wouldn't say that to you...especially not now", I told her.

"How could I have been so stupid?" she asked, mainly to herself.

I rubbed her back to comfort her. "Don't say that Sierra. When you're a trusting person like yourself, you may not see things that are right in front of you", I told her.

She gave me a funny look and said, "Oh really?"

"Yes. But there's nothing wrong with that Sierra. It happens to the best of us."

She looked at me for a few seconds and then she looked over at Eli, who was looking very uncomfortable. As if reading my mind, he said, "Uh...I'm gonna go see what's keeping them."

As he walked out the door, I noticed Sierra was still staring at him. "Do you have a problem with Eli Sierra?" I asked her.

"Why would you ask that?"

"Well, you just seem like you don't like him."

"I've never said that I didn't like him Jade", she replied and started fumbling with papers on the counter to avoid looking at me.

"No, you haven't said it, but I just get this funny vibe from you when he's around."

"Look, I have nothing against Eli. Besides, why should it matter if I like him or not? You're the one that's dating him...not me."

"It matters because you're my best friend and I value your opinion."

She looked me in the eyes for a few seconds. Then she looked away before saying, "I have nothing against Eli Jade. If he makes you happy, then I'm happy."

I was about to respond, when Kiki and Danny walked in carrying the rest of Sierra's products.

"Just put them down beside the rest of it", Sierra instructed.

They placed them down on the counter and Kiki turned to leave.

"Kiki before you leave, I need to get my keys please", Sierra said.

Kiki reached into her pocket and pulled out her keys. We all watched her as she took the keys off of her key ring and tossed them on the counter. Then she headed towards the door.

"You can come back early in the morning to clean out your stations", Sierra said.

Kiki turned around and said, "Danny, you coming

with me or not?"

Danny looked at Sierra. She didn't say anything. She dismissed him with the wave of her hand. He gave me one last look before strutting out the door behind Kiki.

I hadn't finished my discussion with Sierra about Eli. I knew she had a lot going on at the moment, but I needed to know the truth. But before I could ask her anything, she started speaking.

"Jade, if you don't mind, I really want to be left alone right now", she said.

"Are you sure Sierra? 'Cause I can get Eli to just leave and I'll stay here with you", I told her. I really wanted to be there for her in her time of need. I knew she was hurting inside.

"No...that's okay...really I'd prefer to be by myself right now. I have a lot of stuff to sort out. But thanks for the offer." She gave me a weak smile.

"Okay. But if you need me, don't hesitate to call", I told her and gave her a warm embrace. She was resistant at first, but eventually gave in. She released me and let out a deep sigh.

"Thank you Jade...for calling me."

I slapped her on the arm. "Girl, you don't have to thank me."

"Oh yes I do. I don't know what I would've done when I came in tomorrow and saw all of that stuff gone." She shook her head like she was still in disbelief.

"Well, at least they got caught and you don't have to worry about that."

"Yeah, I guess you're right", she said in a way that sounded like she was trying to convince herself.

"Well, I'm gone, if there's nothing else", I told her.

"Okay, goodnight...and once again, thanks for everything."

I walked out the door. I looked to make sure Kiki and Danny were gone. When I got to the car, Eli was leaning against it, waiting for me. "Is your girl okay in there?" he asked as soon as I reached him.

"Understandably, she's still upset. She really put a lot of trust in them. And for them to do that to her, has really crushed her. But, I think she's gonna be okay", I explained.

"That's cool...um...can I ask you a question?"

"Sure, what's up?"

"Does Sierra not like me or something?" he asked.

I pretended to be surprised by his question. "Now Eli, why would you ask a question like that?"

"It just seems like she doesn't care for me too much."

"How can you come to that assumption when you haven't been around her that much?"

"The last couple of times I have been in her presence, she was giving off a vibe. Plus I can tell when somebody aint digging me too tough."

"Oh, is it because she's not drooling over you like all the other women?" I teased him.

"Don't even go there Jade. I'm serious. Why doesn't your girl like me?"

"I think you're just imagining things Eli. She just went through something that upset her tonight. She wasn't herself. Besides why do you care if she likes you or not?"

"Yeah...I guess you're right. I don't care." He opened the driver's side door. "Let's go. It's getting late."

I hopped in the passenger seat. Even though I gave that speech to Eli, I was curious about Sierra's feelings towards him. He had just confirmed what I was thinking.

What I didn't understand was why she felt the way she did. Did she want him for herself? No...that couldn't be the answer. Sierra would never do that to me. Plus, she wouldn't give any man other than Tyler, the time of day.

Maybe she just thought he wasn't good enough for me. Really, I didn't know what her reason was. But I would find out.

Sierra

When Jade called me and told me she saw lights on in the spa, my heart dropped. My mind told me that it could only be one person. But I didn't want to believe it. That is until I walked in and saw it with my own eyes. When Kiki and Danny came out of the back carrying my stuff in their arms, I became sick to my stomach. I wanted to believe I was dreaming.

I knew the time would come for me to find out who the culprit was. I was just hoping for a different outcome...what outcome, I didn't know. And to think they stole from me to get their business up and running, made me furious. I couldn't believe after all I did for those two, they stabbed me in the back like that.

At least Danny appeared to have remorse. Kiki acted like she had an attitude. I walk into my shop and catch *you* stealing from *me* and you act like I did something wrong? Something's definitely wrong with that picture.

Their actions were going to affect a lot of people. I'll have to find replacements for them, not to mention the clientele I'm bound to lose, because Danny is gone. Damn it! I could strangle them for putting me in this situation.

I grabbed my cell phone out of my purse to call Tyler and fill him in. When I got the call from Jade, he wanted to come too, but I told him it wouldn't be good to bring Shelby out so late.

"What's up?" he asked as soon as he picked up the phone.

I filled him in on the activities of the night. Instead of being critical like I thought he'd be, he asked "Are you okay?"

"I'm still pissed, but I'll be okay", I told him.

"Yeah, you will. And at least now you know who it is. So now you can move on."

"Tyler, how could they do this to me?" I started to

cry.

"Why do people do bad things Sierra? No one knows that answer."

"And I feel like such a fool for putting so much trust in Kiki." I cried harder.

"Don't beat yourself up over it Sierra. You had no way of knowing she was going to steal from you." He tried to console me.

"Yeah, but even when I discovered I had a thief, I didn't want to believe it was her when everyone else said it was obvious it was."

"It's over and done with. You didn't want to believe it was her because you trusted her. You just have to learn from your mistakes and move on."

I knew he was right, but I also knew it was going to be a rough road ahead for me.

"I know Tyler. It's just gonna take a little time, that's all."

"So are you on your way home?" he asked.

"Not yet. I just need to take care of some things."

"Can it wait until tomorrow?"

"I really want to get them out the way. Plus, I just want some time to myself to clear my head", I explained. I just called to tell you what happened and to let you know I'm okay."

We said our goodbyes and hung up. I looked at all the product sitting on the counter and decided to get it put back into the supply closet.

As I gathered them up, Alexis crossed my mind. It had been a while since I had spoken to her. I had been trying not to call her because things had been going so well with me and Tyler. The last time we spoke, she wasn't too happy with me. And I gather that's why she hadn't called me either.

Even though I was trying to work on my marriage, I had to admit that I missed her terribly. She always made me feel so good. And not just sexually. She was a great friend and I really wanted to see her.

I picked up my cell phone and speed dialed her number. I let it ring a few times and was about to hang up, but she answered in her professional voice.

"Hi Alexis", I said.

"Hello Sierra. What do I owe for this call?" she asked sarcastically.

"I was just thinking about you and wanted to hear your voice", I told her.

"Aw how sweet. Well now that you've heard it, I'll let you get back to what you were doing."

"Please Alexis. Don't be like that. I really want to see you."

She laughed like I had told a joke. "So you think you can just come in and out of my life when you feel like it? What's the problem? Trouble in paradise?"

I wasn't surprised by her reaction. I knew she was going to feel that way. But I needed to let her know that wasn't the case. "It's not like that Alexis. Things are fine with me and Tyler. I called you because I miss you. And right now, I need a friend."

"Your other friends aren't available?" she asked, with an attitude.

"Come on Alexis. I'm serious...I just caught two of my employees stealing from me. And I'm a little pissed off, to say the least."

"Oh Sierra, I'm sorry. Who was it?" She sounded sincere. I was amazed at how her tone changed so fast.

"Kiki and Danny."

"It figures", she replied.

"Why do you say that?" I asked.

"I mean look at 'em Sierra. They're just as ghetto as ghetto can be...especially that Kiki. And Danny is a faggot trying to come off as high class, but the ghetto always found its way out."

I had never heard Alexis speak that way before. And I could honestly say that I didn't like it. Besides, she wasn't around them enough to speak on their characteristics. For some strange reason, I felt offended.

"That's not very lady-like Alexis", I told her.

"Yeah, but it's the truth", she responded.

"How can you say that? You don't know anything about them."

"I know that Kiki is straight from the hood and Danny is a faggot", she said.

"But that doesn't automatically make them bad people. Plus the term faggot is very offensive. They prefer homosexual."

She started laughing into the phone again. "Sierra, you are so funny. You just caught these two stealing from you and now you're defending them."

"I'm not defending them. I'm just saying that you shouldn't be so judgmental Alexis."

She sucked air through her teeth. "Whatever Sierra...anyway, how did you catch them?"

"Actually, Jade caught them...or should I say Jade saw the lights on in here and called to tell me. So I high tailed it out here. And let's just say they were loading up." Just to talk about it made me angry all over again. But then I had the right to be angry. It was still fresh.

"So you're at the spa now?" she asked.

"Yes."

"So this happened very recently?"

"Yes Alexis. It happened about an hour ago!" I yelled into the phone.

"Oh damn. I'm sorry Sierra. I'm near the area. You want me to come by?" Her voice softened. She had realized how upset I was. I had never yelled at her before.

"Yes, I would like that very much", I told her.

"Okay, I'll be there in a few", she said.

I had to set some ground rules first. I needed to let her know there would be no hanky panky. So I said, "Just as a friend Alexis."

I heard her sigh over the phone. "You didn't even have to say that Sierra. I know you're going through something right now and I would never take advantage of you like that...I'll see you in a few."

She hung up without saying bye. I felt stupid for even saying anything. I'd have to apologize later.

I went back to my task at hand. I couldn't get over how much stuff those two were going to hit me up for. If they wouldn't have been caught, I would've had to do an emergency order or actually buy off the shelf. But lucky for me, Jade was in the right place at the right time.

I guess having Eli in her life did serve some purpose. If it wasn't for him, she wouldn't have been out...I'm sure. If only he wasn't a liar and a cheat. I felt guilty for not telling Jade what I knew. When she asked me if I had a problem with him, I wanted to tell her the truth. But I couldn't bring myself to do it. I just wish I never overheard those women talking that day. Maybe I could just pretend that I didn't.

I had gotten so wrapped up into what I was doing, I didn't lock the door. So when Alexis walked in, she scared me so bad, I almost peed on myself. "Damn Alexis! You could've given me a warning or something. You scared the hell out of me!" I yelled at her, after putting my hand on my chest.

She strolled in, threw her purse on the counter, looked at me and said, "Maybe you shouldn't be up in here with the damn door unlocked."

"Thanks. I'll keep that in mind for next time", I said in my most sarcastic tone.

She looked around and put her hands on her hips. "So, what did the hood rat and faggot get you for?"

I rolled my eyes at her. "Please stop that Alexis", I ordered.

She waved her hand at me and laughed. "Aw lighten up."

"No, seriously...cut it out. I'm not in the mood for jokes...especially tasteless ones." I spoke in a tone to let her know I was serious. I wanted her company, but I wasn't going to entertain her so-called jokes.

"Okay. Calm down Sierra. I won't make any more cracks about your former employees..." She gave me a serious look. "They are former employees aren't they?"

"Of course, they are", I answered.

"Well, you never know. The way you're acting, you might have given them a second chance", she said.

I walked around the counter. "Yeah, a second chance for them to clean me out."

She came and stood beside me. She was closer than what was considered normal, but I didn't say anything. I figured since I had laid down the rules before she came, I didn't have anything to worry about.

"All jokes aside Sierra, how are you feeling right now?" she asked.

I let out a deep breath and squeezed my chin with my thumb and forefinger. I took a few seconds to ponder her question. "Honestly Alexis, I feel a lot of things right now. I feel angry, pissed, humiliated, frustrated, deceived, stupid and so much more."

She had a puzzled look on her face. "Why do you feel stupid?"

I told her the whole story from the very beginning to the end. After I was finished, she didn't say anything. I knew she was trying to come up with something nice to say, to spare my feelings. I could feel tears forming in my eyes. I tried my hardest to control them. I felt a tear escape my eye. I turned my head so Alexis wouldn't see it. But it was too late.

"Sierra baby, please don't do this to yourself", she said.

As soon as she said that, the tears came faster. There was no holding back. I let all of my emotions out in those tears. Alexis came closer and put her hands on my shoulders. She had a genuine look of concern in her eyes.

I wiped my eyes with my hands. "I'm sorry Alexis. You probably think I'm acting like a baby right now", I told her.

She squeezed my shoulders and said, "No, I think you're acting like a woman who's just been deceived by people she trusted. It's okay to cry Sierra."

I put my head on her shoulder and cried even harder. She wrapped her arms around me and held me tight. It felt good to be in her arms again. It felt so natural. She rubbed my hair and back as I cried my eyes out.

That was the type of comfort I craved from Tyler. He always seemed so non-understanding. Or he acted like I just needed to suck it up and move on. I guess women had more compassion than men.

After a few minutes of me crying my heart out, she

released me, looked into my eyes and said, "Are you okay now?"

I wiped my eyes again. "Yeah, I'm okay. I guess I just needed to get that out."

"I understand that", she replied.

I looked at her blouse and saw the big wet spot my tears had left. "I'm sorry about your blouse", I said and pointed at it.

She looked down, smiled and said, "Aw, it's okay. It's just my favorite silk blouse."

"Now, I really feel bad", I replied.

"Really, it's okay Sierra. I'm just glad I could be here for you", she said and winked at me.

We both stood in silence for a few seconds. I could feel the sexual tension between us. She wanted me and I wanted her. But I wasn't trying to go down that road again. Tyler and I were on a good streak, and I didn't want to do anything to jeopardize it. I needed to do something to get my mind right.

"Uh...I need to pack up Kiki and Danny's things from their stations", I told her and walked towards the service areas.

She walked behind me. "You didn't make them get it when they were here?"

"I just wanted them out of here at the time", I explained. "I told them to come back in the morning to get it. So I'm just going to have it ready for them."

"Yeah, that might not be a bad idea", she said.

I looked around for some empty boxes. I didn't see any, so I went back to the supply closet to get some. I grabbed two and went back to join Alexis. She was sitting on the red leather couch picking her nails.

"You want some help?" she asked when she noticed the boxes.

"Sure, why not", I answered.

We got to work on packing up their items. First, we did Danny's. He had enough stuff for three stylists. I guess that's what made him so good...besides the fact that he really had skills. It took both of the boxes to pack up his stuff.

After I located another box, we packed up Kiki's things. She had nowhere near as much stuff as Danny. She mainly relied on my products to do her client's hair. When we were done, we put the boxes up front at the reception desk, where they could grab them and go in no time. The less contact I had with them, the better. They were lucky I was even allowing them back in my place of business.

I was so wrapped up into what we were doing; I didn't realize how much time had passed. I knew Tyler would be calling me soon. Alexis looked like she was going to say something, but I didn't give her chance to. "Uh...Alexis, it's getting late. I better get out of here before Tyler starts getting worried."

She had a look on her face that I had seen many times before. "Sierra, I want you", she said, getting up in my face.

My heart dropped and I could feel the butterflies in my stomach. My body welcomed those words, but my mind was saying go away.

"Alexis...please don't go there", was all I could say.

She licked her lips slow and seductively. "I'm just being honest."

I couldn't even look her in the eyes. I was weak when it came to her. And I knew I needed to get her out of there before I gave into her. Once again, I said, "I really need to go Alexis."

"What are you running from Sierra?" she asked.

Without looking at her, I said, "I'm not running from anything. It's late and I'm sure my husband is home waiting on me."

She looked at me for a few seconds and then laughed. "Your husband?"

"Yes...my husband", I repeated.

She laughed even harder.

"What's so funny?" I asked her.

"I know Tyler is your husband...and stressing that point isn't going to make you want me any less", she said, with a big smile on her face.

"I wasn't *stressing* anything. I was stating a fact.

And you're assuming that I want you", I replied. I did want her, but there was no way I was going to admit that to her.

She came closer to me. I could feel her breath on my face when she said, "Sierra, I don't have to assume anything. I know you want me just as much as I want you."

"The only thing I want right now is to go home to my husband", I lied. I turned to walk away, but she grabbed my arm and said, "I don't know why you insist on lying to yourself."

I pulled my arm from her grip and turned so I was facing her. "Lying to myself about what?" I asked.

She let out a chuckle. "No matter how good things are going with you and Tyler, unless he's changed some things in the bedroom, you are not satisfied."

"You have no idea what you're talking about", I replied, getting defensive.

She put both of her hands on her hips, looked me straight in my eyes and asked, "Has he tasted that sweet pussy of yours?"

My heart started beating faster and I was sure she could hear it. And it took all of my strength to keep standing on my wobbly legs. But I played it cool, like her question didn't bother me. "That's none of your business", I snapped.

She laughed. "I take that as a no."

I didn't want to admit to her that she was right, but I knew I couldn't lie and make it sound believable. So I just said, "You don't know what you're talking about." I was about to walk away, so she couldn't see the look on my face, but she grabbed me by both of my arms. I tried to release her grip, but she wouldn't budge.

She stared at me for a few seconds. Then she said, "Look Sierra, I didn't come here to fight. I came here as a friend. And I'm sorry for prying into your personal business with your husband."

I relaxed under her grip a little. "It's okay Alexis. I'm sorry for snapping at you. I guess I'm just under a lot of stress right now. And I do appreciate you coming here."

She smiled a big smile and said, "Can we call a truce?"

"Sure", I said. She held out her arms for me to hug her. I gave her a hug and regretted it the moment our bodies touched. It was as if there were electric sparks running through my body. The sexual chemistry was there no matter how much I didn't want it to be.

It was then and there that I decided that I had to stay away from Alexis if I wanted to save my marriage. I had to end our friendship. There was no other way.

I pulled away from her and was about to express my concerns to her. She kissed me on the lips before I could say anything. Between the kissing, moaning and groaning, I completely forgot about what I needed to say to her.

We kissed for what seemed like forever. Then she led me to the couch in the hair salon. Within minutes, we were both naked. I knew that I should've stopped her, but my body wanted her so bad. It needed what Tyler wouldn't give to it.

I promised myself that would be the last time. So I lay back and let Alexis please me like I knew she could. When her tongue reached its destination, I was in heaven. She feasted on me like she had been starving for it. I couldn't control myself. I screamed out in ecstasy, wishing the pleasure could go on forever.

"Oh my God Alexis...that feels go good", I cried out.

She stopped briefly to say", I know you miss me munching on this sweet pussy Sierra. Tyler will never please you like I do. This pussy is mine."

I wasn't interested in what she was saying. I just wanted her to finish her task, so I pushed her head back between my legs. She took the hint and went back to work.

Before long, my body was shaking and convulsing, as orgasmic waves crept through me. I let out a scream that caught both me and Alexis off guard.

"Are you okay?" she asked, with a wicked grin on her wet lips.

After catching my breath, I said, "Yeah, I'm fine.

That orgasm was kind of powerful."

"I'm sure", she replied. She sat down on the couch beside me. "It's my turn", she cooed.

I was about to oblige when I heard the spa phone ringing. "Don't answer it!" she yelled.

"I have to answer it. It's probably Tyler calling to check on me", I replied.

"Just let it ring Sierra."

"I can't Alexis. If I don't answer, he's gonna get worried...or worse, come up here." I dashed to the front and picked up the phone. "Hello."

"Hey Sierra...you sound like you're out of breath", he said into the receiver.

"Uh...yeah, I ran to get the phone."

"What are you still doing there? Do you know what time it is?" he asked.

"To answer your first question, I was packing up Danny and Kiki's stuff. To answer your second question, yes, I'm aware of the time, which is why I was just wrapping up what I was doing. I'll see you in a few babe", I told him.

"Okay...but don't make me drag Shelby out of the bed and come out there to get you. Come on home." He hung up before I could respond.

I went back into the hair salon where Alexis was lying on the couch playing with herself.

"What are you doing?" I asked just to be asking.

She smiled at me and said, "What does it look like? Why don't you come join me?"

I gathered my clothes up off the floor. "I gotta go Alexis", I said.

She jumped up off the couch. "Whatta you mean you gotta go?" she asked.

I started putting on my underwear. "Just like I said, I gotta go home."

"So you're just gonna leave me hanging like that?"

"I'm sorry Alexis. I don't know what you want me to do. Tyler is expecting me home", I said while putting my pants on.

"And...your point is?" she asked. She was still

naked and had made no attempt at getting her clothes together.

"My point is if I don't come home now, he's coming up here to get me", I told her.

"He told you that?" she asked skeptically.

"Yes, he did. Now you need to get dressed."

She smacked her lips and started putting on her clothes. "Well, I guess we'll have to finish this some other time", she said.

I had to let her know that would be the last time. I knew she was going to be upset, but it was something I had to do. "Uh...Alexis...I need to talk to you", I said.

She stopped putting on her shoes. "What is it Sierra?"

I just came straight out with it. "We can't do this anymore."

She laughed and went back to putting on her shoes. "Yeah, okay Sierra."

"I am serious Alexis. I can't do this anymore. It's just not right", I explained.

She looked up at me with a look on her face that I had never seen before. "So you're gonna quit me just like that?"

"It's not as bad as you're making it sound Alexis. I mean...you knew I was married before you seduced me", I replied. I wasn't going to let her make me feel guilty. She knew my situation before she persuaded me to be intimate with her.

She got up in my face pointing her finger at me. "Don't act like you haven't enjoyed the time we've spent together. I have given you pleasure that your husband wishes he could give you."

I was taken aback by her outburst, but I wasn't going to let her intimidate me. "Look Alexis, I have enjoyed our time together. But all good things must come to an end. I know what I've done is wrong and I'm woman enough to admit that. I also know that this needs to stop before someone gets hurt. And even though your friendship has been wonderful, we can no longer be friends. The sexual chemistry between us is so strong.

We'll always be tempting each other. And I just can't risk that."

She stared at me for a few seconds. I tried to read her expression, but I couldn't. It was like she was looking right through me. She didn't say anything so I said, "Alexis, are you okay?"

She ignored my question and said, "So is that your final decision?"

"I'm afraid so", I said reluctantly.

"You're going to regret this Sierra", she said and stormed pass me.

I followed her. "What's that supposed to mean?" I asked her.

She grabbed her purse off the counter and gave me a cold look. "It means what it means", she replied.

I had no idea what she meant, but I didn't want her to leave on those terms. "Alexis, I don't want you to be angry with me. I did this for our own good. Can't you understand where I'm coming from?" I tried reasoning with her.

She rolled her eyes at me, threw her purse over shoulder and said, "I have nothing else to say. Just go on home to your husband." She then turned and walked towards the door.

I went behind her. "Alexis, please don't leave like this."

She unlocked the door, opened it and walked out. I didn't bother trying to stop her, because I knew it wouldn't do any good. I watched her as she sped away in her car.

I knew she was going to be upset, but I had no idea it would be to that extent. Alexis was one of those people who didn't deal well with rejection. She was used to getting what she wanted.

Though I didn't want her upset with me, I had to stick with my decision. I had to put a stop to it sooner or later. I couldn't risk destroying my relationship with Tyler. My main concern now was what Alexis meant by me regretting my decision. Did she mean she was going to tell Tyler about us? Even if she did, I'd deny it. Hopefully,

I wouldn't have to worry about that. Alexis was just upset. I figured once she had a chance to calm down and think about things, she'd forget all about me.

I grabbed my purse and headed towards the door. My cell phone rang just as I was locking the door. "I'm on my way now", I said without looking at the screen. I hung up before he could respond.

I thought about Alexis on my short drive home. I hated that things had to end that way, but I had my marriage to think about. Now Tyler and I could go on living our lives together without any interference.

Taylor

"Girl, are you serious?" I asked. Jade had just filled me in on the events at Sierra's spa last night.

"Yes girl. I wouldn't joke about that", she replied.

I was in total shock. Jade and I had assumed Kiki was the one stealing, but to catch her in the act was priceless.

"I know Sierra is pissed and disappointed right about now", I said.

"Yes, she is. You should've seen the look on her face when we walked in on them. And then that hussy Kiki had the nerve to have an attitude. If I hadn't been there myself, I wouldn't believe it."

"That's crazy", I replied, thinking about how Sierra must've felt. "At least now, she's got answers."

"Yeah, that's true. But you know she's gonna be in a foul mood for a while."

"We'll just have to help her get through it", I said.

My phone signaled that I had another call. I looked to see if it was anyone important. It was Exodus. "Hey Jade, I got another call. Can I call you back later?"

"Sure, I need to get back to work anyway", she replied.

"Bye." I ended the call and clicked over to Exodus.

"Hey sexy. What's up?" I said in my seductive voice.

"Hey Taylor...we need to talk", he replied in a serious tone.

"What do we need to talk about?" I asked him.

"I'd rather we talk face to face", he said, making me nervous.

"Is something wrong Exodus?" I asked.

I heard him sigh in the phone. "Can you meet me at our spot?" he asked, ignoring my question.

"Aren't you supposed to be at work?"

"I took the day off", he said.

393

"Are you sick or something?" I asked. The suspense was killing me.

"No, I'm not sick Taylor. Are you gonna keep asking me a bunch of questions or are you gonna meet me?" he answered with irritation in his voice.

"I'm not meeting you for you to kick me to the curb. I don't get dumped. I do the dumping", I told him.

"It's nothing like that. But we really do need to talk. So are you gonna meet me or not?" he asked for the third time.

I hesitated for a few seconds. It could all be a set-up. I meet him and he tells me he doesn't want to see me anymore. But I needed to know what he wanted to talk about. "Yeah, I'll meet you", I finally answered.

After we hung up, I went to my bedroom to find something to put on. If he was going to dump me, I was going to be looking good as hell, so it would be harder for him. I grabbed my black *Carolina Herrera* dress that hugged me in all the right places. After touching up my makeup, I slipped it on along with my black open-toed *Jimmy Choo* pumps. I looked at myself in the mirror. There was no way he could dump me, looking the way I looked.

As I drove to meet Exodus, I thought about how my life would be without him in it. I wasn't in love with him or anything, but I knew he was more than just some dick to me. Honestly, I had no idea what it was I really felt for him. My mother always told me that love was for suckers. She said if you didn't fall in love, you didn't get hurt. And after what had happened with Leroy and Brian, I felt she may have been right. So I had grown accustomed to keeping my feelings in check. Then at times, I felt that my mother wasn't the one to take advice from when it came to love or relationships. The only thing she seemed to ever love was money.

Whatever it was he needed to talk about, I had to face it. As I pulled up to our spot, my heart began to beat faster. I had knots in my stomach and my palms became clammy. Damn, I hated that Exodus had that kind of effect on me.

When I reached my destination, he was already there waiting on me. "Damn Taylor, you looking sexy as hell", he said as soon as he laid eyes on me.

I did a seductive twirl and said, "Thank you. You don't look so bad yourself."

"You want something to drink?" he asked me as I sat my purse on the bed.

"No, I'm okay", I replied.

He stood there watching me, licking his lips and rubbing his hands together. I knew what he had on his mind. But there was no way I was going to let him get inside me before telling me what he wanted to talk to me about.

To confirm my suspicions, he walked over to me and put his arms around my waist. "Taylor baby, you look good enough to eat", he whispered in my ear.

I pushed him away and said, "I'm sure I do."

"What's wrong with you?" he asked me.

I sat down on the bed next to my purse. "What do you need to talk to me about?" I asked him, getting straight to the point.

His face became very tense and he started pacing the floor. After doing that a few more times, he stopped and looked at me. "I don't know where to start", he said.

I leaned back on the bed on my elbows and crossed my legs. "I got time. I'm not going anywhere. So why don't you start at the beginning", I replied.

He rubbed his hands over his face and let out a deep sigh. "Okay...here goes..."

I held my breath as he began to speak.

"...Um, my meeting you outside of David's office was no accident", he continued.

I gave him a puzzled look. "I don't understand", I said.

"Well...uh...my meeting you was part of a plan", he responded.

I stood up and got closer to him. "A plan? What kind of plan?" I asked.

He stepped away from me and walked over to the kitchen area. I followed him. "What kind of plan?" I asked him again.

He hesitated before answering my question. "...It was part of David's mother's plan..."

"You mean Claire?" I asked, like I didn't already know the answer.

"Yes", he said, without looking at me.

I began to pace the floor, trying to figure out what in the hell was going on. "So how do you know Claire?" I asked him.

He let out another sigh and scrunched up his face like he didn't want to answer me. "Uh...she hired me", he said.

I was confused. "What do you mean she hired you? David's your boss."

"She hired me to seduce you", he said nonchalantly.

I couldn't believe what I was hearing. That witch had actually paid someone to sleep with me. She hated me just that much. "So you're telling me that the day we bumped into each other was all a set up?"

"Yes", he answered.

I lost control and began slapping him in his face. He grabbed my hands and tried holding me. "You son of a bitch", I screamed, still trying to hit him.

"Calm down Taylor!" he yelled.

I pulled my hands out of his grasp. "Don't tell me to calm down. I can't believe this shit!"

"I'm sorry Taylor. I never meant to hurt you", he said.

"You're sorry alright. How can you fix your mouth to say you never meant to hurt me? Your goal from the very start was to deceive me." I shook my head back and forth in disbelief. "So how did you end up working for David? Was that part of your plan too?" I asked him.

"She got me the job with David and then she propositioned me to do a job on the side. At first I said no. But when she told me all the money I could make, I gave it a shot. I mean, David pays me well, but Mrs. Claire was willing to pay top dollar. She made me an offer I couldn't refuse. Plus, I didn't know you then. You were just a name to me at the time", he explained.

"Does David know about us?" I asked.

"No...he doesn't...at least not yet", he answered. He looked at me with a sad look in his eyes. "Taylor, I know you don't believe me, but I really am sorry", he said.

I rolled my eyes at him and turned up my lips. "You're right...I don't believe you. You're a fake and a fraud", I told him, pointing my finger in his face.

"You have a right to be upset with me. But I do care for you Taylor...which is why I decided to come clean with you", he said.

I laughed at his comment. "You care for me...the same person you were paid to fuck? Give me a fucking break Exodus. Is that even your real name?"

"Yes, to answer both of your questions", he replied.

"So you decided to tell the truth because you care for me?" I asked once again to make sure I understood him correctly.

"Yes...and Claire was starting to put pressure on me", he said.

"Put pressure on you how?" I asked.

"She was saying that it was time to let David know what kind of tramp he married. She said it had been long enough and we should have enough evidence to work with", he explained.

I thought back to her last visit when we were going to the mall. She was giving me a chance to get out when she offered me that money. When I turned her down, I guess she decided to go on with her original plan.

I just couldn't get over all that had transpired. Exodus had been paid to set me up and my mother-in-law paid him to do it. I was in a bad situation and I had to figure a way out of it.

"So what's going to happen now?" I asked him.

He hunched his shoulders. "I guess she's going to tell David?"

"And just how is she going to tell him?"

"I really don't know. She never let me in on that part. Originally, you were to never find out that she hired me. I guess our affair was supposed to come out accidentally", he said.

All sorts of things were running through my mind. Of course I was furious with Exodus for deceiving me like he did. And I was certain that I would never speak to him again, after everything was said and done with. But my main concern was David. He was going to be crushed if he found out. He would be upset with Exodus, of course. He considered him one of his best employees. And of course he would be upset with me, because he trusted me. And then he would be upset with his mother for doing something so dirty. But knowing her, she would talk her way out of it and I'd end up being the one he hated the most. I just had to do something.

"Can't you say that you have no idea what Claire's talking about or just deny it all?" I asked.

He tilted his head to the side and looked up at the ceiling. "Uh...I guess I could, but what about Claire?"

"What about her?"

"She's already paid me a lot of money Taylor and I don't think she'll be too happy about me turning on her", he said.

"Do you think I give a fuck about her feelings Exodus? My damn marriage is at stake here!" I yelled.

"Taylor, you need to calm down", he said for the second time.

"I told you to stop telling me that. I have every right to be furious. And you're the last person I want telling me to calm down. You're lucky I'm not some psycho bitch", I replied.

"Taylor, I'm sorry. You're right", was all he said.

I started pacing the floor again, trying to think of how I was going to get myself out of the situation. How in the hell could I let this happen? Because of some dick, I was getting ready to lose my extravagant lifestyle. The more I thought about it, the madder I got and the more I wanted to kick Exodus' ass. I walked over to him and started punching him again. He grabbed my arms and pushed me onto the bed. He then got on top of me so I couldn't get up.

"Get off of me Exodus!" I screamed into his ear.

"I will if you promise not to hit me again", he said.

"I can't promise that", I replied, out of breath from trying to wrestle from under him.

"Well, I'm not gonna let you up", he said.

"Okay, okay. I promise", I said, giving in to him.

He eased off of me, still holding my arms. "I'm gonna let you up and we're gonna sit here and talk."

I sat up on the bed and he released my arms. He kept staring at me and wouldn't say anything. I finally broke the silence. "Everything was a lie Exodus", I told him.

"In the beginning it was Taylor. But I was attracted to you the minute I laid eyes on you", he said.

"All those times we got together, you did it because you were paid to do it", I reminded him.

"But I enjoyed every bit of it. I would've done it for free", he said.

"Yeah, but you didn't", I replied.

He looked down at his lap. "No, I didn't."

I grabbed my purse and stood up. "I need to get out of here."

"No. Wait Taylor", he said, grabbing my arm. "Please don't go."

"Give me one good reason why I should stay here with you Exodus", I said. I put my hands on my hips and waited for an answer. When he didn't say anything, I said, "That's what I thought", and walked to the door.

When I opened the door, he said, "Taylor...I think I love you."

I stopped, closed the door and turned to look at him. "You think you love me? Exodus, don't confuse love with lust. You don't love me. If you did, you would've never done what you did."

He stood up and walked over to me. "Don't you see? I fell for you in the process. Of course I didn't love you in the beginning. But as I got to know you, my feelings for you changed", he said.

"You don't love me...you don't even know me. And I damn sure don't know you. All of our time together was spent between the sheets. What kind of love is that

Exodus?"

"We can get to know each other", he said, sounding desperate.

"I need to figure out how I'm going to save my marriage. I don't have time for this", I told him.

"You don't love him Taylor", he said.

"You don't know what you're talking about."

"I know that you don't give a damn about that man. It's all about financial security with you", he responded.

I couldn't even say anything. He was right. I couldn't recall how many times he had heard me say that I married David for his money. "There's nothing wrong with wanting financial security...You should know, seeing how you took on an affair with me for money. So what can you say about me?"

He didn't say anything at first. He looked like he was in deep thought. Then he said, "I got a solution for your problem."

I was curious, so I said, "What is it?"

"You can tell David everything, leave him and we can be together", he said, with a serious expression on his face.

I couldn't believe he let that come out of his mouth. There was no way in hell I was going to leave David to be with him. "Exodus, you must be on some shit if you think I'm going to leave David for you." It seemed kind of harsh, but I had to be honest with him.

"I can take care of you...if that's your concern", he said.

"How are you going to take care of me? David's going to fire your ass after he finds out about us."

"I told you the old lady hooked me up. I'm set for a minute", he responded.

"I need more than a minute Exodus. With David, I'm set for a lifetime."

He let out a chuckle. "You may not be once all this shit comes to light."

I rolled my eyes at him, pissed that he had the nerve to laugh at the situation. "I'll worry about that when the time comes...And I'm so glad you think this shit is funny."

"I don't think it's funny...I just think we need to be realistic", he replied.

He did have a point. I would be left with nothing. Being dumb, I let David talk me into signing a prenuptial agreement. He told me that was the only way he would marry me. I tried to act hurt, telling him that if he really loved me, he wouldn't say that type of stuff. He said he had worked too hard to get where he was and he wasn't going to just give it away in a split-up. I was pissed, but if I wanted him to marry me, I had to oblige. Then to top it off, he told me that if I really loved him, I wouldn't care about his money.

Damn it! Why did I sign that prenup?" I said out loud before I realized it.

"Prenup? What prenup?" Exodus asked, like those were unheard of for someone with David's money.

"What prenup do you think I'm talking about?" I asked him.

"I'm just confused. Claire told me you didn't sign a prenup."

"What would make her think that?" I questioned.

"She said that's what David told her...That's also why she offered you that money", he said.

I frowned at him. "What money?"

"The money she offered you to leave him when she was here."

"She told you about that?"

"Yeah, she told me everything."

My curiosity had gotten the best of me. "Exodus, did you fuck her?" I asked him.

He made a face at me. "Fuck who...Claire? Hell no! I already told you I don't do white women. A brotha loves his sistas. And even if I did decide to dip in some vanilla, it damn sure wouldn't be an old prune like Claire. In the words of Fred Sanford, 'aint nothing on this earth uglier than an old white woman.' If I'm going that route, it will be a Cameron Diaz or a Jessica Alba type."

I threw my hands up. "I was just asking."

"But back to the subject at hand. Are you saying that you did sign a prenup?"

"Yes, I did. It was one of the conditions David laid out before he would marry me", I explained.

"Well why did he tell his mother you didn't sign one?" he asked.

"How in the hell am I supposed to know?" I yelled.

"Are you sure you signed one?"

"Of course I'm sure. We had a discussion about it before I signed it." I told him about the discussion.

He rubbed the top of his head. "Well either he lied to you or he lied to his mother."

I was more confused than ever. Why would David lie to me about the prenup? Was he testing me or something? Nothing made sense anymore. I could feel a headache coming on and I was without my pills. I looked over at Exodus, who was watching me like he wanted to say something. He didn't say anything though, so I took that as an opportunity to depart.

"I need to go Ex", I said.

Once again, he grabbed my arm. "Think about what I said about me and you Taylor...please", he whispered.

"There's nothing to think about Exodus. You want us to go on like nothing happened. You deceived me and I can't get over that", I told him.

"It's no worse than what you're doing to David. You don't love him Taylor", he replied.

I didn't take the time to come up with a response. I just walked to the door. Once I opened it, I turned to look at him one last time. I shook my head at him and walked out the door, slamming it behind me. That chapter of my life was closed. I just had to figure out how I was going to explain everything to David. And most importantly, find out about that prenup.

Jade

"It won't be long before you're the head nigga in charge babe", Eli said to me.

We were lying in bed after a few rounds of earth shattering mid-day sex.

"Don't use that word Eli. It's so degrading. Black people shouldn't say it no more than white people should", I lectured him.

"Calm down Jade. No need to get all Martin Luther King Jr. on me. I won't say it anymore", he said.

"Thank you. I appreciate it", I replied.

He frowned at me. "Now back to what I was saying. You still nervous?" he asked.

"Yeah, a little bit", I answered, honestly.

"You'll do fine. Stop worrying", he assured me and kissed me on the forehead.

"I hope so", I said.

"You will."

My thoughts drifted away from my problem and back to Sierra's. I felt so bad for her. I couldn't imagine going through what she was going through. She trusted those two so much. Not to mention, they were her top stylists.

Even though I felt bad for her, I couldn't help but think about how she was acting towards Eli last night. It just seemed like she was looking at him with disgust in her eyes. I've never seen her react that way to anyone. She's the type of person that likes everybody. And I just couldn't understand what she had against Eli. Or maybe it was my imagination.

"So you're ignoring me now?" Eli's question interrupted my thoughts.

"Uh...no...did you say something?" I asked him.

"I've been talking for the last five minutes.....So you mean you didn't hear anything I just said?" he asked.

"I'm sorry Eli. I was just in deep thought", I told

him.

"About work?"

"No, not really."

"Anything you wanna talk about?" he asked.

"I was just thinking about what happened to Sierra. And I was wondering if she was okay", I told him.

"I told you before, you worry too much."

"Yeah, I know", I said, sarcastically.

"Well, you do. You should be more like me...just plain carefree", he said.

"I know, but it's hard. If what happened to Sierra happened to me, I would be finished", I said.

"I'm sure you would be, but you can't let that stuff get to you", he replied.

I couldn't understand how he could seem so nonchalant about everything. "But how can you not let it get to you Eli? Two of the people she trusted the most were stabbing her in her back. That's got to be a letdown", I explained.

He motioned with his hands as he talked. "First off, I don't put all my trust in people. Second, I don't have high expectations of people. And last, but not least, I feel that people only do to you what you allow them to do...not all the time, but some of the time. Some things are beyond your control."

I looked at him like he had lost his mind. "You have a crazy way of seeing things", I told him.

"How is that? Everything I said makes sense. You just might not agree with it", he responded.

"Okay, maybe the one about not putting all your trust in people works, but I'm not too sure about the other two", I said.

He sat up in the bed and got closer to me. "Okay, let me break it down for the mentally challenged who don't understand."

I nudged him with my elbow. "So you got jokes now?"

"No ma'am...just trying to help you out", he said with a smirk on his face. "But back to the lesson of the day. I don't have high expectations from anyone. My family has taught me that. You don't expect much, you don't get disappointed. I expected my father to be around. I expected my mother to be a caring and loving mother, who was there for her kids. I expected my brother and sister to do something with their lives, regardless of our upbringing. But what happened? They did the opposite of what I expected. So now, I don't expect anything from anybody. It is what it is and you do what you do. It's just that simple.

As far as people doing to you what you allow them to...that's a gray area. I mean, I couldn't control my father walking out on us. But my mother could control letting him crawl back in her bed long enough to get her pregnant with another child he had no intentions of taking care of."

I could see the emotion in his face as he talked about his mother and father. It was definitely a soft spot for him and I could see why. I didn't want to pour salt into the wound, so I didn't say anything...even though I wanted to. Instead I said, "Since you put it that way, it all makes sense to me now."

"I know it does", he said, smiling like he had accomplished something major.

"Is that how you feel about me Eli?" I asked him, not really sure if I wanted to hear the truth.

"What do you mean?" he asked. He knew what I meant. He was just buying time.

I played along. "Do you not have expectations of me or how far our relationship will go?"

He stared at me for a few seconds. I could feel my heart beating faster as I waited for his answer.

He took a deep breath and then he spoke. "Honestly Jade, I'm just going with the flow. You know I care about you, but I'm not planning a future in my head. I mean, I'm just taking it day by day and enjoying the time we spend together."

I didn't know how I should comprehend his answer. He did say he cared about me and enjoyed our time together. On the other hand, he pretty much said he wasn't looking forward to a future with me. I knew how men were when it came to commitment. But that still didn't stop me from hoping for one with Eli. I was in love with him and hoped he felt the same about me.

I decided not to ask him if he did. I couldn't handle it if he gave an answer I didn't want to hear. I would save that conversation for another time.

"I guess taking it day by day is all I can ask for", I told him.

He looked at me and smiled. I could tell he was happy I didn't push the issue. I would let him think I was content with his answer. But little did he know I wasn't finished with him. We had a lot more to talk about...a whole lot more.

Sierra

Kiki and Danny had come early this morning to get their things, after I called them. Danny was still trying to apologize and plead his case. Kiki still had the same funky attitude she had last night. I asked her again why she did what she did. Her response was, "A sista gotta do what she gotta do to make it in this world."

"But I trusted you Kiki. I gave you a key to my place", I told her.

She smirked and said, "Maybe in the future, you should watch who you trust...and FYI, you got a few more folks up in here you might want to keep an eye on."

"What are you talking about?" I asked her.

"I'm not about to give you any dirt, if that's what you getting at. I'm just saying watch your back." She took her stuff and left.

When Danny came back in to get the last of his stuff, I asked him what she meant by her remark.

"Don't pay Kiki any mind Sierra. She's just bitter 'cause she got caught. You have nothing to worry about", he said and smiled at me.

I didn't return the smile. I couldn't believe he was smiling at me after all that had happened. He noticed my frown and stopped smiling.

"Well, I guess I better get going", he said.

"Yeah, I guess you better", I replied.

He looked at me one last time before walking out the door.

I called them so they could come before the others started coming in. Even though they had betrayed me, I didn't want to cause a scene by having them come when everyone else was here.

Everyone had started arriving and asking questions about why their stations were empty. I knew I had to explain everything that had happened. So I gathered everyone in the hair salon. The room was buzzing with questions and conversations about what was going on.

"Okay everybody, I need you all to settle down. I have something very important to say", I yelled.

"What is it this time?" Kiona asked in a sarcastic tone.

I decided to ignore her, for the time being, because once I popped the news on them, she would shut her mouth.

"Will you just listen and let her talk?" Latoya jumped in.

Ever since her make over, she exuded a confidence she didn't have before. It wasn't in a bad way. It was like she was self-assured and knew her worth. She was no longer intimidated by the others. I was so happy for her.

Kiona didn't respond. She just looked over at Michelle and they both rolled their eyes at Latoya. She looked at them like she was daring them to say something.

So things wouldn't escalate, I continued with my news. "Like I was saying....I have some news for you guys. Unfortunately, Kiki and Danny are no longer with us." I paused for a few seconds to observe everyone's reactions. I noticed Kiona and Michelle looking at each other.

"What happened? Did they find another job or something?" Destiny asked.

"Not quite", I answered. I looked around at the eager faces. For some reason, I was having a hard time telling them the truth. Part of me felt it was because I was still blaming myself for what happened.

"So what is it Sierra?" Michelle asked in a demanding tone.

I overlooked her tone, because I knew they were all anxious to know what was going on. "Well...late last night, I caught them in here stealing", I said.

The room was dead silent. Everyone looked like they had seen a ghost. Then Kiona said, "I don't believe you."

"Why would she lie about something like that?" Angel spoke up.

Kiona was about to respond, but I cut her off.

"You don't have to believe me Kiona. Why don't you ask Kiki yourself, when you see her?"

She rolled her eyes and neck at me and said, "What makes you think I'm gonna see her?"

"Oh, I'm sure you will...but that's not the issue right now", I told her.

"I can't believe you actually caught them in the act", Latoya said.

"Yeah...I wouldn't believe it myself, if I hadn't seen it with my own eyes", I replied.

"So how did you catch them?" Michelle wanted to know.

I told them how the events played out. They all seemed to be shocked. Kiona and Michelle didn't have too much to say. They just kept stealing glances at each other.

"So what are you gonna do about new stylists?" Destiny asked. "I can do my fair share of hair, but I can't take on both Kiki's and Danny's clients."

"I guess I'm going to have to put an ad on Craig's List or something. You guys can also get the word around that I'm looking for two stylists", I said.

"I can help out until you get someone", Angel replied.

Everyone gave her a look of surprise.

"You?" Kiona questioned. "What do you know about doing hair?"

"I know a lot", she answered.

"You never said you knew how to do hair", I said.

"That's because you never asked", she responded.

"So you're telling us you know how to do hair?" Michelle asked, as if she didn't understand her the first time.

"Yes, that's what I'm telling you...I use to do hair before I got into massage therapy", she answered.

"So...what happened?" I wanted to know.

"I was a makeup artist as well. I guess you could say I got tired of it. So I went and got certified in massage therapy...and here I am."

"Oh, that's great Angel. I could definitely use your

help until I get some replacements", I told her.

Kiona started laughing. "Not to be rude, but how do we know you're good enough to replace Kiki and Danny?"

Before Angel could respond, I said, "The only person that needs to know how good she is, is me. The last time I checked, I made the decisions around here."

She mumbled something under her breath.

"You got something you want to share with the rest of us?" I asked her.

"I was talking to myself", she answered.

I looked at the clock and noticed it was almost time for the clients to start rolling in. I knew some of Kiki's and Danny's clients were going to be upset once they realized they were both gone. A lot of them probably wouldn't even allow someone else to do their hair. I sure hope Angel knew what she was doing. Destiny did an okay job, but she was no Kiki or Danny.

"Okay guys. We need to start preparing for the day. Our first clients are about to start coming in. Be prepared to deal with some upset and irate people. Just be polite and let me deal with them. And whatever you do, don't disclose any information about why Kiki and Danny aren't here", I explained.

"Why not? Their clients should know what thieves they are. Why should we save them from embarrassment? They didn't think about that when they were ripping you off", Destiny ranted.

I tried calming her down. "Destiny, I understand where you're coming from. But this is not about saving them from embarrassment. This is about maintaining a professional environment. I don't want rumors circulating about what happened. I would appreciate it if you all just stick to saying they no longer work here. If asked why not, just simply say you don't know."

"So you want us to lie?" Destiny asked, with a frown on her face.

"Why are you so ready to spread the news about what happened?" Kiona asked Destiny, glaring at her.

I responded by saying, "Oh, I'm pretty sure you'd

like to protect your friend's reputation.

"Aint it funny how people turn on you when things go wrong?" Michelle jumped in.

"I'm not even talking to you Michelle. So mind your business", Destiny shot back at her.

I threw my hands in the air. "Okay guys, let's settle down. This was not meant to be an opportunity for you guys to turn on each other. I just ask that you respect my wishes...okay?"

Everyone said okay and retreated to their stations. I stopped Angel before she could go to her massage room.

"Angel, I really appreciate you stepping up like that. I would've never known you could do hair", I told her.

"It's not something I talk about a lot."

"Don't let Kiona get to you. She's just jealous", I said.

"Sierra, I couldn't care less what Kiona or anybody else thinks of me. And to prove to you that I know what I'm doing, I'll go to my car and get my portfolio", she replied.

I could tell she was aggravated. "You don't have to do that Angel", I assured her.

"No...I think I do...I'll be back", she said and walked out the door.

Even though I believed her about being able to do hair, I still wanted to see her portfolio, just to check out her skills. When she came back in, she plopped the portfolio down on the counter. I hesitated for a minute. I didn't want to seem eager.

She nodded towards the counter. "Go 'head and take a look. I know you want to."

I opened it and started skimming through the pages. "You always keep this in your car?" I asked her.

"Yes, I do. Actually, that and a few other things from my past", she answered.

I had to admit, I was quite surprised by her talent. She was as good as...or maybe even better than Kiki and Danny put together.

"You have a lot of talent Angel. Why did you stop?"

She let out a big sigh. "My ultimate goal was to be a hair stylist and makeup artist for the stars. When that didn't happen, I decided I didn't want to do it anymore. I didn't conquer my goal, so I didn't see a need to continue on that path. I felt like a failure. So I decided to try something else...massage therapy."

"You shouldn't have considered yourself a failure just because you didn't get to be-"

She cut me off. "Sierra, I really don't want to talk about it. I've said too much already. Like I said before, I'll help out as much as I can...until you get someone else."

"Uh...okay...thanks once again", was all I could say.

She walked towards the massage rooms. I held her portfolio up. "Hey...don't you want this?" I asked.

She turned around and said, "No. Leave it there. I think some folks might need to see that I'm not a joke." Then she disappeared.

I continued admiring her work, dreading the day ahead. I knew it wasn't going to be easy, but I was hoping for a miracle.

Taylor

As soon as I got back home, I hurried to David's office. I needed to find that prenup he had me sign. Since talking to Exodus, I was more confused than ever. What else could David be hiding from me? First, a sister. Now, a prenup. Or should I say lack of a prenup?

I looked carefully through each and every drawer, hoping to locate it. After searching for about fifteen minutes, I realized it wasn't going to be in there. But I knew I had signed one. So where could it be? Then it hit me. It was probably in that briefcase of his...the one he kept under lock and key.

"Taylor, what on earth are you doing in here?" Ms. Hazel's voice boomed.

"Oh...Ms. Hazel, you scared me", I said, ignoring her question.

She gave me a disapproving look. "Taylor, you know Mr. Morgan wouldn't be too happy about you being in here."

I stood up and put my hand on my hip. "And why wouldn't he? I *am* his wife."

"And as his wife, you know that he's very private about this office. I can only clean it when he's in here to supervise", she said.

"Well, what is so special about this damn office anyway?" I asked.

"Honestly, I don't know. But I respect his privacy, and so should you...wife or not." She gave me a look like she was daring me to challenge her.

"Ms. Hazel you know I have a lot of respect for you, but I'm gonna need you to stay outta my business. There are some things going on around here that I need to get to the bottom of", I told her in my most stern, but polite tone.

"Things like what? Are you still going on about this so-called sister of Mr. Morgan's?" she asked.

"It's more than that. And I really don't want to get

into that with you right now", I explained.

"Okay...let's suppose what you say is true. You think snooping through his office is going to give you the answers you need?"

"What else can I do?" I asked.

"How about just coming right out and asking him what it is you want to know? Did that cross your mind?"

Before I could respond, she said, "Obviously, it didn't. Or you wouldn't be in here sneaking around."

"You make it sound so bad", I said.

She grunted. "It is bad. And how did you get into that file cabinet? He always keeps it locked."

I pointed to the key on his desk.

"Where did you get that from?" she asked.

"Uh...I got it from under his desk...He has a special space for it under there."

"Oh Taylor, how could you?" She gave me a pitiful look.

"Don't judge me. You don't know what I'm going through!" I yelled at her.

She stepped back. "You're right...I don't...And I hope you find whatever it is you're looking for." Then she turned to leave.

"Ms. Hazel...are you going to tell David I was in here?" I asked her.

She turned to look at me. "He will eventually find out what you're up to, but it won't be because I told him." Then she walked out the door.

I immediately felt bad for what I was doing. I was feeling guilty for everything, including the affairs with Exodus and Charles. It's like my conscious kicked in for a few seconds.

I looked around me and saw the mess I had created. I sat down in David's chair to pull myself together. I don't know what happened to cause my conscious to rear its head. Then it hit me. All these years, I strived to be the opposite of my mother. I realized I was like her in more ways than one. The lies. The men. The love of money. The only difference between us is that I would've been a better mother than she was. There is no way I could do to my daughter what she did to me. No matter how much I love money, I couldn't pimp out my child the way she did me. And there's not a day that goes by that I don't think about the baby that was taken away from me right after birth. And not knowing what really happened to her has haunted me for years.

I ran away from my mother years ago. Yet she had been living inside me every day. I had become my mother. And admitting that was one of the hardest things I ever had to do. The sad part is I knew I wasn't willing to change. It is who I am.

I was living the life most people dreamed of, but I wasn't truly happy. I had been living a lie. Having designer clothes, driving a luxury car, living in a big fancy house and having tons of money at my fingertips wasn't enough. With that being said, I was still terrified of losing it all.

David was going to put my ass out on the street and I had no one to blame but myself.

Sierra

Things at the spa went better than I had expected. Most of Kiki's and Danny's clients were upset when they realized they were gone. But once I convinced them to give Angel a chance and discounted their services, they calmed down. The good thing is, they all left very much satisfied.

The rest of the week went off without a hitch. Things couldn't have been better...until Angel approached me. "Sierra, have you had any luck with finding replacements for Kiki and Danny?"

The problem was that I hadn't even put the ad on Craig's List. Since Angel was doing so well, I had completely forgot about it. And to be honest, I was hoping I could convince her to take on the position and I'd find a replacement for her. "Well you know it's only been a couple of days Angel. These things take time", I explained.

She gave me a suspicious look. "You haven't even put the ad out there...have you Sierra?"

I looked away and started fumbling with some papers that were on the counter. I didn't want to lie to her, but I didn't want her to know the truth either. So I just repeated my statement. "Like I said Angel, these things take time. Plus, I want to get some good quality people I can trust."

She didn't respond right away. She just stared at me for a few seconds. Her whole attitude had changed this week. It was as if she had two personalities. The quiet sweet Angel that did the massages had disappeared. Something about doing hair seemed to bring out the aggressiveness in her. She wasn't rude or anything. She just had more bite and cockiness in her. The clients were pleased with her work, so I guess I would have to deal with it...at least for a little while. If she started getting nasty with me, I would have to put her in check.

"Sierra, I made it clear that this was only

temporary. So if you got something up your sleeve, you can cancel it", she finally spoke.

I responded in my most innocent tone. "I have no idea what you're talking about Angel."

"Yeah...okay Sierra. Just remember my job title is massage therapist, not hair stylist", she replied.

"I know that", was all I said.

She gave me one last look and walked away.

I wasn't going to challenge Angel. I would put the ad on Craig's List just so I wouldn't be a liar. But I had no intentions of hiring anyone else...at least not a hair stylist.

I went into the salon to check on the others to make sure everything was going okay. Destiny was finishing up one of her regulars and had one waiting. Kiona was doing a fill-in and Michelle was doing a pedicure. Latoya was in a corner studying before her next client. Even with all the drama that had went down, business was going smooth. My life was great. My marriage was back to normal and my business was booming. I couldn't be happier.

Taylor

I had been avoiding David most of the week. It wasn't too hard to do, considering how much he worked. We saw each other in the mornings before he went to the office. And when he'd finally make it home, I was either out shopping or pretending to be asleep.

He seemed like his normal self. So I had assumed that witch mother of his hadn't told him about my infidelity. I didn't know how much longer I could keep up this charade. I would have to face the music sooner or later. I just wish I had a little more time to come up with a plan.

My phone startled me out of my thoughts. I recognized Exodus' number. He had been blowing my phone up all week. And each time he called, I let it go to voice mail. I really had nothing else to say to him. I hit reject to end the call. I didn't feel like dealing with his nonsense.

My phone started ringing again, flashing Exodus' number across the screen. He was really being persistent. "What do you want Exodus!" I yelled into the phone after answering it.

"We need to talk Taylor", he responded, sounding desperate.

"I've heard all you had to say", I told him.

He sighed into the phone. "Seriously Taylor...I really need to talk to you."

I put my hand on my hip like he could see me. "I'm listening."

"I don't want to talk on the phone...I need to talk to you face to face", he replied.

"Exodus, I don't have time for your games. And I have no intentions of meeting you. So whatever it is you need to say to me, say it or I'm hanging up on you." I was really getting irritated with him. I knew he was bluffing. He wanted to see me with the hopes of seducing me.

"Damn it Taylor! I'm serious", he yelled into the phone.

I held my finger up...again, as if he could see me. "I know you are not yelling at me. You done lost your damn mind."

"I'm sorry Taylor. Please don't hang up on me", he begged.

I had never heard him sound like that. He sounded like a kid who had been caught with their hand in the cookie jar. So against my better judgment, I said, "Where do you want me to meet you?"

"Well, I'm about to go to lunch. So why don't you meet me at that diner around the corner from the office?"

I laughed out loud. "You want to meet me around the corner from David's office? Won't that be a little risky Exodus?"

"I guess you're right...you suggest a place."

I thought for a moment. "Why don't we meet at *Northgate Mall* under the parking deck?"

"Cool. That'll work. See you in a few."

We hung up. I didn't know what Exodus was up to. But if he had any plans of us living happily ever after, he was going to be greatly disappointed.

I threw on some clothes, did my makeup and flat ironed my hair. Just because he wasn't getting any, didn't mean I couldn't look good.

As soon as I stepped out the door, my cell phone rang. David's office number flashed across the screen. I was tempted not to answer, but thought better of it.

"Hi sweetie", I cooed into the phone.

"Hello my beautiful black angel", he responded.

"What's up?" I asked, wanting to hurry him of the phone.

"I was hoping I could have lunch with my beautiful wife since I've abandoned her most of the week."

I put on my best sympathetic voice. "Aw baby I'm sorry, but I'm already out with Jade. She called me earlier and said she needed to talk to me. I wish you would've called me earlier."

"It's okay. I understand...is she okay?"

"Oh yeah, she's fine. We're just having some girl talk...that's all", I lied.

"Tell her I said hello."

"She's in the restroom right now...but I will be sure to tell her you asked about her when she comes out."

"Okay...well...I guess I'll let you get back to your lunch. Maybe I can take a rain check."

"Okay...I'll see ya' at home later." I hung up before he could say anything else.

When I got to the mall, Exodus was already there waiting for me. I parked my car beside him and slid into the passenger seat of his Escalade.

"So what do you want to talk about?" I asked him as soon as I closed the door.

He ignored my question. "You look nice."

"Thanks...so what do you want to talk about?" I asked more forcefully.

"It's right down to business with you huh?"

I grabbed the handle of the door to open it. He grabbed my arm. "No Taylor...don't leave."

I snatched my arm form his grasp and rolled my eyes at him. "I suggest you say what you have to say."

"Okay...Claire is about to spill the beans to David", he said.

My heart started beating faster. And I felt sick to my stomach. "What do you mean spill the beans?" I asked just to say something.

"What in the hell do you think I mean Taylor? Now is not the time to ask stupid questions", he responded.

I deserved that, so I didn't even get mad. "How do you know she's going to tell him?" I asked him.

He laid his head back on his head rest and looked straight ahead. "She had been blowing my phone up all week. But I was ignoring her ass."

I laughed to myself at the irony because I had been doing the same thing to him.

He continued. "I guess she got tired of me avoiding her so she called me at the office."

"David's mother called you at his office?" I asked just to make sure I heard him correctly.

"I guess she got someone else to ask for me or something. Hell, I don't know. All I know is that when I answered the line, she was on the other end, pissed off. She asked me why I hadn't returned any of her calls. When I couldn't come up with anything to say, I just came out and told her I was backing out of our deal. Of course that didn't sit too well with her. She told me that no one backed out on her. I even told her I would give her back all the money she gave me. She said she didn't want the money. She wanted her son back from the nasty black bitch he was married to."

He looked over at me. What she said didn't faze me any. I had been called worse. I nodded for him to continue.

"I told her I just couldn't go through with it. She called me every name under the sun and told me I would regret the day I double crossed her. I was already regretting the day I met her."

"What now?" I asked, wanting him to get to the point.

"She said she would deal with me later, but she needed to have a heart to heart with David. So I knew what that meant."

"Did she say when she was going to talk to him?" I asked.

"No. Not really. But considering the type of woman she is, I wouldn't be surprised if she paid him a surprise visit. I talked to her this morning, so she's probably making her plans as we speak."

I could feel my blood boiling through my veins. Exodus had a point. That old hag would probably show up at David's office and cause a scene or something. She had to be stopped. The problem was I didn't know how.

"I gotta go", I blurted and reached for the door.

"What are you going to do?" Exodus asked with a worried look in his eyes.

"Honestly...I have no idea."

"Well what about us?" he asked.

"This is really not the time Ex. I can't deal with that right now. You're not going to like what I have to say anyway." I opened the door and hopped out.

He was trying to talk to me. I slammed the door in his face, jumped into my car and sped off.

All the way home, I kept thinking about how I was going to get myself out of the mess I had gotten into. It was time to face the music. I had to take the situation head on. I would beat Claire at her own game.

Taylor

I had decided I was going to tell David everything. If I come clean before his mother can get to him, I will come out being the better person...I hope.

I called him after I left from meeting Exodus. "Is everything okay?" he asked when I reached him.

"Yes, I'm fine...physically, but we really need to talk. So I hope you don't have any plans or meetings after work", I told him.

"Uh...no I don't. What's going on Taylor? You planning a romantic evening or something?" he asked, sounding concerned.

He was probably afraid that he would have to have intercourse with me. Our usual routine consisted of him eating me until I came. He'd fall asleep afterwards and I'd go in the bathroom to finish off what he started. Damn I'm gonna miss Exodus.

"No. Nothing like that. I just think we need some quality time together. Plus, I feel bad about not having lunch with you earlier", I told him.

"Okay, that sounds great. I gotta get back to work so I can make sure I'm out on time this evening", he responded, sounding a lot more chipper.

We said our goodbyes and I headed back home. Hazel was in the kitchen when I got there.

"Good, you're here", I said to her when I entered.

"Where else would I be on a Thursday?" she asked.

I ignored her sarcasm. "What are you making for dinner?"

"I have a duck in the oven with garlic roasted potatoes and I'm sautéing some veggies I picked up from the Farmer's Market."

I wasn't a big fan of duck. It just seemed so oily and it had a weird texture to me. Since being with David, I had grown accustomed to eating a lot of things I hadn't eaten before. A southern girl like me grew up on fried chicken, collard greens, macaroni and cheese and all that type of stuff. Duck was never on the menu. But I kept my opinion to myself and said, "That sounds great."

She wiped her hands on her apron and gave me a once over. "What are you up to?"

"I was thinking about riding to the mall to do a little shopping", I answered.

"Hmm...your favorite thing to do...like you need another pair of shoes, or anything else for that matter."

"Actually, I'm going to find something to wear later tonight", I told her.

"Where are you going...if you don't mind me asking?"

"Nowhere. David and I are going to have a quiet dinner tonight."

"And you're going to buy something to sit at home?"

"Yes...and I wanted to tell you that you could take off early...after you finish preparing dinner."

She laughed. "You don't have to tell me twice."

"Well, I'm about to go. You'll probably be gone when I get back. So have a good weekend."

"But I'll be here tomorrow. You know I'm here every other Friday."

"Well, I'm giving you tomorrow off as well. I got a feeling it's gonna be a long weekend." I gave her a wink.

"Oh, so you're going to get that type of outfit", she teased.

"Yeah, we're way overdue", I laughed. I don't know why, but I felt comfortable talking about that with Hazel...even if it was a lie.

"Well, don't let me stop you honey. Go handle your business and I'm gonna finish up in here", she said and went to check on the food.

"See ya'. Have a good weekend", I said before walking away.

"You too...and don't hurt the man too much", I heard her yell as I entered the foyer.

"I'll try not to!" I yelled back.

If she only knew. Sex with David was the last

thing on my mind. The only reason I gave her the day off was because I didn't know how the night was going to end. And I didn't want her around tomorrow because things may still be popping. And then there was the chance that David's mother might show up.

I headed to the *Streets of Southpoint*. I decided I would head to *Macy's* and grab something. Considering what I was about to face, shopping should've been the last thing on my mind. But I figured I could still look my best, with the hopes that David would show me some mercy.

After leaving the mall, I realized that I needed to get some cash. If David put me out, I would have no money. I had access to the house account, but I'm pretty sure David would block that after everything went down. And I had a checking account of my own, the one I had before I met David. I had a little money in there, but it was nothing compared to the house account I had with David.

I took all of my credit cards and got the maximum amount of cash advances I could get on them. It wasn't much, considering what I was used to. But it would have to do. I could try to get more tomorrow morning before David closed them out. I put all the cash in a paper bag and shoved it under my seat. I would deposit it into my checking account when I got the chance. I looked at my watch and realized that I needed to get home.

My heart beat faster, the closer I got to the house. It was going to be a long night.

"You look beautiful Taylor", David said to me as soon as I came downstairs. I had been waiting for him and wanted to meet him when he came in.

"Thank you David", I said nervously.

"So what's on your mind?" He got straight to the point.

"Don't you want to eat first?" I asked him. I wanted to stall as long as possible.

"Honestly Taylor, I don't have much of an appetite right now. I've been anxious ever since I talked to you today", he replied.

"Okay...uh...well, I guess we'll talk now." I thought my heart would jump out of my chest, it was beating so fast.

"Come on...let's go in there." He pointed to the den.

"Okay", I said, but I didn't budge.

He held out his hand for me to go. I went in and he followed me. He sat down on the loveseat, but I remained standing. I was too nervous to sit. I started pacing the floor, trying to think of a way to break the ice.

"You're really scaring me Taylor", he said.

I stopped pacing, rubbed my palms together and took a deep breath. "Okay David...there's no easy way to say this...I've been having an affair."

The expression on his face didn't change much. It was if he didn't hear what I had said.

"Did you hear what I said David?" I asked just to make sure he did hear me.

"Yes, I heard you. You said you've been having an affair", he replied.

"Aren't you upset...mad...hurt...anything?"

He smirked. "Of course I'm upset, mad and hurt...surprised...no."

"I don't understand David. I expected you to be furious with me. I had even expected you to put me out when I told you", I confessed.

He patted the seat beside him. "Come sit down", he instructed.

I sat down beside him. He grabbed my hand and held it firmly. "Taylor, I know that I don't satisfy you sexually-"

"Don't say that David. I-"

He put his finger up to my lips. "Please...don't Taylor. You don't have to try to spare my feelings. I've known for a long time."

I was quite surprised. "But you never said anything."

He stood up and walked around the loveseat. "What was I supposed to say? What man wants to admit

426

that he can't satisfy his wife? I'm one of the most powerful men in the county and I can't even please my wife in bed. I sometimes think that's why I work so much. It's a way to make me feel manly and possibly avoid the issue."

Even though he was telling the truth, I didn't want him to think that way. I stood up and walked around the seat to face him. "Don't be so hard on yourself. I'm the one that stepped out on our marriage. I can't believe you can even stand to look at me right now."

"I'm not going to sit here and act like I'm not hurt by this...Taylor, I am hurt...but I know we can get pass this. When I married you, I married you for better or for worse. I may not like the fact that you cheated on me, but I do understand why."

I still couldn't believe how well he was taking the affair. All of my worrying had been for nothing. I wasn't going to have to give up the life I had grown accustomed to. Being my mother's daughter, I knew that was all that really mattered to me.

"I do have one question though...What made you decide to tell me now?" he asked.

It was time to drop the other bomb. I had to tell him the rest of the story. I took a deep breath. "The truth is David, it's someone you know."

His face became beet red. "Is it Charles?"

His question caught me off guard. Even though I had been with him, I didn't consider that an affair. And unless he had some proof, I wasn't going to come clean about it. "No, it's not Charles."

"Then who is it?"

"Exodus." There...I had said it. The cat was out of the bag. There was no turning back.

The look on David's face was one I had never seen before. He looked like he was ready to kill. I tried to reach out to him, but he backed away from me. He ran his fingers through his hair and grabbed the back of his head with both hands. "Exodus...You've been fucking Exodus? Of all the men you could've chose, you chose Exodus?"

"It's not what you think David", I tried to explain.

He glared at me. "Oh, really? Because I could've sworn you just confessed to me that you've been having an affair."

"Yes, I know. But he approached me", I said.

"Oh, so that makes it better. He's my employee for Christ's sake Taylor!" he yelled.

"But I didn't know that at the time", I lied.

He tilted his head to the side and looked up at the ceiling. "Wait...wait...so you're telling me that you had already been sleeping with Exodus before I introduced him to you?"

"Yes", my voice came out in a whisper.

"So all this time you two have been screwing each other?" he asked again.

I knew I should've told him how his mother had set me up, but I decided that I would let her tell on herself. Besides, I didn't think he could deal with any more surprises. "Yes, David. All this time."

"I can't believe this shit! My wife and my best employee...fucking...each other."

"I'm sorry David. I really am."

He ignored my attempt at apologizing. "You two have been making a fool out of me all this time...probably laughing at me behind my back."

Once again, I reached for him and once again, he backed away. "Seriously David, it wasn't like that. You gotta believe me."

"I gotta get out of here. Don't wait up", he said and rushed out of the den.

I ran behind him. "Wait, David. Please don't leave like this."

He didn't respond. He grabbed his keys off the table in the foyer. "Where are you going?" I asked him.

"I just need to clear my head...like I said, don't wait up."

He stormed out the door and slammed it. I rushed to get my cell phone. I hit number five on my speed dial list.

"What's up?" he answered after the first ring.

"I hope you're still not at the office."

"Why?"

"I just told David about our affair. And let's just say he's beyond pissed."

"No I'm not, but I'm going to have to face him sooner or later", he replied.

"Good luck", I said and ended the call.

I hit number one on my speed dial list. It went straight to voicemail. David had turned off his phone. He really was angry. I had a lot of apologizing to do...if only he would accept it.

Sierra

I was in a good mood, so I wanted to surprise Tyler the way he had surprised me before. I left the spa early, came home and cleaned up the house a little. I even took Shelby to the babysitter's. I was going to surprise Tyler with a nice quiet dinner alone. After I had laid out what I was going to put on, I hopped in the shower. I shaved all the right areas, making sure everything was baby smooth. I dabbed some Dolce & Gabbana Light Blue behind my ears, since it was one of Tyler's favorite scents

As I was rubbing body oil over my skin, the doorbell rang. I grabbed my robe, threw it on and tied it up. When I got downstairs and opened the door, no one was there. I was about to close the door when I noticed a large brown envelope lying on the porch. I picked it up and saw that my name was printed on it in big letters. I wasn't expecting anything, so I had no idea what it could be.

I hurried back into the house and ran upstairs with the envelope. I sat down on the bed and stared at it for a minute or two. I felt a little hesitant about opening it. But I was very curious about what was inside. So I took a deep breath and opened it.

Sometimes following your first instinct is a good thing. What was inside that envelope was enough to make me wish I hadn't opened it. There were very explicit photos of my husband with another man. My hands were shaking as I flipped through the photos.

On a couple of the photos, Tyler was giving this man some oral pleasure. His eyes were closed and he looked like he was enjoying it. There were a few of him getting his manhood sucked by who I assume was the same guy.

And just when I thought it couldn't get any more disgusting, there were two of him giving it to the other man in his ass. But what really put the knife through my heart were the ones of Tyler on his hands and knees receiving it from the other man.

I had to be dreaming. It couldn't be real. I closed my eyes real tight and opened them again. Nothing had changed. The filthy photos were still in my hands. How could Tyler do this to me? Maybe he had found out about me and Alexis and was seeking revenge. But that didn't make sense. No straight man was going to seek revenge on his wife by sexing another man.

All sorts of thoughts started running through my head. He was so adamant about us not engaging in oral sex, but there he was doing it with another man. The thought of it all made me even more disgusted. His attitude and different mood swings all started to make sense.

I needed to talk to someone, get some advice. So I picked up the phone and dialed Jade's work number. As soon as she picked up, I said, "Jade, it's me...Sierra. Remember when you said if I need to talk, you're here? Well, I really need to talk to you."

"Okay, what's up?"

"No...I can't talk to you over the phone. I need to see you in person."

"Uh...okay."

"Are you busy after work?"

"No. Not really."

"Good. Call me when you get off."

"Okay. I'll come see you-"

"No, I'll come by your place", I blurted.

"Okay...Sierra is everything okay?"

"No, it's not", I answered.

"But we'll talk later."

When I hung up with Jade, I put the photos back in the envelope. I got dressed and paced the floor. I just couldn't sit still. My husband was cheating on me...with another man. How ironic. I was cheating on him...with another woman.

How could my life get turned so upside down?

Jade

When Sierra called me today and said she needed to talk to me, she didn't sound like herself. So I called Eli and broke our date. I told her I didn't have any plans because she sounded like she really needed me. I called her when I got home. And she had just called me to let me know she was on her way.

When I opened the door for Sierra, she was holding a big envelope and she looked like she had been crying.

"Hey Jade. I'm sorry to intrude on you like this, but I didn't know who else to call", she said as she stepped inside my apartment.

I put my hand on her shoulder and said, "Girl, it's no problem. You know I'm always here for you."

"Thanks...I really need you right now", she said as tears formed in her eyes.

"Sierra honey, what's wrong? Let's go sit down." I pulled her into the living room.

"It's Ty-Tyler...he's ch-cheating on me...with... here...this will explain it all." She shoved the envelope she was carrying into my hand.

"What's this?" I asked.

"Just open it", she ordered.

I opened the envelope and pulled out its contents. My jaw dropped when I scanned the first photo. I flipped through each photo several times, hoping that my eyes were playing tricks on me.

Then I finally spoke. "Sierra, what in the hell is going on?"

She threw her hands up. "I don't know Jade!"

"Where did you get these from?" I asked her, pointing at the pictures.

"Someone delivered them to me today."

"You don't know who it was?"

"No, they rang the doorbell. When I went to answer the door, they were gone and those were left on the porch."

I couldn't believe what was happening. I knew Sierra had to be devastated. "Do you know who this man is?"

"No! You can't see his face in any of the pictures Jade!"

"I just thought maybe you knew who he was."

"It may come as a surprise to you Jade, but I had no idea that my husband was fucking another man behind my back!" She was upset and she had a right to be.

"I'm sorry Sierra. I didn't mean to upset you any more than you already were."

"It's okay Jade. I didn't mean to take my anger out on you. I'm just in shock right now."

"Sweetie, you have a right to be. I don't know what I'd do if Eli did that to me."

"I don't mean any harm Jade, but you and Eli haven't been married for over six years. So I don't see how you can compare the two."

"I'm well aware of that Sierra. But I would be hurt none the less", I said, crossing my arms over my chest.

She looked at me and shook her head. "We're getting way off track here. My husband is having an affair with another man." A sound resembling that of a wounded animal escaped her.

I went to her and wrapped my arms around her. "Everything is gonna be okay Sierra. I know it hurts, but you can get through this. I'm sure there's an explanation", I told her.

"What kind of explanation can there possibly be for my husband sucking another man's dick Jade?" She took a deep breath then continued. "Or for him fucking him in his ass?"

I stroked her hair, hoping to calm her down. "You're right Sierra. I don't think there's anything he can say that will explain his actions. You know I've been hearing a lot about this down-low stuff. It seems to be on the rise these days."

Sierra wiped her eyes with the back of her hands.

"What does that mean?"

I was surprised she had never heard of that. But I didn't dare say that to her. "Basically, it refers to men who lead normal lives with wives or girlfriends, but they're sexing men on the side."

"That's disgusting", she replied.

"That may be true, but it's very common now." I hesitated before I continued. "You know I have to ask. Did Tyler show any signs at all?"

She threw her hands up in the air and shook her head. "I don't know. What kind of signs?"

"You know...uh...like has he been acting different...or staying out late...stuff like that?"

She tilted her head to the side and closed her eyes like she was in deep thought. She then opened her eyes and took a deep breath. Then she spoke. "Things had gotten really crazy between us."

I thought back on that night he called looking for her. "What do you mean?" I asked.

"We had been arguing a lot. And Tyler had been so cold towards me at times; I didn't even want to say anything to him. We were barely speaking to each other at one point. But lately, things have been going okay...or so I thought."

I stood up. "He hasn't hit you has he?"

"Girl, sit down. No he hasn't hit me."

"Damn Sierra, I had no idea you were going through that. I'm sorry."

She rolled her eyes towards the ceiling. It's like he's got two personalities. One minute, he's being a royal asshole. Then the next minute, he's apologizing for being an asshole, telling me how much he loves me. Then the next thing I know, he's an asshole again."

"Damn Sierra. I'm sorry. I had no idea. How long has this been going on?"

She leaned back on the couch and ran her fingers through her hair. Then she looked up into the ceiling as if she were searching for words. "Like I said earlier, things have been great over the last couple of weeks. But before that, things had been funny with us for a while. I'm kind of embarrassed to say it, but I had gotten bored with our sex life-"

I waved my hand at her. "Girl, that's nothing to be embarrassed about. That's normal."

"You didn't let me finish", she said and sat back up on the couch. She looked down at the floor. Then she continued. "Tyler and I have never had oral sex."

"Are you serious?" I asked, hoping she wasn't.

"I'm afraid so."

"But why? I mean why haven't you?"

"Tyler said it's nasty and disgusting...yet here he is feasting on this man's dick like it's his last meal." She motioned to the explicit photos that were now spread out on my coffee table.

"So he wouldn't let you do him either?" I asked.

"No, he wouldn't!" she yelled.

"That's crazy. Don't too many men turn down getting a blow job." I felt so bad for her.

"Well he did. I even tried to just do it one night, like seduce him. Girl, he almost knocked me off the bed and told me I was acting like a whore."

I couldn't believe what I was hearing. All this time I had been thinking Sierra had the perfect life. She was beautiful with a super fine husband and a precious little girl. She was a successful business owner and lived in a nice house in a good neighborhood. I guess things aren't always as they seem.

I tried consoling her. "Sierra, I'm so sorry. I really had no idea."

She let out a laugh, one that was almost scary. "What are you sorry for? You're not the one being a hypocrite...telling me one thing and doing something else."

She gathered up the photos and put them back in the envelope.

"Sierra sweetie, are you gonna be okay?"

"Yeah, I guess so", she responded dryly and stood up.

I stood up also and put my hand on her shoulder. "You know I'm here for you, if you need to talk, or cry, or if you just need a shoulder to lean on."

"Thanks Jade. I appreciate that." She forced a weak smile.

"Girl, you're my best friend. I would do almost anything in the world for you", I told her, meaning every word.

She gave me a look that sort of confused me. It was almost a look of pity. But it could've just been my imagination. She was going through a lot. We both stood there in an uncomfortable silence that seemed to last forever.

Then I finally spoke. "Are you sure you're gonna be okay?"

She let out a sigh. "Yeah...I guess. I just need to figure out how I'm gonna handle my situation."

I didn't know what else to do, so I reached out to her and gave her a warm hug. "Everything's gonna be okay", I told her.

She started crying again. So I held onto to her until the crying subsided. She wiped her eyes with the tail of her shirt. "Okay Jade I've taken up enough of your time. And I need to get going."

"Just remember what I said...call me if you need me."

"Thanks Jade. I will. Please don't say anything to anyone...not even Taylor."

"I won't...I promise."

I watched her walk to her car with the envelope of filth in her hand. I stood in the doorway for a few minutes replaying the photos in my head. I couldn't even imagine what Sierra must be feeling. That's a hard pill to swallow. I would be devastated if Eli deceived me that way.

Sierra

Those photos were like a train wreck. No matter how disgusting they were, I just couldn't stop looking at them. Tyler looked as if he was in heaven. In all the years we had been together, I couldn't recall ever seeing that look on his face when we were making love. It all seemed so natural to him. My husband was fucking another man.

I know I did my dirt...but it was different. It's socially acceptable for women to have sex with each other. Men fantasized about it all the time. But men who had sex with other men were straight up gay. No woman wanted to see her man with another man. That just wasn't cool. There was nothing sexy or exciting about seeing two men get it on. And any man that had sex with another man and said he wasn't gay, was a liar.

I started thinking about that down low stuff Jade was talking about. It didn't make sense to me. If a man wanted to be with another man, why didn't he just be with one? Why drag an innocent woman into the mix?

I grabbed my laptop and googled down low. Several links popped up. I clicked on the one for Wikipedia. After reading the article, my stomach was in knots. I felt like such a fool. All these years, my husband had been living a secret life. I was just a trophy for him. And what about AIDS? Never in my life had contracting AIDS crossed my mind. I had been with the same man since I gave up my virginity. I knew Tyler wasn't a virgin when we had sex for the first time. But I had assumed that there was no one else after me.

Was the man in the photos the only one he had been with? There were so many questions that I needed answers to. Jade had asked if he had shown any signs that he was gay. I really couldn't recall any particular behavior. I compared him to Danny and there were no similarities. Danny was very open about his homosexuality and made it clear that a woman couldn't do anything for him. Tyler didn't act like Danny at all. He acted like a man. Danny was more feminine than some of the ladies at the spa.

I was racking my brain, thinking of anything that could've been a clue. He was always particular about his clothes and most of the time it took him just as long as it took me to get ready. He didn't like hair on his body and had it removed on a regular basis. But I always contributed that to the fact that he use to model. Plus, I liked him hairless.

Now I had some things to think about. How was I going to approach him with my findings? What was going to happen to our marriage? Would I confess about my relationship with Alexis? How would all of this affect Shelby?

Damn you Tyler for putting our family into this situation.

Taylor

Even though David told me not to wait up for him
last night, I did. And he never came home. I called his
phone over and over, only to get his voice mail. I have to
be honest. Not knowing where he was had me worried. In
the few years we've been married, I've never not known
where he was.

I looked at the clock on the night stand. It was
after nine, so he should be at his office by now. I called
and let it ring until the answering service came on. There
was no way he'd not open up his office. He had to be
there. I dialed Exodus' number.

"Have you seen David?" I asked, as soon as he
answered the phone.

"Yes, he did pay me a visit last night."

"At your place?" I asked.

"Where else? I told you I wasn't at work when you
called me last night."

I had no idea David knew where Exodus lived. I
didn't even know where he lived. "So David knew where
you lived?" I asked him.

"Yes, he did. He had been to my place on many
occasions. Even though David's my boss, we hung out a
few times...nothing major."

"You never told me where you lived", I pouted,
sounding like a child.

"You never asked. You seemed content meeting at
hotels. So I assumed you weren't interested."

He had a point. I never asked him anything. I
didn't know if he had any kids, if he had any family in the
area, where he was from...nothing. I always refrained
from asking questions, because when you start asking
folks about their personal lives, they were bound to do the
same to you. And that was something I didn't want to
deal with.

"Yeah, yeah, you're right. But back to David...what

did he say or do?" I asked.

"Man, he was furious. He called me everything but a child of God. For a minute, I thought he was gonna try to swing on me. But I guess he thought better of it, 'cause he knew I would've kicked his ass."

"So what did you tell him?"

"Hell, I told him the truth. I mean...I couldn't lie. You had already told him everything. And from what I gathered, you hadn't told him about his mother's role in everything. So I figured if you hadn't told him, I shouldn't either."

"So where are you now?" I asked him.

"I'm at the office."

"You mean to tell me that after all that has happened you still went to work today?" I was in disbelief.

"I said I was at the office. I didn't say anything about working. I'm cleaning out my desk. David fired my ass."

"Are you serious?" I asked, not because I was surprised. It was the only thing I could think of to say.

"Yes, I'm serious. I told you that was gonna happen. I don't know any man that would allow a man to keep working for him after he found out he was doing his wife. And to be quite honest, I wouldn't feel comfortable working here anymore."

"So is David there now?" I asked.

"Yes, he's in his office."

"Well, I called there before I called you and no one answered the phone."

"Yeah, he told Autumn to let all calls go to voice mail."

"Does she know what's going on?"

"I hate to say it, but everyone here has an idea of what's going on", he replied.

"Damn what did you do, go around the office bragging about it?"

"If you must know, I went to David this morning to try to talk to him again. It got kind of loud. Of course that nosey ass Autumn was somewhere listening. As soon as I stepped out of David's office, she was in my face. She started pointing her finger at me, saying she knew all along that something was going on between us. I couldn't deny it, so I just walked away. She followed me, asking a bunch of questions that I had no intentions of answering. Within minutes, the whole office knew what had happened."

"I never liked that bitch", I said out loud, mainly to myself. "I'm sure she's somewhere gloating, thinking she has a chance with David now."

"Well, I don't know about all of that..." He paused. "...I've got everything packed, so I'm about to be out. David made it clear he didn't want to see my face again...Look, I need to cut this short. I got a lot of shit I need to do."

"That's fine. I need to handle some things myself", I told him.

"Okay. Well I'll see you when I see you...and Taylor...once again...I'm sorry...about everything", he said.

"Yeah Exodus...I know."

After I got out of my lounge clothes, I put on some clothes and did my makeup. I jumped into my BMW and headed straight to David's office. I was going to force him to talk to me. I needed to know where I stood.

When I pulled into the parking lot of David's office, I looked for Exodus' Escalade. It was gone. I wouldn't have gone in if he was still there.

When I walked in, I came face to face with Autumn, as I had expected.

"What are you doing here?" she snapped. "If you're looking for Exodus, you just missed him."

Under normal circumstances, I would have cursed her out and told her to mind her own damn business. But I had more important things to deal with. So instead of responding to her, I ignored her and attempted to walk away. That bitch had the nerve to stand in front of me to block my path.

"Autumn...I advise you to get out of my way", I said in a calm, but firm tone.

She put her hands on her hips and got all up in my face. "What are you gonna do Taylor...hit me? Show me that ghetto bitch that you've been hiding all this time?"

I could feel my heart beating faster. It was taking all the strength I had not to beat Autumn's ass. She was really testing me in the worst way. "I'm going to say this one more time Autumn...get out of my face."

"I knew you were screwing Exodus. You are such a whore. You don't deserve a man like David. I should be with David. I would know how to treat him. Once he dumps your cheating ass, David will be mine-"

"Autumn what in the hell are you doing?" David's voice came from behind us.

"Uh...I...uh...was just...uh-", she stuttered.

"She was just harassing me and confessing her true feelings for you", I said.

A look of embarrassment appeared across her face. "Uh...David...I was just trying to-"

"Save it Autumn. I'll talk to you later." He then turned his attention to me. "What are you doing here Taylor?"

Autumn was still standing there with that stupid look on her face. "Don't you have something to do?" I asked her.

She didn't respond and looked at David. He gestured for her to leave. She rolled her eyes at me and walked away.

I turned my attention back to David. "You had me worried sick last night", I told him.

"I told you not to wait up for me."

"I know...but you are my husband David", I said.

"You should've thought about that when you were creeping around with my employee", he said, loud enough for anyone around to hear.

"Can we please go back to your office to discuss this? I don't think the whole office needs to know all of our business", I said, looking around to see who could be eavesdropping.

He didn't answer. He walked back towards his office and I followed him. As soon as we entered, I closed the door.

David sat on the edge of his desk. He crossed his

arms across his chest and stared at me. His blue eyes were sad. I could see that he was really in pain. I don't know how it happened, but I felt a tear trickle down my cheek. Then another one came, and then another. I was crying and I couldn't stop it.

"That's the first time I've ever seen you cry Taylor", he said.

"That should say something", I told him.

"Say what?"

"That I'm sorry. David, the last thing I wanted to do was hurt you", I replied, truthfully. Even though I didn't really love David, I considered him a good and decent person. Hurting him was something I wasn't proud of.

"Then why did you do it Taylor...why?"

I hunched my shoulders. "Honestly David...I don't have an answer", I told him.

We all knew the truth. I wasn't satisfied. But I wasn't going to make matters worse by admitting that to him.

"Was he better than me?" he asked with a look on his face that told me he really didn't want to know the answer.

I wanted to say 'hell yeah', but instead I said, "David, I really don't want to talk about that."

He looked defeated, like all the air had been sucked out of him. "Is it over between you two?" he asked.

`I walked closer to him. "Yes, it is."

"Are you sure?"

"Yes, I am...I told him it was over when I decided to confess."

"What made you decide to tell me what was going on? I mean, why now?"

That would've been the perfect time to tell him about his mother's part in everything. But I was smarter than that. It would come across a lot worse if she implicated herself. That way David would finally see what a bitch she really was. "I guess my conscious finally got the best of me", I told him.

"So what's next?"

"I don't know David...you tell me", I replied.

"I guess you want to go on like nothing happened."

"Up until you found out it was Exodus, that's what you were willing to do", I explained.

"Well, that changed everything. To cheat on me was one thing, but to cheat on me with my employee...that's just wrong."

"All I can do is, say I'm sorry and it won't happen again."

"Taylor, I want to believe you...I really do", he said.

I walked up to him and kissed him on the lips. "Then believe me", I whispered.

He stared into my eyes before wrapping his arms around me. I melted into his arms because I knew at that moment we were going to make it.

"I love you Taylor...Promise me you won't ever hurt me again", he whispered in my ear.

"I promise", I whispered back.

He gripped me harder and looked me in my eyes. "Taylor, I'm giving you a second chance. Don't make me regret it."

His tone was firm and serious. I had never seen him be so forceful, at least not with me.

"You won't regret it baby. I promise", I told him.

I had come to close to losing everything and I wasn't going to risk it again. I knew I was feeling guilty before about my actions, but the truth was I loved living the good life and I didn't want to give it up. Being poor again just wasn't an option.

He grabbed my hand and led me to the door. "I don't mean to rush you off, but I do have some work to do...including finding a new rep."

He opened the door and we walked out to the reception area. Autumn was sitting at her desk. When she looked up and saw us holding hands, the expression on her face changed. She was furious and it showed. I wanted to piss her off further, so I planted a big sloppy kiss on David's lips. "I'll see you later tonight baby", I said in my most seductive voice.

"You sure will", he said and patted me on my ass. "But wait...before you go, I need to address something." He walked over to Autumn's desk.

"Autumn, Taylor is my wife. If I ever hear you be disrespectful to her again, you will be looking for another job. And if you have any feelings for me that aren't work related, I suggest you get a handle on them...Do I make myself clear?"

She gave me a cold look before saying, "Yes Mr. Morgan", in a sarcastic tone.

David didn't say anything about her little attitude, but I knew he would deal with her later. I was just glad to finally see him put her in her place.

I was quite pleased when I left David's office. Everything was going in my favor. I couldn't have been happier. Now the real problem was going to be keeping my promise to David. I had sexual needs that David couldn't fulfill. And there was no way in hell I was going back to the battery operated satisfaction kit. It was okay for every now and then, but it didn't take the place of the real thing. I would have to find some new meat. Charles was too needy and obsessed. Exodus was definitely out of the picture. After he deceived me the way he did, there was no way he was getting any more of the goodies. I would find some fresh meat...when the time was right. I had to build David's trust in me again. And just when I get him where I want him, I'll go back on the prowl.

Jade

I had just finished eating breakfast and was cleaning up the mess I had made. My breakfast of French toast drenched in blueberry syrup made from fresh blueberries, scrambled eggs and turkey bacon had hit the spot. I had even made fresh squeezed orange juice. I usually didn't eat such a big breakfast, but today was all about relaxing and pampering myself. I had no intentions of even leaving my apartment.

I thought about calling Sierra, but I knew she would call me if she needed to. I dried off my hands and went to the living room. I scanned my coffee table for something to read. I spotted the Eric Jerome Dickey novel I had purchased, but never got around to reading. Eli had been taking up most of my spare time. So a lot of the things I use to do got put on the back burner.

I picked up the book and flopped down on my recliner to see what adventure EJD was going to take me through. As soon as I got comfortable, there was a knock on the door. I wasn't expecting any company, so I was going to ignore it. But the knocks got louder and harder. I got up and opened the door, without inquiring who it was.

A slim attractive white female was standing there smiling, with a big black bag in her hand.

"Uh...can I help you with something miss?" I asked her.

"I'm promoting a new line of cosmetics and skincare", she said, holding up the black bag.

"I'm happy with what I use now. So I won't be interested", I responded. I was about to close the door in her face.

"Please, just let me show them to you. If you're still not interested afterwards, I promise I will leave and not bother you anymore", she pleaded with me.

I hesitated for a moment. "Oh...okay. But I'm

telling you, you're wasting your time."

"I'll take my chances. You never know until you try."

I opened the door wider and waved her inside. "Come on in."

"Thank you." She looked around before saying, "You've got a nice place."

"Thanks...have a seat." I motioned for her to sit down. "Would you like something to drink?"

"No thank you. I'm fine."

I sat down. "So what is this wonderful line you have?"

She unzipped the bag. "Well...I've gotta be honest with you. I really don't have a line."

"I don't understand", I replied.

"You will in a minute...Jade", she said.

"How do you know my name? Who are you?"

She started fumbling through her bag. "To answer your second question, my name is Amanda. And to answer your first question, I'm the wife of the man you've been screwing for the last several months."

My stomach dropped. "Are you referring to Eli?"

"Unless you're sleeping with someone else's husband also...yes."

"You're a liar. Eli isn't married", I said.

She laughed and shook her head. "You are one dumb bitch."

I stood up. "Look Amanda, I think you need to leave."

"I'm not going anywhere. We've got some unfinished business", she said.

I went to pick up the phone. "If you don't leave, I'm calling the police."

"I wouldn't do that if I were you", she said and pulled a gun out of her bag.

I put the phone down and stood there, afraid to move. "Are you crazy or something?" I asked her, already knowing the answer.

"Yeah, I'm crazy...crazy to have put up with Eli's infidelity for all these years."

"Look Amanda, I didn't know Eli was married. So your problem is with him, not me", I said, trying to reason with her.

She pointed the gun at me. "How could you not know he was married?"

I kept my eyes on the gun. "Maybe I was just in denial. Maybe I didn't want to believe he was married."

She waved the gun at me. "Go sit down. You standing there, is making me nervous."

"You're the one with the gun. So I should be nervous", I said. Then I sat down in the seat across from her.

We sat there in silence for a while. Then she spoke. "The average woman would've left Eli's lying, cheating ass by now. But not me. I couldn't. He's the only man I've ever loved. When I married him, I vowed to stay with him for better or for worse. I don't want our kids to be without their father."

I sat there listening to her and felt sick. She said they had kids. Eli was married...with kids. "You have kids?" I asked in a whisper.

"Yes...four."

"I can't believe this. How could I be so stupid? My mother tried to warn me. I didn't want to listen to her", I said out loud, but mainly to myself.

She gave me a look of surprise. "So you really didn't know Eli was married?"

"No, I really didn't...I mean...I always thought he was hiding something. I use to ask questions all the time, but he would get upset with me. Then one day he finally opened up to me about his family. After that, I just assumed he was so secretive because he was ashamed of his family."

"Did you have a home number for him?"

"No, but that's normal. A lot of people don't even have home phones anymore."

"Have you ever been to his place?"

"No."

"Did you even know where he lived?"

"No."

"Have you met any of his family or friends?"

"No, but I just told you he was ashamed of his family."

As I answered each question, I realized I had been a fool. Eli had me so open I believed everything he told me.

Amanda stood up and circled the living room. "I will say this...out of all of Eli's little whores, you've got to be the dumbest."

"I'm not a whore! And I'm not dumb. I was just...in love."

She stopped pacing and looked out the window. "Yeah, Eli can have that effect on you. He's charming and irresistible. And the sex..." She turned around to look at me. "...well, you know how the sex is."

"What are your intentions with me?" I asked her.

She ignored my question and continued talking. "Eli has always had a way with women." She started pacing the floor again. "He was a playboy before I married him. But silly me...I thought he would change once we became husband and wife."

I asked just out of curiosity. "How long have you been married?"

"Ten long years. But we dated a long time before we got married. He took my virginity. So I'll be damned if I'm going to just let him go."

I was starting to feel sorry for her, even though she had a gun in her hand. "Look Amanda. I'm sorry about what happened with Eli. But you can't blame me for something I wasn't aware of. Hell, I'm hurting too right now. And now that I know Eli is married, I can promise you that our relationship is over."

She started laughing. "Oh, you better believe it's over. It's over because I say it's over." She came towards me with the gun.

I knew right then that my life was in jeopardy.

Sierra

I had made up my mind. I was going to confront Tyler about the photos. I couldn't take it any longer. I had been walking around like everything was okay...and it wasn't. I know I did my dirt, but I would face that if it surfaced.

While Tyler was out for his Saturday morning jog, I stayed home from the spa and took Shelby over to the babysitter's.

I heard the front door open alerting me that Tyler was home. He came into the kitchen, smiling. He kissed me on the cheek. "Hey Sierra I thought you'd be at the spa by now."

"Uh...actually, I had some things I needed to do."

"Oh. Where's Shelby?"

"I took her to Nikki's."

"Why?"

"Because I wanted us to be alone Tyler."

He gave me a seductive look. "Oh...you got something up your sleeve?"

"No. It's nothing like that Tyler."

"Well, then what is it?"

"We need to talk", I said.

"Aw come on Sierra. Why you gotta spoil my good mood?" He threw his hands up in the air.

I rolled my eyes at him. "Tyler, why do you have to assume that I'm trying to spoil your good mood?"

"Anytime a woman says 'we need to talk', it's never anything good."

"Could you please wait here? I need to get something."

I went to the home office and took the envelope out of my purse. I could feel my legs getting weaker as I made my way back into the kitchen.

He saw me standing there with the envelope behind my back. "What's up with you Sierra? If you got something you want to say, say it."

I threw the envelope on the counter and said, "You want to know what I have to say? What do you have to say about this garbage?"

He picked up the envelope and opened it. As he scanned the photos, a look of shame and embarrassment came across his face. "Sierra, I...uh...how...where did you get these?"

"Is that all you can say Tyler?" I screamed.

"This is not how it looks."

"Oh...so you're not really sucking another man's dick? And he's not really fucking you in the ass? And I guess that's not you fucking him in his ass? So what you're telling me is that my eyes are deceiving me?"

He walked over to me and tried to hug me. "Sierra, I'm sorry. I never meant for you to find out."

I pulled away from him. "Find out what Tyler...that you prefer another man over your own wife? That all those times I wanted you to give me oral pleasure, you wouldn't because I wasn't a man?"

"I love you Sierra. I really do", he pleaded.

"How can you say that? All these times I tried to spice up our sex life, you always made me feel like I was dirty for wanting to try new things. You told me I was nasty for wanting to please you. But nothing I've ever tried to do to you is as nasty as the disgusting acts on those pictures. At least now I know why you've been acting the way you have."

He grabbed me by my shoulders. "Come on Sierra. We can get pass this. It's not as bad as you're making it out to be."

I pushed him away from me. "Are you fucking kidding me? I have pictures of my husband in sex acts with another man and you're telling me it's not as bad as it seems?"

"Marriages come with a few ups and downs Sierra. There's no such thing as a perfect marriage."

"Are you listening to yourself Tyler? You're acting as if this were some simple little thing that you've done."

"Think about Shelby Sierra. How will this affect

her?"

I couldn't believe he let those words come out of his mouth. "Oh...so now you're thinking about Shelby? You weren't thinking about her when you were getting it on with your lover."

"Once you calm down and have time to think things over, you'll be able to forgive me and we can put this behind us."

I sat down at the table and put my face in my hands. I could feel Tyler watching me. We remained that way for a few seconds. I finally looked up at him, with tears in my eyes. Then I spoke. "Time to think about it? I've been thinking about it for the past two days."

He gave me a surprised look. "So you've had these pictures for two days and didn't say anything? Why?" he asked.

"I don't know Tyler. I guess a part of me wanted to pretend I hadn't seen them...sweep them under the rug. But I couldn't. Those photos haunted me. They consumed all my thoughts. And I had to address them...sooner or later."

I had told myself I wasn't going to cry. I was going to be strong. But Tyler's nonchalant attitude and demeanor had gotten to me. As I watched him standing across from me with that look on his face, I became even more disgusted. There were so many questions that I wanted answered. Yet, I was afraid to know the answers. And once I got the answers to those questions, what would I do? How would I feel? All types of thoughts were running through my mind. A part of me wanted to run over to Tyler and claw his eyes out. The other part wanted to understand why he did what he did. Every emotion I was feeling exploded inside of me and the tears came like rain.

Tyler rushed over to me to console me. "Sierra baby, I'm really sorry...Please forgive me."

"Tyler...please don't. The way I'm feeling right now, I don't think it's a good idea for you to be this close to me." I then stood up and walked over to the island. I turned my back to him and wiped my eyes with my shirt.

He spoke again. "Sierra, I know you're hurting right now. But I know we can get pass this."

I didn't say anything at first. I pondered the questions I had in my head. I knew I had to ask them, regardless of the outcome. I took a deep breath. Then I spoke. "Tyler, I have a few questions to ask you. I probably won't like the answers, but I really need to know them...Be honest."

He hesitated before saying, "Okay Sierra."

I turned to face him because I needed to look into his eyes to see if he was being honest. "Was that the only time you had been with him?"

He looked like he wanted to be anywhere, but there. His eyes begged me to not push the issue. But I wasn't backing down. He answered. "No...it wasn't." Then he looked down at his feet.

My stomach dropped. I felt as though all the air had escaped my lungs. My husband had admitted to having sex with a man on more than one occasion. Life hadn't prepared me for this. My legs buckled under me. I leaned on the island for support. But I wasn't finished yet. I still had questions. I took another deep breath and asked, "Is he the only man you've been with?"

He was still looking down. For the longest time, he refused to look up at me. Then he said, "Sierra is this really necessary?"

"Answer the damn question!" I screamed.

He looked up at the ceiling. He looked out the window. He looked everywhere, but at me. Then he said, "No."

He said no. That one word felt like a ton of bricks crashing down on me. All sorts of things ran through my mind. Was my husband gay? He had to be. There was no other explanation. My head was pounding. My heart was aching. The pain I felt was turning to anger. I picked up the vase of flowers that was sitting on the island. Before I could stop myself, I hurled it at Tyler's head. Lucky for him he seen it coming and had enough time to duck. The vase crashed into the wall. Glass, water and flowers came tumbling down...just like my marriage.

"Are you crazy woman? You could've hit me!" he yelled.

"That was my intention, you bastard", I replied.

"You said you wanted the truth. So I told you the truth."

"I know what I said Tyler...I was just hoping for a different outcome."

"Well, I'm sorry you didn't get the answers you hoped for."

"You have destroyed our marriage and that's all you can say? How could you do this to me?"

He came towards me and stood directly in front of me. "Before you start pointing the finger, let's get something clear Sierra."

"What's that?" I asked, putting my hands on my hips.

"I'm not the only one with skeletons in my closet", he said.

"And what is that supposed to mean?" I asked.

"Oh, you know what it means. I'm not the only one doing dirt."

"I have no idea what you're talking about Tyler", I responded. Then I walked away so he couldn't see the guilt in my eyes.

He followed me. "Oh, but I think you do."

I turned around to face him. I poked my finger in his chest and said, "Don't you dare try to turn things around on me."

He grabbed my finger and squeezed it. "Give it up Sierra. Your so-called ignorance is not appealing."

What was he talking about? I hadn't done anything...other than my little fling with Alexis. And there was no way he knew about that. Maybe he did see me at that sex club. That had to be what he was talking about. Either way, I wasn't about to admit to anything. My stand was innocent until proven guilty.

Jade

Amanda was laughing hysterically. "You should've seen your face. You thought I was going to shoot you, didn't you?"

My heart was beating so fast, I had to take a few seconds to get myself together. "That shit...isn't funny...You shouldn't play with guns."

She ran her fingers through her hair. "Believe me, I'm not playing. I came here with a purpose...to save my marriage."

I didn't quite understand how her coming to see me was going to save her marriage. And I let her know that.

"You're a threat to me", was her response.

"I don't get it. You said Eli's been cheating on you your whole marriage", I said.

She walked back over to the window, making sure she still had an eye on me. "Out of all the women Eli has been with, you're the first one he's carried on with for such a long time." She started crying. "I think he might be in love with you", she continued through her tears.

I sat there in disbelief, listening at this woman tell me that her husband might be in love with me. I didn't know if I should be flattered or disgusted. I knew how I felt about Eli, but all of that changed the minute I found out he had deceived me. Now I was feeling hatred for him and pity for his wife, even though she was in my apartment with a gun in her hand.

I watched her as she stood looking out the window, obviously hurt by her husband's cheating ways. She was tall, slim and in great shape. Her strawberry blond hair was cut in layers that framed her oval shaped face. She had deep blue eyes, a small button nose and full lips that appeared to be the result of injections. She was a beautiful woman and I'm sure she would have no problem getting a man.

"Amanda, you're a very attractive woman. You don't have to put up with a man who continues to cheat on you. As a woman, you deserve better. He isn't worth it. No man is", I told her.

She glared at me. "Don't say that about Eli. He is worth it to me. I am his wife damn it!" She pointed the gun to her chest. "I have given him the best years of my life. I gave him everything!" She started pacing the floor again.

"I gave up on my modeling career to become his wife. I gave him three kids that I didn't even want to have. And I even took in his bastard child and raised him as my own when his mother got hooked on drugs. So I'm not giving him up...to you or anybody else."

"He's not going to change", I said, wanting her to face the truth.

She looked around my apartment and said, "You sure do bounce back quickly."

"What do you mean by that?" I asked her.

She continued to walk back and forth, holding the gun in her hand, ready to pull the trigger if she felt the need to. "No one would guess that your place was trashed and destroyed not too long ago", she said.

"How do you know about that? Did Eli tell you that?" I asked.

She laughed. "Yeah, my husband told me about his girlfriend's place getting vandalized", she said, sarcastically.

I started thinking back to that night and how nothing was stolen. Everything was destroyed like someone had a personal vendetta against me. As Amanda stood in front of me brandishing her gun, I realized it was her. "You did that to my apartment...didn't you?"

"You're not so dumb after all", she said.

"What I don't understand is how you did it", I replied.

She explained to me how she made a copy of my apartment key from the one I had given to Eli. But I never gave Eli a key to my apartment. It just never came up. Somehow he got a copy made.

She said she followed him that night when we went out to eat. She let herself in and destroyed my apartment the way I was destroying her marriage.

"Was Eli aware of your actions?" I asked, hoping she would say no. I couldn't handle knowing he had a part in it.

"Of course not. He wasn't aware of any of the things I did to you", she said, with a smirk on her face.

"What things are you talking about?" I asked her.

She came closer to me, like she was daring me to make a move. "The phone calls...the Bratz doll...your car..." Her voice trailed off.

"*You* did those things to me? All this time, I thought it was Paige." I shook my head from side to side. I felt like such a fool. The thoughts of Paige and I rolling around in the parking lot of *Food Lion* stuck out in my head. She said she hadn't done it, but I didn't believe her. I was so sure it was her. How was I to know that Eli had a crazy wife at home?

Amanda started laughing again. "You know the funny part was watching you and that other woman go at each other. Now that was entertaining."

"How did you know that both of us were going to be there?" I asked her.

"I knew you were there because I followed you from your job. It was just pure luck that the other woman was there. Things couldn't have worked out any better."

I just couldn't believe what was happening. How could I get myself into such a situation? Not only was Eli married with children. But his wife had damaged my apartment and my car, while making harassing calls to me. And here she was holding me hostage with a gun. I was starting to wish that I hadn't got out of bed this morning.

For the second time I said, "Amanda what are your intentions with me?"

She looked down at the gun and then at me. She then turned her head to the side, like she was in deep thought. Then she said, "My intentions are for you to stay away from Eli...for good."

457

"I told you now that I know Eli is married I want nothing else to do with him. I don't do married men...at least not knowingly."

Suddenly my cell phone vibrated on the coffee table alerting me I had an incoming call. I looked at the phone and then at Amanda. "Don't even think about answering that," she commanded.

I did as she instructed. I watched the cell phone until it stopped ringing, wondering who it was.

As soon as my cell phone stopped ringing, the sound of the house phone ringing echoed through the apartment.

"Someone's really trying to get in touch with you. It's probably that no good husband of mine", she said.

"Well whoever it is, they're going to know something's wrong because I always answer my cell phone when I'm not working", I told her truthfully.

"By the time they do realize something is wrong, it will be too late", she replied and snatched the phone cord out of the wall.

My heart started beating faster. I begin to realize that I was running out of time. I had to come up with a plan. If she didn't have that gun, things would've never went this far. I knew I could take her, but a loaded gun was another story.

I tried reasoning with her again. "Look Amanda, I know you're hurt and upset. You have a right to be. But I'm not the person you need to be angry with. As you already know, I didn't even know about you. Eli needs to be made accountable for his actions."

She shook her head from side to side, like she didn't want to hear what I was saying. "You don't understand...if you're not around, he won't want you anymore. That's why I have to get rid of you."

"So you get rid of me and your problems are solved right?" I asked. "No, they're not. Why? Because he's moving on to the next woman...and the next woman. The cycle continues...until you decide enough is enough. It's time to face the truth. Eli is the problem here...not me...not you...not even all the other women."

She walked back over to the window. "In his line of work, women are always throwing themselves at him. I know beautiful women can be a temptation for men, especially men like Eli. He loves everything about women. I know he loves me too. It's just that his love for women sometimes outweighs his love for me. In the end, I'm the only one that counts because I'm the one he chose as his wife. I'm the one who gave him kids and I'm the one he comes home to."

He really had her nose open. But deep down inside, I knew she didn't really believe that crap she was unloading on me. "Amanda, if you really felt that way, you wouldn't be here right now. The fact is, you're tired", I told her.

"You don't know me. You don't know how I feel!" she screamed.

"No, I don't know you. But I do know that any woman in your position would be fed up by now."

I saw her body soften. It appeared that maybe she was finally taking in what I was saying. She didn't put the gun down, but she loosened her grip on it. She started crying again. Even though I felt hurt and betrayed by Eli, I wished there was something I could do to help her. No woman deserved what she was going through. But how could I help a woman who hated me for having an affair with her husband?"

She cleared her throat and wiped her eyes. "You sound like my mother. She's been telling me for years that I need to leave Eli. I keep telling her that it's not that simple. I know I deserve better, but I don't think I can go on without him. I depend on him for so much."

I was about to respond, but there was a knock on the door. Amanda held the gun up. "Don't say a word", she whispered.

The knocking got louder and more forceful. I was tempted to run and open the door, but I wasn't taking any chances with a woman scorned.

I didn't have to open the door. As soon as the knocking stopped, there was a key inserted into the lock. The knob turned and the door flew open. Eli walked in.

He looked like he seen a ghost when he saw Amanda standing there with the gun in her hand.

When he finally found his voice, he said, "What in the hell is going on here?"

Taylor

I woke up feeling rejuvenated and as giddy as a teenager...not because my husband and I had so-called made love last night. I felt that way because I was still a millionaire's wife. My fairy tale hadn't ended yet.

To show David I was serious about my promise to him, I convinced him to stay home from playing golf today. We had a nice breakfast that I prepared myself. It was only pancakes and sausage, but the fact that I fixed it meant a lot to him.

After we had both showered, we went for a stroll around the neighborhood. Of course, it was David's idea. I wanted to go shopping or take a trip to Sierra's spa. But if I wanted to stay on his good side, I had to do whatever he wanted to do. As we walked along and took in the surroundings, I came to a conclusion.

"David, don't you think it's time to leave this neighborhood?" I asked.

"Why...what's wrong with it?" He looked at me skeptically.

"Nothing's wrong with it. I just think we've outgrown it", I replied.

"You've only been here two years Taylor."

"Okay...you've outgrown it then."

"I haven't outgrown it. I love it here. I've been here since I made it in the business", he beamed.

"Yeah, that's my point. You are a millionaire many times over. Yet you're living here in *Croasdaile Farms.*"

"Take a look around you Taylor. These are beautiful homes!"

"I'm not saying they aren't David. All I'm saying is that with your money, you could be doing so much better."

"I don't want to do better. I'm content with where we live", he argued.

"But you shouldn't be. It's time for an upgrade

461

David", I responded.

He stopped walking and looked at me. "I guess your ideal home is one like the celebrities...with like 20 bedrooms, 15 bathrooms, movie theaters, bowling alleys, indoor and outdoor pools, ten car garages and all that other nonsense."

I threw my hands up. "Yes...if you can afford it, why not?"

"I guess you didn't hear me when I said it was nonsense", he replied.

"I don't think it's nonsense. I mean really David...what's the purpose of having all that money if you're not going to make use of it."

"I do make use of it. I donate it to charities, put it in the bank...and the rest, you spend", he said with a smirk on his face.

I smacked my lips at him. "Funny...but seriously, you can still do all of that and have a nicer house."

"Taylor, we do have a nice house. Do you know how many people would love to live here?"

"I know we have a nice house and I know that there are a lot of people that would love to live in a place like this-"

He cut me off. "Then why are we even having this discussion Taylor?"

"Because I want you to admit that I'm right", I said.

"I'm not going to admit you're right. I don't think it's okay for people to throw money around just because they have plenty of it. Yes, it's nice to know you're set financially...and don't have to worry about where your next meal is coming from. But buying over expensive things just because I can doesn't do anything for me. Helping people who are less fortunate is what makes me feel good. Why would I want a bigger house when it's just the two of us? It just doesn't make sense to me. That's the problem with most of the rich and famous. They get some money and just start blowing it on unnecessary things. Then a few years later when their career is over or they are no longer relevant, the money runs out and before long, they have nothing to show. When they were spending money like it was going out of style, they should've been saving and planning for their future."

I wasn't expecting him to go off on a tangent like that. All I was trying to do was get us to live like we should be living. "Okay...I didn't know I was going to get a lecture. I just thought it would be a good idea to consider house shopping...that's all", I said, trying to sound pitiful.

He started laughing. "I'm sorry baby. I guess that's just a touchy subject for me."

"Yeah...I see", I replied.

"Well, if you don't mind, I'd just like to drop the subject all together", he said.

"Uh...sure. That's fine", I answered. I would bring it up again later. I was determined to get the mansion of my dreams. No matter how stern David was when it came to certain things, he would bend a little when it came to making me happy. The affair was still fresh in his mind. So I knew he wasn't going to give in to me right then. But it wouldn't be too long before I had him eating out the palm of my hand again.

We continued our walk in silence, which was fine with me. It gave me plenty of time to plot my next course of action. After we agreed the walk had done our bodies some good, we headed back home. Just as we were walking up, a cab pulled up to the house.

"I wonder who that could be", David said.

I didn't have to wonder. I already had an idea of who it was. And my suspicions were confirmed when the cab driver got out, opened the back door and Claire Morgan stepped out.

"What is she doing here? She didn't tell me she was coming." He looked at me. "Did you know she was coming?"

"Like your mother would actually talk to me", I said, rolling my eyes in annoyance.

The cab driver was unloading her bags just as we reached them. "Thank you, young man", she told him and handed him some money.

He looked down at the money. A big grin came across his face. "Oh, you're welcome ma'am...anytime.

You have a good one." He hopped back into his cab and drove off.

"Mother, what on Earth are you doing here?" David asked as soon as we reached her.

"Is that any way to greet your mother?" she asked.

He reached out to hug her. "I'm sorry mother. I'm just surprised to see you."

She hugged him and kissed him on the cheek. "It's okay son. I know you weren't expecting me." She glanced at me with her usual disappointing look. "Taylor...you look...well...you look like you always look."

"And Claire you look amazing as always", I replied with my fake smile in place.

Obviously trying to ease the tension, David said, "So...Mother, you never did say what brought you here...not that I'm not happy to see you."

She looked over at me and then put her arm around David. "Well, I have some business to take care of."

"What kind of business?" he asked.

"Oh, nothing you need to worry about dear...but I really wanted to spend some time with you", she said.

"Aw, that's great Mother", he said. He reached for her luggage. "Come on...let's get you settled in."

David was the first to enter the house. Claire threw me a dirty look before going in behind him. I returned the favor, just to let her know I was not intimidated by her.

"Are you hungry Mother?" David asked her after we were all inside the house.

"No, I'm fine dear. Don't make a fuss over me. You just go back to what you were doing", she replied.

The way she kept calling him dear made my skin crawl. To be honest, I think everything she did made my skin crawl...especially since I knew why she was really there.

"It's no fuss Mother. Taylor and I just came from a walk and we were just coming back to hang out a little", David told her.

"Oh", she said dryly.

"Why don't we take your bags upstairs to your room so you can get comfortable", David said and grabbed her luggage off the floor.

"Yes, I do need to freshen up a bit."

They made their way upstairs and I searched for my cell phone. I had to find an escape before David tried to put his mother off on me. After I located it, I dialed Jade's number. It rang until her voice mail came on. She must've been busy, because she always answered her cell phone on the weekends. Maybe she and Exodus were getting busy...lucky girl. I didn't even bother calling Sierra, because I knew she would be at the spa.

I went to the kitchen and poured myself a glass of grape juice. I had to figure out how I was going to get away from the witch and her son. It wasn't that I had a problem being with David. I just couldn't deal with the two together. She treated him like he was a child and he basked in it.

Then there was the sole purpose of her visit. When and how she was going to spring the news to David? But then again, it didn't matter anyway. She was going to get the shock of her life. Then I realized that I wanted to be around when she decided she would reveal my deception. I wanted to see the look on her face when David told her he already knew.

I heard them coming down the stairs laughing and talking. They entered the kitchen as I was finishing up my grape juice.

"It's a little too early to be drinking, isn't it Taylor?" she asked.

"Not when it is grape juice...besides I'll leave the drinking to you. You look like you like to enjoy a stiff one every now and then."

David gave me a disapproving look. I pretended not to notice and washed my glass out in the sink.

"Taylor, I'm not going to stoop to your level. I have way too much class", she said and straightened her blazer.

I was about to respond, but David spoke up. "Hey...I've decided to take my two favorite ladies out to lunch."

"Oh, I was hoping you and I could spend some time together...alone", she said before looking over at me.

"Well...Mother I was hoping I could spend time with both of you...and I did promise Taylor that we would spend the day together since it has been a while. Besides, I didn't know you were coming...remember?" He looked at her with pleading eyes.

She crossed her arms and said, "If that's how you want it, then I guess I have no other choice...do I?"

He stood closer to her and put his arm around her shoulder. "Please don't lay a guilt trip on me Mother. I hate it when you do that." He motioned for me to come closer with his free hand.

I hesitantly walked over to them. He wrapped his other arm around me. "There's enough of me to go around. So we're going to go out and we're going to have a great time."

'It's going to be an interesting day', I thought to myself.

Sierra

"Tyler I'm not going to stand here and let you point the finger at me when you're the one out here screwing another man!" I yelled at my husband.

He started laughing and shaking his head.

"What in the hell is so funny?" I asked him.

"You are", he answered. "Actually, you're more like an Academy Award winning actress."

I had no idea what Tyler was getting at, but he was really talking crazy. Maybe that was his way of trying to get off the subject at hand. Whatever it was, I wasn't going to play along for too much longer.

"I know what you're trying to do Tyler and it's not gonna work. I'm not gonna just sweep this shit under the rug. So if you got something you want or need to say, just say it."

"I can do better than that Sierra. You think you're the only one that knows something? You're a hypocrite...that's what you are", he said, pointing his finger at me.

"I don't have to put up with this", I said and was about to leave.

He grabbed my arm. "No...I need to show you something."

"What do you need to show me Tyler? What could you possibly have to show me?"

He held his hand up. "Just wait here and I'll be back."

I was tempted to just leave, but I was curious about what he was up to. So I stood there waiting for him to come back. When he came back, he had some type of cd or DVD in his hand. "What's that?" I asked him.

"Oh, I will be glad to show you what it is."

I knew he was stalling, but that didn't stop the knots from forming in my stomach. "So let's see it", I said confidently, even though I was nervous inside.

He left out the kitchen and I followed him. We went into the den. "Are you sure you want to see this?" he asked, holding up the disc.

"Just admit that there's nothing on there. You're just trying to throw me off your cheating ass", I said.

He turned on the TV and popped the disc into the player. There on the big screen was me with my legs spread wide open and Alexis' head buried between them. The expression on my face was one of sheer pleasure.

A lump formed in my throat and I could hardly speak. "W-where...d-did...y-you...get that Tyler?"

"I guess the same place you got those photos Sierra", he said, with a satisfied look on his face.

I walked towards the TV. "Cut that off. I don't want to see this!" I yelled.

Tyler stood in front of me. "Oh no! You need to see it. Plus there's more." He grabbed my wrists and forced me to sit on the couch. He picked up the remote and hit fast forward. He stopped on a scene where I was pleasing Alexis.

Then there was the time she used the strap-on with me, the time with that Boris guy and so much more.

I felt like I was going to be sick. I couldn't take anymore. "Tyler, please turn it off. I can't watch anymore", I pleaded with him.

He turned it off and said, "How in the hell do you think I felt Sierra...watching another man fuck my wife?"

"I'm sure it was no worse than watching your husband get it on with another man", I snapped.

He didn't respond. He sat down on the couch next to me. We both sat in silence for a while. I was more confused than ever. How did someone get into Alexis' house to record me and her together all of those times? And why did they do it? Was it the same person that sent me those photos? Who would try to split us up? Nothing was making sense.

"So, I guess we're even now...huh?" Tyler asked, with a stupid grin on his face.

"What? You can't be for real. How in the hell are we even Tyler? This isn't a joke. You were screwing another man, in case you forgot." I was furious.

"And you were screwing another woman...and another man, as well", he replied.

I stood up. "Yes, you're right...but that only happened because I was unhappy and dissatisfied with our sex life...I was bored Tyler. At times, you made me feel like you didn't want me. Then Alexis came along ...and somehow she made me feel sexy and desirable again. She did things to me that you wouldn't do. I kept telling myself it was wrong, but I couldn't stop. It's like she had me under a spell or something. And as far as Boris goes, that was a onetime thing. I only did it because Alexis wanted me to...She had me so sprung, I would've done almost anything she asked me to do. Then you started acting all wonderful lately, and that made me feel guiltier. I kept trying to part ways with her. She didn't seem too happy with my decision and kept persuading me to continue the relationship."

I paused long enough to check Tyler's reaction. He was looking at me with a serious expression on his face. I couldn't tell if he was angry or not. I continued. "But the last time I was with her was the night that I caught Kiki and Danny stealing. She came by, which is why I got home so late. After we were intimate, I told her it was over. She stormed out and I haven't seen or talked to her since."

It felt good to get all of that off my chest. It didn't change the fact that we had both cheated, but at least my conscious was clear. Tyler leaned back on the couch and blew air out of his mouth. He then looked up at the ceiling.

"I know you're upset Tyler...and you have a right to be but-"

He looked at me and said, "Sierra, I think you need to sit down...I have a confession to make."

My heart started beating fast. What else could he possibly tell me that was worse than what I had already found out? "What is it Tyler?" I asked.

He patted the cushion beside him. "Please...sit."

I did as he instructed. He took a deep breath.

"Okay...here it is. It's my strong belief that your meeting Alexis was no coincidence."

"I don't understand."

He held his hand up to me. "Look Sierra, I'm gonna need you to not interrupt me...Just let me talk first. Then you can ask all the questions you want when I'm finished...okay?"

I shook my head and he continued. "As I was saying, I don't think it was a coincidence. You see...that man on the photos ...that's Demond, Alexis' ex-husband."

I felt my stomach drop and my heart felt as though it was going to jump out of my chest. Had I heard him correctly? Did he say he was screwing Alexis' ex-husband? I wanted to jump up and leave, but I knew I needed to hear the rest of what he had to say.

"Demond and I originally met at this sex club called *Twilights*. We formed a friendship and realized we had a lot in common. Our friendship went to the next level, as we expected it would. We both knew we were attracted to men, but were afraid to act on it in the past. Since we were both married and had a lot to lose, we decided to act on our sexual desires with each other. Everything was going fine until Alexis caught us. We would always get a room, but he said it was okay to be at their house because Alexis was out of town on business. I guess she came back earlier than what he expected. We were in the middle of having sex, and she walked in on us. As to be expected, she was furious. She even grabbed a knife and tried to cut him...Let's just say it was a big mess. She filed for a divorce because he told her he was attracted to men and couldn't promise her he would stop being with them. So that night when she showed up at the restaurant and you introduced her as your friend, I panicked. I just assumed she was going to tell you about me and Demond. I knew nothing good would come out of your friendship, which is why I didn't want you around her. It was like waiting for a bomb to go off. Then that day when you told me she caught her husband with another woman, I relaxed a little. I don't know why, but I did. I guess I figured that if she was going to tell you

470

anything, she would've told you by then. But in the back of my mind, I knew shit would come to light eventually. Never in a million years would I have thought that you two were having an affair. That was the furthest thing from my mind...until I got that video."

I was stunned, upset, hurt and dumbfounded all at the same time. I couldn't believe what I just heard. And even though he had given me plenty of details, I was still a little confused with the whole situation.

"Are you okay?" He asked and reached for my hand.

"I still don't get it", I said, ignoring his question.

"What is it that you don't get Sierra?" he asked.

"You said Alexis planned meeting me so she could tell me about you, but she didn't."

"Oh, but she did...when she sent you those pictures", he said.

"What makes you think that she sent them? She didn't take them did she?"

"Of course she didn't take them. How she got a hold of them, I don't know", he answered.

"Then that proves she wasn't the one that sent them. How do you know that Demond didn't send them?" I asked him.

He let out a dramatic laugh. "Sierra, you can't be that naïve...I mean seriously...It's obvious what's going on here", he said.

"Well apparently not to me."

"Listen very closely and I'm gonna break it down for you...Alexis blamed me for her and Demond's split up, so she wanted to get back at me. She befriended you and apparently seduced you. I guess her goal was to hurt me the way Demond and I hurt her. I assume she had video cameras set up in her house to record your intimate moments. And when you broke things off with her, she decided to make her move. She sent you those pictures and sent me that video."

Everything he said made sense, but I still didn't want to believe it. Alexis had been so attentive and so good to me. There was no way that was all an act. She

471

always made me feel so good. It had to mean something to her. Maybe it was just a coincidence that I was the wife of the man she caught her husband with. Even as I thought that to myself, it sounded unbelievable. Either way, I had to find out for myself. I had to know the truth.

I stood up to leave. "Where are you going?" Tyler asked.

"I have to find out what's going on Tyler", I told him.

"Sierra, I just told you what was going on. We both screwed up. So let's just put this behind us and get on with our lives."

"It's not that simple Tyler…and you know it. I need some answers. And I need them from Alexis.

Jade

"What does it look like?" Amanda said to Eli.

He looked at me and then back at her. "Amanda, put the gun down. Don't do anything you'll regret."

She pointed the gun at him. "The only thing I should regret is marrying your no good ass."

"Are you okay?" he asked me.

I rolled my eyes at him and looked away. I didn't even want to be in the same room as him. If his crazy ass wife didn't have that gun in her hand, I probably would've jumped on him and scratched his eyes out.

"Is she all you care about Eli? What about me? I'm your wife!" she yelled.

"Amanda, you need to calm down and put that gun away before someone gets hurt", he demanded.

"That's my intention. Someone is going to pay for my pain...and it's going to be your little girlfriend here." She pointed the gun towards me again.

"Jade didn't do anything to you. She didn't even know you existed. So if you want to hurt someone, hurt me", he told her.

"But I love you Eli. You're the only man I've ever loved. I could never hurt you", she whined.

He walked towards her. "Then put the gun down."

"You come any closer and I swear I will shoot that bitch", she said, still pointing the gun at me.

Eli stopped in his tracks and held his hands up. "Okay okay...I won't come any closer. Please don't shoot her."

She pointed the gun at him and said, "Since you care for her so much, go sit beside her."

Eli did as he was instructed. When he sat down beside me, I turned away so I wouldn't have to look at him. I should've hated him, but I didn't. Of course I hated that he deceived me, but I still had those feelings of love for him...that I couldn't just turn off.

Amanda started pacing the floor again. Then she started crying. "Why don't you love me the way I love you Eli?" she cried.

He glanced at me before answering. "Amanda baby, I do love you. You know that."

"If you did, you wouldn't cheat on me the way you do", she replied.

"Come on Amanda. Don't start that shit again", he said.

"Don't start what Eli...telling the truth?" she asked.

"Just because I cheat on you, it doesn't mean I don't love you. You're the mother of my kids."

"Then why all the women Eli? Why? Am I not woman enough for you!" she screamed, with tears running down her cheeks.

"Those women don't mean shit to me Amanda. It's all about sex", he answered.

"So is that all I was to you Eli...a fuck...something to do?" I asked him. I couldn't believe he admitted to that with me sitting right beside him.

He looked back and forth between me and Amanda. I could tell he didn't want to answer that question.

"Why don't you answer the question Eli? You can't hurt me no worse than I'm already hurt. I already know the truth", she said.

I put my hand up to his face. "Don't even worry about it. It doesn't matter anyway..." Then I turned so I could face him. "I don't know if you care or not Eli, but I was really falling for you. I was hoping that we could one day take our relationship to the next level. Your actions not only hurt your wife, they hurt me too."

For the first time since everything went down, I broke down. Eli's deception had finally gotten the best of me.

"Why are you crying?" Amanda asked me. "Hell, I'm the one that has to deal with his lying and cheating on a regular basis."

"But you don't have to", I said through my tears. "I told you, you deserve better Amanda."

"Don't be trying to turn my wife against me", he said.

"In case you haven't noticed, you've done that yourself Eli", I told him.

"You know Jade, you are so right. All this time I've spent hating the many women that have been in and out of Eli's life, I should've been hating him." She turned her attention to him. "I have put up with your infidelity for so long, that it just seems natural. But it's not natural. No woman should have to share her husband with woman after woman. Just like Jade said, I deserve better. I have been a good damn wife to you Eli. I've given you three kids and even took in your other son. I do your cooking, your cleaning, wash your dirty drawers and sit home every night waiting for you to come home from being with whatever bitch you're screwing at the moment. I wanted to hurt Jade because I could tell that you were really feeling her. But even with her out the picture, things won't change. You'll just move on to the next one. I can't deal with this shit anymore...I want a divorce", she told him.

"You don't mean that Amanda. You're just upset right now", he replied. He had a cocky look on his face that made me want to slap the taste out of his mouth.

She held the gun up. "Don't tell me what the hell I mean. Of course I'm upset. I have a right to be." She shook her head. "I've come to realize that our marriage is a fucking joke Eli. There's no communication, no romance or passion. We don't even spend time together. I'm more like a servant than your wife to you. You don't respect me or treat me as your equal. To be honest, I don't know why I've stayed with you for so long."

"You stayed with me because you love me and because you know I love you...no matter what", he replied.

She let out a hearty laugh. "Love doesn't cut it anymore Eli. I need more than that damn it!"

"You're not going anywhere Amanda. You're not strong enough to make it on your own", he told her.

"I'm stronger than you may think", she responded.

"It doesn't matter, because you're not taking my

kids anywhere."

"Oh please Eli. You don't give a damn about those kids. When was the last time you spent some time with any of them? You spend all of your time with work and your many women", she answered, waving her hand in my direction. "You have no idea what it's like to keep making excuses to your kids about why their father is never around." She then pointed the gun to her chest. "I'm the one that's there for them. I'm the one they depend on. I may as well be a single parent."

He gave her a cold look. "Like I said, you're not going anywhere bitch!"

She rolled her eyes towards the ceiling, took a deep breath and said, "You're right, I'm not going anywhere...but you are."

The next thing I heard was gunfire, after Amanda pulled the trigger.

Taylor

As I had suspected, the outing with David and his mother was very trying. She challenged everything I said or did. And every time David decided he would buy me something, she figured out a way to talk him out of it. But what irritated me the most was the way he kept defending her. When I had finally had enough and felt like I would explode, she decided she was ready to go home and call it a day.

After we had arrived back home, David went upstairs to take a shower. She approached me in the kitchen.

"I'm giving you another chance to walk out of my son's life with a little dignity...while you can", she said to me, with a smirk on her face.

I smiled at her. "What are you talking about woman?"

She looked behind her to make sure David was still upstairs. "The last time I was here, I offered you money to get lost. You should've taken the offer, because I'm asking you to get lost again. But this time, there's no money involved. You are leaving this sham of a marriage the same way you came into it...broke."

I walked over to her and got up in her face. "Claire you might intimidate other folks, but not me."

She laughed and put her hands on her hips. "Someone should've told you...I'm not one to be taken lightly. I can be your worst nightmare. I've got stuff on you that will surely make David send you away with your tail between your legs."

Of course I knew what she was talking about. And the fact that David already knew, was making the whole conversation more fun. I couldn't wait to see the look on her face when he told her he already knew. "Whatever it is you think you have on me doesn't compare to what I have", I told her.

"And what is that?" she asked.

I licked my lips seductively and said, "This sweet black pussy that your son can't seem to get enough of."

"You filthy whore. I don't know what David ever saw in you. Of all the classy, sophisticated women he came across, he chose you...a nappy-headed, money hungry low class slut!"

Before I knew it and without thinking, I slapped her so hard, she stumbled backwards. She immediately grabbed her face, which was already turning a shade of red. I had never hit another woman, especially someone older than me. I always respected my elders, but she deserved it.

After she gained her composure, she said, "You black bitch. You just signed your death wish."

I was about to say something, but David walked in. Claire was still holding her face.

"What's going on in here? Is everything okay?" David asked, looking back and forth between the two of us.

Claire pointed at me with her free hand. "That wife of yours hit me!"

David gave me a shocked look. "Is that true Taylor?"

I stood up straight and put my hand on my hip. "Yes, it is."

"Why on Earth would you do something like that?" He asked, grabbing his mother's arm.

"Why don't you ask her?" I replied and tilted my head in her direction.

"I'm asking you Taylor!" he yelled.

"Your mother is a racist snob David...that's why I slapped her!" I yelled back at him.

"My mother may be somewhat of a snob, but she is not a racist! And even if you believe that to be true, that doesn't make it okay for you to put your hands on her", he said.

I didn't even bother responding. I knew I couldn't win that battle.

Claire rolled her eyes at David. "Son, how can you

call your own mother a snob?"

He turned to face her. "Mother, that's not the issue right now...I walk into the kitchen and find out that my wife has slapped my mother and I want to get to the bottom of it."

"It's obvious son. Your wife is out of control and she has no class, which is what I was telling her when she decided to deck me", she replied.

"Oh, you said more than that", I told her.

"It doesn't matter what she said Taylor. Slapping her was uncalled for", he scolded me like I was a child.

"Oh, you haven't heard the worst of it son", she told him.

He looked at her and then looked at me. "What is she talking about?" he asked me.

I shrugged my shoulders. "I have no idea."

"I'll tell you what I'm talking about...That no good wife of yours is having an affair with your employee Exodus", she said with a big grin on her face.

David had a confused look on his face. "I know that Mother..." He looked at me and then back at her. "...But how did you know?"

The smile on her face vanished when she realized he said he already knew. "You mean to tell me you knew this and you haven't thrown her out on her cheating ass?"

"We've talked about it and I've decided to forgive her", he replied.

"Just like that?" she asked.

"Of course I was upset when she told me, but we talked about it and she assured me it wouldn't happen again", he told her, like it was her business.

She threw me an evil glance. "And you believe her?"

"Not to be disrespectful Mother, but this is really between me and Taylor", he replied.

She put her hand on his shoulder. "I understand that dear. I just don't want you making decisions you may regret later."

He patted her hand. "I am an adult Mother and I have to make my own decisions...whether you agree with them or not", he said.

That was the first time I ever heard him stand up to his mother...at least when it came to me. I was so proud of him. I wanted to stick my tongue out at her, but thought better of it, considering how childish it would've been.

"Well...if that's how you want it David, what can I say?" she asked, sounding upset.

David still had a puzzled look on his face and I knew why. "Mother, you still haven't told me how you knew about Taylor and Exodus." He then looked over at me. "You didn't tell her about it...did you?"

I let out a chuckle. "Like, I would tell her that."

He asked her again. "How did you know?"

She looked at David and then at me. Then she looked down at the floor. The only sound that could be heard was the humming of the refrigerator.

"Mother, I'm waiting", David said.

The look on her face was priceless. I had never seen her look so passive. After another bout of silence and not being able to take anymore, I said, "I'll tell you how she knew."

Her eyes pleaded for me not to say anything...like I would actually save her from ridicule. "She knew because she hired Exodus to seduce me."

I told him the whole story from the beginning. When I finished, I could see that he was furious.

He glared at her and said, "Is that true Mother?"

She reached for his hands and held on to them. "Son, you must understand that everything I did was for your own good."

He pulled his hands away from her grip. "How could you do such a thing?"

"I did it because you aren't smart enough to see that this woman isn't good enough for you and is nothing but a whore", she said as if I wasn't in the room.

"You are talking about my wife Mother!" he yelled.

"Don't you dare raise your voice at me David Morgan", she replied.

"I'm sorry Mother, but you have crossed the line",

he said.

"Why are you angry with me? All I did was prove what I had been thinking all along. If anything, you should be thanking me."

"Thanking you? Do you hear yourself? What you did was deceitful and underhanded...to me. When you were putting your plan together, I'm sure that didn't cross your mind. You were so busy trying to set my wife up that you didn't think about how it would affect me."

"I did it for you son. Can't you see that?" she replied.

"No Mother...you did it for yourself...just like everything else you do."

I was starting to feel uncomfortable just standing there while they argued back and forth. Even though she deserved it, I had never seen David so angry with her. I was almost feeling sorry for her...until she said, "I can't believe you're going to side with that tramp instead of your mother."

It was time for me to step in. "Look Claire, I'm getting sick of you talking about me like I'm not in the room."

David held his hand up to me. "I'll handle this Taylor. This is between me and my mother."

"Well, since she keeps calling me everything under the sun, I'm involved also. And I'm not about to stand here and let her keep insulting me David. Now either you put her in her place...or I will", I told him.

"What are you going to do? Hit me again?" she asked.

"If that's what it takes", I said, getting closer to her.

David stood in front of me. "There's going to be no more hitting around here."

I stepped back and took a seat on one of the bar stools. If David hadn't been there, Claire would've surely gotten a good old fashioned ass whipping. I was fed up with her constantly putting me down and everything around her. Then she was always turning things around on you, when she was in the wrong. How David and Mr. Morgan put up with her is beyond me.

Then I started thinking about Deanna. Maybe she was like me...she got tired of her mother and left home the first chance she got. As overbearing as Claire was, it wouldn't be hard to believe.

I took a deep breath and tried to compose myself. "Maybe I was wrong for hitting you..." I told Claire, even though I didn't mean it. "...and I apologize."

David nodded his approval and then turned to her. "Okay Mother...it's your turn", he said.

She let out a grunt. "You're not buying that feeble attempt at an apology are you David? If she did it once, she'll do it again. It's probably the way she was brought up."

I stood up and slammed my fist on the countertop. "That's it! I'm not putting up with this bullshit anymore", I said, staring Claire straight in the eyes. "You are a first class bitch who likes to put down and control everyone around you!"

The look on David's face let me know he wasn't too pleased with my outburst. But he knew I had reached my breaking point, so he didn't say anything.

Claire cleared her throat. "David, are you going to just stand there and let her talk to me that way?"

David looked at me and then back at his mother. He was in deep thought, torn between the women he loved. He had a big decision to make.

Tired of waiting for him to respond, Claire threw her hands in the air. "Don't stress yourself about it David...What can I expect? I guess it's the woman in you."

Her statement surprised me and confused me at the same time. I looked to David for an explanation, but he was glaring at Claire. "Mother...don't go there...please", he said.

Don't go where? What was he talking about?

Claire started laughing. "Oh...that's right. Your wife doesn't know, does she?"

"Mother, I'm begging you...please don't", David pleaded.

"Oh come on son. You shouldn't be keeping secrets from your wife", she said before letting out another laugh.

I was really getting concerned and wanted to know what was going on. "What is she talking about David?" I asked him.

"Nothing, Taylor. She's just blowing hot air. Don't pay any attention to her", he replied, without even looking at me.

I knew he was lying and the beads of sweat on his forehead proved it. My stomach was in knots and I felt like I was going to lose my lunch. I wanted to know what was going on. But in the back of my mind, I was wondering if it was something I could handle.

"Taylor my dear, what I have to say is something you'll definitely want to hear", Claire said in her fakest sweet voice.

She was really irritating me. "Look Claire, if you have something to say, say it...or I'm gonna assume you're blowing hot air like David said...maybe trying to get the attention off of yourself and your wrong doing.", I told her.

She looked over at David, who had turned as white as a ghost and then back at me. "Okay Miss Thing, you want to know what I have to say. David is not my son", she said.

I let out a sigh of relief. "What do you mean he's not your son? Is he adopted?"

"I gave birth to him, but he's not my son...He was born as my daughter Deanna", she said with a big grin on her face.

I became weak in the knees and had to sit down to keep from falling. And just as I sat down, my lunch came back up.

EPILOGUE

Sierra

How did my life get turned so upside down? That was the one question I had asked myself repeatedly.

To those on the outside looking in, my life was perfect. I had married the one and only man I ever loved. We had a beautiful daughter together. I had a successful business and lived in a nice house. But as we all know, things aren't always as they seem.

I had mixed feelings when I found out Alexis' ex-husband was behind everything. I was relieved to know that Alexis hadn't deceived me. Yet, I felt appalled to know that he went through all of that to have Tyler to himself. He wanted me out of the picture and was willing to do whatever it took.

Alexis wasn't totally innocent. Her original plan was to come in and ruin my marriage, but she had a change of heart when she realized she was really falling for me.

"Mommy...Daddy's here!" Shelby yelled, jarring me out of my thoughts.

"Hello Sierra", he said as he entered the room.

"Uh...Shelby sweetie, why don't you go to your room and play?"

As soon as she left the room, I turned to Tyler. "I don't recall hearing the doorbell", I said.

"I didn't think I needed to ring the doorbell at my own house", he snapped.

I blew air out of my mouth. "Tyler, we had a deal. You moved out remember?"

"My moving out was your idea...in case you forgot", he replied.

I rolled my eyes. "I didn't forget. I also didn't forget that you wanted to go on like nothing had happened Tyler."

"We could've made it work Sierra", he said.

"Oh yeah...you, Demond and I living together happily ever after", I said sarcastically.

"Don't act like I'm the only one that was doing dirt."

I could feel my temper flaring. Ever since everything came out in the open, he had been slinging mud. I knew what I did was wrong, but he had set things in motion. And I was getting tired of him making light of his infidelity. I decided I wasn't going to let him get to me. I was going to be the mature one.

"Tyler, exactly why are you here?" I asked him.

He hesitated for a few seconds. "To be honest Sierra, I didn't come here to argue with you. I came to talk to you", he said.

"About what?" I asked.

"About us", he replied.

"Us...there is no us."

He grabbed my hand and held onto it. "Come on Sierra. We got a history together baby. I was your first love and the one that took your virginity. You're the mother of my child for Christ's sake."

I looked down at our hands. Then I looked into my husband's eyes. He was the most handsome man I had ever seen. I couldn't deny the fact that I still loved him. At one point, I couldn't imagine life without him. But a lot has happened and things have changed. There is no way I could go on with our marriage like nothing happened.

I pulled my hand from his grasp. "Tyler...you're gay. And the sooner you admit that, the better off you'll be."

He got in my face like he wanted to hit me. "I am not gay! And I don't ever want to hear you say that again", he said through clenched teeth.

His attempt to intimidate me didn't get to me. He was in denial and I wasn't about to hop on the bandwagon with him.

"You've had sex with other men...and in today's society that makes you gay", I told him.

"What about you? You slept with Alexis. I guess

that makes you gay also", he said.

"What happened between Alexis and I is more accepted than what went on between you and Demond. If a man has sex with another man, he's gay. If a woman has sex with another woman, she can be considered bi-sexual or just experimenting. There are men out there who would love to see their woman with another woman", I explained.

"You actually sound like you're an expert or something", he replied, with a smirk on his face.

"Let's just say that the Sierra you married is long gone. I'm no longer the timid naïve woman who is oblivious to what's going on around her."

"So what in the hell does that mean?" he asked.

I threw my hands up in frustration. "It means that I'm going to start living my life to the fullest Tyler. No more going through every day the same ole' way. I want to start going to new places and doing new things."

"We can do that together Sierra...if that's all you want", he said with hope in his voice.

I shook my head from side to side. "No Tyler. It's over. I really need you to understand that. And you're lying to yourself if you think we still have a chance. I have been nothing but a trophy for you. All this time you've been living a lie. You did what was expected, but your heart was somewhere else. I now know that and have accepted it. Now it's time for you to admit it and accept it too."

He looked at me for a few seconds. "Is there someone else?" he asked as if he hadn't heard anything I said.

I couldn't help but to let out a chuckle. "This is about me Tyler. Right now I'm focusing on Sierra", I told him truthfully.

We talked some more and I continued trying to get him to see things from my point of view. He appeared to accept the facts, but I know deep down inside he was still hopeful.

He decided to take Shelby for a few days to give me some time to myself. Plus we wanted her to spend equal time with each of us. Even though we weren't together we didn't want her to feel slighted.

With free time to myself, I didn't know what to do. Then I decided it was time to do what I said I was going to do. It was time to start living my life to the fullest

I grabbed my phone and brought up the speed dial list and punched in the number and hit send.

"Hey, what's up?"

"I want to be spontaneous for a change", I said.

"What do you have in mind?"

"I want to go to a place I've never been before", I answered.

"Where's that?"

"Jamaica!" I yelled into the phone.

"Well you should do it."

"You think so?"

"Yes. Why not? You know I got connections. So I can get us a nice deal and we can be on our way."

"That sounds great", I said excitedly.

"What about your daughter?""

"Oh, she's with Tyler. He's taking her for a few days."

"That's nice of him."

"He's her father. It is part of his responsibility", I snapped.

"Okay. Don't get so touchy. Are you down for the trip or what?"

"Of course I'm down. It was my idea", I replied with agitation in my voice.

"Well get your stuff together and meet me at my house in an hour. I'll handle all of the arrangements."

"Okay. I'll see you in an hour", I said and ended the call.

I packed my bags and an hour later, I pulled up to Alexis' house. I know I gave Tyler the impression there was no one else, but no matter how much I tried, I couldn't stay away from her. I was like an addict and she was my drug of choice.

I was going to Jamaica and I was going to have the time of my life. And the relationship between me and

Alexis would continue to be my little secret.

Jade

When Amanda had pulled the trigger, Eli saw it coming and was able to avoid being shot in the chest. He ducked and the bullet hit him in the shoulder. He was able to wrestle the gun away from her before she could pull the trigger again.

After finding out the type of person Eli really was, a part of me wished she had killed him. Even after everything that happened, he expected me to go on with our relationship. He told me we were too far gone to call it quits. I was furious with him. His wife was about to be charged with attempted murder and he was still pursuing me.

I told him that I never wanted to see his face again and I meant every word. It's amazing how you can be head over heels in love with someone one minute and the next minute, you hate them with a passion. Eli had made me fall for him...hard. I had all these visions of our future together. He was the perfect man for me...minus the wife and kids.

Eli had proven what I had said all along...men couldn't be trusted. That was the motto I had lived by in the past. Then he came along with his charm and aggressiveness and won me over. As soon as you let your guard down, shit happens. Things were about to change. The next man that gets a taste of my goodies is going to have to prove himself to me.

On a better note, work has been going great. I jumped into my role with great ease. I did such a good job, Mr. Lawson decided to make it permanent. With my salary increase, I will never have to worry about money again. I won't have David's money, but I will be well taken care of. Mending my heart was another story and something I wasn't sure would happen anytime soon.

Taylor

David was born a female. That thought played over and over in my head since Claire confessed it that night in the kitchen. I listened to him tell me the story of how he knew he was supposed to be a male from the time he was eight years old. Deanna didn't like to do things that little girls liked to do. Her parents brushed her off and just labeled her as a typical tomboy. But as time went by and she was becoming more and more masculine, they realized they had a problem on their hands. At first they thought she was gay, but she dropped a bomb on them by telling them she wanted a sex change. Her father was dead set against it. Deanna had made up her mind and was going to live her life the way she wanted to. She started taking testosterone and then eventually took the plunge...David was born.

I kept asking myself how I could not have known. There were so many things that stood out, now that his secret was out. I thought about how he never wanted me to touch him and how he always wanted the lights off when we made love. He always went into the bathroom to get dressed. All that time, I took it as him being self-conscious of his size. Never in a million years would I have thought it was because he didn't want me to see his man-made dick.

It was only when he became a successful business man, that his father accepted him. His mother was always supportive and in his corner...until he married me. She hated everything about me and would do almost anything to split us up. When the affair with Exodus didn't work, she became desperate, which is why she ended up spilling the beans about David's big secret.

Well, she finally got her wish. After discovering that David was born a female, I decided that there wasn't enough money in the world to make me stay with him. I know I could go on like nothing happened. But his being born a female would always be in the back of my mind.

At least now I have a leg to stand on. Before, I thought my affair with Exodus would cause me to be left with nothing. Now things were different. I'm not an expert on divorce, but I have a feeling that finding out your husband was born a female is far worse than cheating on your husband. Our whole marriage was a lie and I'm going to make sure I get what's coming to me.

CPSIA information can be obtained at www.ICGtesting.com
Printed in the USA
BVOW011205100413

317780BV00010B/321/P

9 781618 634030